# SUSAN LEWIS

# DON'T BELIEVE A WORD

HarperCollins*Publishers*

HarperCollins*Publishers* Ltd
1 London Bridge Street,
London SE1 9GF

www.harpercollins.co.uk

HarperCollins*Publishers*
Macken House, 39/40 Mayor Street Upper
Dublin 1, D01 C9W8, Ireland

This paperback edition published 2025
4

First published by HarperCollins*Publishers* Ltd 2025



A catalogue record for this book is available from the British Library

ISBN: 978-0-00-847210-8 (PB)



Set in Sabon LT Pro by HarperCollins*Publishers* India

Printed and bound in the UK using 100% Renewable
Electricity at CPI Group (UK) Ltd



FSC
www.fsc.org
MIX
Paper | Supporting responsible forestry
FSC™ C007454

This book contains FSC™ certified paper and other controlled
sources to ensure responsible forest management.

For more information visit: www.harpercollins.co.uk/green

# DON'T BELIEVE A WORD

Susan Lewis is the internationally bestselling author of over fifty sensational novels across the genres of family drama, thriller, suspense, crime and romance – including the Richard and Judy picks *One Minute Later* and *I Have Something to Tell You*. She is also the author of *Just One More Day* and *One Day at a Time*, the moving memoirs of her childhood in Bristol during the 1960s. Following periods of living in Los Angeles and the South of France, she currently lives in Gloucestershire with her husband, James, and their beloved, naughty little dog, Mimi.

To find out more about Susan Lewis:

www.susanlewis.com
/SusanLewisBooks
@susanlewisbooks
@susanlewisbooks
@susanlewisbooks

**Also by Susan Lewis**

**Fiction**
*A Class Apart*
*Dance While You Can*
*Stolen Beginnings*
*Darkest Longings*
*Obsession*
*Vengeance*
*Summer Madness*
*Last Resort*
*Wildfire*
*Cruel Venus*
*Strange Allure*
*The Mill House*
*A French Affair*
*Missing*
*Out of the Shadows*
*Lost Innocence*
*The Choice*
*Forgotten*
*Stolen*
*No Turning Back*
*Losing You*
*The Truth About You*
*Never Say Goodbye*
*Too Close to Home*
*No Place to Hide*
*The Secret Keeper*
*One Minute Later*
*I Have Something to Tell You*
*I Know It's You*
*A Sicilian Affair*

**Books that run in sequence**
*Chasing Dreams*
*Taking Chances*

*No Child of Mine*
*Don't Let Me Go*
*You Said Forever*

**Featuring Detective Andee Lawrence**
*Behind Closed Doors*
*The Girl Who Came Back*
*The Moment She Left*
*Hiding in Plain Sight*
*Believe in Me*
*Home Truths*
*My Lies, Your Lies*
*Forgive Me*
*The Lost Hours*
*Who's Lying Now?*
*No One Saw It Coming*

**Featuring Laurie Forbes and Elliott Russell**
*Silent Truths*
*Wicked Beauty*
*Intimate Strangers*
*The Hornbeam Tree*

**Featuring Cristy Ward**
*Nothing to See Here*

*To Chap and Sallie Jo Mitzell. The world always feels like a better place when we're together, no matter where in the world we are.*

# Prologue

'Tell me I'm seeing things.'

Mia, who'd spoken, didn't look round as her sister, Lottie, came quietly into the room behind her. Her eyes remained fixed on the mystery of what she was studying through the picture window of their hilltop home. Rented for the summer season.

Amused, perhaps a little irritated, by the way Mia was peering around a curtain as if afraid of being seen – it would have to be by a bird, or a paraglider or someone hanging upside down from the roof to get eyes on her here – Lottie took centre stage to investigate the focus of interest.

'Where are you looking?' she asked, searching the sunlit slopes of lush green fields that rolled from their outside terrace down to the scrubby beach below.

'You'll see,' Mia said softly.

Lottie already had and as her heart slowed with surprise she blinked uncomprehendingly at the sight of a small child in a blue anorak and yellow wellie boots sitting all alone on the gritty sand. Her back was turned so they couldn't see her face – she was too far away for it to be more than a blur anyway – and her white blonde curls were being tossed about in the breeze. Her tiny hands looked to be clutching her knees.

What on earth was she doing there all alone? That was how it appeared. And what could she be staring at? There was nothing to see apart from the churning might of the Severn Estuary and mountainous terrain of South Wales on the horizon.

Had someone gone into the water and not come out again?

There seemed no panic in the child, so presumably not that.

'How did she get there?' Mia asked, almost peevishly, as if

someone might be playing a trick that she couldn't quite get a handle on.

Lottie looked up and down the coast as far as she could see. There was no one else in sight, no parent or fishing boat, no sign at all of how the child might have got to the bottom of their hill and onto that godforsaken stretch of stony shoreline. It was as if she'd been washed up by the waves and simply left there like flotsam – or some kind of offering?

Mia would like that.

So would Lottie, although maybe for different reasons.

Of course, the child must have walked, it was the only way, but she was surely no older than two so she couldn't have done it alone.

'Her mother, or someone, must be nearby,' Lottie said, 'we just can't see them from here.'

They continued to watch and wait.

Eventually, the little girl stood up – she really was tiny. She turned towards the long grass that swept up the far side of the field towards a small spur of a track that wound on up to the South West Coast Path. There was a stile, not visible from the sisters' window, where the occasional hiker or rock pool explorer could gain access to this remote, rather dismal bay. Lottie expected the child to wave, and maybe start running to someone coming her way – a parent who would appear from the wings any second to scoop her up and carry her away.

No one came, and after a few stumbling steps the child sat down again, her back still turned. This time her tiny hands seemed to be covering her face.

Mia's deep brown eyes moved to meet Lottie's.

Both women were in their mid-forties, their birthdays just a year apart, Mia – Emilia – being the eldest. Both were tall and slender, with a regal sort of bearing. There the similarities ended. Mia was brown-haired and pale complexioned, with a slightly too prominent jaw and close-set eyes. Lottie – Carlotta – with her lustrous dark curls and fine-boned features, was often described as a beauty.

'She can't be alone,' Mia said, disbelievingly.

Lottie continued to watch and wait. This was all wrong, a tiny speck of humanity alongside a vast, amorphous sea with no one to mind her. It was making her heart thud with unease, and stir with a sense of protectiveness – something she instinctively felt towards children, in spite of having none of her own.

'It's starting to rain,' Mia said, noticing a gauzy mist drifting like a veil across the landscape. There was a small crease between her brows as she created all manner of scenarios to fit the tableau of small child seemingly abandoned on a beach.

Lottie didn't answer, simply dug her feet into a pair of old hiking boots and tied the laces.

Mia said, cautiously, 'Edwin won't like it.'

Lottie regarded her sister in scornful dismay. Her tone was cool as she said, 'Your husband isn't here.'

Mia flushed and seeing how much she'd hurt her Lottie was momentarily torn between contrition and an urge to slap her.

Pulling open the door she paused and turned back. 'She's probably too young for tea,' she said, 'so heat up some milk,' and stepping out into a lively gust, she crossed the terrace to begin the descent to the beach. It wouldn't matter, she told herself, if someone showed up when she got to the child and told her to mind her own business. She didn't mean any harm, and besides, if anyone should be indignant about the situation it ought to be her. After all, what right-thinking person allowed a little mite like that to venture close to the sea on her own, even if the tide wasn't likely to come in any further today? All she, Lottie Winters, wanted was to make sure the child was in no danger then she'd go happily on her way. Well, maybe not happily, for her curiosity would want to be satisfied by the reason the girl had come to be there in the first place.

As she strode effortlessly down the hillside she could feel Mia's eyes boring into her back, and could actually sense her unease. It wouldn't be so much about the mission Lottie was bent on, although that would be a part. It would be all tied up in Mia's constant fear of what she'd do if Lottie ever found a husband of her own – someone whose need of Lottie, whose right to her time and devotion, would necessarily trump Mia's own.

Lottie was, according to most, beautiful, exotic, adventurous, desired by many men and yet, over the years, she'd spurned them all to remain free, answerable to no one but herself. Should that ever change Lottie knew Mia would do her very best to be happy for her. She often said that no one deserved love more than Lottie, but how would she, Mia, fill the gaps, the veritable chasms, that would open up if Lottie wasn't there any more?

Poor Mia. She'd never been good at making friends, the way that came so naturally to Lottie. She was too shy to travel alone, something Lottie did often. And she was too cautious to take risks, especially the kind that drove Lottie to help those in perilous states of fear and destitution around the world. She was, she knew, too independent, too wayward and strong-minded to bend to any man's will and in the end most men didn't like that.

'You're as bad as Mummy,' she'd grumble whenever Mia loyally, if not convincingly, echoed their mother, 'thinking, no believing, that no woman is complete without a husband. Do I look unfinished to you? Do I behave as though half of me isn't functioning? I have sex when I want it, thank you very much, good male friends who spoil me and demand nothing in return, so why would I want to saddle myself with the burden of having to please someone else when it's so much more fun pleasing me?'

She wasn't that selfish really, or not all of the time, and as frustrated as she often felt with Mia, she was ready to accept that they were as close as sisters could be, and, to a certain degree, quite interdependent. Their inherited fortune was shared as were their lives, 24/7, when Lottie wasn't travelling. In fact, they were so attuned to one another's thoughts and so exclusively in their own world at times that Edwin had once described them as each other's oxygen – and he hadn't meant it in a kind way.

By now Lottie had reached a small gap in the hedge at the bottom of their field where the air was saltier and more bracing and the noise of the tide almost drowned the gulls. She pushed on across the gritty sand towards the water's edge still not entirely certain what she was about to do, and still expecting someone to appear from behind the dyke to whisk the child away.

No one did, and as she came to a stop beside the tiny creature her heart caught on a great wave of feeling. The tiny, damp face tilted up to look at her, big brown eyes swimming in tears and hair plastered to her mottled cheeks. She was as pretty, and as tragic, a picture as Lottie had ever seen. She was trembling and frightened – and clearly lost.

Sinking down to the girl's height, Lottie said, 'What are you doing out here on your own? Is someone with you?'

The child only stared at her.

Lottie looked over her shoulder, up and down the coast and even out to sea, but there was no one in sight.

When she turned back the girl was still watching her, lips quivering, eyes timid and tearful. Instinctively Lottie drew her into her arms and felt the pleasing heft of her as she filled the space meant for a child. 'There, there,' she soothed, stroking the wet hair and feeling a surge of protectiveness wrap itself around the girl's loneliness and fragility. 'It's all right. I'm going to take care of you.'

The child didn't pull away, simply rested her sweet little head against Lottie's shoulder.

'What's your name?' Lottie asked in her ear. Not receiving an answer, she drew back to look at her again. 'Where's your mummy?' she asked softly.

Two small tears dropped from the girl's eyes.

'Did she bring you here?'

No answer.

'Do you know where you live?'

The little girl sucked her lower lip between tiny white teeth.

Lottie glanced up at the house, already knowing she was going to take the child there – what else could she do? Leaving her here simply wasn't an option and it was a long way into town. To her surprise she saw that Mia was outside, on the terrace and frantically waving. Was she trying to warn her of something? What was she saying? Lottie looked around, but there was still no one to be seen.

'We're going to sort this out,' she told the little girl, and taking her tiny hand she led her across the beach to begin the climb up the hill.

It was too hard going for such small legs, so she scooped her up and carried her the rest of the way. How many children had she carried to safety in her time, she wondered. Certainly hundreds, but numbers hardly mattered. Each wretched little soul was as special as the next, as worthy as those who'd gone before and still others yet to come.

Mia met them beneath the terrace and quickly took the child into her waiting arms.

'She's so lovely,' she crooned, stroking the girl's drizzle-soaked cheek with the back of one hand. 'So sweet and tiny. What's her name?'

'I don't know,' Lottie replied. 'Why were you waving?'

Starting, as if suddenly remembering, Mia said, 'Someone was there. Not far from the stile. They were watching you, but when you picked her up they turned and ran away.'

Lottie looked towards the stile, barely visible through the overhang of trees and tangle of bushes. 'Male or female?' she asked, unable to make sense of anything.

'Hard to be certain at this distance.' Mia was already carrying the girl onto the terrace. 'They were wearing a hooded jacket.'

'Maybe I should pop out to the lane to see if anyone's still there?' Lottie said.

Mia nodded, distracted now by her need to dry the child and make her feel safe. Once inside the kitchen she set her down and dropped to her knees in front of her. 'Are you OK?' she whispered softly.

The girl's eyes welled with tears.

'There, there, sweetheart,' Mia soothed, wanting to smother her in an embrace, but afraid it might scare her. 'No need to cry. We've got some lovely milk to warm you up, and . . .' her eyes brightened playfully, 'a delicious homemade cookie.'

Ten minutes later, Lottie returned to find Mia sitting in a cosy armchair with the child on her lap, a half-drunk glass of milk and partly eaten cookie on a small table beside them.

'No sign of anyone,' Lottie said, peeling off her coat. 'I don't understand it. Why would—'

'There's a note,' Mia interrupted. 'There. On the table.'

Lottie glanced at it, then back to Mia as if she might explain further.

'It was in her coat pocket,' Mia said softly.

Lottie picked it up and as she absorbed the words she felt the strangest confliction of feelings coming to life inside her.

> Her name is Sasha. She will be two years old on May 14th. I know you are good people. Please take care of her until I can come back for her.

# CHAPTER ONE

*TWENTY-THREE YEARS LATER*

NEW YEAR'S EVE

'And you found this, where?' Cristy asked, looking up from the pages she'd just spent the past few minutes reading, pages that had taken her briefly to another world where clearly something wasn't right. She already wanted to know more.

'It was amongst my aunt's papers,' Sadie Winters replied. She was sitting up tall, a little stiffly – nerves, Cristy suspected – and her voice wavered slightly as she spoke. Her beauty was something Cristy hadn't especially noticed when she'd come into the room; now it seemed almost mesmerizing in its subtle form of radiance. In fact, it was as if the beauty itself was undecided on how far to go, how much it wanted to be recognized. Her hair was golden blonde and fell in soft, luxuriant waves to her shoulders; her forehead was high, her almond-shaped eyes brown and intelligent, hesitant, as well, Cristy thought. Right now they conveyed a sense of hope along with a quiet determination to stay focused on why they were there.

Sitting beside Sadie at the conference table in this spacious office in St Peter Port, with its vast picture windows framing the harbour and all manner of nautical-themed fixtures on the walls, was Sadie's best friend, Anna Gaudion.

'It could make a brilliant podcast,' Anna declared eagerly, clearly thinking Cristy needed more persuasion. Perhaps Cristy did, although she had to admit she was already more than half on board. Whatever the mystery, presuming it was based in fact –

two sisters, a child on a beach, an enigmatic note . . . would it be right for *Hindsight*, the true-crime podcast series that she and her partner produced? 'That's why we've come to you,' Anna ran on.

Cristy had to smile. This girl, young woman – she and Sadie were both mid-twenties – was as outspoken and excitable as she was rash and lovely.

Anna was still speaking. 'It blew my mind when I read it the first time,' she said. 'It's totally surreal, don't you think? Like something out of a movie, only it really happened.' She turned uncertainly to Sadie. 'Well, we think it did,' she added. 'I mean, it must have, because it explains everything.'

Sadie's voice was gentle, her smile still hesitant as she said, 'Actually it doesn't explain anything, which is why we're here.'

'Of course,' Anna agreed. 'But all the names are real,' she continued, turning back to Cristy. 'Mia and Lottie are Sadie's aunts, and we think, well we know, that Lottie, who died just before the lockdowns, so four years ago, wrote what you've just read. It was her thing, you see, short stories. She had lots published, back in the day, but then she stopped. Well, we thought she did, but since Sadie started going through all her stuff she's found dozens of them, all printed out, and not necessarily complete.'

'And then I found that,' Sadie added, nodding towards the pages in front of Cristy.

Cristy sat back in her chair barely noticing the torrents of rain streaking the windows behind the girls while gale-force gusts chopped up the sea and tossed fishing boats about like toys. She was about to speak when Anna said, 'It's a brilliant story, what we know of it so far. We just need someone to help us find out the rest. So if you're interested, I know you do cold cases . . .'

From the doorway David said, 'Anna, why don't you let someone else speak?'

Cristy had to laugh even as her heart warmed to find him standing there, his dark-blond hair and handsome face wet with rain, his expression wry as he took in the scene and came to a quick conclusion about his daughter's part in it. 'Sorry if I'm interrupting,' he said, his eyes on Cristy's, 'but I felt someone should.'

Anna said, indignantly, 'I'm just trying to get things going here, Dad. You know how shy Sades is . . .'

'She's just not loud,' he corrected, 'otherwise she's perfectly capable of speaking up for herself.'

Anna's eyes shot darts at him. 'You shouldn't even be here,' she told him. 'I thought you had a meeting in town.'

'It got cancelled, so I thought I'd call in and see how you're getting along.' As he came to stand behind Cristy she lifted her face and smiled as he kissed her.

'They keep doing that,' Anna grumbled to Sadie. 'And it's not like they don't have a room.' To her father, she said, 'You have to go now or you'll just end up taking over the way you always do.'

With a laugh, he said to Sadie, 'Should I take her with me so you can get a word in?'

Apparently enjoying his tease, Sadie said, 'She's OK.'

With a smile, he dropped another kiss on Cristy's forehead and was already answering a call as he left the room.

Taking a moment to refocus – why wasn't Cristy over these teenage flutterings yet, it had been almost a month since they'd first 'become official' great euphemism, introduced by her nineteen-year-old daughter, Hayley. 'Sadie,' she said, firmly, 'why don't you tell me about yourself and your life today. I'd like to have a fuller picture of who you are, what you do, where you live, although I take it it's here on the island.'

As Anna took a breath to answer, Sadie put a slender hand over hers and said, 'There's not all that much to me, really . . .'

'Not true!' Anna protested.

'Maybe we need to call your father back,' Cristy suggested.

Anna scowled as Sadie laughed and said, 'I'm soon to be twenty-six – at least I think I am – and I've lived in Guernsey for most of my life. Anna and I went to school together, that's how we know one another. I left for a few years when I went to uni in London and I worked there for a while after. I came back when one of my aunts fell ill. She recovered, thankfully, but by then I'd already decided I was going to stay on. Jasper – my fiancé – works here in St Peter Port, he's an investment analyst, and I'm trying to set myself up as a freelance editor of fiction. No clients yet, but it's still early days.'

'She's going to be brilliant,' Anna insisted.

Sadie's eyes sparkled as she said, 'We all need an Anna when it comes to confidence boosting. Anyway, that's what I do when I work, which actually isn't all that often. Jasper and I have a small house on my aunt's estate just a couple of miles along the coast from here. She's on her own now, since my other aunt passed away, so I'm glad to be nearby, although J and I spend a few days a month near Bath with his parents. He's not from the island, you see, so he feels the need to escape now and then, and I guess I do too, but I don't like leaving Mia for long.'

'The two of you are close,' Cristy concluded.

Sadie nodded. 'We have been for as long as I can remember. Her name's Emilia, Mia. I grew up with her and my other aunt, Carlotta – Lottie. They were the best parents anyone could ever wish for. Real characters, in their different ways, often unpredictable, generous to a fault, sometimes bossy especially with each other, far too forgiving, but not gullible, never a great idea to get on the wrong side of them, but on the whole they were just . . . *kind*.' She thought for a moment and added, 'Controlling as well, but there again, aren't all parents? Anyway, since Lottie died, just before Covid, it's like Mia has . . . This is going to sound strange, I know, but she seems to get confused about who she is. She often talks to Lottie out loud, asking what she thinks about something, or what she, Mia, should do in a certain situation. Then she answers herself and laughs at how "dotty" she must sound.'

'She's not demented or anything,' Anna put in, 'well, maybe she is, a bit, but what matters for our purposes today is that she just won't answer questions about Sadie's parents.'

Cristy's gaze returned to Sadie. 'What exactly have you asked her?' she prompted.

'Lately, not very much,' Sadie admitted, 'but a while ago, I mean a few years back, I started looking into my roots and that's when I discovered that I'm not their dead brother's daughter, the way they've always claimed. In fact, I can't find any record of them having a brother at all.'

Understanding how alarming that must have been, not to

mention disorientating, Cristy said, 'So are you thinking now that the child on the beach is probably you?'

Sadie swallowed dryly. 'I think it's possible, yes. And my aunts either kept me because whoever wrote the note didn't come back, or . . .'

'Or they stole her,' Anna finished, clearly having reached her own conclusion. Then not quite so certain she added, 'There's also the chance they might have bought her and what we've read is a kind of cover story?'

Intrigued by both possibilities, random as they were, Cristy said, 'Just to be clear . . . these pages here are written like fiction, but it's your belief they are, in fact, or could be, a record of how you came to your aunts'. . . What shall we call it? Care?'

Colour seeped into Sadie's cheeks as she said, 'It's the way she's used our names,' she explained, clearly worried that Cristy had already concluded she was reading too much into a few random pages.

'We reckon this could be a fictionalized version of fact,' Anna said, spelling it out helpfully.

Cristy nodded, still not entirely sure what she thought, although she was ready to accept that there might well be something more . . . sinister? manipulative? at play. 'How old is your aunt?' she asked Sadie. 'The one that's still living.'

'She's seventy,' Sadie replied.

'And still quite glam,' Anna added, 'in a bit of a funky way. I mean, she likes the Sixties look, flicked-up hair, mini-dresses, fake leather trousers and all that sort of stuff, but it kind of suits her.'

'Lottie, on the other hand,' Sadie continued, 'preferred a more masculine sort of style, although her features and her mannerisms were entirely feminine. She loved baggy trousers and men's shirts. She'd even go to balls dressed in a tuxedo at times.'

'She wasn't gay,' Anna insisted. 'She really liked men, didn't she? I mean, it says so in these pages, and she was always messing with the blokes around the yacht club here on the island.'

With a wry sort of smile, Sadie said, 'Mia used to accuse her of liking men a bit too much, and Lottie would accuse her of being jealous, or frigid, or tell her to loosen up and get a dildo.' She laughed and Cristy did too, as much at the unexpectedness of it as the comedy. 'Not that Mia didn't have her share of "admirers",' Sadie continued. 'I mean, she was married once. I never knew him, and they never really talked about him, or about anyone Lottie was involved with. She used to keep her affairs, or flings, or whatever we want to call them, to when she travelled.'

'So are your aunts from the island?' Cristy asked.

'No. They're from London originally.'

Anna said, 'We think the house mentioned in those pages is somewhere their grandparents took them a few times when they were young.'

Cristy frowned curiously. 'Why do you think that?'

'Because my aunts used to talk about it. They told me about going to Somerset as children when their parents were in more exotic places. They described it as an adventure, somewhere different, more rustic with no rules and lots of freedom. Lottie told me once, years later, that on a whim they got someone to find it for them, and they rented it for a while. She joked that they weren't as much into the rusticity or bad weather then, so they didn't stay as long as they'd intended.'

Seeing how the girl's mind was working, Cristy said, 'So what exactly did they tell you about your parents, and how you came to live with them?'

Sadie took a breath and clutched her hands together as she said, 'They told me that my father, their brother, and my mother, were killed in a car crash when I was two years old, and that's when they became my legal guardians.'

'And are they? Your legal guardians?'

'I haven't found any documents to support it, but I guess it's academic now, considering my age.'

Conceding the point, Cristy said, 'But you know that they never had a brother?'

'Not that I can find any record of.'

'Do you have a birth certificate?'

Sadie swallowed as she nodded. 'It says I was born on the fourteenth of May 1998 and that my father's name was Martin Winters.'

*She will be two years old on May 14th.*

'What about your mother?' Cristy asked.

'She is down as Vanessa Winters, née Jameson. I've tried, but I can't find any trace of them – at least not as a couple with a daughter who'd be my age.'

'And when you discovered your aunts didn't have a brother, what did you do?'

'Nothing – then. I didn't know how to bring it up without it seeming as though I was being mistrustful, and spying on them.'

'But you must have asked about your parents before that, while you were growing up?'

'Yes, of course, and they'd tell me lovely stories of how much they'd adored me and how proud they'd be of me if they could see how well I was doing. They even had photographs of me as a baby, and of them, but I'm not sure now how real any of it was.'

Cristy sat with that for a moment until Anna said, 'We're actually pretty certain her aunts stole her. You'll understand what we mean when you see what else Sadie found in Lottie's desk.'

Cristy looked at Sadie, a prompt for her to explain.

'It was during the pandemic that I first started to go through Lottie's things,' Sadie began. 'There's so much, honestly, I knew it was going to take forever, and Mia kept telling me it could wait . . . I realized she didn't want to help in any way, and I didn't mind, I understood it would be a lot more painful for her than it might be for me.'

'But she was OK with you doing it?' Cristy prompted.

Sadie nodded. 'I guess so. I mean, she never tried to stop me, so I just got on with it. Not every day, you understand, not even every week, but then, quite recently, I opened one of the hundreds of box files prepared to find more bank statements, or postcards of places Lottie had been, brochures, various knick-knacks, she kept everything . . . But in this particular box there were two large brown envelopes. The first turned out to contain photographs that I recognized right away. They were the ones I mentioned just now that used to be dotted around the house when I was growing up. Me – or a child who was supposed to be me – as a baby either with my "parents", or alone. A couple of my "parents" on their wedding day, my christening, that sort of thing. What I never noticed when I was younger, but I did when I studied them more closely recently, was that there are no early photos of me with my aunts, or of them with my parents.'

'Have you asked your aunt Mia about that?'

'Not yet. I guess I'll have to at some point, but the last time I brought up the subject of my parents . . . Actually, it was before Lottie died, and I'm afraid it didn't go well. I'd eventually plucked up the courage to ask about their brother and Mia got angry, saying I should leave things alone and stop bothering them with memories they'd rather not revisit. Lottie was pretty angry too. She asked if I was unhappy, and if so I didn't have a right to be. She said, "Haven't we given you everything?" and they had, of course, I could never deny that.'

Thinking how spiteful that sounded, Cristy said, 'You mentioned two envelopes just now.'

Sadie nodded. 'The other one contained the pages you've just read. You can see they're a printout, but I can't search Lottie's computers to see if there's more because, after Lottie died, Mia had them returned to factory settings and shipped off to various schools in Africa. She said it's what Lottie would have wanted.'

'Didn't she make back-ups of Lottie's files?' Cristy asked.

'I don't think so, or not that I've found so far. They could be in Mia's office, of course, but I don't have any reason to go poking around in there.'

'And what about these pages? Have you shown them to your aunt?'

'Not yet. I wanted to find out first if I'm just being fanciful or paranoid . . .'

'We want to know what you think,' Anna said for her.

Regarding them both, Cristy said carefully, 'You understand, Sadie, I'm sure, that if this does turn out to be fact rather than fiction your aunt could be in a lot of trouble.'

Sadie looked horribly pained. 'I do, but honestly, if you knew what it was like to have no idea who you really are, to have no real sense of belonging . . . I'm sorry if that sounds selfish, but I don't know if I can carry on not knowing any more. And as for my aunt, I promise you, it won't be anything she can't handle. She'll just throw money at it, the way she does with everything.'

Thinking that no amount of money could buy off a case of child abduction, Cristy's eyes moved to Anna as she said, hotly, 'What matters is that Sadie should know who she really is.'

Cristy looked at Sadie again. 'Have you done a DNA test to find out if you're related to your aunts in any way?' she asked.

Sadie swallowed. 'Yes, I have, and no, I'm not.'

In spite of having expected the answer, Cristy couldn't help feeling the girl's bewilderment and sadness. How on earth must it feel to find out that the space you should be filling in the world is empty?

Anna said, 'You never know, Sadie's real parents could be out there somewhere, desperate to find her . . .'

'If they're still alive,' Sadie put in quietly, 'and I like to think they are.'

As Cristy's eyes swept her face, she was wondering about the people who'd made this stunningly lovely young woman and what could have happened to tear them all apart. As privileged a life as Sadie had led, there was clearly a whole other story folded into her genes, running untold through her veins. She wasn't the person sitting here today, or she shouldn't be. There was someone else inside her who needed to be heard, to be recognized for who she really was.

In the end, she said, 'What about your aunt? How's she likely to take it if you do find your real family?'

Sadie shook her head helplessly. 'I guess a lot depends on who they are and what they say happened to separate us,' she said.

Silent echoes of the mysterious story seemed to fill the room before Anna said, 'Please say you'll help.'

# CHAPTER TWO

Much later in the day Cristy was standing alone at the window of David's bedroom staring through her own pensive reflection down to the ornamental lake at the heart of the Gaudion estate's small valley. A veil of mist was drifting across the glassy water where a floating platform of fireworks was being prepared for the New Year's Eve celebrations at midnight. Daylight was fast disappearing, yielding to the murk of a damp winter's night, but the earlier storm had subsided leaving everyone hopeful for a grand display at the magical hour.

On a good day she'd be able to glimpse the sea from here, which made her think of Sadie's aunts and the hilltop holiday home overlooking the Severn Estuary. Where exactly could that have been, she wondered. Presumably, somewhere on the Exmoor coast. She'd read the printed pages again, and had found herself drawn quite easily back into Lottie's rescue of the little girl on the beach. What a strange thing to happen, presuming it did. Who on earth would leave a child alone at the edge of such a dangerously tidal stretch of water? Who had created the small girl who'd grown into such a beauty?

She was intrigued by the aunts too, seeming so reclusive on the one hand, and yet clearly not, given Lottie's promiscuousness and overseas travels. If the story was based in fact then Sadie Winters' real name was Sasha. More importantly, and intriguingly, had she really been found on a beach, or was this odd sort of memoir a purposeful rewriting of history? If so, it couldn't have been concocted with Sadie in mind, given the sisters' efforts to pass the girl off as their niece. So who had it been for?

Before coming upstairs she'd scanned the pages in David's

home office and sent them to Connor, her partner on the podcast, to get his take on things. They'd talk in the morning, or maybe he'd call after he'd read them.

Hearing the door open she turned and smiled as David came into the room looking puzzled and concerned, clearly wondering why she was up here when there was so much going on downstairs.

'Sorry,' she said, as he came to embrace her. 'I just needed a few minutes. I'll come now to help get everything ready for this evening.'

'There are caterers,' he reminded her.

'Nevertheless . . .'

He stopped her with a kiss and then another that deepened with the kind of promise not easy to resist.

'Dad! Are you in there?'

He groaned as his head fell back in frustration. 'Go away,' he shouted.

'Can I come in?' Rosaria shouted back.

'No!'

Cristy laughed. 'At least she's asking,' she said, reminding him of this morning when Rosie had waltzed right in without knocking. Luckily they'd simply been lying in bed, covered by a sheet. Had Rosie arrived a few minutes earlier . . .

'I want to,' Rosie grumbled.

Caving in, Cristy went to open the door and felt such a rush of affection for David's eldest that she spontaneously drew her into an enormous hug, despite Rosie being a grown woman. Rosie was simply the sweetest, gentlest and kindest soul in the world whose extra chromosome seemed, for some reason, to make her love people and enjoy life more than anyone else Cristy knew. Thirty-two she might be, with Down's and an autoimmune condition, but nothing ever upset her for long, or held her back from sharing a secret, or dampened her enthusiasm for a project.

'Granny's too busy to take me to the theatre,' she told her father, 'and we've got a show at seven, so you'll have to drive me there.'

'You're on stage tonight?' he exclaimed in alarm.

'You know I am, but I'll be back in plenty of time for the party. I can't let everyone down, Dad, so *please*.'

Clearly not thrilled David said, 'Does it mean I have to sit through *another* performance of *Beauty and the Beast* in order to bring you home again? I've already seen it a hundred times.'

'He hasn't,' Rosie told Cristy, 'because it hasn't been open that long. Oh, I know!' she suddenly cried excitedly, 'Anna can take me and bring Sadie. Sadie hasn't seen it yet and she said she wants to. I'll go and find Anna.'

As she raced off to find her sister, Cristy closed the door and laughed at the way David was thanking God for his narrow escape.

'Speaking of Sadie Winters,' he said, going to the small bar he kept on a trolley next to the fireplace, 'how have you left it with her? Does the story interest you?'

'Yes, it does,' Cristy admitted, sinking down on the sofa. 'Have you read the pages she brought to me today?'

'I have,' he replied, handing her a Scotch. 'I found the resonance, perhaps I should say possibility, of truth in the story . . . unsettling?'

Cristy nodded as he sat down with her. 'Made more so by the use of real names. Anyway, I'd certainly like to read more – presuming there is more – but if Lottie's computers have gone . . . Why would she only have printed out a few pages? Why print out any at all?'

'I've no idea about that, but if you're not able to leave tomorrow maybe you could meet Mia Winters. She's an . . . interesting character.'

'How so?'

He tilted his head as he thought. 'I'd say she's . . . mercurial. The minute you think you've pinned her to something you realize she "left the room" a while ago. Lottie was far easier to deal with; straight-talking, a woman of her word, and of the world; a real dynamo, especially when it came to fundraisers, sailing and tennis. She certainly liked to win; in fact she was on the court when she died.'

'Heart attack?'

He nodded. 'Quite sudden and very shocking given she was

only mid-sixties. Mia took it hard; Sadie did too. Lottie was the life-force in that house – and if anyone knew how to throw a party it was her.'

Starting to feel sorry that she'd never meet her, Cristy said, 'I'm not sure if Sadie will want me to speak to Mia. She hasn't told her about the pages she found yet.'

'Mmm, I guess that doesn't surprise me. She's very protective of her aunt, and obviously nervous of what she might discover the further into this she goes, but it'll be hard getting to the truth if you can't question Mia. On the other hand, even if you do, like I said, she's a hard one to pin down.'

Cristy sipped her Scotch as she thought. 'It's early days,' she said, 'and Sadie's going to carry on looking for more pages that might connect with the ones we have so far. Apparently there are dozens and dozens of boxes full of ideas for short stories, chapters from some, the ends or beginnings of others, even complete ones apparently.'

They sat quietly for a while, each with their own thoughts, hers mostly still with Sadie and her aunts, until their drinks were finished and it really was time to go downstairs.

'Incidentally,' she said, as they reached the door. 'Where is Juliette staying?'

David's brows rose in surprise, as if he hadn't even considered his ex-partner's needs, although he clearly had, because he said, 'She's in the second bed in Laurent's room.' This kind of made sense since Juliette was Laurent's mother – Laurent being the youngest of David's children, aged twelve. 'The cottages are all taken, bar one,' he continued, 'but it seemed a bit mean to put her out there on her own when the rest of the family is going to be here.'

Cristy smiled. *Family*. 'I'm sure Laurent's already loving having his mum around,' she said, 'and I'm looking forward to meeting her.'

Seeming pleased by that, he said, 'I think you'll like her. She's very . . . *French*, in a good way . . .'

'Is there a bad way?'

He laughed. 'She kind of has that coined too, but she's a good mother to Laurent . . .'

'Even though he lives here, with you?'

'It makes more sense. He's settled in school, his friends are here and he has family around him. In Paris there's only Juliette and her aristo-arty set who aren't really interested in children.' His eyes narrowed as he regarded her closely. 'Are you OK with her being here?' he asked warily.

'Of course,' she insisted, though not entirely sure this was true. 'Why wouldn't I be?'

He smiled. 'No reason I can think of. Now, we'd better go down before Mum sends up a search party.'

*

There were only a few minutes to go before midnight when Cristy looked around the crowded party in search of David. She hadn't seen him in a while, but there were so many people here. It seemed half the island had come and the volume of chat along with the music was so loud it was almost impossible to hear what anyone was saying. *Papillon*, as Rosie called the Gaudion estate in honour of her dead mother's love of butterflies, was apparently *the* place to be on New Year's Eve. Cristy briefly reflected on Lexie Gaudion, the great love of David's life whose terrible and tragic death had been the focus of Cristy's last podcast series. She wondered if Lexie and David had thrown parties like this, everyone in black tie and evening dresses, glasses brimming with fine wines, champagne on ice ready for midnight and trays of delicious canapés being passed around by uniformed catering staff.

Spotting Cynthia, David's mother, with her other son, Richard, and his wife, Astrid, Cristy slipped through the throng, clinking glasses with as many strangers as extended family as she went, until she almost stumbled into Richard, laughing as he caught her, and asked if any of them had seen David.

'He went down to check on the fireworks,' Cynthia told her, her dear, crumpled face flushed with delight as a waiter refilled her glass with a classic white Bordeaux. 'Five minutes to go!' she cheered joyfully.

'Have you heard from your children yet?' Richard shouted in Cristy's ear.

'Just,' she shouted back.

Laughing, Richard, who was very like David to look at, only shorter, greyer and stockier, raised his glass to 'absent friends' as his wife leaned in to say, 'I saw you talking to Juliette earlier. How did it go?'

Having struck up an easy rapport with Astrid over Christmas, Cristy was able to say, dryly, 'To quote David, *Elle est très française*.'

Astrid threw back her head as she laughed, while Cynthia said, 'She's a canny one is Juliette, and frankly, I'm not too sure she's happy about you being here.'

'She's not,' Cristy confirmed, but decided not to elaborate. Juliette, with her swanlike neck, voluptuous mouth and boyish cap of sleek dark hair, could have stepped straight from the pages of *Vogue*. And this evening she was all chic sophistication and supreme elegance in a black silk sheath dress that showed the toned perfection of her shapely body to an annoying degree. It was no wonder David had been captivated by her, she was sensational and sensual to an almost indecent extreme.

'You look stunning,' Cristy had told her, trying to be friends, while already knowing it wasn't going to happen.

'Sank you,' Juliette had responded in a throaty French accent. 'David has always had good taste in women.' She hadn't even tried to temper the immodesty with a smile, unless of course it was meant as a compliment to Cristy as well. 'How long are you staying?' she'd asked, her eyes holding to Cristy's as she took a sip of her drink.

'I'm not sure,' Cristy replied, unwilling to give her the satisfaction of knowing she was planning to leave in the morning, weather permitting.

'I do hope we have some time to get to know one another,' Juliette smiled. 'I hear you're quite fascinating.'

Cristy wanted to laugh, so she did. 'It's lovely of you to come and see the New Year in with Laurent,' she said.

Juliette's pretty head tilted to one side. 'How could I not when David was so insistent?'

*Touché*, Cristy thought, feeling the warmth drain from her smile.

'He gets very lonely here all alone on this island,' Juliette continued. 'I feel bad for 'im, but it was not possible for me to stay. I adore *Paris*, it is in my blood, and there is too little here in the way of sophistication. I am sure you have found the same, *non*?'

'Not really,' Cristy replied smoothly. 'I think it has a lot going for it.'

Appearing surprised, Juliette said, 'So will he persuade you to stay?' Before Cristy could reply she leaned in closer and whispered, 'I sink it is only fair to tell you that 'e 'as asked me, only today, if I'd reconsider moving back here. Not only for Laurent's sake, you understand, for his too. You see, we still have a strong connection, and neither of us can quite break it, though I am not sure that we try very 'ard.' She drew back to gaze deeply into Cristy's eyes before raising her glass to her lips again and turning to greet someone close by.

There was no sign of her now, not that Cristy was keen to find her. However, with David also missing she couldn't help wondering . . .

'OK, everyone!' Richard shouted above the din. 'Time to get your coats if you're going outside. Heating's on in the garden room if you want to watch from there. Three minutes to go!'

'Garden room?' Astrid invited, linking Cristy's arm.

Allowing herself to be ushered along with the others, Cristy looked around for David again, but there was still no sign of him. Deciding he must still be down at the lake she took the frosted flute of champagne Astrid was passing and followed Cynthia to the huge picture windows. Though it was inky dark outside there was a small sea of torchlights bobbing about in the valley, reflecting on the water and making everything seem spectral and enticing.

'Where's David?' Cynthia cried in Cristy's ear.

'I've no idea,' Cristy shouted back.

'He should be here. Oh, will you look at Rosie out there without a coat.'

It was only when everyone was yelling 'Happy New Year' and the first fireworks soared and exploded into the sky that Cristy finally spotted him outside, walking quickly towards the house.

Then she saw Juliette, watching him from the entrance of a gazebo, and it was impossible not to think that they'd just stolen some moments together.

Feeling the phone buzz in her hand she checked the screen. It was Matthew, her ex-husband, wishing her Happy New Year in spite of it still being only four in the afternoon where he was, in LA. *Can we talk? I need you. Mx*

'Cristy! Happy New Year!'

She looked up to find Sadie and Anna bearing down on her, both slopping champagne over their fingers, eyes bright with excitement.

'I've found some more,' Sadie told her as they embraced. 'It's only a few pages, but it's definitely the same story.'

'There you are!' David cried, taking Cristy's arm and turning her around. 'I'm sorry for missing the big moment, but Happy New Year.'

'Oh God, they're going to snog,' Anna groaned. 'There's something really ick when it's your father.'

'Then don't look,' he said, and planting a hand over her face he pulled Cristy to him. 'Happy New Year,' he whispered against her lips.

'Happy New Year,' she echoed, yielding to the kiss. Then pulling back she searched his eyes. She could find nothing duplicitous in them, no trace of guilt or anger or of wanting to be elsewhere. Even so, she couldn't help noticing that along with the scent of cool night air and his own musky cologne there was a trace of Juliette's distinctive *eau de parfum*.

# CHAPTER THREE

'She's asleep,' Lottie said quietly, as she came down the creaking wooden stairs.

Mia was standing at the bottom, her expression torn between concern and fear, her slim hands clutched tightly together. She was a worrier, always had been and always would be. It irritated Lottie; however, on this occasion she was ready to concede that her sister had good reason to feel anxious.

'What are we going to do?' Mia asked, following Lottie along the hall into the kitchen where the remains of a beans on toast tea with orange squash and squishy marshmallows were still on the vinyl-covered table. It wasn't a large kitchen – nothing about the house was large, which had actually been its greatest charm when they were small, coming here with their grandparents. It could hardly have provided a greater contrast to their parents' five-storey, Regency townhouse in the heart of Kensington.

'She's been here for three days now,' Mia stated, as Lottie started to clear the table.

'Yes, I know that.' Lottie's back was turned as she ran hot water into the sink and squirted in a short stream of Fairy Liquid. She almost never did any washing-up, at least not here in England. When she was on the ground in places of suffering and severe hardship she turned her hand to just about anything. Tonight she was finding the process pleasingly therapeutic in a 'clean everything off ready to start again' sort of way.

'You're planning to keep her, aren't you?' Mia blurted.

Unfazed, Lottie said, 'It's what we've been asked to do.'

Mia grabbed a tea towel and started to dry. 'Why hasn't anyone come looking for her?' she demanded, as if her indignance could somehow justify the fact that they hadn't reported the child missing themselves when they both knew they should have. 'There hasn't been anything on the news and we haven't even seen anyone since you brought her up from the beach. It doesn't make any sense.'

Lottie was perfectly aware of that, although it clearly made sense to someone, somewhere.

For the past three days they'd waited expectantly, fearfully even, for a knock on the door, either from whoever had written the note, or maybe from the police, but so far no one had come near the place. So how long were they supposed to care for the child? Would someone contact them again soon? It was as if time was standing still, holding its breath, waiting to find out what would happen next, and into the void tumbled all sorts of crazy scenarios. At least for Lottie. She wasn't entirely sure what Mia was thinking from one minute to the next, but that was Mia – no sooner had she had a thought, than it was changed with the passing wind.

Yesterday Mia had driven into town to buy the child clothes and toys and books to crayon in, while Lottie had stayed behind helping small fingers to piece together a jigsaw they'd found in the cellar. At least no one, when they eventually came for her, would be able to say she hadn't been well taken care of. Exactly how they were going to explain not contacting the authorities as soon as they'd found her was an awkwardness they'd deal with when, if, they had to.

'Mrs B is due tomorrow,' Mia stated, as if Lottie wasn't already aware of that.

Their housekeeper, Gita Brinkley, was a sweet-natured woman of Indian origin who wasn't much good at cleaning or laundry, but boy could she cook. She lived in an old fisherman's cottage on the outskirts of the nearby town, drove a noisy Mini, helped organize events for the local WI and took care of pets when their owners were away. Her husband, Charles, was, as far as Lottie and Mia could make out, usually drunk by the middle of the day. Poor Mrs B, she deserved so much better.

'What are we going to tell her about . . .?' Mia asked, glancing towards the ceiling as though to remind Lottie of who was up there.

'Do you have any ideas?' Lottie countered, handing over a soapy plate.

Taking it, Mia said, 'Actually, I have. I was thinking we could say that she's our niece come to stay for a while.'

Lottie turned to her, eyebrows arched incredulously. 'And when her mother or some other relative comes looking for her, what then?'

Mia shrugged. 'Maybe no one will,' she ventured, and Lottie knew exactly what was in her mind now. Hadn't she been thinking the same herself? Wasn't it why they'd already started to call the child Sadie instead of Sasha? Nothing had been said about that, Lottie couldn't even be sure who'd used the name first, it was simply something they'd slipped into, and the dear little soul was going along with it.

Having now voiced her greatest hope, Mia's heart was floating in waves of dreamy expectation of how life could be going forward. There would be so much more of the joy they'd shared in the last few days, Sadie's sweet face watching their every move, and the music of her laughter when Mia tickled her. She liked to jump and play peek-a-boo, and she was learning to set her own place at the table. She didn't make a fuss when it was time for bed and she loved listening to stories, often gazing up at Mia or Lottie as they spoke the words softly until she finally fell asleep. She even sat quietly when Lottie brushed the tangles from her golden hair. Of course she cried for her mummy, it was only to be expected, but she allowed herself to be comforted with the promise that 'Mummy will come soon.' No one had mentioned Daddy.

Lottie suddenly said, 'Let's agree that we're developing a fondness for her, and it's nothing to be ashamed of when she's a little angel. I just wish we knew why someone put her into our care, and why they did it in such a . . . furtive and dangerous way when they could simply have brought her to the door.'

'If they had we wouldn't have accepted her,' Mia pointed out. 'I mean, how could we when we know nothing about her, or the people she's been with until now? Do you think it was her parents?'

'How on earth would I know?'

'She's said "Mummy" a few times,' Mia pointed out.

Lottie wasn't listening. 'Maybe the person you saw running away had stolen her,' she said, 'that's why they didn't want to be seen.'

Mia shook her head. 'I think it was her mother. She waited until she knew we had her before she ran.'

Lottie's hands stilled in the dishwater as she continued to think. 'Should we be actively trying to find out who she is?' she asked, knowing of course that they should. 'Or do we just keep her here until someone comes?'

'I say the latter,' Mia replied. 'I mean, we don't know if she's in danger from someone and I think she probably is, that's why she's here, to be kept safe.'

Lottie didn't disagree, after all it was what the note had said. 'But why us? We're not from around here, so who knows enough about us to feel they can trust us with a small child and make sure she comes to no harm?'

Since the question was rhetorical Mia didn't attempt an answer.

'The trouble is,' Lottie continued, 'the longer she's with us the harder it'll be to let her go, and we'll have to eventually, you know that.' Such cunning, so much artifice and planning all wrapped up in the right words.

'Why?' Mia wanted to know, falling into the trap. 'If someone is so irresponsible as to abandon a child on a beach – or to leave her with two complete strangers – maybe they don't deserve to have her back.'

'Well, we can't just randomly keep her, especially not if she has a mother who wants her . . .'

'Who left her. The authorities will take a very dim view of that . . .'

'And they won't much like us either when it's discovered that we didn't contact them as soon as we found the child. We could end up being charged with abduction or kidnap or something worse.' Get it all out there, voice the biggest fears, it was the only way to beat them.

Mia's eyes were wide with alarm as she said, 'Maybe this is the start of a blackmail attempt. If we don't give someone what they want they'll report us for stealing the child.'

Lottie was about to scoff when she realized Mia could have a point. Before she could speak a little voice behind them said, 'Can't sleep.'

They turned, hearts in their mouths as they wondered how much she might have heard. She was standing in the doorway, her angelic face all flushed and sleepy, her lively curls tumbling around her tiny shoulders. She was like an apparition, a dream they were sharing that had somehow manifested into a disconcerting reality.

Mia went to scoop her up and sat with her at the table while Lottie prepared some hot milk. 'Would teddy like some?' Lottie offered.

Sadie nodded and hugged the shiny new bear to her chest. When Mia had handed it over she'd lit up as if it was what she'd always wanted. 'Teddy,' she'd whispered. It was one of the few words she'd spoken since they'd taken her in.

'Did you have a dream?' Mia asked softly, stroking her hair.

Sadie lowered her head.

'Do you want to tell us what it was about?'

Sadie looked up at her, but didn't answer.

'I hope it wasn't a scary one,' Lottie said with a play growl.

Sadie shook her head, and squeezed her teddy again. After a moment she tilted her head back to look at Mia again. 'I want Mummy,' she said quietly.

Mia's eyes shot to Lottie's as she drew the child in tighter.

Bringing the milk to the table, Lottie set it down and sat as she said, 'Can you tell us your mummy's name, Sadie?'

Sadie kept her face hidden in Mia's shoulder.

'If we do contact the authorities,' Mia said later, after they'd tucked Sadie back into bed and read her a story, 'they'll probably take her into care and what good would that do anyone?'

Recognizing the question for the excuse that it was, Lottie said, 'Even if we pass her off as our niece to Mrs B, that's just the beginning. What do we tell our friends? And isn't Edwin threatening to come at some point soon?'

As Mia's heart contracted, she went to a cupboard to take out a bottle of whisky. It probably wasn't a good idea to drink with a child in the house, but surely one wouldn't hurt and if they were going to get onto the subject of Edwin . . .

Fetching down two glasses, Lottie said, 'He knows we don't have any nieces or nephews, so how would we explain her to him?'

'He might not come,' Mia responded dolefully.

'He will, he's the proverbial bad penny, and if she's still here . . .'

Mia was finding it hard to think.

'We're doing everything wrong,' Lottie declared irritably. 'As if there's a right way, for God's sake. Do you know what I'd do if I was writing this?'

Mia eyed her warily.

'I'd make you end your farce of a marriage, that's what I'd do.'

Mia stared at her open-mouthed.

'You should never have married him in the first place,' Lottie scolded, 'and I shouldn't have encouraged it. He's only ever been interested in your money . . .' She stopped at Mia's stricken look. 'I'm sorry,' she said quickly, 'but you know it's true. You're worth so much more than he could ever offer, so let's pay him off, get rid of him once and for all.'

'And that,' Mia said hoarsely, 'is how you'd write my life?'

'It's how I'd write ours, going forward,' Lottie replied. 'So now, drink up if you want to hear the rest.'

# CHAPTER FOUR

'It's definitely got me intrigued,' Connor declared, his voice booming around the electric Smart car that Cristy had borrowed from David's mother that morning. She hadn't found the volume control yet, but at least she'd managed to hit the right button when Connor's name had flashed across the screen letting her know he was calling.

'It's different,' he continued. 'Usually this kind of story is all about someone who's gone missing never to be seen again. Here we have the victim, so to speak, we just need to find out who lost her.'

'Or gave her away, or whatever,' Jodi added. Connor's wife always took a keen interest in their podcasts and Cristy always welcomed her input.

'Presuming the chapters we've seen so far aren't fiction,' Connor said, 'and I don't reckon they are, not with the names being the same and dates tying in . . . I'm seeing them as more of a . . . confession?'

'Purging of conscience?' Jodi suggested.

'It's hard to say when there's so little to go on,' Cristy said, taking a careful right turn onto a heavily wooded road where almost nothing was visible through the dense fog that had fallen overnight.

She'd scanned and emailed the latest chapter first thing this morning while David was still in bed sleeping off a few too many glasses toasting in the New Year. With so many friends and family at the party and him being the host, he'd found himself in such demand that Cristy had barely seen him after midnight. She'd lost track of Juliette too, not that she'd been keeping an eye out for her, though she'd noticed her when she'd appeared on the dance floor – with David. How closely and well they'd moved together, and how intimate they'd seemed, until David had caught her eye and winked. Anyway, she was determined not to start exercising herself over his past, it was clearly what the woman wanted and Cristy was damned if she was going to allow herself to be dragged into childish games. She just hoped Juliette had slept well on the bunk in Laurent's room while David had crashed out in his own bed next to Cristy.

'Are you still there?' Connor's voice was slightly broken as he asked.

'Sorry, yes, just not a great reception. Anyway, I'm clearly not getting off this island today, there are no flights or ferries probably until tomorrow, or Wednesday, so I'm on my way to meet Mia Winters. Unsurprisingly, Sadie doesn't want me to reveal why I'm there, so I'm just a new friend who's visiting the Gaudions, while actually getting a take on how batty, or not, the old lady is. That's Anna's word, by the way. Sadie insists she's quite lucid when she wants to be and uses her battiness to avoid things she doesn't want to do, or discuss.'

'Sadie's got to have realized that if it turns out she was abducted her aunt's going to have some hard questions to answer,' Jodi pointed out. 'Is that really what she wants?'

'All I can tell you,' Cristy replied, 'is that she believes there's a lot more to her story than we've seen so far, and I don't think we can argue with that. So let's try not to jump to obvious conclusions before we have a fuller picture, and whether we get that through more pages, or hard research, remains to be seen.'

'Do you have any recording equipment with you?'

'Only my phone, but I'm not about to go covert on the old lady.'

'I wasn't meaning that. You could just lay down a description of the house, grounds, that part of the island, et cetera.'

'If I could see it, I would,' she retorted wryly, as she plunged into a deeper morass of fog. 'I don't think I should be out in this, to be honest. There's no one else on the roads . . . If I can find the place without going over a cliff it'll be a miracle.'

'Maybe turn back,' Jodi suggested. 'It's not as if it's urgent. Wait for the weather to clear and go then?'

'It's not far now, and Sadie's waiting for me. With any luck she might have found more pages by the time I get there.'

'Call us again when you have news from the aunt, or Sadie,' Connor said. 'Meantime I'm going to start working on what we already have.'

'It's New Year's Day!' Cristy cried, and immediately gulped as she almost hit a roadside rock. 'I really should ring off,' she said, 'I need to concentrate on where I'm going.'

As the call ended, the sudden silence that descended felt oddly disorientating, leaving her with a disturbing sense of isolation in this tiny car that was inching along a barely visible highway with only the satnav to guide her through the virtually invisible mass of fallen cloud.

Keeping the speed right down she followed the map on the screen, mounting a hill, dipping around a bend and climbing another before a disembodied voice suddenly bellowed, 'You have reached your destination.'

Certain she was in the middle of nowhere Cristy came to a halt, praying that nothing approached from behind, or in front, to slam her and the little Smart car into the great beyond. She looked around. It wasn't until a space briefly opened in the drifting fog that she saw the towering gates to Villa des Roches, the Winters family estate.

Relieved, and amazed she'd actually got here, she turned gingerly into the welcome layby and decided to call Sadie rather than try to find a bell to gain entry. However, the gates were already starting to swing slowly open, telling her that someone must be watching on video.

She'd moved forward only a few yards when Sadie appeared out of the mist and gestured for her to open the passenger door. 'That's where Jasper and I live,' she said, jumping in. 'The lodge, not that you can see much of it in this. It's a bit clearer down at the house, or it was when I left half an hour ago. Are you OK? I'm surprised you came.'

'So am I,' Cristy muttered, and quickly swung the car to the right as she mounted a low, grassy bank.

'It's more or less straight now,' Sadie told her, 'and it's all downhill.'

'So the house itself is on the coast?' Cristy asked, eyes glued to the tarmacked drive.

'Not exactly, it kind of overhangs, but for some reason the fog never seems quite as bad in our cove as it does elsewhere. Great party last night, wasn't it?'

Cristy nodded. 'What time did you leave?'

'Around two, I think. Jasper's not in the best shape this morning, so I left him in bed while I went to check on Mia. I had a bit more of a dig around in Lottie's rooms while I was there, but nothing new, I'm afraid. What did you make of the pages I gave you last night?'

'I've just spoken to my partner, Connor, and he's as intrigued by what we've seen so far as I am. So you need to fill me in on everything you've done to try to find out where you came from.'

With a sigh, Sadie said, 'Not very much, is the answer, I'm afraid. I mean, the obvious stuff, like DNA and Google searches, but when I have so little to go on . . . Ancestry-dot-com can't help without the names of my mother and father – I put in Martin and Vanessa Winters, but that was never going anywhere without dates and places of birth. And anyway, we already know that my aunts didn't have a brother. Sorry, it's sounding a bit hopeless, isn't it?'

'Don't let's give up yet,' Cristy advised, and felt a slight unravelling of tension as a truly spectacular Arts-and-Crafts-style mansion, with towers and turrets, whitewashed walls and red-brick chimneys, emerged from the haze like a fairy tale castle. 'It's impressive,' she murmured, coming to a stop outside a wide, arched front door with enormous pots of topiary either side and a church-like stained-glass window above.

'It's insane, really,' Sadie declared, 'but it's home and I think you'll like it inside. They've always kept it up together and there's plenty of space for entertaining. Lottie loved to throw parties. Come on, the door's unlocked so we can go straight in.'

The hexagonal entrance hall turned out to be every bit as grand as Cristy had expected, and was, she suspected, most likely flooded with light on a good day from the ornate ceiling lanterns high overhead. The walls were painted a creamy white, the floor was pale oak and the furnishings, so many of them, were colourfully and tastefully in keeping with the distinctive turn-of-twentieth-century period.

'Lottie's rooms are over there,' Sadie announced, pointing towards a set of oak-panelled double doors, both closed, with exquisite fan-shaped wall sconces either side, 'but come and meet Mia first.' As she trotted down three steps to lead the way through another set of panelled doors, Cristy followed, admiring everything they passed, from the sumptuous William Morris wall coverings and Klimt-style paintings (maybe they were originals?) to the art-deco cabinetry and a fascinating collection of vases and lamps.

Eventually they were in a kitchen-cum-living area, which, though large, was much simpler in décor than what she'd seen so far. A superb and vast hand-carved cast-iron fireplace with a log fire burning in the grate was between two sumptuous cream-coloured sofas, while a round eight-seater table and matching chairs filled a circular breakfast area where tall windows offered uninterrupted views of a mist-shrouded sea. The kitchen itself was almost discreet with teal-coloured units and a wraparound bar.

'Ah, ha, you must be Sadie's new friend.' Mia Winters entered the room from another door, all smiles and quirky elegance in a beige-mix tartan pinafore and cream rollneck sweater. She was in good shape for seventy, no doubt about that. Her chin was an arresting feature, seeming a little large for her face, while her abundant, expertly coloured hair was carefully flicked up at the ends, and the dark amber jewels in her ears matched the colour of her eyes. 'I'm Mia,' she said, offering a slender hand, 'and I'm very pleased to meet you.'

'Likewise,' Cristy said warmly. 'You have a beautiful home.'

Mia smiled. 'Thank you. Please, won't you sit down?'

'I'll make coffee,' Sadie said and scooted round to the kitchen area. 'How do you take yours, Cristy?'

'Black, no sugar, thanks,' Cristy replied.

'A girl after my own heart,' Mia smiled, touching a hand to her meagre chest. 'You're a guest of the Gaudions, I hear. And didn't you make a podcast about the girls' mother? David's dead wife?'

As Cristy blinked in surprise, Sadie exclaimed, 'How do you know that? I never told you.'

Mia smiled craftily. 'I don't rely on you for all my information,' she replied. To Cristy she added, 'It was an addictive series. I binged the whole thing in two sittings. What an incredible job you did, and how utterly marvellous that you and David have now become close. I do believe the hand of fate was at work there . . . Well, it is in everything, of course, but sometimes it reveals itself more clearly than at other times.'

Wondering if Mia believed that fate had washed a near-two-year-old girl up on their beach almost twenty-four years ago, Cristy said, 'I'm glad you enjoyed the series.'

'You're a dark horse, Mia,' Sadie scolded.

'Oh, that was Lottie, not me,' Mia corrected. 'My sister had so many secrets,' she told Cristy. 'She was probably a spy. I always used to think so, but she'd never admit to it. If I'm right, then I'm sure she was a jolly good one. Lottie was good at a lot of things, wasn't she, Sadie?'

'The best,' Sadie confirmed, bringing cups and a coffee pot to the table, 'but one thing's for certain, she was absolutely useless at keeping her paperwork in order.'

Mia's laugh was slightly too high. 'That's true,' she assured Cristy, and turning to a long-case grandfather clock next to the fireplace, she blinked in surprise, as if it had struck. 'Is that the time already?' she asked.

Since the hands were showing twenty-past eight, it had either stopped, or was three hours slow – or maybe it had sped off to the evening.

As though her aunt hadn't spoken, Sadie finished pouring and handed a cup to Cristy as she said, 'I was telling Mia about last night's party earlier. The fireworks were sensational, weren't they?'

'I've always loved fireworks,' Mia confided. 'We had them all the time at our parties, when Lottie was alive. She didn't care for them so much, but she knew I did so they were a must.'

'Actually, it's you who doesn't really like them,' Sadie reminded her. 'Lottie was a fiend for them.'

Mia nodded agreeably. 'That's true. And you take after her in that way. Did you have sparklers? You've always loved them, especially on birthday cakes. She's never grown out of it,' she told

Cristy. 'We don't with some things, do we? Are you staying long in Guernsey?'

'Just until the fog clears,' Cristy replied, picking up her coffee.

'Oh, that's a shame.' Mia smiled and took a sip from her delicate cup.

Not entirely sure what to say next, Cristy willed Sadie to come to the rescue for it was clear already that David was right about trying to pin Mia down. She wasn't going to stay on subject if she didn't want to, and even when she did there was no knowing how much of what she might say was true.

'May I ask where you live, Cristy?' Mia said, sounding interested.

'Bristol,' Cristy replied, glad to be on safe territory. 'Close to the harbourside.'

'Oh, very nice. Not that I've ever been there, but it sounds idyllic.'

Amused by the overstatement, Cristy dared to say, chattily, 'How long have you lived in this house?'

Mia frowned as she thought – and thought.

Cristy waited, knowing it was going to be easy to check the land registry, or Guernsey's equivalent, so she was really very interested to hear Mia's answer.

'I think it must be about twenty-three years by now,' she said, looking to Sadie for confirmation. Receiving it, she added, 'It wasn't like this when we moved in. In fact it was quite run-down, but thanks to Lottie's vision and some very talented builders we've come to what you see now.'

'Are you actually from Guernsey?' Cristy ventured.

Mia gave a nostalgic little sigh. 'No, Lottie and I hail from London. Kensington, to be exact.' After a pause she added, 'We kept the house after we left – it was Mummy and Daddy's of course, we inherited it after they passed – but then we decided to sell. We weren't going back, so there seemed little point in keeping it. It was really quite large. Do you have parents, Cristy?'

Admiring how astutely she was running the conversation, Cristy said, 'Not any more, sadly.'

Mia's tone was heartfelt as she said, 'I'm sorry to hear that. It's hard when they go, isn't it?'

Mindful of Sadie's birth parents, Cristy tried to think of a way to turn matters in that direction without seeming obvious, but Mia was speaking again. 'Lottie and I were in our thirties when it happened to us. Such a shock, losing them both the way we did. There one day, gone the next.'

'How did they die?' Cristy asked politely.

Mia frowned, as though not entirely sure, or maybe she'd belatedly realized she was heading towards a place she didn't want to be. 'Are you a reader, Cristy?' she asked brightly.

With a quick glance at Sadie, Cristy said, 'Yes, I am. Are you?'

'Oh yes. It's one of my favourite pastimes. Do you happen to have read any of my short stories? I haven't had any published for a long time, but quite a few were, back in the day.'

'It was Lottie who wrote,' Sadie reminded her.

Mia laughed. 'That's what we used to tell everyone, but really it was me. I wrote them all. I just didn't want the fuss and bother of finding an agent and editor, and all the business that goes with getting them into the public's hands. Or the clutches of reviewers.' She gave a shudder of distaste. 'Heaven save us from them, is what I always say.'

Feeling the sands shifting again, Cristy said carefully, 'Do you still write?'

'Oh no. I gave it up a long time ago. I just read now, and listen to the occasional podcast.' She twinkled charmingly and put her coffee cup down. 'It's been lovely talking to you, Cristy. Thank you for coming, but I have a lot to be getting on with today so I shall leave Sadie to show you around. She's very good at doing tours. Are you interested in the Arts-and-Crafts style?'

'Uh, yes, I find it quite fascinating,' Cristy assured her, wondering if Mia now thought it was the reason she'd come, to view the house.

Mia was on her feet. 'Do feel free to take photographs if you'd like to,' she said, 'but we'd rather they didn't show up in unsuitable magazines, if you don't mind. Sadie will give you a list of those we've approved.' She checked the grandfather clock again, but said no more as she left by the door she'd come in through.

With a laugh, Sadie said, 'And there you have my aunt Mia. Mad as a box of frogs, or is that just what she wants us to think?'

Wryly, Cristy said, 'It's a tricky one. But tell me, do you think she actually did write the stories?'

'No, I know she didn't, but that's what I mean about her seeming to mix herself up with Lottie. She does it all the time. Tomorrow she'll be the spy and Lottie will acquire some other sort of mystery, or hang-up, or bizarre little hobby. Anyway, I'm happy to give you a tour if you'd like one, or we can just take a look at Lottie's suite. You'll see for yourself what I'm up against.'

A few minutes later, Cristy was surveying first one, then another, and another of Lottie's spacious rooms, all opening off one another, each with high ceilings and elaborate French doors leading onto terraces that hung over the sea, way below. The endless clutter of boxes, books, filing cases, ornate chests, sports equipment, odd musical instruments, exercise paraphernalia and so much else, all stacked against walls, on desks, under tables and every other available surface, was almost overwhelming.

'It could take years to go through all this,' she remarked to Sadie.

Sadie didn't disagree. 'What's worse,' she said, 'is that nothing is in order. The pages I gave you last night? I found them by chance, clipped to the back of some notes that had no relevance to them at all, or not that I could find.'

Cristy checked her phone as it buzzed with a text. David wanting to know where she was.

'Do you have anyone who can help you with this?' she asked, looking around again and feeling increasingly daunted by the seemingly impossible task.

'Anna,' Sadie replied. 'And Jasper when he has time.'

Cristy nodded thoughtfully, and turned back to the entrance hall where they found Mia waiting and holding up Cristy's coat.

'You left it in the sitting room,' she said, handing it over. 'I thought you'd be needing it.'

Cristy smiled at the gentle irony in her tone, while feeling slightly wrongfooted again. Was she being told it was time to leave?

'Thank you,' she said. 'Your sister has certainly collected a lot of things over the years.'

Mia waved a dismissive hand. 'She was such a hoarder. Had all sorts shipped in from all over with never a single idea of what she was going to do with it once it got here. But you know, it's not only her stuff she kept, mine is in there too . . . Journals and notebooks, travelogues, endless photographs, and of course all her short stories.'

So they were Lottie's now.

'I'm sure she wrote six a day sometimes,' Mia ran on. 'They just came tumbling out of her in an unstoppable flow and I think I've probably read every one. They're very good, but of course I'm biased. Shame so many were lost when we reset her computers, but she never wanted to keep them anyway.' She turned away and disappeared back into the depths of the house.

Cristy turned to Sadie and smiled as the young woman shrugged.

'I'll keep going,' Sadie promised, 'and let you know as soon as I find anything else – presuming I do.'

'It could drive us all nuts if you don't,' Cristy told her, 'but you do realize, of course, that as soon as we go live with the story your aunt is going to know about it. And considering what serious ramifications there could be for her she'll almost certainly try to stop us.'

Sadie pulled a face as she nodded. 'I've been thinking about that,' she admitted, 'and I really don't want to hurt her, or make her think I'm in any way unhappy or ungrateful for all she and Lottie have given me, because I'm neither of those things. But like I said before, I really do want to find out who I am. It's like I *need* to. I hope you can understand that.'

Looking into her troubled eyes, Cristy said, 'Of course.' Who wouldn't understand that, she was thinking as she put on her coat and turned to the front door. But did Sadie really have a full grasp on what it could do to her aunt?

*

A few minutes later, Cristy was back in the welcome layby outside the villa's grounds, calling David.

'Hi, where are you?' he asked when she got through to him.

'Mum said you borrowed the car to go see Sadie and Mia. Please tell me you're still in one piece.'

'I am and I'm just heading back.'

'The conditions are serious out there,' he said gravely. 'You shouldn't have gone in the first place. Would you like me to come get you?'

'I think I can manage, thanks. How are you feeling?'

'You mean apart from the sore head? Like I'm in need of three pints of water and seeing you. Are you driving at the moment?'

'No, I've stopped to make this call.'

'Good. So tell me, how did you get on with Mia?'

'She's much like you described, but I'd say a lot smarter than she wants anyone to think.'

'You could be right about that. Tell me more when you get here. Mum's throwing together a late lunch . . . Will you be joining us?'

'That's certainly my intention. Who's still there?'

'Just about everyone who stayed last night. The fog's too thick to go anywhere, although it apparently didn't stop you.'

'I'm suitably contrite,' she assured him, 'and I'll also be extremely glad when I get there, but the satnav has served me well so far. No reason why it should let me down now. If I get into any difficulties I'll call.'

*

By the time Cristy walked into the Gaudion family's wonderfully warm kitchen to be assailed by mouthwatering aromas of bacon and hot toast, at least two dozen bodies were scattered about the place either drinking coffee, sipping water or, in a few hardy cases, getting stuck into Bloody Marys.

Realizing no one had noticed her yet, she removed her coat and watched Anna and Rosie whizzing about with plates of hot food while Juliette, looking very much at home, slid a delicious-looking frittata from an oven and Cynthia sautéed a pan full of rosti. She looked around for David and found him stacking extra wood on the fire while chatting with his brother who was laughing at whatever they were saying. She didn't want to tear her eyes away, simply wanted to carry on looking at David, taking in his hands, his back, the length of his legs as he stood. She thought of the way he made love, the power and gentleness of him, his taste and smell . . .

Suddenly, out of nowhere, she seemed to be caught up in some sort of surreal moment, as she wondered how she'd come to be here, at the heart of someone else's family, when her own was far away doing other things.

She watched David turn around, prompted by Astrid, and couldn't be sure of how pleased or not he was to see her. He was frowning and his expression didn't lighten as he picked his way through everyone to come and greet her.

'What's wrong?' he said quietly. 'Has something happened?'

'No,' she said in surprise, 'everything's fine. I just . . .' What was going on in her head? Why had she felt that unsettling moment of detachment? Breaking into a smile, she said, 'Looks like the party continues.'

Glancing round to survey the gathering he said, 'I have a feeling it won't stop until at least tomorrow. How are the roads out there?'

As she answered she could feel Juliette's eyes on them. 'Still not very passable,' she admitted, 'but I don't think anyone here is having a problem with being fogged in.'

'Apart from you?' he countered.

Her eyes went to his. 'I'm happy to be with you,' she told him, 'but I have to admit I'll be glad to see the children.'

Seeming to accept that, he said, 'I'd like to hear more about your first meeting with Mia, but come and get something to eat first.'

Aware that he hadn't kissed her, or even touched her, she followed him over to the kitchen and again ignored Juliette's scrutiny, preferring instead to react to the way Rosie lit up when she saw her.

'Happy New Year's Day,' Rosie cried, sticking out her bottom as she leaned in for an air-kiss. 'I've got a secret,' she whispered, loud enough for everyone nearby to hear. 'You're not allowed to tell anyone.'

'We already know,' David teased.

Cristy laughed, then realized he was looking at Juliette.

Juliette's smile was playful as she said, 'I don't think you do.'

'Don't be so sure,' he murmured.

Wondering how innocent banter with Rosie had suddenly become a flirtation between David and Juliette, Cristy took the plate of food Cynthia was offering, not entirely sure how hungry she was now, and searched around for somewhere to sit.

'Over here,' Astrid, David's sister-in-law, called out, and elbowed her husband off one of the sofas onto the floor. 'Come sit by the fire and get warm.'

Grateful for the invite, Cristy picked her way across the room, laughing and joking with those she passed. Settling herself in next to Astrid, she said, 'Is there vodka in that tomato juice?'

'There actually is,' Astrid confirmed, holding up her glass to examine it. 'Why don't you join me? It's very good.'

Considering it, Cristy smiled up at Anna as she brought over some hot buttered toast.

'How did you get on with Mia?' Anna asked. 'Whacky or what?'

'She's definitely her own person,' Cristy said dryly. 'Apparently she binged on the last series of *Hindsight*.'

Anna blinked in amazement. 'No way! You mean the one about our family?'

Cristy nodded and took a mouthful of cauli hash brown.

'I had no idea she even knew what a podcast was,' Anna exclaimed.

'I don't think Sadie did either, so seems best not to make too many assumptions about Mia Winters. In fact, now I've had time to consider it, I can't help wondering if her admission was a little warning shot across Sadie's bows, letting her know that she's perfectly aware of why I was invited there.'

As Anna's eyes rounded, Astrid laughed and said, 'Never underestimate those Winters women, is my advice. They've always been as canny as they come and twice as shrewd, and I wouldn't be a bit surprised if Lottie's playing you from the grave. It's the kind of thing she'd have a lot of fun with.'

Amused by that, Cristy said, 'Does that mean you don't believe in the story Sadie's unearthed?'

Astrid shrugged. 'From what Anna's told me about it, and what I knew of Lottie, I'd say it probably contains elements of truth, but exactly what those elements are . . .'

Unable not to notice David leaving the room with Juliette, Cristy forced herself to listen as Anna said, 'If you're thinking Lottie set this up, remember she died suddenly, so there was no time . . .'

'But you don't know when she did it,' Astrid pointed out. 'Listen, all I'm saying is I have a feeling there's going to be a lot more to this story than you might think.'

'As if we don't already think that,' Anna muttered.

Astrid said to Cristy, 'It's interesting, certainly, that the Winters sisters chose to come here twenty-odd years ago. It can't have been long after Sadie was found on the beach – if we're presuming that part of the story is real . . .'

When she didn't continue, Cristy prompted her to finish her thought.

Astrid smiled and her voice was a little slurred as she said, 'Speaking as a member of the Gaudion family . . . We know how easy it is to keep secrets on this island, don't we? Your last podcast proves that. In fact, there's nowhere better, given that the whole place is practically built on them. *Nullas quaestiones, nihil mentitur*, or something like that.'

'What does that mean?' Anna queried.

'Ask no questions, told no lies,' Cristy provided.

'It's the unofficial motto in these parts,' Astrid explained. 'So where better for two wealthy women to relocate when planning to pass off a small child as their own?'

Refraining from saying that they'd already figured that part of it out, Cristy watched David come back into the kitchen, grab a bottle of wine and disappear again.

Distracted by her phone, she saw it was a family What'sApp from both her children who she hadn't yet spoken to this year. 'I need to take this,' she told Astrid, and after asking Hayley and Aiden to give her a moment she headed through to the summer room.

Once comfortably seated with the noise of the party barely audible through the closed door, she broke into a smile to see

Hayley's and Aiden's cherished faces on the screen – although neither, she realized, was looking particularly happy.

'How are you?' she asked. 'Isn't it a bit early in LA for you to be calling now?' Even as she said the words her heart gave a jolt of unease. 'What's happened?' she asked before either of them could speak. 'You're OK, are you?'

'We're fine,' Hayley assured her, 'but you might need to be sitting down for this.'

'I already am,' Cristy told her.

White-faced and clearly not celebrating, Hayley said, 'Marley's had the baby.'

Cristy's insides turned cold. Marley, the unpredictable, irrational child bride who'd stolen Cristy's husband and wrecked her family, and who'd turned out to be quite unlike anyone Cristy had ever known, had given birth to Matthew's child. Hayley and Aiden now had a half-brother or -sister.

Given her children's expressions, Cristy's first thought was that there was something wrong with the newborn, until Aiden said, 'Dad's not allowed to see it.'

'Not *allowed*?' Cristy echoed incredulously.

'It's a boy,' Hayley continued. 'Two weeks early, but he's OK and so is Marley, apart from the brain hiccup that's making her keep Dad out of the room. He's going nuts, shouting at people, demanding his rights, and then he got into a fight with a security guard.'

'Someone called the cops,' Aiden ran on, 'and he's been arrested.'

'*Arrested!*' Cristy choked, certain she couldn't have heard right.

Both children nodded.

'Where is he now?' she asked.

'In some cell, I guess,' Aiden answered miserably. 'Scott, Marley's dad, is talking to a lawyer to try and get him out, but, Mum, we really don't want to be here any more.'

'I've checked flights,' Hayley said, before Cristy could respond, 'and there's availability on one tomorrow night – well, tonight I guess, it's three in the morning here. It's just massively expensive so we were hoping . . .'

'We feel really bad bailing on Dad,' Aiden cut in, 'but we thought we'd be one less thing for him to worry about if we weren't here any more. And you know we didn't really want to come anyway.'

It was true, they hadn't wanted to go, but Matthew had been so hurt by their reluctance to spend some time with him in LA over the holidays that Cristy had ended up talking them into going for New Year. And now, this.

Picturing them at Scott Dukes's Laurel Canyon home, worrying about their dad, desperate to get away, feeling guilty about it and yet checking flights anyway, she said, 'Use the emergency credit card, and ask Scott to arrange a ride to the airport.'

'Thanks, Mum,' Hayley said. 'Sorry to put this on you now . . .'

'Don't worry about me. Just get yourselves home safely.'

A few minutes later Cristy was back in the kitchen – still no sign of David or Juliette – but Cynthia seemed to notice right away that all was not well with her.

'Has something happened?' Cynthia asked, drawing Cristy aside so no one could overhear.

Cristy gave a mirthless laugh. 'Marley's had the baby; Matthew's been arrested and the children are flying home tonight.'

Cynthia regarded her steadily. 'Maybe we need to sit down?' she suggested.

Following her back into the summer room Cristy felt a moment's overwhelming – even unsteadying – affection for the woman who reminded her so much of her own mother.

'So which part of it are you the most worried about?' Cynthia asked, as they took a chair each, overlooking the gardens.

Cristy smiled ruefully. 'I guess, for the moment, I'm pretty focused on getting home in time to meet Hayley and Aiden off the plane. But they'll be OK. Hayley has an emergency credit card so she can pay for the bus or a train to Bristol and from there they'll be able to get to my flat.'

'So that's sorted. What about Matthew? How on earth did he get himself arrested?'

Such a good question – although Cristy wasn't having much trouble imagining the chaos he'd created. 'Apparently he got into a dust-up with a security guard at the hospital,' she said, 'because

Marley won't let him see the baby.' Thinking of the tiny, innocent little creature at the heart of the madness, she became aware of a deep, churning sensation inside. It was dark and worrying and reminded her of how she'd felt when Aiden had first told her Marley was pregnant – as if a silent, raging tide was rising up to demolish what was left of her marriage. 'It's a boy,' she added. 'I don't know his name.'

'Why won't she let Matthew see him?'

Cristy shook her head. 'I've no idea. The last I heard Marley wanted Matthew to bring the child back to the UK when it was born so I could help him bring it up. Obviously that was never going to happen, apart from in Marley's head. But apparently it's all changed now and Matthew, who, as far as I knew, was dreading being a dad again, is in a prison cell for thumping someone who tried to get in the way of him seeing his son.'

Cynthia sighed as she pondered this bizarre set of events. 'I don't suppose any of this has been easy for him,' she commented. 'From all I've heard he now knows what a mistake he made in letting you go . . .'

'It's too late for that,' Cristy interrupted, not wanting to hear it. 'We have to deal with where we are now, except it actually isn't my problem, is it? Or it wouldn't be if he weren't my children's father, and I just know he'll be on the phone to me as soon as he's able to get to one.'

'Expecting what?'

'I've no idea. I just hope he doesn't think I'm going to fly over there to try and talk some sense into his crazy wife.' Cristy's eyes went to Cynthia's and after a beat she found herself almost wanting to laugh. It was all so messed up and farcical, and actually it *was* comical, provided Matthew got out of prison, of course – and as long as it didn't start impinging on her life the way he no doubt expected it to. But what about the press? Someone was bound to get hold of it sooner or later. With Marley being the daughter of a movie and theatre legend, and a successful actor in her own right, and Matthew's much lesser fame as a news anchor (OK not in the States but he'd already won a lot of notoriety in the UK for destroying his marriage over a child superstar in the first place), this was a story that was going to excite the tabloids, that was for sure.

'Why don't you let David make some calls?' Cynthia suggested. 'You know he has contacts all over, even in LA, and he'll arrange for a car to pick the children up at Heathrow.'

'No, I don't want to put him to the trouble . . .' Cristy said, perhaps a little too quickly.

'It won't be any trouble. You just need to let us have the flight details . . . And I'm guessing you'll be wanting to leave in the morning?'

Wishing she could go right now, Cristy said, 'If there's a flight, yes. I just hope the fog will have lifted by then or I'll be stranded. Maybe for days. Oh God, what a mess.'

'It's going to be fine,' Cynthia assured her. 'When does Hayley return to uni?'

'I think it's the fifteenth, but she was planning to fly to Edinburgh on the seventh to meet up with her boyfriend. Aiden starts back to school on the eighth so I definitely have to be there for that, or knowing him he'll find something "more interesting" to do.'

Cynthia laughed. Having got to know Aiden a little over Christmas, she, like everyone else, had taken quite a shine to him. 'I'm sure we'll get you off this island in time to keep him on the right path,' she said. 'Now, let's go and track down David so we can—'

'Actually, I'll catch up with him later,' Cristy interrupted, really not keen to find him if he was with Juliette – actually not even wanting to think about that. 'Right now I should ring Connor and Jodi to let them know the children will soon be on their way. I'm sure they'll insist on collecting them, or at least on putting them up until I can get back to Bristol.'

*

As it turned out Cristy was able to get a flight the next day. She left early, before anyone else was up, and after leaving a note for David, assuring him she'd be in touch as soon as she got home. *Thanks for a wonderful Christmas and New Year*, she added. *Sorry I was asleep when you came up last night; and I didn't want to wake you this morning. Your mum will tell you about Matthew and the children. Never a dull moment with them.*

She'd struggled with how to end it, as she'd wondered, not for the first time these past twenty-four hours, how she really felt about him. The situation with Juliette was bothering her a lot. Having been cheated on once, by Matthew, she never wanted to go through anything like it again and if there was still something between David and his ex . . . Maybe she, Cristy, was getting too involved, too soon, taking things way too seriously. And when it came right down to it, did she actually want their relationship to continue? How could it when his life was here on this island and hers elsewhere?

# CHAPTER FIVE

It was a week into the new year and Cristy and Connor were at Quinns' Podcast Studios on Bristol's harbourside. They'd already been given clearance from the company's owners, Harry and Meena, to move back into the once elegant and airy drawing room of a vast converted Georgian property at the heart of Spike Island, which was now a spacious ground-floor office reserved for prestigious productions. If *Hindsight*'s success continued, it was possible they'd soon outgrow this, but for now they were more than happy to be here. With such illustrious neighbours as the world-renowned SS *Great Britain*, only yards from their front door in its restricted dry dock, and the internationally loved and highly acclaimed Aardman Animations, home of *Wallace and Gromit* and *Shaun the Sheep*, just across the cobbled walkway outside their car park, it was a pretty desirable place to be.

CRISTY: 'Hi, I'm Cristy Ward . . .'

CONNOR: 'And I'm Connor Church. Welcome to a brand-new series of *Hindsight.*'

CRISTY: 'Before we get into the curious and compelling mystery we've chosen to investigate over the following weeks, we'd like to thank you all for the amazing support you gave our last series *Nothing to See Here . . .*'

CONNOR: 'Which, for those who haven't yet heard it, can still be found wherever you get your podcasts. Also, all the usual extras – photographs, video and extended versions of interviews featured in the series – remain available on our website.'

CRISTY: 'As our next story develops we'll be posting a lot more for you to view or interact with, and you'll soon understand what a vital role you might play in helping to solve this highly unusual case.'

CONNOR: 'We're going to begin by admitting that we aren't yet sure what the crime is here – bear with us and you'll see what we mean as the mystery unfolds. It begins with a written story, or an extract from one, that has its roots, we're sure, in some pretty strange facts.'

CRISTY: 'It was brought to us by a young woman called Sadie Winters who has no idea of who she really is, where she came from or what actually happened to her when she was just under two years old. But something certainly did.'

CONNOR: 'It's important to say now that so far we've found no reports of a missing child from around the time Sadie was found on a deserted beach on the west coast of England.'

CRISTY: 'Obviously, we'll be carrying out a much deeper dive into police files and missing persons registers as we move on with the investigation, and we'll let you know what we find as more details come to light. For now, here is Sadie reading two extracts from the written story she found amongst her aunt's papers after the aunt died suddenly in early 2020. Just keep in mind as you listen that the child she's telling you about is almost certainly her.'

As they ended the series intro Cristy sat back in her chair to listen once again to the audio file Sadie had painstakingly recorded over the past couple of days. It included everything from the moment Mia had spotted a child on the beach, right through to Lottie's suggestion that Mia should end her marriage if they wanted to keep the child they'd begun to call Sadie. There was now a third extract, found only yesterday, that was due to be recorded later today via a live link from Guernsey.

By the time they'd finished listening to Sadie's earlier recording, Cristy had brewed a fresh pot of coffee in their corner kitchenette and Connor was standing back to survey the headshots he'd just lined up across the top of the whiteboard. Mia's and Lottie's had been taken from old photographs provided by Sadie, while the one of Sadie herself had been sent by Jasper this morning. Though she wasn't smiling, it still managed to show just how lovely she was.

'I don't think Sadie should be between them,' Cristy observed. 'There are almost certainly going to be two separate backstories here, so the sisters should have one half of the board, and Sadie the other.'

Seeing the logic of that, Connor quickly rearranged the small gallery, giving space for two threads, before taking the coffee Cristy was passing him and returning to his desk.

'So Harry and Meena are due back at the end of the week,' he commented. 'Which reminds me, have you contacted Clover and Jackson yet to get them on board for the duration? I reckon we're going to need our crack research team at full throttle for this.'

'I spoke to Clove at the weekend,' she assured him, 'and lucky for us neither she nor Jacks have any conflicting assignments, so they're already familiarizing themselves with what we have so far. They'll join officially as soon as we have a budget fixed.'

'I say let's pull them in right away. We'll get what we want, no doubt about that, definitely enough to cover their contracts – and maybe to up our own a little? Have you crunched any numbers yet?'

'I have. I'll send my suggestions over so you'll see that I've built in an increase for us all. What we don't know yet, of course, is how much has to be greenlit by this new Sponsorship Liaison Group after consultation with the chosen sponsors. I'd say probably all of it.'

Connor was immediately hostile. 'Bollocks to that,' he grunted. 'If kow-towing to idiots is what success brings then let's live without it.'

'Or let's carry on the way we intend to right now. With any luck, by the time they make their minds up about anything, especially content, we'll be too far down the road to change course. Now, back to Sadie and the aunts – does that sound like a pop group?'

'A what? No one says that any more.'

Laughing, Cristy said, 'Listen to you, pushing thirty and still getting down with the kids? You're a father now, a grown-up producer and early-nighter . . .'

'Your point being?'

'I'm not sure, but those youthful good looks of yours could be under threat if your little darling starts depriving you of sleep. Then what will all your fans do?'

'I expect move on to Superman, from whom I stole them in the first place.'

She laughed again, for Connor did indeed resemble a young Christopher Reeve with his inky dark hair, large black-rimmed glasses and devastating smile. Cristy checked the time and finished her coffee. 'We're due to connect to Sadie in the next ten minutes,' she alerted him. 'So, just to be clear, we're definitely up for this in spite of having no idea where it might take us, or what kind of trouble it could end us, or anyone else, in?'

He grinned. 'Isn't not knowing the best part of it? And this latest extract she's found has really got me going.'

'Yeah, me too. I just hope she's tracked down more by now, because it's definitely raising more questions than it's answering.'

'Sorry to disappoint,' Sadie grimaced when Cristy put the question to her a few minutes later, 'but don't worry, we're still looking.'

'There's got to be at least another page,' Connor declared, as if his determination could somehow make it appear.

On his screen Sadie grimaced helplessly.

'OK,' he said, 'let's go with what we have so far. Are you OK to read?'

Sadie nodded eagerly. 'It's so short I almost know it by heart.'

'Excellent. There are a few rays of sunshine falling over your face, so if you could change angle slightly . . .'

As she adjusted, Cristy could tell that in spite of her bravado she was nervous, so she said gently, 'Don't worry if you stumble or lose your place, we can always do it again, just know that you have a great voice for podcasts.'

'As opposed to face?' Sadie quipped.

Cristy laughed. 'The video's only for the website, and we won't use anything you'd rather we didn't.'

Sadie nodded, and her eyes moved back to Connor as he released one ear from his headset and gave the thumbs up.

Before Cristy could speak Sadie said, 'This is the first time I've actually seen you, Connor. Did anyone ever tell you you look like Clark Kent?'

As Cristy sniggered, Connor refrained from saying, *Only about a million times*, and peered meaningfully through his glasses. 'Just don't put me near a phone box,' he cautioned.

'Or he'll get his knickers in a twist,' Cristy explained.

Sadie burst out laughing and Cristy ducked as Connor aimed a pencil at her head.

'OK, I'm going to disappear from the screen now,' he told them, 'it's just you and Cristy, Sadie, and she'll lead you in.'

After his habitual, though unnecessary, countdown Cristy began.

CRISTY: 'So, Sadie, you're going to read a third extract from what appears to be the same story, written by your aunt?'

SADIE: 'That's right. It's another scene, or part of a chapter, set in the hillside house. It's only a couple of pages that we found mixed in with other papers at the back of a drawer.'

To Connor, Cristy said, 'We need to get some footage of Lottie's rooms to put on the website so everyone can see just what a monumental task Sadie is facing. Is there any chance you can shoot that for us on your phone?' she asked Sadie.

'I should think so,' Sadie agreed. 'You might have to talk me through how to do it to make sure I get everything you need, but it shouldn't be hard. Provided Mia isn't watching.'

Cristy frowned at the reminder of what else she had to say during today's call. 'We'll come on to that,' she said. 'For now let's carry on with the reading. Are we still recording?' she asked Connor.

He gave a nod and she said, 'OK, in your own time, Sadie.'

SADIE: 'It starts mid-sentence, and this is what it says: . . . when Mia came into the room and shook Lottie awake.

"What time is it?" Lottie asked groggily, as she turned onto her back, blinking at the blaze of sunlight trying to stream through the curtains. "Just after seven," Mia whispered. "Sadie's still sleeping. Someone's knocking at the door."

'Registering the words Lottie came suddenly awake. "Have you looked out to see who it is?" she asked worriedly.

'"I didn't want to risk being seen. No one ever comes here, apart from Mrs B and Pete, the gardener, and neither of them knock."

'Lottie reached for her robe. Her heartbeat was suddenly unnaturally fast, her limbs shaky, and she could see it was the same for Mia. Had someone come for Sadie? It had to be that, so what were they going to do? They should have left here already. What fools to have stayed this long.

'They stood quietly in the semi-darkness, listening for more knocks and bracing themselves in case whoever it was refused to go away.

'The silence ticked ominously on, smoothed by the distant wash of waves and haunting wail of seagulls.

'"I think they might have gone," Mia whispered.

'Going out to the landing Lottie peered over the banister to the bottom of the stairs. No silhouette through the frosted pane in the front door, no muted crunch of footsteps on the gravel outside, or sound of a car engine. It was a long walk to get here on foot, but with the South West Coast Path not far away it was possible.

'She glanced back at her sister, and went into the next room to check on Sadie. There was no reason to think anyone had broken in and taken her – Mia had already told her she was still sleeping – but Lottie just needed to see for herself.

'She was there, beneath her new pink-frilled canopy and magic glow of fairy lights, all curled up around her teddy, eyes closed and mouth half-open as she breathed steadily, peacefully and so sweetly that Lottie's heart seemed to fold around her.

'"Lottie," Mia whispered.

'Leaving Sadie's door ajar, the way she liked it, Lottie

returned to the landing. Mia was at the top of the stairs staring down at something. Lottie followed her eyes and her own immediately widened with surprise and unease.

'An envelope was lying on the mat, just inside the front door, large and brown and apparently unsealed.

'Thinking immediately of blackmail, ransoms, all kinds of craziness, Lottie indicated for Mia to stay close to Sadie and started down the stairs. She had a horrible feeling that someone was watching her, but who on earth could be?

'Everything outside remained silent as she stooped to pick up the envelope, almost afraid to touch it in case it was some sort of booby trap. It wasn't addressed to anyone and not at all heavy, so she reached into it and pulled out the contents. At first she felt confused, until understanding dawned and she gasped in shock.

'"What is it?" Mia cried, coming quickly down the stairs.

'Lottie's face was pale and frightened as she handed over the envelope's contents and watched her sister register what had been delivered to their door.

'"Oh my goodness," Mia murmured, clasping a hand to her mouth. "Is there a note?"

'Lottie checked and shook her head. "That's all there is," she said.'

As she finished reading Sadie looked up to the camera, waiting to be told what to do next.

Cristy said, 'Well done, you read that very well. How do you feel?'

'You mean apart from frustrated and mad keen to know more?'

Cristy smiled. She could see the girl was shaken.

'It feels kind of sinister, don't you think?' Sadie said. 'Two middle-aged women alone in a remote house with a child they seem to be in the process of abducting and suddenly, out of nowhere, something – God knows what – comes through the door.'

Cristy had to agree, it did feel sinister.

Sadie glanced up as someone, out of shot, handed her a mug.

'Who's with you?' Cristy asked, not really thinking it would be Mia, but feeling the need to check anyway.

'Just me,' Anna answered, stooping to join Sadie in the shot. 'Great stuff, isn't it? But we have to find out what was in that envelope.'

'Jasper's down at the house now seeing if he can turn something up,' Sadie informed them.

'Shall I stop recording?' Connor asked.

Cristy shook her head. 'I'm just going to do a little spiel,' she told Sadie, 'and then we'll get into the interview we discussed yesterday if that's OK?'

'Take it away,' Sadie responded. She sipped her coffee as Cristy waited for Connor to bring the script to the screen, then began.

CRISTY: 'I know, beyond frustrating that the latest extract ends where it does, but what we do get from it is that whatever was inside the envelope scared Lottie.'

CONNOR: 'And Mia. What we don't know from this though is how long Sadie had been with the sisters by then.'

CRISTY: 'And it's possible that other pages or chapters exist that detail events leading up to this scene.'

CONNOR: 'In other words, there's every chance Lottie's story isn't going to be revealed in order, which could end us up with answers before questions are asked, or pieces of the puzzle that could belong to another picture altogether.'

Though they were still recording, Cristy said, 'We might have to cut that last bit. We could lose our audience if they think we're just going to confuse them.'

'It's the truth though,' Connor countered.

'So maybe we record the whole series before going to air?'

'I thought we were hoping for leads from the public, by posting the pods weekly?' Sadie interjected.

'Without them we might never actually have a story,' he pointed out.

Aware of that, Cristy frowned as she said, 'We've just got to be careful we don't start irritating the listeners. Pods leap back and forth all the time, I know. But with this one there's far more potential for getting things wrong either through misunderstanding, or just not knowing enough to make sense of where we're at in the story.' To Sadie, she said, 'Let's go ahead with the interview now and discuss this further when we're done. Are you ready?'

'As I'll ever be,' Sadie replied.

Cristy waited for Connor to register the timecode and began.

CRISTY: 'Sadie, since you found this extract have you had any thoughts on what might have been in the envelope?'

SADIE: 'Well, I think for me, the most obvious answer is some kind of blackmail threat, although Lottie herself kind of dismisses that . . . Not altogether, it's true, but it wouldn't be normal for her, a natural storyteller, to presage the truth in such a clumsy way.'

CRISTY: 'For the benefit of our listeners, here's a reminder of Lottie's words: *"Thinking immediately of blackmail, ransoms, all kinds of craziness . . ."* But we can't rule out blackmail?'

SADIE: 'No, we can't, and as I said, it is the most obvious answer.'

CONNOR: 'Mia asked if there was a note, but it doesn't seem that there was.'

SADIE: 'That's true. I was thinking, maybe it was a photograph of some kind. There wouldn't have to be any words, the image could speak for itself.'

CRISTY: 'You mean, for example, it could show Lottie taking the child from the beach?'

SADIE: 'Something like that.'

CONNOR: 'The fact the envelope arrived after Sadie had been with them for a while could suggest that someone had been waiting for the right time . . . Lottie says in the story that she felt as though someone might be watching.'

Cristy signalled for Connor to stop the recording while at her end Sadie waited, clearly not entirely sure what was expected of her now.

Eventually, Cristy said, 'I can't see how we can continue with this, Sadie, until you've spoken to your aunt. Even if she won't tell you what was in the envelope, presuming she remembers – and I understand she might say she doesn't when she does – it's crazy to go ahead without at least trying to get her involved.'

Sadie's eyes showed her unease. 'If you're saying you want to interview her, I really don't think she'll go for it.'

'She already knows you're looking into your past . . .'

'Well, we haven't actually discussed it.'

'But she has to have guessed it's why I was at the villa on New Year's Day.'

'Yes, I suppose so, but she hasn't mentioned it since.'

'OK,' Connor said firmly, 'let's go back to what we do know. Tell us what she said when you first asked her why you couldn't find any trace of her brother, your supposed father? When was that, exactly?'

'A few years ago,' Sadie replied, 'and it was actually Lottie I asked.'

'And she said?'

'Before she got angry and all self-righteous on me, like I told you before, she kind of pulled a Mia on me, saying it was all a long time ago, and everything had probably been lost along the way.'

Cristy said, 'Which tells you precisely nothing, apart from the fact that she was lying, or at least avoiding the truth. Sorry if that's brutal, Sadie, but no one talks about their dead brother that way.'

'I agree,' Sadie responded, 'I just didn't know how to force anything out of her, any more than I know how to get it out of Mia now.'

Connor said, 'I don't suppose any memories have resurfaced for you of those early days on Exmoor?'

Sadie tilted her head as she said, 'I've been thinking about it a lot, and there was someone: a man, tall, dark-haired, he wore sunglasses, and a hat. I think I remember liking it when he picked me up.'

'Do you have any sense of where you might have been when you were with him?' Cristy asked.

Sadie shook her head.

'Did you call him anything? Such as Daddy?'

Sadie continued shaking her head. 'I don't think so. It's not coming to me, anyway.' Connor said, 'Any chance it was Edwin, Mia's husband?'

'I'm not aware of ever meeting him,' Sadie replied.

Wondering if they might end up putting her through some sort of regression session, Cristy said, 'Anything else?'

'I'm sorry,' Sadie said defeatedly. 'I realize it would all be a lot easier if I could remember more than I do, but I'm hopeful, as we continue going through Lottie's things, that they'll prompt more memories – or at least give us some better leads than we have right now.'

# CHAPTER SIX

Much later, having spent most of the rest of the day googling the Winters sisters, something both she and Connor had been doing regularly this past week, Cristy was still mulling it all over as she joined a handful of fellow commuters in the early evening gloom to take the last cross-dock ferry to the opposite pier. Ordinarily she'd have walked along the harbourside to cross at Prince Street Bridge, but this evening she needed to call into Tesco to pick up a particular pizza for Aiden's tea.

She'd already learned from David that the aunts' wealth stemmed from their paternal grandfather, William Winters, and the expansion of his own father's electronics business into a multi-million-pound, global enterprise by the time he was forty. Apparently William's only son, Alfred Winters – Lottie and Mia's father – had floated the company on the New York stock exchange back in the Sixties, increasing the family fortune to quite dizzying levels before he'd gone on to lose, some said half of it, through bad investments. The daughters had inherited what was left when Alfred and Martha, the girls' mother, had been killed in a car accident at the end of the Eighties. Presumably this was what had inspired their story about losing a brother and his wife.

'Their estimated worth at the time of inheriting,' David had gone on to tell her, 'was said to be in the region of forty million. I've no idea how it stands now, only that their affairs have long been handled by Crosswell Haigh, a risk-averse wealth management firm in the City of London.'

'So it's possible their fortune has increased over time rather than diminished?' Cristy had asked.

'I'd be amazed if it hadn't, given who's handling it, but there are ways of finding these things out. If you think it's important, I'll look into it for you.'

Although its relevance wasn't clear, Cristy had accepted the offer just in case something interesting came from his research. He hadn't got back to her yet, and nor had she chased him for there really wasn't any rush. At the moment, they considered Lottie's and Mia's lives prior to 2000, when Sadie was presumed to be two years old, to be far less significant than the years that had come after. The source and size of their wealth, as well as the kind of women they'd been in their younger years, were simply part of the due diligence she and Connor, as journalists, necessarily carried out at the start of a project.

Recalling how they'd once subjected David to similar scrutiny for a podcast, she huddled deeper into her padded coat and stepped ashore ready to fight the driving wind and rain. She wondered what he might be doing now, and immediately felt her knots of anxiety tightening. They weren't only caused by him and the fact that they'd barely been in touch since she'd returned to Bristol over a week ago, although she had to admit that was bothering her a lot. She had no idea if Juliette was still in Guernsey with him, but imagined it was the reason he hadn't rung. It was certainly why Cristy hadn't called him. She was equally, if not more, concerned about her ex, Matthew, and the children. Not that there was any reason to be worried about Hayley and Aiden – Hayley had been perfectly fine when she'd flown off to Edinburgh yesterday, and Aiden, for once, hadn't found an alternative plan to starting back to school today. She guessed worrying about them simply went with being a parent, although the fact that they were still concerned about their father's state of mind wasn't helping.

Matthew, for his part, was fretting about how much he must have upset them while they were in LA for them to have flown home so soon. This was when he wasn't raging down the line to Cristy over Marley and the baby who, apparently, was going to be called Bear.

'Have you ever heard anything so ridiculous?' he'd shouted when he'd rung to tell her. 'Why the hell would you call a child *Bear*? And why don't I get a say, is what I want to know?'

Seeing no point in getting into that, Cristy said, 'At least she's speaking to you, finally, and the photo you sent of you holding him is lovely.' She'd hated it, actually. Not the child, obviously, but the painful reminder that no one, least of all her, could ever have foreseen during the happy days of their marriage that this improbable, inescapable mess was in their future. They should still be together, going about their lives in the Leigh Woods house where both children had grown up and where they'd been so happy for so many years. Until apparently Matthew had decided he wasn't any more.

Well, he certainly wasn't now, and though the schadenfreude of his betrayal backfiring on him so spectacularly probably ought to be giving her some satisfaction, it wasn't. For whatever reason it was bothering her a lot that he seemed to have no idea how he was going to be a father to his new son, never mind husband to his shockingly unpredictable child bride. Moreover, he was presumably due back at work and on air any day now at the TV station where he was a main news presenter so he'd have little choice but to leave them in LA and return home. What the heck was going to happen then?

Sighing at the thought of how it was all unravelling for him, Cristy lowered her hood and pushed into the welcome warmth and bright lights of the Tesco Express.

Minutes later she was outside again, complete with requisite pizza and bottle of wine and hurrying past crowded bars and cafés, across Millennium Square, and over Pero's Bridge with its landmark horn-shaped sculptures towards Queen Square. She wished she was feeling more cheerful, but January really was the dreariest month and right now she couldn't think of much to feel cheerful about.

*Picture snowdrops and fat robins*, she could hear her mother urging, *bracing walks on cold sunny days, hot chocolate in front of the fire, cosy evenings and piping hot stews.*

It had been her mother's way to find something uplifting to think about in darker moments, something to help raise their spirits when they were slumped in the blues. *First footprints in snow*; *icicles hanging from trees*; *starry skies*; *hot toddies*; *snuggling up with someone you love.*

God, how she missed her mother, even after all these years.

It probably didn't help that Cynthia, David's mother, was so like her with her abiding love of nature and the kindness that radiated from her so selflessly and reassuringly.

Finally crossing the puddled courtyard of her apartment complex she let herself in through the main door and heaved a sigh of relief to be out of the wind – and to see a light shining under her own front door. Unless she'd left it on this morning it must mean Aiden was home, as he'd promised he would be by the time she got back from work.

'Hi! It's only me,' she called out, unzipping her coat and dropping her heavy bag on the hall table. 'Something smells good,' she added in surprise.

'Hey!' he called back. 'Dad's here and we're making a spag bol.'

Cristy stopped. Had he really just said his father was here?

*Oh God no.* She desperately didn't want to deal with Matthew tonight, or any night actually. However, it seemed she had no choice, because here he was, coming out of the kitchen, wearing one of her aprons – the cheek of him – and carrying a large glass of wine, presumably for her.

'Hope you don't mind,' he said, attempting – and failing – to look sheepish. 'I flew in this morning and I was really keen to see Aiden, so he said to come here . . .'

'That was your suggestion,' Aiden shouted from the kitchen, 'so don't blame me, you bellend.'

Matthew started. 'What did he just call me?' he demanded.

'And the spag bol was my idea,' Aiden continued. 'I was planning it as a surprise for you tonight, Mum, but then Dad rang so I got enough for three. Six probably, looking at it, but we can always call a few mates.'

'He's not a bad cook,' Matthew told her, pressing the wine into Cristy's hand. 'I had no idea, did you?'

Deciding not to share the fact that David's mother had taught Aiden her bolognese recipe while he and Hayley were in Guernsey over Christmas, Cristy looked at the wine, then back to Matthew, and almost laughed when he ducked.

'Please don't,' he implored. 'It's a really good vintage and think of the mess.'

Still not sure what to say, or do, she followed him into the kitchen-dining-sitting room to discover that candles had been lit, the table set for three and right next to her usual place was the sweetest little bunch of snowdrops in a glass jar. It was as though her mother had prompted someone to put them there specially.

'I got them because I know you love them,' Aiden said, coming to embrace her with a wooden spoon in one hand, and a pepper mill in the other. When had he suddenly become taller than her? Surely he couldn't have grown that much in a day, and she was sure she'd still had the edge this morning.

Since he wasn't in the habit of buying her flowers, she gazed into his faintly bearded handsome face (far too like his father's) and said, 'You are the most adorable person I know, Aiden Jennings. Thank you.'

Shrugging, as if his thoughtfulness simply went with being him, he returned to his cooking saying, 'No rows tonight, OK? I've had a tough first day back at school and I don't need to be refereeing you two.'

Cristy laughed. 'Who are you and what have you done with my son?' she teased.

'Yeah, funny. Dad, can you grate some more Parmesan, I don't think there's enough, and if you're serious about making Mum feel special tonight you can start by pouring her a glass of wine. Oh, you already have. Good man.'

Avoiding Matthew's eyes, Cristy sat down at the table and took out her phone.

'Expecting a call?' Matthew asked, going to deal with the cheese.

She wanted to say, yes, from David, if only to remind him that there was someone else in her life now, but how was she going to explain it if the call didn't come? He'd notice, because Matthew was like that – or he'd become that way since deciding he'd made the biggest mistake of his life in ending their marriage. His vigilance, his concern for her and interest in anything she did, were all about trying to win her back, and though it might be the last thing she wanted, right now she realized she was almost starting to feel glad he was there. At least it would distract her from thoughts of David, and his apparent reconnection with Juliette. Not that he'd admitted to anything rekindling between them, but something was going on there, she could sense it as surely as she'd seen it when they'd disappeared for at least two hours on New Year's Day. And with a bottle of wine.

'Aiden tells me you're about to kick off a new series,' Matthew said chattily. 'Am I allowed to ask about it?'

Reminded of the easy domesticity they used to enjoy at the end of most days when they'd discussed various projects while one of them cooked and the other kept the wine topped up, she began telling him about the curious case of Sadie Winters.

'That sounds a good title for the series,' Aiden commented, setting a steaming bowl of pasta in front of her. 'Will you dish up? Or shall we help ourselves?'

'Bring me some serving spoons,' she instructed, 'and we've already got a title. *Who's That Girl*.'

'The Eurythmics, 1982,' Matthew informed them, untying his pinny and taking more wine from the fridge.

'1983,' she corrected, and winced as he began singing the song.

'Can you do that?' Aiden asked, shoving a spoonful of bolognese sauce into his father's mouth to shut him up. 'Pinch someone else's title?'

'That's hot!' Matthew protested.

'You can't copyright a title,' Cristy replied, reflecting on how relaxed and actually happy Matthew seemed given the mess he'd left in LA. 'And it's not the actual title anyway.'

'Still think *The Curious Case of Sadie Winters* is better,' Aiden decided, and bringing spoons along with the main dish to the table, he sank down in his usual chair leaving Matthew to sit at the end in much the way he always had over the years.

'OK, bon ap,' Aiden said, getting stuck in as soon as Cristy finished serving. 'Any complaints, don't bother talking to the chef.'

'Wow, it's good,' Matthew told him after the first taste. 'Since when did you know how to pull together more than a sandwich?'

As Aiden's eyes came to hers, Cristy said, 'My son has many hidden talents . . .'

'Our son,' Matthew corrected.

Wanting to get off the subject before it reached David's mother, she said, cheerily, 'So how's Bear?'

She hadn't meant to laugh, hadn't even realized it was coming until Aiden sniggered and she spluttered an undignified guffaw. It wasn't funny, it really wasn't, and yet apparently it was, for the next thing Matthew was struggling to hold back his own mirth, and before they knew it they were in the grip of uncontrollable laughter.

In the end, as Cristy dabbed her eyes with a napkin, Aiden said, 'Is she really serious about calling him that? I mean, it's a cool name but . . .'

'At least it's not Bobby Bear, which was her first choice,' Matthew responded.

As they collapsed into laughter again, Cristy noticed her phone vibrating on the table beside her. Seeing it was David she turned it over, and let the call go to messages.

No point changing the mood of the evening when it was going so well, and besides, it was probably a good thing not to be available the instant he decided to get in touch – especially if, after a week of silence from him, the reason behind it was to tell her that his feelings no longer matched hers.

# CHAPTER SEVEN

By the end of the week the *Hindsight* office was fully up and running with Clover and Jackson, their regular and trusted researchers, back at their usual desks and all new contracts provisionally agreed. Harry and Meena, now returned from a six-week trip to India, were pretty jetlagged as well as a few pounds heavier, but clearly fully on board for *Who's That Girl.*

'I admit I'm quite fascinated by it,' Meena declared at their first production meeting of the series. She was her usual delightful self, exuding calmness and mischief in equal measure, and showing not a single sign of ageing in spite of her fifty-plus years. Harry, on the other hand, her ever faithful and long-suffering husband, was wearing the slightly dazed expression he always wore following a prolonged stay with his in-laws and extended family.

'But before we go any further into it,' Meena continued, 'I know you're keen to hear more about the sponsorship we have on board. Actually, I'll email the details, for now I'll just mention Isabelle Penny who's going to be dropping in to introduce herself, I think sometime today. She's already working on marketing and publicity strategies to help promote *Hindsight* as the series launches – and she also, I believe, has some great ideas for how you can work with each of the sponsors. You're going to love her. Well, love might not be the right word, but I'm sure you'll find it after you've met her. So now, back to the important stuff. Is there anything else we need to catch up on with *Who's That Girl*? Great title by the way. I'm told all the sponsors love it.'

'But what they think doesn't really matter,' Connor pointed out, making clear his hostility towards any kind of outside involvement, even if the players were providing money and, so far, encouragement.

Meena batted her eyelids.

Cristy murmured a thanks to Clover who'd apparently read the room and decided it was time to pass around coffees. The spritely twenty-eight-year-old's colourfully beaded dreadlocks and dazzling smile invariably brightened the day, no matter the weather outside, or mood inside. She was a joy to have on board, as was the lightly bearded, spiky-haired Jackson whose tech expertise was as invaluable as his many geek contacts. 'We've given you everything we have so far,' she told Meena.

'Apart from the footage Sadie sent yesterday,' Connor said, 'of her dead aunt's rooms at their amazing fuck-off mansion overlooking the sea.'

'Great description,' Harry commented dryly. 'I think I have just the right picture of it now. So, has Sadie discovered any more little gems from her aunt's stash for you to puzzle over?'

'Apparently she has,' Cristy replied, 'but she's going to be in Bradford-on-Avon this weekend so she's bringing it rather than sending by email.'

'Any idea what it is?' Meena queried, her honey-coloured eyes glittering with intrigue.

'Only that she found it – I quote – "a bit disturbing, and difficult to get her head around".'

Meena's eyebrows rose as Clover said, 'Is it another chapter, or page of the story?'

'She didn't say that,' Cristy answered, 'so I'm inclined to think it might be something else. We'll find out when I see her on Sunday.'

'What we have so far ends with the envelope coming through the door,' Connor reminded them.

'Is it possible,' Jacks put in, 'that Sadie's found what was in it?'

'No idea until I see her,' Cristy replied. 'However, what I can tell you is that we've managed to track down Gita Brinkley, the aunts' housekeeper at the time they were at the hilltop house on Exmoor. Luckily for us – and for her – she's still in full control of her faculties at the age of eighty-six, or she certainly sounded it when we spoke on the phone. She's in a retirement village near Minehead, so Connor and I will be heading down there early next week.'

'Did you ask if she remembers a child suddenly appearing out of nowhere?' Harry prompted.

'I did, and she does,' Cristy replied, 'but she didn't want to discuss it on the phone.'

'I've been carrying out a search for Edwin Prosser, Mia's ex-husband,' Clover informed them. 'Not much to report yet, I'll be going in for a deeper dive as soon as this meeting's over.'

'We've tried contacting Lottie's publisher,' Connor continued. 'Apparently, Felicity Green, now retired, was Lottie's editor up until the last collection of short stories was delivered.'

'What do you hope to get from her?' Harry asked.

'We won't know until we speak to her,' Connor replied. 'She's travelling around Mexico at the moment, due back sometime next month, but in her email she says she was very disappointed when Lottie decided to stop being published.'

'Remind me again when that was?' Jackson said.

Checking her notes, Cristy said, '2005, by which time Sadie would have been around seven.'

'Anything relevant about that?' Harry wondered.

'Not that we know of – yet.'

'Speaking of Guernsey,' Meena interrupted, 'which we were, kind of, I've yet to hear all about your Christmas and New Year. OK, now's not the time, but drinks later at the Mud Dock?'

Having expected this and actually welcoming it, Cristy said, 'It's a date, but it was a terrific Christmas . . . just not such a great New Year,' she confessed, 'and things have been going steadily downhill from there.' She smiled to cover her feelings as everyone regarded her with as much interest as concern. 'It's OK,' she assured them, 'it won't get in the way of what we're trying to achieve, although it might make any upcoming visits to the island slightly awkward, at least for me. However, nothing I can't handle. In fact, I'm waiting for David to send what he's managed to find out about the aunts' financial situation. I'm guessing he hasn't obtained a full picture yet and will let us have it when he does.'

'How is it relevant?' Harry wanted to know. 'OK, I get that money always is, but are you looking for something specific?'

'Evidence of blackmail would be helpful,' Connor pointed out, 'massive pay-offs, dodgy-looking investments . . . But that's asking for fine detail and getting that out of the kind of firms that run estates like the Winters' . . . Well, let's say we're not holding our breath, but maybe Sadie can help there.'

'She must be quite a wealthy young lady now that one of her aunts has passed,' Meena commented. 'I don't understand why she'd want to risk blowing the rest by putting the other aunt through this?'

'I don't think it's about money for Sadie,' Cristy said. 'She's protective of her aunt, or is trying to be, and is mindful of, shall we say, difficulties further down the road, but she wants answers. And I for one don't blame her.'

'Me neither,' Clover piped up. 'I mean, who wouldn't want to know where they came from and who their parents really are? I know I did, and it worked out really well for me in the end.'

'But you always knew you were adopted,' Cristy reminded her, 'and no one ever stopped you trying to find your birth mother. Or, more to the point, lied about who you were and who she was.'

'So we're satisfied,' Meena said, 'that Martin and Vanessa Winters have never existed?'

'Not as the aunts' brother and sister-in-law,' Cristy replied. 'Or as Sadie's biological parents.'

'Because she's done a DNA test?'

'She has, and no matches, which only means that no one has registered on any of the ancestry sites who can be tied to her.'

'I've never tried one of those sites, have you?' Meena asked, clearly intrigued by the idea.

Harry was already alarmed. 'No, no,' he protested, holding up his hands in defence. 'You already have enough family to populate a small nation, any more and I swear I'll leave you.'

Laughing, Meena started to pack up her things. 'We've got a meeting at the Beeb in an hour,' she reminded him. To Cristy she said, 'I'm sure Isabelle Penny will be in touch today, so be nice to her. Any thoughts yet on when the first episode is likely to drop?'

'It could go quite soon,' Cristy assured her. 'The envelope on the mat is a great cliff-hanger. We just have to gain an idea of what we're moving on to – and, of course, we'll need to top and tail with appropriate credits – and sponsor acknowledgements, I guess.'

'Isabelle will be able to help with that.'

After Meena and Harry had gone, Clover commented quietly, 'Definitely not liking the sound of this Isabelle person.'

'We don't want her getting in the way of things,' Jacks added. 'How often is she going to be here?'

'I've no idea yet,' Cristy replied, 'so let's hope not very, and deal with her when we have to.' She broke off as someone came in the door.

Seeing who it was her heart sank, or flipped, or . . . She had no clear idea what it was doing, only that she really hadn't been expecting Matthew, nor was she thrilled to see him.

'Hi,' he said cheerily, as if he dropped in like this every day.

'What are you doing here?' she asked coldly. 'I thought you were on air tonight.'

'I am. We're doing a live feed from the SS *Great Britain* – the PM's attending some sort of dinner on board later, so . . .' He shrugged. Then with a slightly awkward glance at the others, 'Can I . . .? Could we . . .?'

Swallowing her impatience Cristy got to her feet and led him across the hall to the main meeting room. It was only as she closed the door that she thought of Aiden. 'What is it?' she demanded. 'Has he bunked off school again . . .'

'No, no, nothing to do with him,' he assured her. 'Although apparently he wants to stay with me tonight.'

'I know, he texted. So what's this about? You can see we're—'

'In the middle of something, sure. I'm sorry, I tried calling but you didn't pick up—'

'Because I was in a meeting. I still am, so if you can come to the point—'

'OK, well, this probably isn't the right time, but as I was nearby I thought . . . I've been wanting to talk to you since the other night when we . . . Well, you know, you were there.' He laughed uneasily.

She eyed him stonily, having no idea what he was building up to, and not at all keen to find out.

'I just wanted to ask how serious it is between you and this . . . David,' he blurted, looking so unsure of himself, and so like their son during his rare moments of uncertainty, that it took the fire out of her anger surge.

Sounding more long-suffering than impatient, she said, 'It really isn't any of your business, Matthew, and frankly, I resent you asking.'

He swallowed. 'OK, I deserved that, but after we . . . spent that time together the other night . . .'

'It's sounding to me as though you're reading far too much into that . . .'

'No. No, I'm not, I was just afraid you might and . . . Well, it's not that I don't want us to get back together, you know I do . . .'

'This conversation's over . . .'

'No, wait,' he cried, as she made for the door.

She turned back, eyes blazing. 'If you seriously think I have spent a single minute thinking about the other night and the fact that for some deranged reason I let you *sleep* in my bed, then you are beyond delusional. For God's sake, Matthew! You start off by asking how serious I am about David, now you seem to think I've got designs on you . . .'

'I just wish you did,' he cried helplessly, 'and that everything could go back to the way it was. And you can hardly blame me for trying to find out how the land lies with Mr Guernsey . . .'

'I've already told you, it's none of your business, so if that's all you're here for . . .'

'Actually, I wanted to see you,' he admitted. 'I don't know why, but the world, everything, feels better when I'm with you . . .'

'But you're not *with* me. You have a different wife now and a child. Have you been in touch with them? What's happening over there?'

Pushing a hand through his hair, he said, miserably, 'Apparently Bear is missing me, although how that's possible when I've only held him once for about three seconds, God only knows.'

She blinked. A long moment passed before he said, 'Please don't laugh.'

'I wasn't going to,' she lied. Then, 'You do realize that's Marley saying *she* misses you, don't you?'

He shrugged. 'I guessed you'd have a clearer understanding of it than I do.'

Unable to believe how dense he could be, Cristy said, 'So you're here for me to tell you what to do next?'

'I'm just not sure how to play it,' he confessed. 'One minute she doesn't want me anywhere near her, or the baby, the next they're missing me . . . I can't just fly over there. I've got a job and a son here to think about and if she's determined to carry on living there . . . Well, how's that going to work for anyone?'

'I've no idea, Matthew, but as it isn't my problem I'm not going to spend any more time on it. Now, if you don't mind . . .'

'Will *he* be there for Aiden's gig tomorrow night?' he asked, as she opened the door.

Realizing he meant David, she stopped, gave herself a moment and said, 'No, he won't, but before you start reading anything into *that* please let me tell you again . . . We, you and I, do not have a future together outside of being parents to our children,' and before he could say any more she walked back into the production office and slammed the door.

'Oh dear, is this a bad time?'

Cristy looked up to find a short, plump woman with a playful pink bob and flashy red glasses staring at her sympathetically.

'Isabelle Penny,' she said, holding out a hand to shake. 'But please call me Iz.'

*

'Holy shit,' Meena murmured later, when Cristy finished telling her all about Matthew and David. They were at the Mud Dock Café with a bottle of wine between them on the table and a couple of menus they'd yet to look at. 'Your personal life is all kinds of weird right now,' she stated, 'and frankly I don't know what to tell you. Apart from the fact that you *know* your ex is a cheating bastard. I'm not sure I'd be able to trust him again if I were you . . .'

'It's not even in my head to try,' Cristy broke in heatedly.

Still seeming dubious, Meena refilled their glasses and, after they'd selected a few small plates to share, she said, 'What about David? Do you really think he's back with *La Française*? What's she like, by the way?'

As she pictured Juliette, Cristy only wished she could shut the image down, or turn her into something that resembled a frog. 'Think Sophie Marceau at her sultriest,' she said.

Meena's eyes widened with alarm. 'Oh, dear,' she murmured.

'And she's at least ten years younger than me.'

Looking even more worried, Meena said, 'But she won't have half your class.'

Cristy only wished it were true.

'So why did they break up?' Meena asked. 'If she's such a goddess.'

'All I know is that she wanted to live in Paris and he was determined to stay in Guernsey, so they went their separate ways and now they only see one another . . . Actually I've no idea how often they see one another, but there's no doubt she's very at home when she's there.'

'Have you talked to him about her?'

Cristy shook her head. 'I'm not quite sure how to bring it up without sounding petty, or jealous . . . Anyway, as I told you, we haven't spoken since I left and for all I know she's still there.'

'But you don't know that for certain.'

'Maybe I don't want to.'

Meena clearly wasn't happy with that. 'You have to confront this, Cristy,' she said bossily, 'and it's not like you to shy away from a situation. Ask him, outright, if he's involved with her again. Sure, it'll be horrible for you if he is, but isn't it better to know the truth so you can start moving on if you need to?'

Unable to deny that, as much as she might not relish it, Cristy said, 'Maybe this way we save one another the awkwardness of having to admit that we – *he* – made a mistake.'

'But you have to be in touch anyway, for the podcast – didn't you say he's getting some information for you?'

'He can give it to Connor, or Jacks, it doesn't have to be me.'

Meena sat back in her chair and fixed her with a long hard stare. 'Do you know what I think?' she said in the end.

'I know you're going to tell me.'

'I think you were so hurt by Matthew that you're going into self-protection mode way before you need to. I mean, it's not as if David hasn't tried ringing, you said yourself he has . . .'

'Once, and I left there over a week ago.'

'. . . and what sort of message do you think you're sending by not calling back?'

Cristy's eyebrows rose sceptically. 'He'll know why I haven't,' she countered.

'Really? Tell me what happened after he disappeared with *La Française* on New Year's Day.'

'With a bottle of wine, don't forget.'

'Didn't you ask him about it when he came back? How long was he gone for?'

'A couple of hours, I think.'

'Was she with him the whole time?'

'I presume so.'

'Did she come back with him?'

'No.'

'So how was he with you after that?'

'To be honest I didn't see much of him – maybe I was avoiding him, I'm not sure, but I'd heard from the children by then so I was worried about them . . .'

'But he slept with you that night? As in, you shared a bed?'

Cristy nodded and felt her heart contract at the way she'd feigned sleep when he'd come into the room. She simply hadn't felt up to any sort of heavy discussion, and still hadn't in the morning which was why she'd left the way she had.

'And you haven't been in touch since?'

Cristy shook her head.

'Not even with his mother?'

'Well, of course I've emailed her and she replied saying they're all missing me. I don't know if David's included in that, but if he is he should be speaking for himself.'

Meena shook her head in dismay. 'You need to have this out with him,' she declared.

'Maybe, but now I want to hear about your time in India . . .'

'Hang on, before we go there, I hear Isabelle Penny dropped in on you today. How did it go?'

'You mean Iz,' Cristy said dryly. 'And what little we saw of her decided us that she's an unusual sort of person that could either grow on us, or drive us mad. Only time will tell. Now, back to you and your trip. How was your wonderful mother? And did you remember to send her my love?'

As Meena launched into a colourful and hilarious account

of her and Harry's Christmas in Mumbai, Cristy found herself laughing and unwinding in a way she hadn't since leaving Guernsey.

Finally, after finishing the bottle and an extra glass each, they left by the iron steps of the old industrial building to wait for Meena's Uber outside the cycle works. The night was icy cold and damp, but alive with Friday revellers as the city's youngsters descended on the hotspots.

'Are you going to be all right?' Meena asked, as her driver pulled up alongside them.

'Absolutely fine,' Cristy assured her.

'Why don't I drop you?'

'Because it's in the opposite direction and it'll take me five minutes to walk from here.' Pulling her in for a hug, she said, 'It was lovely to see you.'

'You too,' Meena smiled. 'Just don't be so hard on yourself, OK?'

'Promise,' and aware of her mobile vibrating she stood back for Meena to get into the car.

*Please let it be him.*

Moments later, as she took the phone from her bag, she saw that it was Hayley and decided not to answer. She simply couldn't face her daughter's wise counsel this evening, so slid the phone back into her pocket and began walking towards the swing bridge. By the time she'd crossed it and reached her apartment complex a message had arrived from Hayley. She waited until she was inside, coat off, kettle on and feet up, before opening it.

*Hey Mum, just checking in on you. Hope you're OK – Dad keeps asking me if it's serious between you and David. I hope it's all right with you but I've ended up telling him 'very'. David's a good guy. He definitely gets my and Aiden's vote.*

*Love you, call anytime.*

*H ♡*

# CHAPTER EIGHT

CRISTY: 'OK, Sadie, can you talk us through what you have there?'

SADIE: 'Of course. I'll be glad to.'

In spite of the bravado in her voice, Sadie hesitated, and took a deep, slightly shaky breath. Jasper was at the small dining table next to her, his treacle-coloured hair slick to his head, his handsome but unshaven face showing his concern. They were at his parents' weekend retreat near Bradford-on-Avon, a converted stable block with far-reaching views of the countryside and so much olde-worlde charm it was like being in a cosy antique shop.

Cristy watched them quietly, sensing their connection, understanding Sadie's uncertainty as well as her gratitude for his support. This wasn't going to be easy for her, Cristy knew she'd be having difficulties too in her shoes, but Sadie had insisted on going through with the recording.

Eventually, she laid her hands on the box file in front of her and began to describe it.

SADIE: 'There's a label on the front that says: "Sadie's Things". The writing is quite faded, as though it was written a long time ago, and the label itself is peeling at the corners.

'It smells a little old and musty, but the contents are mostly intact. There's a toy rabbit; a star-shaped hair slide; a Barbie doll wearing a pink gingham dress; a tiny pair of ballet shoes, and six photographs.'

CRISTY: 'Do you recognize any of these items?'

SADIE: 'I can't say I do, but as you can see each of the photographs features a little girl who I'm guessing could be me, aged one or maybe slightly older. Not much more than a baby, anyway.'

CRISTY: 'Are they the photos that were around your house when you were growing up? The ones you were told were of you and your parents?'

SADIE: 'No, they're not. These are quite different.'

CRISTY: 'Tell us about who's in them.'

SADIE: 'There's a woman who's probably early- to mid-twenties . . . She has shoulder-length, thick blonde hair and she looks, well, kind of like me. I mean, me now, not in the photos. Would you agree?'

CRISTY: 'Yes, I would.'

Sadie's relief and gratitude showed in a smile.

SADIE: 'I have to tell you, it makes me feel quite . . . I don't know, strange, when I look at her, like I'm being transported out of myself, or something. I mean, if she is my mother . . . and it's hard to think she isn't given how alike we are . . . I can't stop wondering why we're not together when here, the way she's holding me . . .'

Cristy paused as Sadie dabbed away a tear, understanding perfectly why she was finding this so upsetting. The photographs quite clearly showed a young mother who adored her child.

CRISTY: 'Can you tell us a bit more about what we're seeing in the photos?'

SADIE: (picking them up one by one) 'In this one she – the woman – is wearing jeans and a white T-shirt that has some writing on the front, but it's not possible to make out what it says. She's lying on the grass side by side with the child. They're holding hands and seem to be staring up at the sky . . . There's a shadow over them, from whoever took the photo. It looks like a man.'

She moved on to the next.

SADIE: 'In this one she's sitting up on her knees and the child is tucked in against her, their faces one above the other, and they're laughing quite hard, clearly having so much fun.

'In the third one . . . they're pulling silly faces, tongues out, eyes pulled down . . . The next two are of the child fast asleep on somebody's lap – you can only see the arms holding her, nothing to say who it is, but they're masculine . . .

'The last one is the child again, riding the shoulders of a young man who's holding her legs and laughing up at her. He's wearing a hat that partially obscures his face, but he has a lot of dark hair, and he's laughing.'

Cristy watched as Sadie continued to gaze at the photos, taking them in and presumably remembering how she'd had a memory of a man in a hat.

CRISTY: 'So you think these two people are your parents?'

Sadie nodded, before remembering she needed to speak.

SADIE: 'Yes, that is what I think.'

CRISTY: 'And since finding these photos . . . Have they jogged any memories for you?'

SADIE: 'Well, as I said before, I have an image of a man in a hat, and of him – I think it was the same man – riding a bicycle with me on the crossbar, and I'm sure I remember being on some sort of carousel.'

CRISTY: 'Do you recall anything particular about the woman?'

SADIE: 'I didn't at first, but then I . . . I think I remember playing with her hair and getting it all tangled up in a brush.'

CRISTY: 'Do you have any thoughts on where you might have been at the time any of these photos were taken?'

SADIE: 'I'm afraid not. Something I remember though, oddly, is a clothes horse full of fresh laundry, and a garden with toys . . . Swings, a trampoline, that sort of thing. There was a big house nearby, or maybe it just seemed big to me . . .'

CRISTY: 'There's something else in the box you've brought today. Something of huge significance. Do you mind telling us about it?'

Sadie reached for a single, folded sheet of paper, straightened it, and cleared her throat a couple of times.

SADIE: 'I'm sorry, it's still making me quite emotional . . .'

CRISTY: 'It's OK. Just take your time.'

Sadie glanced at Jasper and closed her eyes as he leaned in to kiss her forehead. Seeming to take strength from it, Sadie straightened as she began to speak.

SADIE: 'I believe this is the note that was found in my pocket after my aunt brought me in from the beach. It says, "Her name is Sasha, she will be two years old on May 14th. I know you are good people. Please take care of her until I can come back for her."'

Cristy allowed a few moments to pass, giving Sadie time to decide when she was ready to continue.

SADIE: 'It's really strange to think I could be looking at

my mother's handwriting. It makes her seem . . . real, in a way she didn't before. I keep wondering what was going through her mind when she wrote it. What, or who, could have made her give me up?'

Sadie put the note down, and sounded almost impatient as she said, 'Wallowing in questions I can't possibly answer isn't going to get us anywhere.'

Her tone, her frustration, belied the lost and bewildered look in her eyes.

Feeling for her, Cristy continued gently.

CRISTY: 'Do you think she and your aunts ever met?'

SADIE: 'Obviously, it's possible.'

Sadie's eyes dropped to Cristy's recorder and stayed there.

'Would you like me to stop?' Cristy offered.

She shook her head and looked up again.

SADIE: 'You're going to ask me if I've shown any of this to Mia.'

CRISTY: 'Have you?'

SADIE: 'No.'

When Sadie didn't elaborate Cristy glanced at Jasper who raised a hand in a small gesture, seeming to advise giving her more time.

SADIE: 'I'm going to show it to her, obviously. I have to now I've told you about it. I guess I'm just really nervous about what she's going to say. How she's going to explain it.'

JASPER: 'What we really want to know is when the aunts received all these things – we know the note was in two-year-old Sadie's coat pocket, but when did the photos and everything else turn up? And why did they keep it and never show it to Sades?'

SADIE: 'I think – but I have no way of knowing of course – that these photos might have been in the envelope that was posted through the front door that morning.'

CRISTY: 'If you're right, we know, at least according to Lottie's writings, there was no note with them, so what kind of message do you think they were supposed to send?'

SADIE: 'Maybe they were to let my aunts know that I came from a loving home . . . But how loving could it have been for them to have just left me on a beach?'

JASPER: 'We've wondered if sending the photographs was meant to keep Sadie's parents alive for her. Special moments captured on film for her to treasure until they came back.'

SADIE: 'But they never did come back.'

JASPER: 'At least not that we know of.'

CRISTY: 'Do you have any idea yet when the toys might have turned up?'

SADIE: 'No, but there's nothing to say they actually came from my parents. For all I know they're small things that Lottie or Mia might have bought for me and put into the box when I outgrew them.'

CRISTY: 'But the fact they're with the photographs . . .'

SADIE: 'Leads us to believe they're part of what's long been held back from me. It's true.'

CRISTY: 'OK. Let's talk for a moment about the photos you remember being displayed around the house. The ones you were told were of you and your parents. Who do you now think they might have been of?'

SADIE: 'It's a good question. I wondered at first if it was one of my aunts as a child with their parents, but there are albums of photos from that time in our library and they're obviously from a different era. Anyway, they're clearly not the same people.'

JASPER: 'It's possible to buy historical family shots like that. Film and TV companies use them all the time.'

CRISTY: 'Couldn't the same be said of the photos we're looking at now?'

SADIE: 'Of course, but you've admitted yourself how much I'm like the woman, and I definitely remember a man in a hat.'

CRISTY: 'Where did you actually find these photos? I know they were in this box . . .'

SADIE: '. . . which was under the daybed in Lottie's sitting room, inside a suitcase full of old postcards and letters from the children Lottie used to sponsor in various parts of the world.'

Seeming to lose interest in that, Sadie picked up the handwritten note again and stared at it for some time before continuing.

SADIE: 'Why didn't anyone come back for me?'

JASPER: 'Maybe they did, but your aunts had already taken you to Guernsey by then.'

SADIE: 'It surely wouldn't have been that hard to track them down, if someone really wanted to.'

Though they were still recording, Cristy's next comment wasn't really meant for the pod. 'Until you speak to your aunt we're not likely to have any answers to these questions . . .'

Sadie's eyes widened suddenly as she fixed them on Cristy. 'I almost forgot. I've now shown Mia the pages of Lottie's story, the ones we've already recorded.'

Cristy blinked in surprise. 'And what did she say?' she asked carefully.

Sadie's smile was small and even slightly resentful. 'The first thing she asked was if you had seen them, can you believe that? And when I told her you had, she said . . . Wait for this . . . She wants to talk to you.'

Thrown again, Cristy said, 'I'll be glad to talk to her, obviously, but didn't she comment on the pages themselves, or try to explain anything?'

'Not at all. It was . . . Like as if I'd made them up or something.' She looked to Jasper for his opinion.

'You probably already know this,' he said to Cristy, 'but you can never be sure what Mia's thinking. It's possible she didn't even really take in what she read.'

'I think she did,' Sadie insisted, 'or she wouldn't have asked to speak to Cristy.'

'So, does she want me to call her?' Cristy asked.

'She didn't say how she wanted to communicate, and for all we know she'll have changed her mind, or forgotten about it the next time we bring it up.' She frowned slightly as she thought. 'Do you think it would be a good idea for us to record the last bit of this conversation, from me telling you that she wants to talk to you? I'm just thinking it might be harder for her to back out of it if she hears it go out on a podcast.'

'We're still recording,' Cristy told her, 'but let's see if she'll do it without the . . . persuasion. When are you going back to Guernsey?'

'Tomorrow.'

'Then we'll speak over the next couple of days, and you can let me know how things develop once you've spoken to her again. Meantime, would you mind if I take some shots of the box and its contents for the website?'

Sadie opened her hands in a gesture to 'go ahead'. 'I suppose there's an outside chance someone might recognize them,' she ventured.

Already capturing the images, Cristy said, 'I'm sure someone will. Our problem will be sorting out who is, and isn't, genuine before we start following up on anything.'

*

'Crikey, it must have been a shattering moment for Sadie when she found the actual note,' Connor commented when Cristy rang from the car to report back on the interview.

'I think it was,' she agreed, trying to decide which route back to take, M4 or cross-country? 'She didn't say too much about it, but to be honest, I don't think she's even close to processing it all yet. She might think she is, but there's a lot to get her head around. And those photographs! Even I still feel thrown by them, and how closely she resembles her mother – they're so alike they could almost be the same person. The ones of her father, presuming it was him, weren't so easy to make out, but what struck me most about all of them was how young the couple looked, and how together and *normal* they seemed as a family.'

'Any idea where the shots were taken?'

'It wasn't possible to tell – on a grassy knoll somewhere, on a sunny day. I'll give them to Jacks to see if he can get any more detail out of them. Anyway, the interesting – and good – news is that Mia has said she wants to talk to me. We just have to hope she doesn't back out before we can make it happen.'

'OK, that is interesting. Do we know what brought her to that decision?'

'She knows we've seen the pages Sadie found, so I'm presuming she wants to . . . *explain* them? Ask us to forget all about them? Anyone's guess until I speak to her.'

'So does this mean you'll be going to Guernsey?'

Speaking across the lurch in her heart, Cristy said, 'If I do go I think you should come too. Can you get away . . .?'

'No problem!' Jodi shouted out. 'My mum is itching to come and stay, so don't worry about me and the baby.'

'You're assuming I can bear to be parted from you,' Connor retorted.

'You managed last night,' Jodi reminded him.

'Speaking of which,' Cristy said, 'thanks for coming to the gig. Aiden really appreciated it, and you saved me from being landed with Matthew on my own.' Though her ex-husband had insisted on walking her home last night. She hadn't let him in, or accepted more than a hug goodbye, despite his best efforts.

'It was a cool band,' Connor declared, 'if you're into house, and I kind of enjoyed catching up with your ex. If nothing else, he's always good company.'

'And there is nothing else,' Jodi hastily added. 'Anyway, are you OK, babe? You haven't seemed yourself lately, and something obviously didn't go to plan after Con and I left Guernsey at Christmas . . .'

'Stop prying,' Connor scolded.

'I'm just saying, if you want to chat, or come over and hang out with us, you know we're always here for you.'

Cristy smiled past the tightness in her throat. 'Thanks, guys. It means a lot you saying that, but you've got enough going on, getting used to being parents . . .'

'In the bag,' Connor insisted. 'We're naturals, and we love your company even more than Matthew's. A lot more than Matthew's, I should say. Is Aiden still with you at the flat?'

'He's not supposed to be, but I won't know for certain until I get home.' If he was there it might make it difficult for her to ring David, if she decided to, and she really wasn't sure she would when he still hadn't contacted her. 'Actually, there's another call coming in,' she said, realizing she ought to get off the line while tying herself in knots, 'but I'll send Sadie's interview as soon as I've uploaded it to my laptop.'

As she ended the call and indicated to leave the Pennsylvania Roundabout to take the A420 back to Bristol, she decided that rather than obsess over her ridiculous personal life she'd catch up on the latest edition of *The News Agents*. It was one of her favourite podcasts and could generally be relied on to provide suitable distraction as well as an interesting take on the world of politics.

She'd got no further than Lewis Goodall's intro to an interview with a recently disgraced cabinet minister when her phone actually did ring. With an unsteadying surge of nerves she saw it was David, and had already clicked on before realizing that now, while driving country roads in the dark, might not be the best time to talk to him.

'Hi,' he said. 'Can you hear me?'

'Yes, sorry. I'm in the car. The reception might not be great . . . How are you?'

'I'm good. How about you?'

'Yeah, fine. I've just been with Sadie actually, at her boyfriend's parents' place.'

'Anna said you were seeing her today. She also told me about the note, the one that matches the story written in the first pages, about the child's name being Sasha and that she's two years old. Have you seen it?'

'I have.'

'So is it genuine?'

'On the balance of probabilities I'd say it is.'

'OK. So how has Sadie taken it?'

'It's unsettled her, as you might expect. I think she's still in some kind of shock over it.'

'Has she shown it to Mia?'

'Not yet, but she assures me she will. Actually, I can understand her reluctance. Wanting to find out the truth is one thing, dealing with it when it comes can be another altogether.' Realizing she could be talking about herself and their relationship, she quickly added, 'The problem at this stage is that no one is sure Mia can be trusted to give honest, or even helpful answers. There's a chance she might speak to me, apparently.'

'That's good.' After a beat he added, 'Isn't it?'

'It could be, depending on what she has to say and if she actually goes through with it. Meantime, we're heading to Exmoor at the end of the week to talk to the sisters' old housekeeper, and, after that, we could be back in Guernsey.' Her hands tightened on the wheel as she waited for his response. When it didn't come she realized they'd lost the connection.

'. . . still there?' he asked, coming back on the line. 'Can you hear me?'

'I can now,' and deciding not to mention Guernsey again, she said, 'So how are things with you? It seems an age since we last spoke.'

'That's because it is. I've been trying to give you some space after the onslaught of Gaudions over Christmas. I just hadn't realized you'd need this much.'

She gave a laugh of surprise, and relief; his words were so welcome that she almost asked him to repeat them. 'Sorry,' she said, 'I've been pretty tied up with the pod since I got back, and Matthew still seems to think it's my place to sort out his mess. Anyway, it doesn't mean I haven't been thinking about you because I have, a lot.'

'Good to know.'

Suddenly afraid he might burst her bubble, without having any reason to think he would, she quickly said, 'How's everyone there? I had an email from Rosie all about the boyfriend, and from your mum saying she was thrilled to hear Aiden had tried out her spag bol recipe with great success.'

When he didn't respond she realized the line had failed again, and, clocking where she was on her journey, she thought about pulling into the picnic area at the top of Tog Hill with its panoramic views of the lights of Bristol. However, as there was nothing to say the reception would be any better there, and it was a well-known dogging spot after dark, she kept going.

'Are you still there?' he suddenly asked.

'Yes, I am. Sorry, this isn't great, is it? How much did you hear, or was I just rattling away to myself?'

Laughing he said, 'The last I got was something about spag bol.'

'OK, moving on from that . . .' It was on the tip of her tongue to ask if Juliette was still in Guernsey, but she forced herself not to, worried about how it might come out. 'Tell you what,' she said, 'why don't I call when I get home, or this is going to keep happening.'

'Great idea, because we definitely need to talk. I'm out for dinner later, so maybe tomorrow?'

'Sure. Tomorrow's fine. Where are you going for dinner?'

'Actually, it's a place I haven't tried before, in the Second Arrondissement.'

Realizing this meant he was in Paris the bubble burst so fast she almost hit the brakes. 'OK, well, hope it's good,' she said airily, and unable to think of anything else, she ended the call, hoping he might think the line had dropped again, while not really caring what he thought.

*

By the following morning Cristy had decided that there was little point in calling David. She didn't want an argument, or to come across as petty or jealous, or, God forbid, clingy. He had every right to be in Paris, presumably with Juliette. In fact, for all she knew they slept together regularly while still pursuing other relationships and, if that was the case, it wasn't for her. Best to let it go now before she got in any deeper.

He rang as she was passing the M Shed Museum on Prince's Wharf, while walking into work. It was a bitterly cold morning, with icy patches glittering on the water and bright sunlight dazzling the puddled walkways.

'Too early?' he asked when she answered.

'No, it's fine,' she replied, slipping the phone inside her hat. 'How are you? Good dinner last night?'

'Not bad. We'd probably go again.'

Tensing at the 'we' she decided to come right to the point and said, abruptly, 'Are you and Juliette . . .? Are you sleeping with her?' Not exactly how she'd meant it to come out, but it was there now and he wasn't bloody well saying anything.

'OK, not answering is answer enough,' she said, ready to ring off.

'Hang on, hang on,' he cut in angrily. 'Before you start making assumptions, or rushing to judgements, tell me this, have you slept with Matthew since you . . . since he left you?'

Taking that as an admission on his part, and since she was in no position to deny anything after the night Aiden had cooked for her and Matthew – unless she wanted to get into an explanation of how nothing had actually happened, and she didn't – she said, tartly, 'You're just digging yourself in deeper with that question, but it's OK. I'm not your keeper. You are free to do whatever you please with whoever you please. I just wish you'd been a bit more honest about it and not made me drag it out of you . . .'

'For God's sake, Cristy! I don't know what's got into you. I thought everything was good between us . . .'

'As did I until you . . .'

'. . . then Matthew gets himself into trouble, and suddenly you change. It became all about him . . .'

'That's not true!'

'It is. You barely spoke to me after his arrest . . . OK, I understand you were worried, but . . .'

'Please stop! You're using this as an excuse to blame me . . .'

'I'm not blaming you for anything. I'm just telling you how I saw things, and it wasn't great. You wouldn't even let me come into the airport with you when you left . . .'

'You said you had a meeting . . .'

'I told myself you just needed time to work things out and I should give you space . . .'

'I never said that and the way *I* saw things was you coming out of the gazebo at midnight on New Year's Eve, followed by Juliette. You disappearing with her and a bottle of wine on New Year's Day. And now you're in Paris, presumably with her?'

'Yes, as it happens, I am staying with her. Or I was, I'm at the airport now on my way home, but as for what you saw . . .'

'It's OK, you don't need to explain yourself to me. She's the mother of your son, extremely beautiful and you clearly have a great rapport . . .'

'It's true, we do, and you can't tell me you don't have feelings for Matthew . . .'

'What I feel for Matthew isn't the same.'

'And yet I noticed you didn't answer when I asked if you'd slept with him.'

Still unwilling to explain, she said, 'It's clear to me that what we had, what we've shared over the past weeks . . . It was wonderful, I won't deny that. I loved being with you and I adore your family, but maybe our lives . . . I just don't see how we can go forward together with you there, and me here, and certainly not when you're still sleeping with your ex.'

When he fell silent again her heart twisted with the longing to hear him argue, to persuade her she was wrong, and say they could work things out.

'I don't want there to be any hard feelings between us,' she said, turning towards the studios and needing to end the call before she went in. 'So can we say goodbye in a friendly way and just think about all the good things we brought to one another?'

'If that's what you want,' he said tightly, 'then that's how it'll be. You know where I am if you need anything,' and a moment later he'd gone.

Feeling almost as if she'd been struck, she decided she was too wound up to go into the office right away, so clicking off her phone she started to walk on past Quinns' and Aardman towards the Cumberland Road. She didn't get far before she ran into Iz who she was supposed to be meeting . . . right now.

'Hi, good morning,' Iz sang out in an annoyingly, overfriendly way. She was dressed as though she'd just come from the ski slopes, even her sunglasses were goggles. 'You seem to have missed your turn,' she chuckled, tugging off her beanie complete with ear flaps, headlamp and WiFi.

'Sorry, miles away,' Cristy tried to smile. 'How are you?'

'Excited to get the promos in the can,' Iz beamed, tucking the beanie under one arm so she could rub her gloved hands together. 'Have you and Connor had time to look at the scripts yet?' she asked, trying and failing to link Cristy's arm as they started back down the cobbled lane.

'Only briefly,' Cristy admitted, and stood aside for Iz to go ahead into the building. 'We're not actors, you do understand that, don't you?' she added, as they entered the production office to find they were the first to arrive.

Iz laughed. 'You're just being modest,' she said teasingly. 'You'll pull these little scenarios off brilliantly, I know you will, and the sponsors will be so happy you'll probably secure yourselves more backing for years to come.'

Having no choice but to look thrilled by the prospect, Cristy unzipped her coat and went to put on some coffee. 'Connor should be here any minute,' she said, willing it to be right now, this second, so he could take over dealing with Iz.

'I was thinking,' Iz said pensively. 'Would it be possible for me to have a little desk in here? Somewhere in the corner, you know, so I won't get in the way.'

Cristy kept her back turned and filled the machine with fresh beans.

'I'd just love to watch you guys working, pulling it all together. Not that I'd be here all the time, of course, just now and again, and it might be helpful for you to have me at hand.' She laughed. 'I'm not sure how, right now, but you never know.'

Knowing she wasn't in the right head space to deal with this, Cristy was still struggling for a response when Connor came in. Never having felt so glad to see him, she said, 'Good morning. Iz's here already, and she's just had an . . . amazing idea.'

'Oh?' Connor asked, looking from one to the other and, being a bloke, clearly not sensing trouble yet. 'So let's have it, Iz. We're all up for good ideas.'

As Iz repeated her suggestion, Cristy almost wanted to laugh as he failed to hide his horror. 'Well, we don't normally . . .' he began, glancing at Cristy in panic. 'I mean, some things have to be confidential . . . Not that we need to hide anything from you . . .'

'Of course you don't, and I've already assured Cristy I won't get in the way. I'm just delighted to be overseeing this project and I want to do my best for you – and the sponsors, of course.'

Having to give her credit for not actually mentioning the considerable investment she'd brought to the table that, like it or not, actually gave her some clout, Cristy said, 'Well, I'm sure we can work something out. Now, how do you like your coffee?'

'Black, two sugars, please. Shall we take it to the studio? We're booked in from nine so we ought not to waste any more time. I'm sure the techies will be waiting.'

Knowing that time was money to Iz, while to the techies it was a made-to-measure concept, Cristy said, 'Why don't you go on ahead while Connor and I download our scripts? We'll be right behind you.'

Iz beamed in the way only she could, and taking her coffee she got as far as the door before turning back. 'I probably ought to bring this up sooner, rather than later,' she said, 'but we – that's the Sponsorship Liaison Group and I – think you should delay uploading – or is it downloading – the first episode for another week.'

Having already decided they should, Cristy waited for her to explain her thinking.

'We want these promos to gain as much traction as possible before *Hindsight*'s initial airing,' Iz explained. 'As we haven't been able to record them until today, it's not leaving us much time to let your millions of followers know that you're about to hit them with a brand-new series.'

'But even if they miss the opening episode,' Connor pointed out, 'it'll always be there for them to download. It's kind of the point of a podcast.'

Iz coloured slightly, as if she'd actually forgotten that. 'Of course,' she mumbled. 'I . . . I'm just . . . *sharing* our thoughts, and we feel that building momentum through a series of promotions on all platforms during the week before the first episode drops will get us – you – off to a flying start.'

Before Connor could argue further, Cristy said, 'Thank you for considering the dynamics of how to reach our listeners, Iz, and you're not wrong, we could probably benefit from delaying by a week.'

Iz grinned happily, and saluted them with her coffee before taking off for their designated studio.

Connor was regarding Cristy in confusion.

'We're not really ready yet,' she told him, 'so this suits us perfectly.'

'But we have the first episode in the can,' he reminded her. 'And a lot of press releases have already gone out, not to mention our own, unsponsored, promos.'

'I know, but we can use the delay to our advantage, let people think that something . . . *relevant* and even shocking has cropped up to push back the start date. Meantime, an interview with Mia Winters could change things quite considerably . . .'

'If it happens.'

'We'll exert some pressure if need be. In the meantime, letting Iz and her sponsors call the shots over this could be the start of choosing our battles. They only need to be fought if there's an issue of real importance at stake. And whether we start the uploads this week or next doesn't make much difference, especially when we're not at all sure yet how this series is going to shape up.'

'It has the potential of being a great story . . .'

'Potential, yes, but the deeper into it we go – and we're still in shallow waters right now – the more I'm feeling that something's not quite right with it. I mean, there's obviously a lot wrong if we look at it from the perspective of a two-year-old child being spirited away by a couple of middle-aged women, but getting to the bottom of it all and thinking of how long that could take . . . Frankly, I'm already feeling nervous about turning up enough material to meet our weekly commitments. If we don't there's no knowing what the sponsors might do.' She thrust a coffee into his hand. 'So now, on that happy note, let's get these promos in the can, then we can get back to what we do best.'

# CHAPTER NINE

By Wednesday morning, thanks to an hour's meditative yoga, followed by coffee with Jodi and baby Aurora, Cristy was feeling far more relaxed than she had for the past two days. Her conversation with David at the start of the week had left her angry with herself for caring about him and Juliette, disappointed with herself for being unable to stop thinking about him, and furious with Matthew simply for breathing.

Still, she was nice and chilled now – in both senses of the word – and ready to seize the day.

Connor looked up as she swept into the office, red-cheeked and windswept from her brisk walk to Spike Island. 'I had an interesting call while you and my wife were downward-dogging at David Lloyd's,' he announced drolly.

'Tell me,' she encouraged, hanging her coat and going to pour herself a coffee. 'Clove, did you send the edit of Sadie's latest interview to her for feedback?'

'Done,' Clover confirmed. 'No word yet, but the boyfriend got in touch this morning to ask why the first episode wasn't dropped last night.'

'And you told him?'

'What you said, that we're waiting to speak to Mia in case it impacts the story in some way.'

'Great. And nothing from Mia yet, I take it?' Without waiting for an answer, Cristy said, 'Are we being honoured by Iz's magnificent presence today, does anyone know?'

'Apparently not,' Jackson replied. 'She said she has to be in London. I didn't ask why, mostly because she'd have told me and life's too short.'

With a laugh, Cristy said, 'In which case, as it's just us, I have a little announcement to make before we go any further. It's probably best you all know – if you haven't worked it out already – that David and I are no longer . . . together.'

'What?' Clover exclaimed in confusion. 'But I thought you guys . . .'

'No damage done,' Cristy hastily assured her, 'and there's nothing more to discuss. It was just an FYI.'

'But aren't we hoping he'll give us some insight into the aunts' financials?' Jackson asked worriedly.

'I'm sure he'll still come through, and I'll leave it to you to chase him. That way he'll know you're taking on that aspect of the case.'

She watched both researchers look to Connor, as if seeking further explanation or guidance. Since this wasn't news to him, he simply shrugged and said, 'So, who wants to hear about the call I received earlier? The answer is, you all do, so fasten your seatbelts.'

Smiling, Cristy sank into her chair and automatically opened her inbox, not to see if there was anything from David – there obviously wouldn't be – just because it was a habit she'd formed at the start of the working day.

Seeing Marley's name on the list she quickly closed the screen. Her ex-husband's crazy wife was someone she really didn't need to deal with today – or any other, come to that.

'Are you listening?' Connor demanded testily.

'All yours,' she assured him.

'OK, so when we go to Exmoor tomorrow we're not only meeting with the old housekeeper, Gita Brinkley. We're also meeting with her son, Robert, who got in touch this morning.'

Immediately interested, Cristy said, 'Does he remember the aunts? How old is he?'

Dryly, Connor said, 'Funnily enough, I didn't ask his age, but he does remember them – he called them "the sisters" – and he thought it might be useful if he sat in on our chat with his mother.'

Cristy was frowning. 'Did he sound controlling? As if he might try to *edit* or manage what she tells us?'

'Actually, he came across as a pretty regular sort of bloke,'

Connor replied. 'He's got a bit of an accent – I'd say Aussie, maybe Kiwi, can't tell the difference. Kind of cultured anyway, and definitely friendly. Apparently his mother loves to go out, so he's taken the liberty of booking us into the Notley Arms for lunch before, or while we talk.'

Cristy lit up. 'I hope you told him that's fine by us,' she responded, already picturing the warm and welcoming village pub where they'd always stopped for a meal when filming on Exmoor during their TV days. 'God, we haven't been there in too long,' she sighed, choosing not to recall the times she'd stayed there with Matthew. Memories of him always complicated the picture, much as the reality of him made her head spin in ways too annoying to analyse.

'. . . so I've contacted Simon and Caroline,' Connor was saying, referring to the Notley's owners, 'and they've said they'll put the heating on in the garden room just in case we want some privacy to record.'

'They're the best,' she declared. 'I take it you asked . . . What was the son's name again?'

'Robert.'

'Robert, if . . . What's her name again?'

'Gita. She's definitely of Indian origin, as mentioned in Lottie's writings – and Harry's already afraid she might be one of Meena's family . . .'

Cristy laughed.

'She's been in this country for over fifty years and is more English than bacon.'

'Which is mostly Danish,' Jacks pointed out.

'Semantics,' Connor retorted. 'Anyway, she told me that her husband, Robert's father, was from Exmoor, which was how the family came to be living near Minehead at the time the sisters were renting their summer house, as Gita called it.'

'Hang on, I thought you were speaking to the son,' Jacks queried.

'I was, but she kept calling out from the background. She also told me that they, the Brinkleys, lived in London before they moved back to the father's roots in Somerset, but I didn't get into where in London, or why they decamped when they did.'

'Well, the story's not about them, so why would you?' Clover pointed out. 'Did either of them say anything about a child called Sadie who was "living" with the sisters?'

'They already know it's what we want to discuss, and Robert says he can probably be of more help to us than his mother, which is why he's going to join us.'

Cristy's eyes rounded with intrigue, and grew even wider a second later as Iz waltzed in through the door, looking not unlike Noddy in a bright blue conical hat and crimson fluffy duffle coat. 'I thought you were in London,' she commented.

'Sorry, am I interrupting something?' Iz asked worriedly and seemed as though she might tiptoe out again.

'No, not at all,' Cristy assured her. 'I just heard that you were . . .'

'It got cancelled,' Iz told her, 'so I thought I'd drop by to see how you're getting on here, and to ask if you'd heard the first promos yet? They're on all the major radio stations, as of this morning. Never let it be said that our guys don't know how to put a promotional package together.'

'Which of course, we don't,' Connor retorted tightly.

Shooting him a quick warning look, Cristy said, 'You're amazing, all of you. I've no idea how we'd do this without you . . .'

'Oh stop!' Iz laughed modestly. 'We're just doing our bit. Horses for courses, and all that. Anyway, it means the first episode will have to drop next Tuesday come what may, but we've all listened to it and everyone agrees it's a fantastic opener, especially the way the envelope comes through the door at the end. Phenomenal cliff-hanger. Any news yet on what was in it?'

'Only guesses at this stage,' Cristy told her, 'but we think it was photographs . . .'

To Cristy's relief, after Iz had refreshed her coffee, she took herself off upstairs to enjoy 'a little chat' with Meena.

Returning to her emails, Cristy read and replied to each of them, before finally opening the one from Marley.

*Hi Cristy,*

*How are you?*

*I expect you're wondering why you haven't heard from me before now . . .*

Cristy was immediately struck with guilt. Putting aside what Marley had done to her marriage, her entire life, actually, she was still a young woman who'd just given birth and was, as far as Cristy could make out, friendless. So she should have been in touch by now.

*. . . but I've had so much to deal with. Baby Bear is an absolute joy, without a doubt the best thing that's ever happened to me, although I have to confess I was afraid of him at first. He's so tiny and wobbly and he really didn't want me to touch him, or feed him, or so it seemed to me. I was very hurt by that, until the midwife explained that it often happens with newborns, and it soon turned out that I really needn't have worried because we both quickly got the hang of things and now we're inseparable.*

*I expect you've heard about Matthew being arrested. It was my fault, of course. You're probably not surprised to hear that given my ability to cause mayhem without really trying. The problem was, I stopped him from seeing the baby, and nor would I speak to him myself. I got it into my head that he was going to try to snatch Baby Bear from me. He didn't take kindly to that and ended up making an awful spectacle of himself.*

*Luckily, he'd calmed down by the time Baby Bear and I returned home, and with Daddy around to make sure Matthew behaved I wasn't anxious any more. It's so sweet the way Daddy and Matthew have bonded, I suppose them being quite close in age helps, although Daddy is a big charmer, as everyone knows.*

*I hope you're happy to hear from me. Your friendship and our chats mean the world to me. I always feel I can be myself with you in a way I can't with anyone else. There aren't many people who'd be so generous in spirit as you have been considering the way we met. I sometimes think you mean more to me than Matthew, but please don't tell him that, and anyway, I don't know if it's true.*

*I have no idea at this time how M and I are going to move forward in our marriage. One day I feel it's better for it to end, the next I can't bear the idea of letting him go. He's a very complex and conflicted man, as you know, but he has so much beauty in his soul and kindness in his heart that he is impossible not to love.*

*He is, of course, still very much in love with you – he doesn't tell me this, but I can sense it – and I want you to know that I'm not jealous or insecure about it, because I love you too.*

*I wish you would consider coming here to visit for a while. The house is very big with plenty of rooms, and we have an extra car you can use if you'd like one. Daddy can also get VIP passes to Universal Studios and Disneyland, and I'm sure lots of premieres and things will be happening so you'll be invited to them too.*

*Sorry if this message is going on too long. I'm so enjoying talking to you, I just wish you were here so I could see your lovely face as we share your memories of becoming a mother for the first time.*

*I hope you write back.*

*With love,*

*Marley*

'She's clearly bonkers,' Meena stated after reading the email later. 'Why the heck would you want to go to Universal or Disneyland, for God's sake? How old does she think you are?'

Cristy shot her a look.

'OK, not the point, but honestly, the things she comes out with . . . She's so . . . I don't know how to describe her . . . Clueless!'

Cristy sighed. 'She's definitely not properly in touch with the world, or how people tick. Still, at least she's not asking me to bring the baby up, the way she was a couple of months ago.'

'Shame for him,' Meena muttered, 'at least then he'd get a proper name.'

Chuckling, Cristy picked up her wine and took a sip. They were still at the office, in Meena's upstairs suite where a bio-fuel fire was burning in the old Georgian hearth and a cosy arrangement of sofas was making them too comfortable to move very far on this stormy evening.

'She's terribly lonely, isn't she?' Cristy reflected sadly.

Meena nodded. 'It certainly comes across that way. Have you shown the email to Matthew?'

'No, not yet. I'm in two minds about it. On the one hand he probably ought to see it, for any number of reasons, but on the other I'm trying not to initiate contact with him unless I have to.'

Seeming to understand that, Meena stared into the flames as she said, 'Harry and I had dinner with him last night.'

Surprised, Cristy said, 'That's nice. How was he?'

'Complex and conflicted,' Meena quoted. 'Clearly in a horrible dilemma over his new son, and worried about the older one . . .'

'Why is he worried about Aiden?'

Meena shrugged. 'Apparently he's spending more time on building bands than he is on his studies, but, as we know, that's typical of your lad. He's always got something going on somewhere, and his schoolwork seems like a side issue until it comes time for exams – and he sails them.'

In spite of knowing this to be true, Cristy said, 'He shouldn't take it for granted that everything will just fall into place because he wants it to. One of these days he'll get a rude awakening and I fear it'll be when it comes to his A levels and getting into the university of his choice.'

'If he goes to uni at all.'

Stalled by that, Cristy shook her head in despair, and said, 'I guess we won't know until the time comes. You never do with him. Anyway, back to Matthew . . .'

'Actually, I was hoping we could talk about David.'

Cristy's heart flipped as she frowned. 'Why? There's nothing to say apart from apparently it's over, and, to paraphrase you, better sooner than later.'

Meena simply looked at her.

Cristy threw out her hands. 'Sure it hurts,' she admitted, 'and I'm . . . disappointed. But we weren't together for long, and I've dealt with worse, so let's move on, shall we?'

Meena began shaking her head. 'I'm still not convinced . . .'

'Please, Meena. I don't want to talk about him now . . .'

'You struck up a lovely bond with his family.'

Not enjoying the reminder given how she was feeling the loss of them too, Cristy said, 'I daresay I'll stay in touch with them, for a while, but I'm certainly not going to use any attachment I might have to them to keep one going with him. Now, if it's OK with you, why don't we talk about the new series and Iz's involvement . . .'

Meena's hand shot up. 'I know, I know, she's driving you mad, she has the same effect on me, but I urge you to think of the money and everything else she's bringing to the table. We've never had exposure like it before, and you guys deserve full recognition for the brilliant podcasters you are. You were hitting the top spot at the end of the last series, and there's a lot of buzz out there already for *Who's That Girl*. So, you have to admit, annoyingness aside, she's good at what she does.'

With a smile, Cristy said, 'She's certainly that – although I have to say dubbing us the Dream Team during yesterday's photoshoot made us all cringe.'

Laughing Mia said, 'But you loved it really and the shots were fantastic. All four of you at work in the office, walking along the harbourside – I especially loved the one of you laughing at only you know what. She staged it really well, and she'll have umpteen possibilities up her sleeve of where to run them and when.'

'All with the logos of First Family Bank, Rapid Retail Initiative and Open Destiny Holidays in the background . . .'

'What's wrong with that?'

'Nothing. I'm happy for it.' Cristy gave herself a moment to choose her next words carefully. 'It's no one's fault but mine,' she continued, 'that we weren't properly prepared for this series. I should have been firmer about needing to know more about the story before we committed to the proposed timeline.'

'But it's shaping up to be a terrific—'

'It's shaping up, yes, but when it comes to execution and delivery . . . I'm worried about where we could end up – and I'm not only thinking egg-on-face, and public humiliation if the story comes to nothing . . . Actually I don't think that'll happen . . . I just keep getting the feeling we're being played in some way.'

Clearly confused, Meena said, 'By whom? Surely not Sadie?'

Cristy shook her head. 'The dead aunt was once suggested to me.'

Meena's eyes widened in astonishment. 'You mean from the grave?' she exclaimed.

Understanding how ridiculous it sounded, Cristy said, 'I'm not saying she's controlling us, our production, but Sadie, yes, and even her sister, although I'm sure Mia knows a lot more than she's letting on.'

After sitting with that for a moment, Meena said, 'Hasn't Mia agreed to talk to you?'

'She's yet to commit and she doesn't want to answer anything we send by email.'

Meena threw out her hands. 'You just need to share your suspicions, or reservations, even the spooky bit . . . OK, maybe not that . . . with the listeners. They'll lap it up.'

Knowing that to be true, Cristy said, 'Connor and I have already laid something down on that score. I'm not sure yet where we'll use it, a lot will depend on what we can uncover in the next couple of weeks, but it's there as a kind of padding, if needed. There's just no knowing if Lottie, through her writing, or in the chaos of stuff she left behind, has planted the truth of what really happened twenty-three years ago. Or if it's all some kind of ruse to steer us in completely the wrong direction.'

After a beat, Meena said, tentatively, 'Aren't you going to Exmoor tomorrow?'

Surprised, Cristy said, 'I had no idea you were so up to date with our schedule.'

'Iz,' Meena explained. 'Anyway, I'm told you're meeting the ex-housekeeper *and* her son who apparently remembers the sisters and the child. That's got to be a good lead, something to give the story . . . stronger legs?'

Hoping so, Cristy said, 'We've already googled Robert Brinkley and he's . . .'

As she searched for the right word, Meena said, 'Impressive?'

Cristy had to smile. 'You've looked him up too?'

'I had a spare few minutes earlier, and well, wow! Not what I was expecting, that's for sure. Leading heart surgeon down under, regular assignments for *Médecins Sans Frontières* . . . And, I get this isn't important, but you know me . . .' Her eyes twinkled. 'You have to admit, with those looks he could give Avan Jogia a run for his money.'

'Who?'

Rolling her eyes, Meena said, 'The Indian/English—'

'Poet, yes, of course, who's probably half Robert Brinkley's age and isn't he part Irish as well? But OK, I can see the similarity, especially around the eyes.'

‘Smouldering,’ Meena purred mischievously. ‘I was so mesmerized I was tempted to ask if I could tag along tomorrow, but I wouldn’t want to distract him.’

Laughing, Cristy said, ‘You are shameless, Meena Quinn.’

Meena grinned, and raised her glass. ‘What’s important,’ she said seriously, ‘is that I don’t think someone like Robert Brinkley would be giving you his time if he didn’t have something to say that matters.’

# CHAPTER TEN

CRISTY: 'Connor and I have just pulled up outside the Notley Arms in the quaint Exmoor village of Monksilver. If you've never been, do put it on your list, because it's absolutely the best pub in the area, if not the county. It's owned and run by Simon and Caroline who'll give you the warmest of welcomes, and who doesn't want one of those on days as freezing as this one?'

CONNOR: 'The reason we're here is to meet with Gita Brinkley, the Winters sisters' housekeeper from twenty-three years ago, and her son, Robert. Apparently Gita has memories of the sisters from the time they rented a holiday home on Exmoor, but perhaps more crucially, she recalls the child who came to live with them.'

Pausing the recording, Connor said, 'Do you think we need to make reference here to the box of "Sadie's Things"? It kind of expels any doubt that she was the child, so I could say, "The child we *now know* to be Sadie."'

Cristy shook her head slowly. 'Let's do a sound edit on that later.' She was staring along the sunlit, puddled high street to where an elderly couple was coming out of a picturesque thatched cottage with an even older-looking dog. So many of the properties in this secluded valley, with its centuries-old church and cherished spot on the Coleridge Way footpath, could grace a chocolate box, and plenty could probably tell their own colourful stories of past owners and their secrets.

'We should go in,' Connor said, packing up the recording equipment and opening the car door. 'They could already be here.'

Not entirely sure why she was feeling uneasy about this meeting – was it to do with a persistent sense of something not being right about the story, or simply because she hadn't slept well last night – Cristy got out of the car and followed Connor into the pub.

The instant they walked in to be greeted loudly and exuberantly by Simon, the wonderfully eccentric ex-prison governor, now landlord, her misgivings seemed to fade.

'Come in, come in, my lovelies,' he cried, pulling them both into fulsome hugs. 'Great to see you. You're looking very well. Caroline should be down any minute, and your guests are already waiting by the fire around the corner. Now, what can I get you to drink?'

'I'll start with something hot,' Cristy decided.

'Toddy or tea?'

'How about coffee, black? And Connor's been gagging all the way for a pint of Exmoor ale.'

'Coming right up.'

Hefting his heavy bag onto one shoulder Connor led the way round to where a well-stocked log burner was throwing out heavenly warmth and all tables bar the one next to it were empty. 'Hey! You must be Robert,' he cried enthusiastically, as if he and the man turning to greet him had met plenty of times before, rather than over just one phone call yesterday. 'And *you* have to be Gita! No, please don't get up.'

Cristy winced; Gita was in a wheelchair, although he presumably meant Robert who was already on his feet.

'Good to meet you,' Robert smiled, shaking Connor vigorously by the hand. He was every bit as impressive in person as he'd appeared online, she decided, perhaps even more so. Tall, around six-two, with silvery dark hair, perfectly formed features and compelling dark eyes.

'Thanks so much for agreeing to talk to us,' she smiled as he took her hand. His grip was cool and firm, his fingers long, and his answering smile could surely put anyone at ease. Not a bad quality for a surgeon.

'I hope you don't mind,' he said, 'but I looked you up online, so I could say I'm feeling a little starstruck right now.'

With a laugh of surprise, she said, 'We also googled you, so, if anyone's feeling starstruck – well, overawed is perhaps a better word – it's us.'

'He makes me feel like that all the time,' Gita piped up from her chair, 'and I ask you, what sort of way is that to treat your mother?'

With a droll glance at Cristy, he said, 'The last time you were overawed,' he informed his mother, 'was in 1968 when Dad beat you at Scrabble.'

'He only managed it because I was going into labour with you at the time,' she retorted, 'and you've been messing things up for me ever since. He's made a habit of it,' she told Cristy, reaching out both hands to take Cristy's. She was exquisitely twinkly, with as many lines on her face as pearls around her neck, silver-threaded hair clasped loosely behind her head, and a very lovely smile. 'Please excuse me being in this silly chair,' she said, 'it's not that I can't walk, I just find it painful at times and today isn't one of the better ones. Not to worry though, I can still speak and that's what today's all about.'

'She can certainly speak,' Robert said dryly.

As Cristy laughed Gita scowled and patted the chair next to her. 'We saved this one for you,' she said, 'and you, Connor, could give me a lovely hug before you sit there next to Robert.'

Readily doing as instructed, he said, 'I think I already like you.'

Clearly delighted, she gave a cluck of satisfaction and folded her hands in her lap as everyone sat.

'Isn't this lovely?' she declared, looking from one to the other. 'I've been quite excited to meet you, you know. Robert has too, haven't you, dear?'

'I've hardly been able to contain myself,' he agreed. 'Embarrassing me is one of her favourite pastimes,' he informed them. 'Ah, here are your drinks.'

'And the menus,' Simon added, setting down a tray with a flourish. 'No mussels today, I'm afraid, but the chef can do you some lovely scallops instead, if seafood's your thing. I know you're partial to scallops Gita, so we can pop a couple of extras on the plate for you if you like. Robert and Connor, you might be interested in the venison stew with you both having a liking for game, and for you, Cristy, my angel, we've got some delicious baked Cornish hake with lemon and herb dressing.'

As everyone marvelled at his knowledge of their tastes, Cristy threw out her hands saying, 'Sounds like you've got us covered, Simon, unless anyone wants to choose something else?'

'Happy with mine,' Robert and Connor replied, almost in unison.

'Me too,' Gita smiled. 'And I'll have another ginger ale when you're ready.'

'Same again for you too?' Simon asked Robert.

'I'm good with this, thanks,' he replied, nodding towards his almost full pint of ale. Cristy watched his hand go around the tall glass and the way he stretched out his long legs, crossing them at the ankles and seeming as comfortable here as if at his own hearth. She really wasn't sure what to make of him, certainly his friendliness and easy confidence made him likeable, however . . . She couldn't decide what was troubling her, only knew that she felt wary, concerned that his looks might in some way skew judgement, as often happened with particularly attractive people.

Gita said, 'I don't mind admitting it came as quite a shock to me when Connor got in touch. All these years later . . . It seems like a lifetime ago that I worked for those sisters and that dear little dot turned up out of the blue. Well, it was a lifetime, twenty-three years . . . So much has happened since . . .' She smiled up at Simon as he delivered her drink and sighed nostalgically. 'I used to think about them quite a lot at one time, wondering where they might have gone when they left, how the child was getting along. It was a tragedy her losing her parents so suddenly the way she did, but I always told myself she was in the best hands. Her aunts doted on her, there was no doubt about that, and you could tell she'd never want for anything.'

'So you didn't ever doubt that they were her aunts?' Cristy asked, casting a quick glance at Robert. His eyes were down as he listened, making his expression hard to read.

'I had no reason to, then,' Gita replied, 'but after . . . Well, now you're saying she wasn't related to them?'

'She wasn't,' Cristy confirmed.

Gita shook her head as if trying to slot her many thoughts into place, to rearrange perceptions, maybe suspicions . . . Certainly she was showing little surprise.

'Did you have much to do with the child?' Cristy prompted.

Gita brightened. 'Oh, I did, I did. Little angel she was. I remember she had a birthday not long after she arrived, we baked a cake with lots of icing and two little candles . . . She ended up with flour all over her face and in her hair, how she laughed when I popped a dab of cream on our noses. She thought that was the funniest thing in the world. The sisters came to see what was going on and next thing you know we all had cream on our noses.' Her eyes began to drift, her smile wistful as she recalled the happy moment. 'I'm sorry to say she cried a lot too,' she added soberly. 'She missed her mummy, of course, but we did our best to comfort her and they bought her so many toys, everything a child could wish for . . .'

'Did she ever mention her father?' Connor asked.

Gita thought for a moment. 'She didn't actually speak much, just a few words, "Mummy" being the one she said most. And Gita. Or Yita, as she pronounced it. She seemed to like my name because she always smiled when she said it. The sisters had called me Mrs B up to then, but they took to Gita after Sadie came. They were lovely women, very kind, although they had their ways . . . Mia, I think she was the eldest, she could be all airy-fairy one minute and scared of her own shadow the next. Such a funny thing she was. Chatty, without ever really saying anything. Lottie was different, more . . . outspoken, confident, I suppose . . . Lovely to look at, and always lively. She'd sing and dance about the house, run down the hillside with Sadie in tow. I remember them collecting all sorts of horrible little creatures in buckets and bringing them back to torment us all with. Mia and I would put on a show of being terrified and Sadie would laugh . . . It was an infectious sound; I can hear it even now. It was like we were all cheered up by her and I couldn't help thinking what a pity it was that the sisters had never had any children of their own. They took to motherhood like a pair of naturals in spite of being in their mid-to-late forties.'

'How often did you go to the house?' Cristy asked.

Picking up her glass as she thought, Gita said, 'Tuesdays and Fridays, sometimes Wednesday if they wanted me to cook.' Her eyes sparked with merriment again. 'I'm surprised they kept me on, because I wasn't any good at cleaning. Oh Lord, I was a disaster when it came to mops and dusters. I'd never really done any before, you see. Charles and I always had someone living in who took care of those things . . . That was when we were in Hong Kong, but then life took a different turn . . . We had to leave and London didn't work out well for us, so we came back to Charles's roots. He never really liked it here, but we didn't have a lot of money after losing so much and it suited me just fine. He got a right bee in his bonnet about me working, but someone had to or we'd have starved.'

Cristy looked at Robert as, shifting in his chair, he said, 'If you'd told us how things were, you know we'd have helped . . .'

'Oh shush now, it's all in the past and you had your life in Australia with Jenny and the children to be worrying about.' Turning back to Cristy she said, 'I'm just telling you how I came to work for the Winters sisters. Charles and I had restaurants when we were in Hong Kong, but there wasn't much call for my sort of cooking around here, not back then. And he didn't have the heart to start again after we lost everything . . . I didn't blame him. It's hard for a man, isn't it, when it comes to their pride . . . Anyway, I saw the advert in a local shop and got in touch with the sisters and when they interviewed me they decided there and then that I was right for them. It was for the whole summer, they said, but then . . . It wasn't long after Sadie's birthday . . . You should have seen her dear little face when she blew out the candles on her cake. She was thrilled to bits, clapping her hands and laughing . . . Then she shut her eyes tight to make a wish and we all knew what it was . . . She wanted to see her mummy, of course. It broke our hearts, it did. I remember offering to take her up on the moor to show her the ponies, to distract her, but they didn't want me to do that. I don't know why, but looking back, they never did take her far from the house.'

'Do you remember anyone coming to visit?' Connor asked.

'No, I don't, but I wasn't there all the time, and never at weekends.'

'So you don't recall who brought Sadie to the house?'

'I suppose I always assumed one of them had gone to get her, after the accident. Although I remember thinking it was funny that she hadn't brought anything with her. No clothes, or toys, not even any pyjamas.'

Cristy glanced at Connor as he said, 'How long would you say she was with them before they left Somerset?'

Gita frowned as she thought. 'A few weeks, maybe. It must have been early June when I got there one morning to find them all packed up ready to go. They hadn't said anything about leaving the last time I was there, a few days before, but all their things were in the car . . . They paid me right through to September to make up for giving me short notice. We all cried when it came time to say goodbye, I remember that.'

'Did they say where they were going?'

'I don't think so. I presumed it was London.'

'Did they keep in touch after?'

'No. I could have kicked myself for not getting an address, I'd have liked to write to Sadie, send her a little card once in a while, you know, but well . . . Charles wasn't in a good way around the time they left, and then Robert was getting ready to go back to Melbourne . . .'

'About that,' he confirmed. 'When I realized what was happening over here, with my parents, I worked things out at home so I could spend a good amount of time with them . . .'

'He was another one who tried to persuade me to give up my job with the Winters sisters,' Gita told them, 'but I wasn't going to be bossed around by him or anyone else, and nor was I going to let him give us money. He needed it for his family and we were managing perfectly well on what little savings we had left, and my bit of income.'

Cristy was watching him, perhaps too intensely she realized when his eyes met hers and his brows rose in query. Quickly she said, 'Did you ever meet Sadie?'

Robert shook his head. 'No, but it's possible I saw her a couple of times, from a distance. Not at the sisters' house, it was before

Mum told me about their "niece", in fact, and I wasn't ever sure it was the same child. But after Mum got your call we both thought I should tell you about the young woman I met while out hiking . . .'

'It's what he does when he has a lot on his mind,' Gita explained. 'He hikes. And he was on the South West Coast Path when he first noticed this young woman . . .'

'Are you going to tell it?' he asked.

Gita chuckled and put a finger over her lips.

'Sorry if now's a bad time,' Simon interrupted, bringing in their food, 'but I expect you want it while it's hot.'

'Oh, thank goodness,' Gita clucked. 'I was about to faint.'

Laughing, Cristy said, 'Actually, this seems as good a moment as any to break. If it's OK with you, Gita, we'll go back over what you've said when we've finished eating, and commit it to tape? And maybe you, Robert, won't mind if we go straight to record to hear your part of the story?'

'Fine by me. I just need to reiterate that I still can't be certain it was Sadie I saw, but when Mum and I put things together, after the Winters sisters left Exmoor, well . . . You'll be able to judge for yourselves whether or not we came to the right conclusions.'

*

Half an hour later they had moved from the now busy bar area into the garden room where another roaring fire had been lit to warm the cosy leather sofas, and a large pot of coffee was waiting to be poured.

As Cristy did the honours, Connor set up to record and Robert made his mother comfortable with a patchwork woollen throw over her knees and a quick polish of her steamed-up glasses.

'I must say I'm very much enjoying our time,' Gita commented happily as Cristy passed her a cup and saucer. 'Of course, I might be taking a different view if Sadie hadn't turned out well, but she has, hasn't she?'

'I think you could say that,' Cristy assured her, 'but obviously she's very keen to know who she really is.'

'Yes, of course, I can quite understand that.' Then, 'So you're certain she wasn't their niece?'

'We are,' Cristy confirmed.

As Gita sat with that, Connor said, 'If it's OK with everyone, we'll start recording now?'

Robert gestured for them to continue, and as soon as Connor had mic-ed them all up, he sat down with the equipment and gave Cristy the nod to begin.

'OK, Robert,' she said, 'Connor and I will provide the actual intro to this section, but just to make sure we get it right: it was when you saw the photos Connor sent to your mother of a young couple with a small child that you recognized the woman as someone you'd met while staying with your parents back in 2000?'

'That's right. I knew it was her right away. She was very striking.'

'Good. Fine. So, if you could lead us in by telling us about how you met.'

He nodded slowly, and stretched an arm along the sofa back as he rested an ankle on one knee.

ROBERT: 'I'd only been in Somerset for a couple of weeks the first time I saw her . . . She was sitting on a bench in the park at the start of the South West Coast Path. I probably wouldn't have noticed her if the child on her lap hadn't dropped something as I passed. A rabbit, I think it was. I picked it up and handed it over and as the young woman thanked me I remember thinking . . . Bear with me on this, I thought of my father, a lifelong fan of Marlon Brando, *On the Waterfront* being one of his favourite movies. This girl was very like a young Eva Marie Saint. I saw it right away and wondered how often she might have been told that. I guessed she was in her mid-twenties . . . The other thing I noticed was that she hadn't spoken in English when she thanked me. It wasn't a language I recognized, but she didn't seem keen to engage any further, so I just went on my way.

'I didn't think any more about her, and probably wouldn't have again if I hadn't come across her a day or two later, further along the trail. In fact, the only reason I knew she was there was because I heard someone crying. There was no sign of anyone, but the distress, the sobbing wasn't something I could ignore. So I followed the sound down into a nook, and there she was, huddled into a ball crying as though she'd never stop.

'I'm sure she had no idea I was there until I sat down on the grass a short distance from her. She didn't acknowledge me at first, but when she did . . . It took a while for her to bring herself under control, but I was in no hurry. I simply sat with her and when her breathing was steadier I asked if there was anything I could do.

'She thanked me and said she'd be fine. I asked about her child, thinking perhaps something had happened to it and that was why she was so upset, but she said she was fine too. "Playing," she told me, "today she is playing in the camp." I presumed she meant Butlin's, which was, and still is, just along the coast or maybe one of the local caravan parks. She spoke English, quite well, although it was heavily accented. I half-expected her to get up and leave then, but she didn't, and eventually we got talking, about the view and the weather, where I was from and why I was in Somerset.'

CRISTY: 'Did you ask where she was from?'

ROBERT: 'I did, but she waved an arm as if to say it didn't matter. It was pretty clear she didn't want to talk about herself so I didn't press it.'

CRISTY: 'Were you anywhere near the sisters' house at this point of the trail?'

ROBERT: 'I'd say we were probably half a mile or so away, close to where the path forks to start climbing steeply to the moor one way and dips down gradually towards the coast the other.'

CRISTY: 'And this encounter was before your mother told you about the little girl who'd turned up at the sisters' house?'

ROBERT: 'As far as I recall, yes it was.'

CRISTY: 'And you had no reason to think the young woman you were talking to might know the sisters?'

ROBERT: 'Not then, no. As I said, we didn't talk about anything in particular. By the time we'd walked back to Minehead together I still didn't even know her name.'

CONNOR: 'Did she live in Minehead?'

ROBERT: 'I've no idea. When we got to the coastal end of the high street, she thanked me for being kind to her and we went our separate ways.'

CRISTY: 'But you saw her again after that day?'

ROBERT: 'Yes, about a week later. She was in the park, on the same bench. When she saw me she called out and beckoned me over. She seemed a little brighter that day, and I'm pretty sure that was when we properly introduced ourselves. She said her name was Janina and told me that she came to Minehead whenever she could to see her brother who worked at the Butlin's holiday camp. Apparently he'd sneak her little girl in to play with the other children and ride on the carousels. While she was waiting she either went for walks or read books; if it was raining she took refuge in the library.

'I'm not sure how it came up, but I recall how . . . *interested* she became when I mentioned that my mother worked as a housekeeper for two women who'd rented a place on the edge of the moor for the summer. She asked if I meant the Winters sisters and when I said I did she began telling me all about them and the work they did in various parts of the world to help poor communities . . . I remember being surprised that she seemed to know so much, and feeling I was letting her down when I had to admit that I'd never actually met them.'

He stopped talking as his mother gave a feisty little snore. Laughing, he said, 'I often have this effect on her.'

'I'm listening,' Gita assured them, 'just resting my eyes. Tell them about the second time you saw her with the child.'

ROBERT: 'They were in a café close to the seafront. I was passing by on my way to the trail, as usual . . . The child was sitting on the lap of a young man with a hat perched on the back of his head. He appeared to be teasing her and she was trying to grab his face. I wondered if he was the brother Janina had mentioned. She hadn't talked about a husband, at all, or about her child's father.'

CRISTY: 'Did she ever tell you her brother's name?'

ROBERT: 'I found out later that it was Lukas, with a k.'

CRISTY: 'What about her little girl? Do you know what she was called?'

ROBERT: 'I tried very hard after Janina disappeared to remember if she'd told me, but I don't think she did.'

CRISTY: 'And she disappeared *after* your mother told you about the little girl at the sisters' house?'

ROBERT: 'I'm afraid the order of things is far from clear in my mind after all this time, but I can tell you that I had no reason, then, to connect the so-called niece with Janina's little girl. It was only when Mum told me about an awful row she'd overheard between the sisters and Mia's husband that we both started to feel . . . I guess, uneasy?'

GITA: 'Yes, I should have mentioned him just now when you asked if they had any visitors. I actually only saw him once and he wasn't there for long . . . Edward, I think he was called, or something like that. I know Lottie didn't like him, the way she talked about him made that clear. She thought he'd only married Mia for her money and I got the feeling Mia thought the same, although she never said so. Anyway, I don't know what started the row off, I walked into the middle of it when he was shouting about them being insane and thinking that rules didn't apply to them. I slipped out before anyone knew I was there. I didn't want it to seem like I was eavesdropping. I went back to my car and gave it a few minutes before going in again, this time through the kitchen. I assumed Sadie was upstairs, or in the sitting room, but I couldn't get to her without letting it be known I was there, and they were still shouting. I couldn't make out what was being said, but it was very heated, and someone – Lottie, I think – said something about calling the police. He ended up storming out, and he hit Lottie's car with his own as he drove off.'

CRISTY: 'What happened after that?'

GITA: 'Well, they were very upset, of course, but they didn't talk to me about anything. It wasn't until Mia and I were on our own in the kitchen that she told me I shouldn't take any notice of what he'd said about Sadie not being their niece. He was just trying to make mischief, she said. I suppose she thought I'd heard that, but I hadn't, and it never entered my head until that day that Sadie might not be who they claimed she was.'

CRISTY: 'What did you do when Mia told you that?'

GITA: 'I went home and talked to Robert and Charles about it. Charles thought I should mind my own business, but then Robert told me about the young woman he'd met a few times who seemed to be taken with the sisters, and she had a girl of around Sadie's age . . .'

ROBERT: 'It seemed too far-fetched to think they were one and the same child, and I couldn't come up with a single reason why Janina would let her little girl go. Nevertheless I remember keeping an eye out for her after that, hoping to run into her again, or at least to spot her somewhere with her child, but I never did.'

GITA: 'You went to Butlin's to look for the brother.'

ROBERT: 'Yes, I did, and I was told he'd left, quite suddenly, no forwarding address.'

CRISTY: 'Did you happen to get his surname?'

ROBERT: 'It's possible someone told me, but if they did, I can't recall it now. It almost certainly wouldn't have been English.'

GITA: 'Then the next thing we knew the sisters had gone, taking Sadie with them – and Robert was getting ready to go back to Australia and I suppose . . . we just got on with our lives.'

Realizing they were at the end of what Gita and Robert could remember, Cristy signalled for Connor to stop recording. She was thinking now of what it was going to mean to Sadie to learn her mother's name – and that the man in a hat whose shoulders she was riding in one of the photos was probably her uncle.

Where were Janina and Lukas now?

What had happened to them?

What about Sadie's father?

Connor was saying, 'We need to get Gita's account of her time with Sadie on record. Is that OK with you, Gita? We haven't worn you out, have we?'

'Not a bit of it,' she retorted. 'I'm happy to go over things again. I'll probably find better ways of saying them second time around. And while we're doing that, perhaps Robert could take Cristy over to the coast path to show her the house?'

# CHAPTER ELEVEN

'If you're thinking my mother is a very unsubtle, in fact shameless, matchmaker,' Robert commented as he drove himself and Cristy out of Monksilver, heading for the coast, 'then I can only apologize if she embarrassed you as much as she did me.'

Cristy had to laugh. 'To be honest, I wasn't sure if I'd read it correctly. I mean, aren't you married?'

'I am, but that never stops her. She keeps hoping I'll meet someone here, in England, preferably Somerset, get myself a divorce and move back to be closer to her.'

Blinking in surprise, Cristy said, 'I hardly know what to say to that. A mother wanting her son to divorce.'

He laughed. 'Obviously, she knows it isn't going to happen. It's just a little fantasy she has and would probably have let go of a long time ago if she felt warmer towards my wife.'

'Ah, so they don't get on?'

'Let's just say that being on opposite sides of the world works for them both.'

As he slowed to turn onto the A39 Cristy checked an incoming text and choked back a laugh when she saw Connor's message, *Will I ever see you again?*

Deciding that no answer would suffice, she quickly pulled up her emails, found nothing urgent, and returned to the conversation. 'So how come you're in England now?' she asked. 'Is this a regular visit to your mother – don't tell me you flew over just to be here for the interview.'

He laughed. 'I arrived in the UK about a month ago, always with the intention of visiting Mum , of course, but I'm also researching a paper on emergency cardiothoracic surgery. Currently, I'm working with colleagues at the Bristol Heart Institute, so I wasn't far away when she rang to tell me you'd been in touch.'

Cristy nodded thoughtfully as she took this in. 'So we're very lucky to have you. Although, of course, we could have probably got you on Zoom if you were elsewhere in the world.'

'Probably, but where would be the fun in that?'

Finding herself OK with the flirtation – safe given he was married – she said, randomly, 'Have you ever been to Dunster Castle?'

Glancing up to where it was nestled amongst the trees on the hillside, he said, 'Many times. I used to take my children when they were younger and we were over visiting. They loved it here, I guess because it's so different to where they lived, and happily, they always adored spending time with their grandma. Still do.'

'I can understand why. So how many children do you have?'

'Three. Two girls and a boy, all very grown up now. The eldest is going to be thirty this year, and is actually working at the Bristol Children's Hospital. Like her mother, she's a paediatrician, and like her father, she fell in love while on a gap year so she's ended up living on the other side of the world. Her being here played a big part in my decision to approach colleagues at the BRI.'

'So are you staying with her?'

'God no, I don't think either of us could stand that. I've based myself in a small flat in Clifton for a couple of months; she and her husband have a house in Westbury Park, so we're close, but not in each other's space.'

'Does she have children?'

'Not yet, so the joyful experience of becoming a grandfather still awaits.'

Cristy smiled, while realizing soberly that she too was old enough to be a grandparent, although in her case it would surely be another ten years or more before it happened. 'And your other two children?' she asked.

'My son is twenty-seven and living in Sydney where he's doing amazing things in advertising, or so he tells me. And the youngest, she's twenty-four, the darling of everyone's hearts including a whole slew of inappropriate boyfriends. Career-wise, she's still considering her options.'

Laughing, Cristy said, 'I have a sixteen-year-old son who sounds just like her. His name is Aiden, he fancies himself as a free spirit one day, a mentor the next, a great sportsman, a talent-spotter, astronaut, world peace advocate . . . My boy's ambitions know no limits, and would you believe he seems to sail through his exams as if he's worked himself to a standstill all year when he hasn't.'

'I'm liking the sound of him,' Robert responded warmly. 'And your daughter? Hayley, is it?'

Cristy turned to him curiously. 'So you really did look me up before coming,' she said, not sure how happy she was to know he'd gone into so much depth. Although, she had to admit, it was pretty difficult to miss the shitshow of her personal life, thanks to Matthew and his affair turning her into a byword for rejected middle-aged mothers to be more pitied than respected.

'Forgive me,' he said, 'I'm sure you understand that your children weren't the objects of my search, they just came up. I hope you're not offended.'

Realizing she was being too defensive she relaxed and shook her head. 'No, not at all. My ex-husband's story is not how any of us hoped to achieve fame, but here we are. It's one of the first things anyone learns about me if they're looking me up. Not that I'm a journalist, or a podcaster, or even a woman with feelings. Just that I'm the wife Matthew Jennings walked out on to be with an actress barely older than his daughter.'

'It must have been a difficult time.'

'It certainly wasn't the best, but if you knew what was happening now you'd probably . . . Actually, you'd probably laugh it's so ludicrous, or you'd tell me I was making it up.'

'I'm a good listener,' he said dryly when she didn't continue. 'And I always love a human-interest story with elements of the bizarre.'

Deciding they were getting too far from the point of why they were heading into Minehead, she said, 'Maybe another time. For now, if you don't mind, I need us to focus on Janina and Lukas, the Winters sisters and maybe even Butlin's.'

'Of course, and I'm sorry if I seemed glib just then, or to be getting into things that are none of my business.'

'It's fine, honestly,' she said, and it was, because, why shouldn't it be?

Eventually they turned into the tree-lined stretch of Minehead's main street, full of cafés and bars, niche boutiques and colourful beach shops. Many were closed for the winter, although the blazing sunshine today made it look, if not feel, more like mid-summer than mid-winter.

On reaching the seafront Robert took a left into the harbour and just after the Old Ship Aground he pulled into a small car park. As he went to pay at a machine, Cristy organized her recording equipment ready for the great outdoors. It wasn't cumbersome, or difficult, it was simply so bitterly cold – close to freezing – that she had to try to find a way to operate it while wearing hat, scarf and thermal gloves. Still, at least there was no wind and thanks to the glorious sunshine it felt a complete joy to be here.

'I was thinking,' she said from inside her woollen muffler as they headed off to join the start of the South West Coast Path, 'that maybe you could do the intro to this piece.'

'Me?' he cried in astonishment. 'What does it involve?'

'You simply have to tell us who you are, why we're here and describe the surroundings.'

'Oh, is that all? Nothing major then?'

'Give it a go,' she encouraged. 'I have a feeling you'll be a natural.'

His eyes narrowed suspiciously as she handed him a mic.

'You'll need to clip it to your collar,' she told him, 'so no scarf, I'm afraid. Do you think you can bear the cold on your face for a while?'

'Ah, so that's why you've given me the job, so you don't have to get your face out of that thing. Well, lucky for you I'm feeling chivalrous.'

After a few sound tests to make sure his voice was coming through loud and clear, she gave him the cue to begin.

ROBERT: 'My name is Robert Brinkley, I'm the son of Gita Brinkley who was housekeeper to the Winters sisters for a short spell back in the year 2000. I'm about to start walking the first mile or so of the South West Coast Path to where the sisters were staying when Sadie first joined them.'

He glanced at Cristy for approval, and receiving it, pressed on.

ROBERT: 'It's a truly spectacular January day with more sunshine flooding down on us than we get in the middle of an Aussie summer, although sadly none of the warmth. In fact, it's literally zero degrees, but the way the light is sparkling across the iron grey waves of the estuary and throwing itself onto the wooded hills ahead of us makes them more inviting than chocolate.'

Cristy snorted a laugh.

'It was the first thing that came into my head,' he protested. 'What do you think it should be?'

She thought, gave a few suggestions which managed to be even worse than chocolate, and in the end they were laughing so much she had to cut the recording.

'I think you should do it,' he told her. 'I'm just making an idiot of myself.'

'No, no, you started off so well. Let's just lose the analogy and say something like "The way the light is throwing itself onto the wooded hills ahead of us makes it no wonder the region has inspired so many poets."'

'Now, why didn't I think of that?' Then, 'Who are the poets?'

Though certain she was being teased, she said, 'Coleridge, Wordsworth, Robert Southey . . .'

'Didn't Southey write *Goldilocks and the Three Bears*?'

She grinned. 'He also wrote some stunning descriptions of the walk between Dunster and Minehead.'

'Great. Do you know any of them?'

Having to confess that she didn't, at least not by heart, she offered to google them, but he was already quoting from *The Rime of the Ancient Mariner*.

'"*At length did cross an Albatross, Through the fog it came, As if it had been a Christian soul . . .*"'

'Brilliant,' Cristy exclaimed. 'It has absolutely nothing to do with why we're here, or what we're doing, but it's definitely Coleridge. So now, perhaps we should skip naming or quoting and just keep it general about inspiring poets.'

'Got it. Are you going to interview me after I've finished waxing lyrical?'

'Of course. It's the main reason we're here.'

Apparently happy with that, Robert repeated his intro as discussed and added a few extra lines about the spectacular clarity of the South Wales coastline on a close horizon, along with how very blue the sky was, and salty the air.

ROBERT: 'We're now properly into the start of the coast path. The sea is to our right and to our left is the children's play area where I first saw Janina sitting on a bench with her little girl. There's no one here today – as glorious as the weather is, apparently no one is venturing out in the cold. Back then, it was spring so the trees would have been in blossom and there would certainly have been a lot of children's noise coming from the swings and roundabouts. I think this was the bench – there's a pink bobble hat on it today, presumably dropped by a little girl while here playing recently, and if ever there was a sign this has to be one, although of what, I can't be sure.'

CRISTY: 'To keep going?'

ROBERT: 'You mean, like we're on a treasure hunt? OK, sounds good.'

CRISTY: 'Shall we sit down for a moment?'

ROBERT: 'Yes, we probably need a rest by now.'

As they'd come all of fifty yards she had to laugh. Then joining him on the bench, she said, 'Does being here bring back any other memories of Janina for you?' She signalled for him to speak his answer into the mic.

He sat quietly for a moment and Cristy watched him as his

mind travelled back in time, searching for memories that might have been lost but were still there somewhere waiting to be found.

ROBERT: 'It's kind of sad to think of her now, wondering who she really was . . . What happened to make her leave as abruptly as she did? More crucially, why didn't she take her daughter with her?'

CRISTY: 'Did she ever say anything to make you think that she might be planning to leave the child, even for a short time?'

ROBERT: 'No, nothing – at least not that I remember. In fact, I still find it hard to believe that she did.'

CRISTY: 'I don't have it with me, but the note the sisters found in Sadie's pocket said, "Please take care of her until I can come back for her." Do you have any thoughts on that?'

ROBERT: 'I guess the first question for me is, why did she need to leave her? What kind of situation was she in that meant she couldn't take her child wherever she was going? And *did* she ever come back? I guess we have to assume she didn't given that Sadie is still with her aunts all these years later – or one of them at least.'

CRISTY: 'Another big question for me is *why* did Janina put her child into the protection of strangers? It seems so . . . drastic.'

ROBERT: 'Except we can safely say that she chose the protectors carefully – two wealthy women with reputations for doing well by children, and who might not be quite as inclined as some to contact the authorities. It was a big risk, but presumably she took it because she didn't want the child carried off by the state. If that happened she might never have got her back.'

CRISTY: 'But she didn't anyway, which means she either decided to leave her where she was to have a better life than she could provide. Or maybe she did go back and the sisters paid her a huge sum to go away again. Or something else altogether happened.'

ROBERT: 'Keeping in mind that she was probably from somewhere in Eastern Europe, there has to be the possibility of her being deported, or worse. Trafficking was pretty big back then – still is, of course – and once in the hands of those guys, there's no knowing what might happen to a girl, especially one as beautiful as she was.'

CRISTY: 'I'm finding it quite disturbing to think she could have been caught up in something so . . . evil and dehumanizing. But she seems to have moved around quite freely, if we go by the times you saw her.'

ROBERT: 'Indeed, so maybe there wasn't any kind of gang control going on.'

CRISTY: 'What about her brother? If he left the area at the same time she did, and he seems to have, what would that have been about?'

ROBERT: 'You've circled me back to trafficking with that . . . Maybe they were both trying to escape some sort of servitude or tyranny and felt it was too dangerous to take a child with them.'

CRISTY: 'So leaving her with the sisters would seem like a safe option? I guess I can see that, if we're on the right lines, and there's nothing to say we are. We need to be in touch with Butlin's to find out what they can tell us about someone called Lukas circa 2000.'

She was looking back along the coastline to where the holiday camp's flashy conical domes were gleaming brightly in the sunshine.

ROBERT: 'I shouldn't think you'd find it open today.'

CRISTY: 'Even if it was, we wouldn't be knocking on the door for information. We'll have to start by going through official channels, at which point we'll almost certainly run up against data protection, but that's for later . . . For now, shall we walk on?'

ROBERT: 'I hope you're ready for a climb, because just along the trail we're going to run into a pretty steep one.'

Half an hour later, still breathless from the seemingly endless scramble up an insane incline to a – thank God – much friendlier trail with magnificent sea views, Cristy was trying not to be annoyed by how effortless Robert had made it all seem. Still, at least he hadn't laughed at the way she'd lunged about like an idiot trying to gain purchase on tree roots and impacted rocks, or commented on the frequency she'd had to stop to calm down her heartbeat. He'd simply waited patiently, ready with a hand to haul her up over the cruellest terrain, while not slipping once or managing to stick his ass out like a baboon, or get his scarf snagged by a rogue bramble that had almost throttled her. He was, she reminded herself, a seasoned hiker, at least according to his mother, and this adequately proved it.

'Most people can't do that in one go,' he told her, as they strolled on through a leafy glade towards, she presumed, the sisters' hillside holiday place, 'but you managed it.'

'If you discount the several times my ambition and dignity were stuffed by the need to take in oxygen. You made it seem like a walk in the park, so I can only conclude that you've done Everest, Kilimanjaro and Mont Blanc, probably all in the same week.'

He gave a laugh. 'I admit to Kilimanjaro, and the foothills of Everest, but many of the places I've hiked aren't generally that well known. It's something I do, if I get time, when I'm working in Africa, or Asia. It helps to calm the mind and bring a more spiritual perspective to an otherwise terrible world.'

'You're talking about the work you do with *Médecins Sans Frontières*?' she asked.

He stopped to gaze out across the grand expanse of the Severn Estuary. 'It can be harrowing, sometimes to the point of driving you mad . . . You see so many things that should never be possible, that one human being should never inflict on another. And you hear so many promises from the so-called civilized world that sound good for their electorates, for those with a social conscience, but that all too often end up meaning very little to those who are suffering.' He turned to look at her and smiled. 'It makes you appreciate the simplicity and beauty of moments like this.'

'How often do you go to war zones?' she asked.

'They're not all war zones, some are just parts of the world in desperate need of medical care that they can't get any other way. And not as often now as I used to, is the answer. I'm afraid I'm not one of the superheroes of the organization who've made MSF their full-time career. I just go to help out where I can for as long as I can, but I can tell you it plays hell with your mental well-being.'

Easily able to imagine that, she said, 'The rest of the time you're a heart surgeon in Melbourne?'

'Correct. And you're an investigator who's trying to find answers for a young woman in need of knowing who she really is, so let's go and have a look at the house she was taken into at the age of two. It's quite close now.'

Quite close turned out to be another half-mile at least along the track, but it was mostly easy going through random scatterings of winter-bare elder and beech trees, and leafy green tangles of alkanet, brambles and ivy each side of the path. Silently naming the grasses was a habit she'd acquired from her mother who'd loved wild plants and flowers. David's mother was the same, it was one of the first things she and Cynthia had talked about when they'd met, right here on Exmoor, albeit several miles from this particular spot. Naturally, thoughts of Cynthia turned to wondering about David, and how he might be feeling following their break-up. Was he actually feeling anything? She had no idea, only knew that she wished she hadn't thought of him. However, being here today, with Robert, someone so different and fortunately attached, was certainly distracting, and actually quite uplifting.

Coming to a stop beside him as he paused at the top of a vast green field flowing gently down to the water's edge, Cristy looked to where he was pointing and felt a jolt of surprise. Some fifty yards below was an old wooden stile only partly visible through a cluster of trees.

'Is that the stile mentioned in Lottie's story?' she asked. 'The one Mia saw someone running away from?'

He seemed confused. 'I didn't know about that,' he replied, 'I was just pointing out the footpath that you can see in the grass that runs from the stile to the beach. It's almost certainly the one that was used to get Sadie there.'

Following the barely visible tilting of the long grass to where the invisible trail disappeared behind a tangle of hawthorn to end on the gravelly shoreline, so bleak and uninviting in spite of the sunny day, Cristy tried to imagine leaving one of her children there, at any age, and shuddered at the horror of it. How desperate Janina must have been to do such a thing to her two-year-old daughter, presuming she was the one who'd left her, and it was hard now to imagine that she wasn't.

'She presumably retreated to the stile to watch until the sisters came to the child's rescue,' she said. 'Lottie wrote about Mia seeing someone . . . How could Janina be sure the little girl would be found?'

'I don't suppose she could,' he replied, 'but if she was watching she'd have known if the child was in any danger.'

'How on earth did she get her down there without being seen?'

'Well, the house isn't visible from here, and there's nowhere else around, so actually there was no one to see her.'

'So she somehow managed to get her child to stay there alone and wait . . . It's beyond heartbreaking to think of how confused and frightened she must have been. Both of them, actually, mother and daughter.'

'Maybe it's a measure of how afraid Janina was.'

Nodding agreement, she said, 'We need to record what we've just said.'

Minutes later, with their surmising captured, she kept rolling as they walked on towards a curve in the path. It was strange how moved she was now feeling about being here, as if time was warping in some undefinable way to make her footsteps connect with those of long ago. Janina would have walked this path, would have known what was ahead, if not in her life, then at the end of this trail . . . If she'd been in her mid-twenties back then, by now she'd be the same age as Cristy, and thinking of the older Janina made Cristy feel somehow closer to her.

Robert stopped alongside some steps carved into the hillside, pointing ahead and speaking quietly, almost as if not wanting to wake ghosts.

ROBERT: 'There it is. It's been much improved since the sisters were here, but this is the place they rented for the summer of 2000.'

Remembering that she needed to describe it for listeners, Cristy lifted her collar mic closer to her mouth.

CRISTY: 'It's a long, low stone-built house with a steep red-tiled roof, a porched front door looking along the track towards us, and there's a large wooden terrace facing the sea. Someone seems to be at home – there's smoke rising from one of the chimneys – and I can just make out a car through the greenery at the back. Is there a road? I guess there has to be.'

ROBERT: 'It's a narrow lane that runs kind of parallel with the path we're on, and eventually takes you down to the Old Quay.'

CRISTY: 'Which is where we parked? So we could have driven here?'

Robert arched an eyebrow.

Rolling her eyes Cristy went back to her study of the house, trying to imagine the sisters coming and going, Lottie descending the field on her way to rescue Sadie, bringing the child back up again and handing her to Mia . . .

CRISTY: 'I wonder if it's worth asking someone inside if they remember the Winters sisters?'

ROBERT: 'It'll be a long shot if it's still a holiday let.'

CRISTY: 'But who comes here on holiday at this time of year?'

ROBERT: 'Maybe the people inside . . . One of whom is coming to find out why we're not climbing higher up on the path to continue our walk.'

With the recorder still running, Cristy walked forward to meet the portly man whose bushy moustache and ruddy face marked him out as a drinker, and probably a hunter.

'Can I help you with something?' he called out before reaching her.

CRISTY: 'I was just remarking what a lovely spot this is. Do you mind me asking if you live here?'

PORTLY MAN: 'We just rent it during the season.'

Ah, a hunter!

CRISTY: 'Not stags, I hope, or foxes.'

PORTLY MAN: 'You one of the saboteur lot, are you? If so, we don't want any trouble. There's no law-breaking going on around here, and we don't welcome trespassers.'

CRISTY: 'Understood, but would you mind telling me how long you've been coming here? I'm doing some research into someone who rented the place back at the beginning of the Noughties.'

PORTLY MAN: 'You'll need to speak to the landowner's agent about that. His name's Frank Fox, has an office in Taunton and another in Bath. You'll find him online.'

CRISTY: 'Thank you. You've been very helpful.'

The man grunted as he turned to go, raising a hand in a dismissive farewell.

ROBERT: 'You handled him well.'

CRISTY: 'I got the information I wanted.'

ROBERT: 'Which I could have told you, if you'd asked.'

Laughing as she elbowed him, she watched the hunter disappear inside the house and spoke into her mic.

CRISTY: 'It's quite possible Janina hid very close to the spot where I'm standing right now to watch the sisters, maybe even her own daughter playing outside the house. It's also possible that she went right up to the front door, early one morning, to deliver the envelope that so unnerved the sisters.'

She took a long, last look around, trying for another sense of Janina's presence. It was fanciful, of course, and she really didn't expect to spot some sort of ghost flitting through the trees, or to hear a whisper drifting down from the moor. However, she did get the feeling they were in the right place, that it really had all started here.

'Next stop Frank Fox,' she said, turning off the recorder. 'Do you know him?'

'No, I've just heard that he still rides to hounds and to hell with the law. So you should get along well with him.'

*

An hour later Cristy and Connor were driving back up the M5 towards Bristol, having left Robert to return his mother to her residential village, before making his own two-hour journey north. Frank Fox, who indeed managed Hilltop Lodge – his assistant had soon worked out which property Cristy was calling about – would be getting back to them sometime tomorrow when he returned from an extended Christmas break.

'I was honestly beginning to think Cristy had abandoned me,' Connor was telling Jodi on the phone, as if Cristy wasn't there. 'She was gone way longer than I expected, and now I'm so deeply in love with Gita Brinkley I think we might have to adopt her.'

As Cristy laughed, Jodi said, 'Tell me more about Robert. Is he as drop-dead in person as he is online?'

'You've looked him up too?' Cristy cried. 'Honestly, you're as bad as Meena.'

'No one's that bad,' Connor retorted. 'And let's put it this way, babe, he's so good-looking he even makes me swoon.'

'He's married,' Cristy put in quickly, 'and I am so NOT looking for a man . . . Jesus, how can you even think it when you know what's going on in my life?'

'It could be just what you need.'

'Maybe if he weren't married, but he is, and he also lives on the other side of the world. So can we get ourselves a reality check here and talk about serious things such as the real reason you're calling?'

'This is it,' Jodi responded chirpily. 'To find out how your day went. Oh, and to get an idea of what time you might be back? Would you like to join us for supper and maybe give Aurora a bath?'

Cristy turned to Connor. 'I think she means it,' she said quietly.

'She does,' he confirmed. 'It's a great honour.'

'Then I can't possibly turn it down.'

'Yay!' Jodi cried. 'I'll text Aiden, find out what he's doing in case he'd like to come. Should I try Matthew?'

'Maybe not,' Cristy responded.

'I get it. You don't want him thinking we're encouraging his bid to win you back. Gosh, all these men, Cristy. What is to become of you? Have you heard from David, by any chance?'

'Not since we *broke up*, and I don't expect to. Now, I've got a call coming in on my phone that I need to take.'

'Is it Robert?'

'Actually, it's Sadie, so bye, Jodi,' and leaving Connor to end the call with his wife she clicked on before Sadie could ring off. 'Hi, how are you?' she asked.

There was a moment before Sadie appeared fully in focus on the screen. *Eva Marie Saint*, Cristy immediately thought, and, yes, she could see it.

'I'm daring to hope you found out something helpful today,' Sadie said, raising a hand to show crossed fingers.

'Well, here's one thing I think you'll like,' Cristy smiled. 'Your mother's name is Janina.'

Sadie's eyes glistened as she pressed a hand to her mouth. 'Janina,' she whispered. 'It's so pretty.'

'Isn't it?' Cristy agreed.

'Do you know anything else about her?'

'Some, but it's probably best that you listen to the interviews, then you'll hear it for yourself. It won't be long before we're back at the office, I can sort it out then.'

Still close to tears, Sadie said, 'I know it might sound silly, but just knowing her name . . . I can't describe how it feels . . .' Then, 'I expect you'd like me to try, for a recording?'

'When you're ready.'

Sobbing a laugh, Sadie said, 'Thank you. This means so much.'

'There's still a way to go,' Cristy reminded her gently, 'but we'll get there, I'm sure of it.'

Sadie nodded, showing how keen she was to believe that.

'Tell me about Mia,' Cristy said. 'Is she ready to commit to an interview yet?'

'She's still saying she is, she just won't give me a time, but I'll keep on it. Anyway, the other reason I'm ringing is that I've found more of Lottie's story, and it's . . . pretty explosive.'

# CHAPTER TWELVE

Lottie truly didn't believe Mia had the courage to do it.

Mia wasn't so sure either.

However, when it came right down to it, all things considered and all responsibilities weighed, they'd lost their hearts to Sadie so the next steps had to be taken. The child had brought them more joy than they could ever have imagined a few short weeks ago, had opened up all kinds of possibilities that Lottie had hardly even dared consider before, and had given Mia in particular a sense of purpose that she hadn't even realized had been missing until now. They'd also been trusted with her safekeeping until her mother could return. Presuming it was her mother who'd left her. If not, it was surely someone who cared for her considering what had been in the envelope that had arrived a few days ago.

At first it had shocked and even scared them. They simply hadn't been able to work out what it meant. Why would someone hand-deliver a set of photographs featuring a young man and a young woman with a little girl who was clearly Sadie?

'It must be her parents,' Mia had whispered as they'd stared down at the clear, colourful images that must have been taken fairly recently given Sadie's age.

The first was of Sadie and the young woman lying on some grass, holding hands and gazing up at the sky. Then there was Sadie and the young woman making funny faces at the camera. One of Sadie asleep in a man's arms. Another of her hoisted onto the young man's shoulders looking on top of the world. His face was shadowed by a hat, but it was clear he was laughing and so was she.

'She looks happy,' Lottie murmured, worried and jealous and glad to think their sweet little girl hadn't been badly treated before coming here. At least not during these moments anyway.

'I don't understand what's happening,' Mia said wretchedly. 'What are we supposed to do with them?'

Lottie had no idea. There was no note to explain them, nothing to tell them anything at all. Their names weren't even on the front of the envelope, although they could hardly have been for anyone else given they'd come through their door.

Should they show them to Sadie? How upsetting was it going to be for her to see her parents – presuming it was her parents – after being apart from them for over three weeks? She'd want to see them, naturally. And what were they going to say then? They had no idea who these people were, much less where they could be found. And Sadie was settling in so well; she seemed to be flourishing at the centre of their world. All these photographs would do was confuse and distress her.

'What if they're some sort of message?' Lottie said quietly.

Mia's eyes showed confusion as she turned to her sister. 'What do you mean?' she asked.

Lottie didn't know exactly, not yet, anyway.

Steeling herself for an answer she didn't want, Mia said, 'Do you think we should go to the authorities?'

'You mean, for her to be taken into care?' Lottie snapped. 'Because that's what will happen if we do, and I say she's happier and safer with us.'

Mia nodded, then nodded again. 'The note she came with asked us to take care of her, so that's what we're doing,' she said, as if repeating it gave even more weight to the note and thereby justified their actions. Then bracing herself again, 'Does she need protection because she's in some sort of danger? And if she is, does that mean we are now, too?'

Lottie went to sit on a bottom stair, photos still in hand. 'I think,' she said carefully, 'that this could be the beginning of a very clever blackmail attempt. In fact, I'm sure it is, and we have played straight into their hands by keeping the child and telling no one. So, before anyone starts making demands, I say we protect ourselves and Sadie from all nefarious intentions by making plans to leave.'

'To go where?'

'We'll work it out. For now, we need to hide these photographs, along with the note we found in her pocket, and you have to prepare yourself to deal with Edwin. He'll be here in a couple of hours, if he bothers to turn up. Let's hope he doesn't and you can just instruct our solicitor to send him a letter citing his adultery as grounds for divorce.'

Mia looked as though she'd been struck. This was moving too fast, she was struggling to follow Lottie's thinking, only knew she'd just been thrown into a whole other sort of chaos.

'Pull yourself together,' Lottie hissed impatiently. 'You're getting precisely nothing out of your marriage, apart from a whole lot of humiliation and grief.'

'That's easy for you to say . . .'

'For God's sake, the man's not even smart enough to treat you well so you'll carry on letting him live the life that should never have been his in the first place. You need to get him out of our London house . . .'

'Are you planning to take Sadie there?'

'I'm not sure yet, but it can't be an option with him in it, so he needs to go.'

'But where?'

'What the hell do I care, and you shouldn't either. Sadie has to be our priority. If he sees her he'll start asking awkward questions and the next thing we know he'll have blabbed about her all over the place and she'll end up being taken from us, whether we like it or not. What will we tell her parents then, if they come back? More than that, what do you think will happen to us? We'll be seen as child abductors . . .'

'All right, all right,' Mia cried, hands clasped to her cheeks. 'I hear what you're saying and I know you're right. Sadie has to come first – but someone could be on their way to get her right now . . .'

'Then what are the photographs about? I tell you, no one's coming for her until they've managed to squeeze us dry, and do we really want to give her up to someone who'd use her like that?'

'No, of course not. I just . . . Edwin is . . .'

'Let him go!' Lottie growled. 'Do it today, for your own sake as much as Sadie's.'

Mia was nodding in spite of the ache in her heart. He really hadn't ever loved her, and in truth she'd never been sure about her feelings for him. She'd just wanted to be the married sister, the one who had that sort of respectability and status, the one who'd been chosen, and he'd been so charming and funny and attentive to her rather than to Lottie . . . 'Let's hope he doesn't come today,' she said hoarsely. 'It'll be easier to do by letter. But if he does come, what are we going to tell him about Sadie?'

'We'll get Gita to take her onto the moor to see the ponies. She keeps saying she'd like to do that . . .'

'And if someone recognizes her?'

Lottie threw out her hands in despair. 'I don't know, Mia! I don't have all the answers. I wish I did. I just have a very strong feeling that we need to leave here sooner, rather than later, and we can't go back to London if Edwin's still in the house.'

'I don't see how we can go back anyway. Everyone knows we don't have a niece . . .'

'We can say she's the daughter of a cousin and calling her a niece is simpler. For heaven's sake, use your imagination, or at least try to be helpful. You want to keep her, don't you?'

Mia stared at her, wide-eyed. They both knew it was what Mia wanted, she just didn't have the courage to say it out loud.

It was what Lottie wanted too, maybe for different reasons, but God knew she'd come to love that girl every bit as much as Mia did.

'OK,' Lottie said, 'let's focus on how we can go forward in a way that will make sure Sadie is safe and that doesn't end up costing us half – even all – our fortune.'

There were no more arguments. Lottie knew Mia couldn't fight back when her heart wasn't even trying to hold onto Edwin, was only recognizing the need to protect Sadie and if they could keep her, make her theirs . . . Lottie had a way of making things happen, and Mia had learned over the years that it was usually better to go along with her sister rather than to try to stand up against her. And, when it came to something as important as this, why would she even want to?

*

Edwin arrived earlier than expected. Gita hadn't turned up yet and Sadie was in the kitchen when the odious little man drove up to the house, tooting his car horn like Mr Toad and clearly expecting his adoring wife to rush out and greet him.

Lottie could see that part of Mia wanted to, but she blocked the way. 'Get rid of him,' she said through her teeth.

'But where do I tell him to go?'

'To hell would be a start.'

Mia glared at her.

'Get him to take you for a drive so you can talk.'

'He's just come from London . . .'

'For God's sake, stop finding excuses. Come up with solutions. We can't let him see Sadie when we haven't worked out . . .'

Mia swung round as Edwin pushed open the door and waltzed into the hall as if he came every day and was welcome. 'Hey! Hey! Hey!' he sang out as he spotted them. 'And here I find my two favourite ladies all in rush to see me. How blessed I am.'

'Jesus, Edwin,' Lottie snorted, 'try reading the room for once.'

His laugh was more of a bray, at least to Lottie's ears. 'Mia, my angel, I've missed you terribly and you've hardly been returning my calls. It's why I had to come. Slumming it for the summer was already a step too far for me, but now I'm worried you're keeping a secret love from me. Please say it's not true.'

'Excuse me while I go and throw up,' Lottie sneered, and turning away she almost collided with Sadie coming out of the kitchen.

'Well, well, well,' Edwin drawled in amazement, 'and who do we have here?'

Mia and Lottie exchanged frantic glances.

'You're a pretty little thing, aren't you?' he said to Sadie. 'Where did you come from, eh?'

Sadie regarded him with wide, wary eyes, thumb in mouth, teddy under arm.

'Will you tell me your name?' he asked gently.

She hung back, pressing herself into Lottie's legs.

Scooping her up, Lottie said to Mia, 'You know what you have to do,' and folding Sadie in tightly she carried her into the sitting room.

As the door closed behind them, Mia turned to Edwin, nervous, appalled, and trying to summon the determination to prove to herself, and to Lottie, that she could do this.

'So who is she?' Edwin wanted to know, closing the front door and leaning his back against it. His tone, his whole attitude, exuded more derision and scepticism than she could stand.

Blurting the first words that came into her head, Mia said, 'We're taking care of her, for some friends. She's very young and you bursting in here like this . . . You've scared her and I . . . I think you should leave before you do any more damage.'

His eyebrows rose in disdainful surprise. 'Which friends?' he challenged. 'You don't know anyone with a child that age . . .'

'You've got no idea who we do and don't know. Just as I have no idea which of your girlfriends you've currently got living in my house. Well, it has to stop, Edwin. You need to find a place of your own and I have decided I want . . . I want to be free of you.'

He treated her to such an incredulous up and down sweep of his eyes that she almost withered. 'Have you now?' he responded smoothly.

'Please go,' she said through her teeth. 'You'll hear from my solicitor . . .'

'I'm not going anywhere until I've got to the bottom of what you girls are up to here. And there's something, I can tell that just by looking at you.'

'You don't know anything. You're just . . .'

'Who's the child, Mia? Where did you get her?'

Shocked, Mia cried, 'We didn't get her anywhere. She was brought to us, by her parents, who've asked us to take care of her while they travel . . . overseas.'

Clearly not believing a word, he said, 'What are their names? These parents.'

'It's none of your business,' Lottie snapped, coming back into the hall and closing the sitting room door against the noise of the TV. 'Now, do as Mia says and leave. You are not welcome here, and we've already had as much as we're prepared to take of you . . .'

'And I've already told you – or her – that I'm not leaving until I find out who that child is.'

Lottie's lip curled. As if Edwin even cared, he was only ever all about himself. 'I don't know what vile thoughts you've got going on in that loathsome head of yours . . .' she said.

'She's not safe!' Mia suddenly broke in. 'So we're keeping her here until the coast is clear.'

He blinked in astonishment.

'And for the time being,' she pressed on, 'we're telling people she's our niece . . .'

'Enough,' Lottie barked, cutting her off.

'But everyone knows you don't have a brother or sister,' he cried incredulously.

'It's what we're saying for ease,' Mia explained, 'and no one knows what cousins we have, distant or otherwise. Anyway, getting into the detail of reality would be complicated and lengthy and is entirely unnecessary.'

Impressed by her sister's surge of mettle, if not by her failure to rein herself in, Lottie stared at Edwin, waiting for whatever little nugget he now had stored up behind those foul lips of his to issue forth.

'You're insane, the pair of you,' he declared, looking from one to other. 'I don't know what's really going on here, but I do know you think rules don't apply to you. You tell yourselves that just because you're loaded you can do whatever you like and to hell with the rest of the world, along with anyone who might get in your way. Well, I'm not someone who's going to be pushed around by you the way so many others have. I want answers, first of all to why you, Mia, have suddenly decided we shouldn't be married any more, apart from her taking the decision for you . . .'

'It has nothing to do with Lottie,' Mia cried hotly. 'It's about your cheating and lying, the way you humiliate me and behave as though I'm not good enough for someone like you . . .'

'She's worth so much more than you,' Lottie cut in, fiercely, 'and finally she's seeing it. So, once again, feel free to leave. There are some cafés in town if you require refreshment before your drive back . . .'

'What have you done with the child?' he asked darkly. 'Where is she now?'

Mia swept forward, shoved him aside and tore open the front door.

He stared at her, as if not quite recognizing her.

Suddenly realizing they couldn't let him go like this, that they had to seize full control of the situation first, Lottie said, 'The offer you receive as a divorce settlement will enable you to greatly expand the meagre wine-import business you came into the marriage with. It will also allow you to purchase a central London property the like of which you'd never be able to afford otherwise. In short, you'll be a wealthy man with the kind of freedom and standing you are currently enjoying, just without Mia as your wife.'

He regarded her curiously, almost as though she was speaking another language, although the flinty look in his eyes made it clear that he understood well enough what was happening.

'You will never speak of the child to anyone,' Lottie told him, laying out the conditions he must have known were coming. 'As far as you're concerned she doesn't exist.'

He cocked an eyebrow, suggesting he needed to hear more.

'I think you know me well enough,' she said, 'to understand that it wouldn't be wise to cross me.'

He smirked, apparently enjoying himself now.

'We will tell the world about the child when we're ready, and not before,' she pressed on. 'As yet we can't say when it will be, but what is certain is that you will not want to jeopardize her safety, or your extremely valuable severance package, by doing or saying anything, to anyone, concerning matters you know nothing about.'

He wrinkled his nose. 'Severance package?' His tone was mocking.

'Everything you have, Edwin, everything you are, is in our control. Never forget that. We could, if necessary, discredit you to a point where you'd make yourself disappear without a trace to save us the trouble. What we're doing now is offering you the chance to safeguard yourself and your future in exchange for very little on your part. Accept our generosity, forget you've seen the child, and never try to contact either of us again, unless through a lawyer.'

Mia said, 'And be out of the London house by the end of the week.'

As Edwin's eyes moved back and forth between them, Lottie could tell he was trying to calculate what more he might get out of this before yielding.

'The door is right there,' she told him. 'Go through, get into your car and drive away. If you don't, I will call the police to ask someone to come and remove an intruder.'

His expression turned from surprise to scorn, a mask to cover the humiliation of his defeat. He'd be treading into seriously treacherous waters if he tried to take them on, and he knew it. However, leaving without a last word . . . He clearly couldn't bring himself to sink that low.

'Make sure that offer's with me by the end of the week,' he growled. 'Any later and I'm the one who'll be calling the police.'

As Edwin left Lottie and Mia stayed where they were, listening to him getting into his car and starting the engine. They flinched at the sound of him driving into something before he reversed out of the gate and sped away.

'Are you OK?' Lottie asked, as silence descended.

Mia nodded. 'I think so. Clever of you to threaten him with the police.'

'He might have seen through it, but at least he's gone.'

'Where's Sadie?'

'In front of the TV. Gita's in the kitchen.'

Mia turned round. 'Did she hear anything?'

'I think she's just arrived, but I can't be certain.'

'She'll wonder who he is.'

'We can tell her. She doesn't need the details of why he took off in a fury, but there's no harm in saying he's your husband. Oh my goodness,' she murmured, spotting the sitting room door handle juddering up and down and realizing Sadie was trying to get out. 'It's OK, sweetheart,' she called. 'We're right here, the nasty man has gone now.'

As Sadie stumbled into the hall, eyes full of frightened tears, she spotted Gita coming out of the kitchen and ran to her.

Mia and Lottie looked on, both wishing she'd chosen one of them to go to, but never mind. What mattered was that Edwin had gone, Sadie was being comforted and they had just dug themselves even deeper into a situation they had no understanding of at all.

'We have to talk,' Lottie whispered, as Gita carried Sadie into the kitchen. She was chewing a nail, was about to draw blood. 'I've had an idea that I think will work.'

'What is it?' Mia asked. 'Does it involve Sadie?'

'Of course. Everything involves her now. Unless you want to sit around here waiting for her mother, or whoever the hell sent those photos, to get started on their despicable plans to bleed us dry.'

'OK, let me have a word with Gita first, make sure she didn't misunderstand anything – I mean, if she did overhear what was said.'

# CHAPTER THIRTEEN

Cristy was watching Sadie's face on the computer screen in front of her.

Everyone else in the office was quiet. They were allowing Sadie some time following the reading aloud of her aunt's latest chapter describing the scene with Edwin Prosser. Even though four days had passed since she'd found it, it was clearly still affecting her deeply. Cristy understood why; knowing her mother's and uncle's names had brought a whole new depth to her longing for more knowledge of them – and the scene she'd just created with Lottie's words, seemed to be proof that her aunts had stolen her.

What Cristy herself was starting to have even more doubts about, was the finding of Sadie on the beach. Could it really have happened the way Lottie described? Having visited the coast path it seemed both possible and yet not, which was why she hadn't so far taxed Sadie with her concerns.

'Are you OK?' she asked Sadie softly.

The girl's head came up as she took a breath. She was slightly dishevelled and flushed, but her eyes were dry and her voice steady as she said, 'Yes, I'm fine, it's just . . .' She stopped and started again. 'After listening to your interviews with the Brinkleys at the weekend, and putting them together with this . . .' She held up the pages she'd just read from.

When she didn't continue, Cristy said, 'Would you like us to stop recording?'

Sadie shook her head. 'No, it's OK. Just a blip. I've got myself together now.'

Cristy wasn't certain she had, but knew it would be easy to

stop at any point, and edit out anything Sadie wasn't comfortable with if necessary. So, noting the time-code, she began again.

CRISTY: 'It's clear that this extract, or chapter, has stirred up a lot of emotion for you. Do you mind telling us what about it is resonating so deeply?'

Sadie gave a small, mirthless laugh and tucked her hair behind her ears.

SADIE: 'I guess it's a few things . . . I mean, you can tell from what Lottie's written that she . . . that both my aunts were . . . Actually, it's Edwin's words that keep coming back to me. He accused them of living in a different world, playing by different rules . . . That's how they were, so now I'm asking myself, was keeping me some kind of a game to them?'

She stared down at the pages again as if they might somehow reveal more from between the lines if she only looked hard enough.

SADIE: 'Lottie implies that they had different reasons for wanting to hold onto me, but there's no detail of what the reasons might have been.'

CRISTY: 'She writes about you with a lot of affection.'

SADIE: 'Yes, and I don't doubt that they really did care for me . . . They've proved it over and over ever since . . . I just wish . . . I wish they'd tried harder to find my parents, or at least to get to the truth of why I was with them.'

CRISTY: 'We don't know for certain yet that they didn't.'

SADIE: 'No, I guess not, but the way this latest chapter ends with Lottie having an idea . . . I think I know what it might have been. She told me once that their father had looked into moving the family to Guernsey. I guess it was for tax purposes, or maybe he knew the island and felt they could be happy here. They didn't go, or not that I know of, but I'm wondering if Lottie remembered the plan and that's what gave her the idea to bring us all here. You could say they hid me in plain sight, because they weren't known on the island, and everyone says it's the right place to be if you don't want to be asked too many questions.'

CRISTY: 'It certainly sounds plausible, especially given the timings, because didn't they buy the villa sometime in late 2000?'

SADIE: 'Mid-2001. They rented somewhere in town before the sale went through. Anyway, whatever their motives, or reasons, or secrets, I'm becoming more convinced by the day that these writings are Lottie's way of laying some sort of trail for me. She tucked random pages into all sorts of places, knowing that in the end I would most likely be the one to go through her papers. Except, why not just tell me what happened? Or at least keep it all together and put it into a safe somewhere for me to read after her death? It feels . . . cruel of her to do it this way, and she wasn't that.'

CRISTY: 'Have you asked Mia about it?'

SADIE: 'Actually I have. She ended up in tears, and told me I should just burn everything, for my own sake and hers, but most of all for Lottie's . . . I pointed out that Lottie wasn't around any more to care, and anyway she must have wanted me to know everything or she wouldn't have written it down.'

CRISTY: 'And Mia said?'

SADIE: 'That there's no guarantee it is all written down, and even if it is you can never believe everything Lottie tells you.'

CRISTY: 'Do you believe it? What you've read so far?'

SADIE: 'Yes, I think so. I mean, I don't have anything else to go on and at least some of it rings true.'

CRISTY: 'Have you talked to Mia yet about the photographs

you found? Or mentioned that you now know your mother's and uncle's names?'

SADIE: 'I've shown her the photographs, and she's adamant that they're of a lovely young couple who helped take care of me from time to time when I was small. I pointed out that I look exactly like the woman, but she just patted my hand and said that I can't make something true just by wanting it to be. I haven't got round to the names yet, but I will. Although, something I have told her that I know you'll be interested in . . . I showed her the results of the DNA test that prove I'm not related to her. And do you know what she said? "It's not kind of you to make these things up, Sadie, but whatever you do, you are very special to me, and you always will be."'

Cristy glanced up as Clover let out a sigh of frustration, and Jacks mimed a gun to his head. Understanding how they felt, and knowing how much worse it must be for Sadie, she pressed on.

CRISTY: 'What about the interviews with Gita and Robert Brinkley? Has she listened to them?'

SADIE: 'She said she will, but I don't think she has yet. If it's OK, I have a question for you now: have you managed to contact Butlin's to find out if there's any record of Lukas working there?'

CRISTY: 'Our researchers are on it, but it's likely to be a lengthy process, thanks to data protection. Obviously we'll let you know as soon as there's some news.'

SADIE: (voice cracking with emotion) 'Do you think they're still alive? Robert mentioned trafficking gangs, maybe that's why no one came back for me. Something happened to them . . .'

CRISTY: 'I promise we're delving into that too.'

There was a lengthy pause as Sadie took this in, imagining only she knew what, but obviously the mention of gangs had thrown a whole new sinister light onto the search, and into her roots.

SADIE: 'Does it sound crazy to say that since listening to Gita and Robert Brinkley I've felt . . . more lost than ever. Knowing that my mother wasn't English . . . Having no idea where she was actually from . . . It makes me feel like someone who's grown up living a life that shouldn't even have happened. And then I start wondering about the child that got left behind, the one whose life, whose world, just stopped one day on a beach. Who would she be today? Where does she belong?

'Nowhere, of course. She doesn't belong anywhere, because she isn't anyone any more. She's like a pile of dust that just got swept away in a wind; a ghost forever trapped in nothingness.'

Moved by Sadie's distress and understanding completely her sense of abandonment, Cristy allowed some moments to pass before continuing. However, it was Sadie who spoke first.

SADIE: 'It's hard to see how we're ever going to trace my mother when we don't even know where she was from. And what about my father? No one ever talks about him, but who was he? Did he play any part in my life at all?'

CRISTY: 'All very good questions that we're going to do our best to answer.'

As Sadie's head went down, Cristy decided she'd been through enough for now and glanced at Connor, a signal to end the recording. This was going to make a very strong episode with Sadie's emotion and what it meant to her to learn her mother's name being so prevalent.

'We've stopped,' she said softly. 'We can always pick up at another time. Is someone there with you?'

Anna's face appeared on the screen next to Sadie's. 'I am,' she said, giving a little wave.

Cristy smiled as her heart flipped. Although Anna wasn't like David in looks, she was his daughter and being reminded of him had taken her unawares. 'You're being a very good friend,' she told her.

'Do you think,' Sadie said, 'that Robert Brinkley would be willing to talk to me? I mean, I'm not expecting him to tell me any more than he's told you, but the fact that he knew my mother, if only for a short while . . . It feels, kind of like a link, something to hold onto, if you know what I mean.'

Understanding completely, Cristy said, 'I'm sure he'll be more than happy to meet you, in person, or on Zoom. I'll drop him an email as soon as we're done here.' She cast a quick glance around the room in case anyone had anything to add before she let Sadie go. It seemed no one did, so she told Sadie to call her any time, day or night, and promised to be in touch as soon as they had something to report from their end. 'And please send my love to the rest of the family,' she said to Anna.

'Will do. I know they'll want me to send theirs, so big kiss and come see us soon.'

As Connor ended the connection Cristy suddenly felt unaccountably drained and maybe not as on top of this series as she needed to be. Or perhaps she was just tired after struggling to sleep for the past few nights; even when she had slept her dreams were so tangled and strange, almost frightening at times, that she ended up feeling more exhausted than refreshed when she woke in the mornings. She blamed Matthew – mainly because she blamed him for everything – but there was no denying that she was becoming increasingly unsettled by the scenario of two rich women 'finding' a child on a beach. It was a peculiar and incredible story that seemed to be immersing itself deeper and deeper into the kind of sinister portent that the early hours of the morning made a whole lot worse. She kept asking herself, if they'd known at the beginning what they knew now, would they still have got into it?

The answer was yes, of course they would, especially when there was still nothing to say that they were entering into the kind of territory it was best not to tread.

'Question!' Iz piped up from her small desk in the corner.

Cristy looked in her direction while the others studiously failed to respond. 'Shoot,' Cristy invited.

'Why do we actually *care* about Sadie?' Iz asked boldly.

As everyone stiffened and Connor actually groaned, Cristy tried to gather her thoughts.

'I'm not saying I don't,' Iz hastily jumped in, apparently sensing she'd hit a wrong note, 'I'm just passing on something that came up at a meeting this morning.'

'What meeting?' Connor asked darkly.

'With my colleagues at SLD and the reps for your sponsors. One of them, from Open Destiny, pointed out that Sadie has had an extremely privileged life. So why does she even want to know about a mother who abandoned her when she still has an aunt who . . .' Her words dried up as her eyes grew wary. 'And so why would we care?' she finished feebly.

'They're not unreasonable questions,' Cristy put in, before anyone could cut Iz down to an even smaller size than she clearly already felt. 'And if someone from Open Destiny is asking it then we have to accept that a lot of listeners will too. Wealthy girl bleating about identity, getting a podcast made about her, involving the world in her search . . . Who *is* going to care?'

'Anyone,' Clover put in hotly, 'with an ounce of empathy in their soul will want to know why a small child was given up in the way Sadie was. Not to mention what happened to the mother, uncle *and* father, after the aunts made off with her. It's not about who Sadie is now, or what she has, it's about her sense of identity and self, her confusion over nationality and even her culture . . . Most people will understand that even if they're not facing the issues themselves. As an adoptee I've been through a lot of it. I was out there, not knowing who I was once. So, does that answer your question, Iz?'

Iz was already nodding. 'I said more or less the same thing,' she insisted, 'I just thought I ought to flag it up in case . . . Well, I suppose in case any of you thought our Open Destiny guy might have a point.'

'What I want to know,' Connor said, 'is why you were even discussing it with them when the first episode doesn't go live until six this evening. Are you giving them previews, or something?

A chance to have a say? Because it was our understanding that they'd have no editorial control.'

'Oh, it's not control,' Iz quickly assured him. 'It's simply protocol, a courtesy to loop them in ahead of transmission. Do you call it that for a podcast?'

'Did they have any other comments, or useful insights we should know about?' Cristy asked, cutting Connor off.

'No, that was it, really. I mean, in a negative sense, if we can call it negative, which I don't think it was, really. More . . . constructive. Otherwise, they were all intrigued to know more – remember episode one finishes with the mysterious envelope arriving, and I promise I haven't given anything away.'

Clearly still far from happy, Connor said, 'You can only keep your desk here if we can trust you, Iz. I get that you're not actually on our side, you're working for them, but we're going to end up in a serious falling-out if you don't keep us informed about your meetings.'

'And from now on I will,' she promised, looking more like an overanxious child than a highly successful PR exec with each word she uttered. Maybe this was her superpower, Cristy reflected: always appear vulnerable and make the other person feel they're in the right even if they weren't. It could be a winning technique.

'OK, I think we've gone far enough with that,' she said, stepping in. 'Everyone will start arriving soon to celebrate the first drop, so let's do a quick talk through the recent chapter. Has it thrown anything up for anyone, I mean apart from the obvious?'

After hitting a few keys to change his screen, Jacks said, 'Edwin Prosser. I've managed to get an email address for him now. No idea if it's still current, but I haven't had a bounce back yet, and it's Hotmail UK, so he could still be in the country.' He glanced up, saw he still had his audience and moved on. 'As you know, I've made contact with Butlin's head office about Lukas and a very helpful-sounding person in HR said she'd get back to me, hopefully sometime this week. It could be no more than a polite brush-off, but she didn't mention data protection, at least not yet, so if I don't hear anything I'll definitely try again.'

With a nod of approval, Cristy said, 'Clove, where are you at with your enquiries?'

'OK, so I recorded a video chat with Frank Fox yesterday, the bloke who works for the landowner whose ownership of half of Somerset includes the hilltop house rented by the sisters. Mr Fox is not your archetypal land agent, as you'll see when you watch: all mullet and machismo with a healthy love of himself, kind of sets the picture. Unsurprisingly, he was still a schoolboy in 2000, but before our hook-up he'd very obligingly checked with his predecessor who apparently remembers the sisters, but only because they came for such a short time before taking off again at short notice with the whole summer paid for. He knew nothing about a child, or where the sisters went after they left the house, and a delve into the files didn't turn up anything useful. So, not much more to be achieved there.

'On a more positive note, I'm on the verge of making contact with a retired Avon and Somerset detective who was with the force working out of Taunton back in the late Nineties, early 2000s. I'm told she was involved in undercover ops in west Somerset, gang related, so yes, it was happening at the time Janina and Lukas were around. I've also dug out a few local press articles that are relevant. Currently, I'm ploughing my way through an organized crime report from the Council of Europe dated 2001. It's possible there was some sort of covert activity going on in the area that not even the locals knew anything about.'

'Great,' Cristy responded approvingly. 'Everything's worth exploring even if we end up down a blind alley. You never know which one will break us into a new light. Now, I'd better send an email to Robert Brinkley about Sadie, while the rest of you get ready for the drinks. Who's coming, by the way?'

'All the usual suspects,' Connor answered, 'Meena, Harry, Jodi – this will be Aurora's first grown-up drinks gig.'

As everyone oooh-ed their appreciation Cristy noticed Iz's hesitant smile and said, 'Iz, I take it you're staying to mark the occasion of the first episode dropping with us?'

Starting with surprise, Iz said, eagerly, 'If I'm invited. I'd love to be here. Who's Aurora, if you don't mind me asking?'

'Connor's six-week-old daughter,' Cristy replied.

Iz practically melted. 'I love babies,' she swooned. To Connor she said, 'If I'm nice to her, which obviously I will be, do you think you might like me a bit better?'

Cristy had to laugh as Connor, clearly thrown, failed to find words to respond.

'He will,' Cristy promised, realizing she was warming to Iz in spite of her being a royal pain in the arse, 'and we'll all really love you if you can pop out to get the champagne.'

Iz shot to her feet. 'On it,' she declared. 'Just tell me where to go.'

'So tempting,' Jacks muttered under his breath.

Stifling a laugh, Cristy said, 'Clove will come along to help you carry it.'

'I will?' Clove cried.

'She can't carry a dozen bottles on her own,' Cristy pointed out.

'A dozen!' Iz exclaimed, as everyone blinked.

'It'll save us going out again next week,' Cristy explained. 'Actually, let's put in an order for six bottles to be delivered every Tuesday.'

'You have a party every week?' Iz cried in amazement. They all turned to her and she quickly added, 'Wow! I've clearly come to the right place.' Then, 'And obvs all drinks will be on me!'

*

It was after nine by the time Cristy arrived home that night, slightly tipsy, very tired, but at the same time quite agitated. She wasn't entirely sure what was getting to her, maybe it was the relief – and nerves – of a first episode now being out there in the big wide world and all it was likely to bring from hereon in. Perhaps it was the way Lottie's story was hitting so many wrong notes for her, while still managing to ring with truth – how could that be possible? More likely – at least easier to reach for – was the fact that Matthew had invited himself and Aiden to the party.

'What the heck are you doing here?' she'd demanded as they'd breezed in through the door, bringing bottles of wine and beer like they were students on a gatecrash.

'Great to see you too,' Aiden had grinned in his impossibly winning way, and of course she was pleased to see *him*.

'We were just passing,' Matthew explained, lying badly.

'Have some champagne,' Meena insisted, filling two glasses and handing them over, while Harry shook Matthew warmly by the hand and Iz just had to tell him what a big fan she was, and how honoured she felt to meet him.

Of course he'd settled in as comfortably as if he came to the drop of every episode – even though he'd never actually been to one before – and of course everyone had been their usual friendly selves, even baby Aurora who'd gazed at him adoringly for a full five minutes.

Quite what this had done to him, given his own recently born child was nearly six thousand miles away with a totally mazed mother, Cristy had no idea. However, she did know that her failure to reply to Marley's email was starting to weigh on her.

'She'd like to hear from you,' Matthew had said quietly, before he and Aiden had left, 'but you shouldn't feel as though you have to have a relationship with her. I mean, obviously great if you did, it would make life a lot easier for us all considering how besotted she seems with you, but I understand you have your own life to lead.' It wasn't a long pause before he added, 'Aiden tells me you're not seeing the Guernsey guy any more.'

'His name's David,' she'd snapped, 'and if you think that changes anything between us – you and me – then you need to book in for a head-check.'

Quite why the conversation had rattled her so much, she couldn't say now, although obviously she hadn't enjoyed being reminded by *him* that her first relationship since their break-up had fallen apart so fast.

And then there was Anna's call during her walk home.

'Haven't listened to the pod yet,' Anna had confessed, 'just wanted to let you know that Sadie's biggest fear at the moment is that she's going find out she's the child of a gangster or a rapist and that's why Janina gave her up. Maybe Janina reached a point where she couldn't bear to have the awful reminder around her any more.'

Understanding Sadie's concerns, for how could she not when

that very scenario, and worse, had occurred to her, Cristy said, 'Please don't tell me she wants to pull out . . .'

'No, no, that's not why I'm calling. It's simply to let you know what's in her mind because she couldn't bring herself to say it during the interview earlier. If it turns out she's right, she'll deal with it, she's just glad she's not going through it alone.'

'Having you is clearly meaning a great deal to her, especially with her aunt being so difficult, but it's not easy to support someone through trauma . . .'

'I can handle it. And anyway, she's not only talking about me, she means you and everyone else on your team, and even your listeners – provided they don't turn on her, I suppose, but I can't see why they would. She says she'd probably feel like she was disappearing down a rabbit hole otherwise, and I think even Jasper's a bit overwhelmed by it all.'

Wondering now if they were already down the rabbit hole anyway – it was certainly where she felt she was heading in a personal sense – Cristy slumped down on the sofa and checked her phone. Within an hour of the pod being dropped the feedback had begun, plenty echoing the question Iz had posed earlier: why should they care about a rich kid who hadn't known a day's hardship in her life? Others were demanding to know where the crime was, or accusing *Hindsight* of failing to live up to all the publicity. And of course there were those who'd engaged fully with the story and were already hoping Cristy and the team could help Sadie find the answers she deserved.

As usual Clove and Jacks were going through everything carefully in case someone with vital, or even useful, information was in touch. It wasn't always easy to tell as some trolls and many nutters were extremely clever, and nothing had come through yet to warrant any further action. Still very early days. Many weeks, or even months, could go by before the podcast found its way to the right person.

Would that be Janina? Or Lukas? It was hard to imagine, almost impossible in fact after all these years, but with no reason to rule it out Cristy wasn't going to.

Starting as her phone vibrated, she looked down half-expecting it to be Matthew, but it was a text from Robert Brinkley.

*Great first episode. Hope you're happy with it. (Am I right in thinking the Brinkley interview runs next week?) Only just picked up your email, and no problem about speaking to Sadie. Do you want to record it? Or will it be a private chat? Happy either way. Please feel free to pass on my details. Best, Robert.*

Wondering if it would be a good idea to record him and Sadie when they met, Cristy got up to put on the kettle. Another glass of wine might be more welcome, but she'd had enough earlier, any more would end up making her maudlin – as if she wasn't already.

Replying to Marley was going to do nothing to cheer her up, but unfortunately it had to be done, so she might as well get on with it.

She'd got no further than *Dear Marley, I'm sorry not to have been in touch sooner*, when her laptop's FaceTime app burbled into life. Seeing who it was she immediately clicked on. 'Mia,' she said, as the connection focused, 'this is a surprise. How are you?'

Mia's face was slightly averted, as though she didn't really want to engage, but she surely wouldn't be calling if she didn't have something to say. And on a video link too. 'I'm very well, thank you,' she said, her voice a little clipped, though not entirely unfriendly. 'I thought it was about time we spoke before things start to get out of hand.'

Wishing she was recording this, Cristy said, 'Out of hand in what way?'

'This . . . *nonsense* Sadie is feeding you. It really can't go on.'

'Why do you say it's nonsense?'

'Because it is. If you'd known my sister, if you *knew* Sadie . . .' She sighed irritably, seemed to reset and said, 'My niece has had *issues* for most of her life . . . Of course we've always got her the best help, done everything to make her feel as special as she is. I thought we were getting somewhere, but now, with all of this . . . It must be some sort of delayed shock following Lottie's death. They were very close and Sadie misses her terribly . . . We both do . . .'

When she didn't continue, Cristy said carefully, 'I take it you've listened to the first episode?'

'Yes, of course. Very well done, and a gripping tale, if any of it were true.'

'So there was no child on a beach? No hooded person running away? No mysterious envelope coming through the door?'

Mia's mouth tightened.

'I believe you've seen what Lottie wrote . . .'

'How do you know it was Lottie? And did it not occur to you that Sadie herself might have put the photographs into a box to present them as something . . . they aren't?'

'So you're saying that the young couple featured in them, with Sadie, are *not* related to her?'

'As I told Sadie when she showed them to me, they were very nice people who babysat her from time to time, during our first year here, in Guernsey. They left even before we moved into this house and we never kept in touch.'

Cristy didn't want to call her a liar, so instead she said, 'OK, I could perhaps be persuaded of that if the young woman didn't look so much like Sadie, and if I hadn't interviewed Gita Brinkley and her son, Robert. I showed him the photos and he remembers seeing the couple, in Minehead, at the time Sadie came to live with you on Exmoor. He's even named them.'

Mia's face seemed to twitch; her hands bunched tightly together. 'I've no idea what Gita Brinkley and her son have told you,' she retorted sharply, 'but all you're doing, all of you, is feeding into Sadie's fantasy of having a mother, or father, who could be out there somewhere wanting to know her. I can assure you that she does not need to know them, and nor should she be encouraged in this quest for information that will only end up causing her a lot more harm than good.'

Taking it carefully, Cristy said, 'That sounds as though you're admitting your brother was not her father . . .'

'We told her that because it was easier and it would have stayed that way if she hadn't suddenly decided to question it. Since finding out she's not related to us by blood she's cast us variously as villains, fairy godmothers, crazy people, glamorous benefactors, whatever comes into her head on any given day. I ask you, please don't let her draw you any further into her illusory world. As I've already said, it won't end well, especially not for her.'

'But you're clearly hiding information about her parents that she surely has a right to know.'

'That is your understanding of things, no one else's. I have spent many years protecting my niece, and believe you me, I won't stop now.'

'But what does she need protecting from?'

'If you value your reputation, Ms Ward, and I'm sure you do, then ask yourself this: how is it possible that these extracts, supposedly written by Lottie and randomly hidden amongst Lottie's papers – how is Sadie managing to find them in the correct order? Isn't that what's happening?'

Cristy felt a beat of unease. It was true, they were coming up in a kind of linear way, although she had no idea if any further extracts were missing from what they had so far.

'Sadie is writing them herself,' Mia repeated, tartly. 'Now, I'll leave you to the rest of your evening and I hope all this digging about in a fabricated past will soon be at an end.'

# CHAPTER FOURTEEN

'Well, it's clear she was trying to portray Sadie as a nutjob,' Connor reflected when Cristy reported the conversation to the team the next morning. 'And – presuming we're all agreed that there's nothing wrong with Sadie – the only reason I can see for Mia doing that, is because whatever she's hiding is pretty damned bad. Remind me what she said again?'

Checking the notes she'd made right after the call, Cristy read aloud, '"I have spent many years protecting my niece and I'm not going to stop now." Obviously I asked for an explanation of that, but she just started in about my reputation, and asked how I thought Sadie was managing to find Lottie's story in order.'

'Because Sadie herself is writing it?' Clove said incredulously.

'Even if we believed that,' Jacks said, 'and I don't think we do, there have to be far easier ways of trying to find out about your past. Going to all this trouble would be just, well, nuts!'

'Although you have to admit,' Clover put in, 'it *is* weird that the story is "being found" more or less in order.'

'That's if you discount the possibility of there being other extracts covering the in-between times,' Cristy pointed out. 'For instance, there could be something about Mia's shopping trip to pick up supplies for their new charge, or more about what was in the envelope. That hasn't come to light yet, and I presume it exists. Having said that, in my opinion, what we've read so far has been written by a more mature hand than Sadie's, and the style seems consistent with some of Lottie's published short stories.'

'Anything in them to warrant further investigation?' Connor wanted to know.

'Nothing that I've come across so far. Most are set in foreign lands . . . I get the impression she's drawn on her personal experience of working with NGOs and charities to create certain aspects of the stories.'

'Anything set on Exmoor, or Guernsey?' Clove wondered.

'Not recognizably so, and no characters that stand out as being based on Sadie or Mia.'

'Remind me when she gave up being published,' Connor said, checking the board to see if it was there. Finding it, he read out, '"Last book 2005, discuss with editor Felicity Green, returning UK Feb first. Can speak sooner if necessary." So did something significant happen in 2005 to make her want to pull out? Sadie would have been how old by then? Seven. So well settled in Guernsey and at primary school.'

'Do you want me to set up a Zoom with Felicity Green?' Jacks offered.

After considering it, Connor said, 'Hold fire for now. It's feeling like a bit of a distraction when what we really need is to get to the bottom of what went on in May of 2000, and why Sadie was left on the beach.'

'If she actually was left on the beach,' Cristy stated. As everyone looked at her, she said, 'I'm just putting it out there that she might not have been. But as we've no idea what's true or false about that scenario, I guess we keep going with it for the time being.'

'But what's making you doubt it?' Clover wanted to know.

She shrugged. 'I suppose it just seems so unlikely, far-fetched even, and what I'm wondering is if Lottie wrote it to try and establish an early false record of how Sadie came to them.'

'In order to cover up . . . what?'

'The fact they had her, of course, but I have no theories yet on who, why, what, or when; I'm simply saying that I think we need to keep open minds.'

'Do we mention any of this to Sadie?' Connor asked.

'To be honest, I think she has her own doubts. Remember she – and Anna – were the first to suggest she might have been bought, and Lottie's version is really all about abduction. That's bad, obviously, but the alternatives are a whole lot worse.'

After a brief spell of reflection, Jacks said, 'So where do we go from here?'

Turning back to the whiteboard and its list of those they wanted to interview, Cristy said, 'One of us needs to have a chat with "Corny" – Cornelia – the long-time housekeeper for the sisters at their Guernsey home, the Villa des Roches. Apparently she lives in Cobo Bay now, on the island's west coast, with a small menagerie including a mute parrot.'

'Chances are she'll be prepped by Mia,' Connor warned. 'What about Mia herself? Is it worth trying to talk to her again?'

Cristy's eyebrows rose. 'After her call last night I wouldn't be surprised if our next communication with her is via her lawyer . . . Which reminds me, I'm guessing we still haven't received anything from David Gaudion regarding the aunts' finances?' She was looking at Jacks.

'You're right, we haven't,' he confirmed. 'I'll chase it.'

'I don't think we've made a decision yet,' Connor pointed out, 'on what we tell Sadie about her aunt's call last night.'

Having already made up her mind on that, Cristy said, 'She needs to know what Mia said about "protecting" her. She'll almost certainly challenge her aunt over it, and hopefully end up in a position to be able to report back with something useful. Incidentally, Robert Brinkley's happy to talk to her about Janina and Lukas. I'm not sure how much further it'll take us in the overall discovery process, but it could be good emotional stuff that the listeners will engage with as long as Sadie's OK with us recording it.'

'When are they getting together?' Clover wanted to know, preparing to write it up on the board.

'Perhaps you could follow up with Robert,' Cristy replied. 'It would be great if it could happen at, or near, the house on Exmoor. I'm sure Sadie will be keen to meet Gita again, presuming Gita's up for it, and I can't see why she wouldn't be. I'm inclined to leave that with you, Clove, and if you can tie it in with an arrangement to meet with the retired detective from around those parts . . . Any more news on that front?'

'Ah yes, I have a name now – ex-Detective Sergeant Catherine Shilling. She's living in the Chew Valley these days, so kind of on the way to Minehead.'

'Has she given you a sense of what she can tell you?' Connor asked.

Clover's eyebrows waggled as if she had great news to impart. 'I haven't actually spoken to her yet,' she admitted, making them laugh and groan. 'But I'm told she's happy to talk. I'll set something up as soon as I've nailed down Sadie and Robert.'

Turning to Cristy, Connor said dryly, 'I thought you'd want to see Robert again.'

Cristy's eyes narrowed at the tease. 'I think I'll just ignore that,' she told him, 'and, Clove, I've changed my mind about the detective. I think she's someone Connor and I should talk to just in case she has a lovely little bombshell to throw into the mix.'

'No probs,' Clove agreed, writing Catherine Shilling's details on the whiteboard.

'OK, Jacks, an update on where you are with your enquiries?'

With a grimace, he said, 'Afraid still no word from Edwin Prosser. I'll send a follow-up right after this, and obvs I'll continue pursuing other possible avenues of contact. Same goes with my HR person at Butlin's, but definitely not giving up on her yet. Also, still reading the organized crime report that Clove has dumped on me. Depending on where Janina and Lukas were from, it's quite possible they weren't in this country legally back in 2000 so that's going to make them even harder to trace, especially if there was gang involvement.'

'But Lukas had a job,' Cristy pointed out. 'I can't see a company like Butlin's hiring an illegal . . .'

'Maybe not knowingly. But who knows what might have happened at the local level, or what sort of papers he might have had when he came, false or otherwise. Same goes for Janina. If they were trafficked, sorry to say this, their names might not even be Janina and Lukas.'

'Oh God,' Cristy groaned, 'please don't tell me that.'

'I'm just flagging it up, but definitely working with what we have for now. It's always possible, once we've dropped the next episode, someone will get in touch with more info.'

'Why? What's in the next episode?' Meena asked from the door.

Turning to her, Cristy said, 'Robert and Gita Brinkley's interviews where Sadie's mother and uncle are named. It could trigger something for someone. It's also when we'll put the images of Janina and Lukas with Sadie on the website. Anyway, to what do we owe this pleasure?'

'Actually, I was just passing and thought I'd drop in. No Iz this morning?'

'The question no one was asking,' Connor informed her.

Meena chuckled. 'As if words might rub the lamp and whoosh, there she is?'

'Something like that.'

'Well, you seemed happy enough to drink her champagne last night, and you might like to know that when I spoke to her half an hour ago she was buzzing with the stats she has so far. I believe some platforms are still reporting, and obviously we're expecting the numbers to go up, maybe exponentially, over the coming days, weeks, as the downloads increase. But, suffice it to say, you're off to a blinding start, both domestically and internationally.'

'Yay!' Clover cheered, as they gave themselves a round of applause.

'So you have to give Iz credit for getting you the right publicity,' Meena continued. 'Aren't you doing more interviews for her today?'

'Connor is,' Cristy replied, checking her watch. 'In fact, you probably ought to be going, Con, you don't want to be late.'

As he shot her a look, Jacks said, 'What's happening?'

'It turns out,' Connor replied tersely, 'that Iz, last night, managed to sweet-talk Jodi into a family photoshoot, thereby exploiting my six-week-old daughter for our sponsors' gain.'

'For *Hindsight*'s gain,' Meena corrected.

'Whatever, it just better not end up in *HELLO!* magazine, is all I can say. And how did she manage to get a photographer so fast, that's what I'd like to know.'

'More proof of her superpowers?' Cristy suggested. 'And try to smile. You look so much more like Clark Kent when you do.'

Slanting her another mean look, he began to gather up his things.

'What's the social media feedback so far?' Meena asked Jacks.

'Mostly positive,' he assured her. 'Some seriously disgusting suggestions of what could have been in the envelope, starting with an ear, or a finger, and going on to bodily waste, that sort of thing. A lot seemed to favour a blackmail note – proves how much attention they were paying – and a good number guessed photographs.'

'And what did they think they might be of?' Meena said.

'Again lots of puky suggestions – you've got to seriously wonder about some people, or not, best just to shut them down, I say. Anyway, lots reckoned they were of the child being abused; others went for something unspecified from the sisters'/aunts' past; the favourite was of the aunt leading the child from the beach, a lead up to the aforementioned blackmail.'

Meena nodded. 'OK, well, plenty of engagement is what we want, however it comes. I guess nothing particularly helpful yet?'

'Not from the listeners,' Cristy replied, 'but we're making some headway with other avenues.'

'Good, then I'll leave you to it. Enjoy the photoshoot, Connor, can't wait to see you in *OK!* magazine.'

As Meena left with a wave, he rounded on Cristy. 'Tell me she wasn't serious?' he growled.

Laughing, Cristy shrugged. 'I've no idea who or what the shoot's for, but think of it this way . . .'

'No! You're going to say something outrageous, I know it, so let me get in first. I shall expect some serious progress to have taken place by the time I'm back, because in spite of what you just told Meena, as far as I can see right now, we've hit a wall and no one has a plan for how to get past it.'

*

An hour later, with Clove and Jacks out for lunch and Connor still posing for the press, Cristy was alone in the office reflecting on his parting shot. He wasn't wrong, of course, they were at something of an impasse, although she wasn't unduly worried given how many balls they had in the air. He was just grumpy because he didn't like Iz any more than he enjoyed publicity. Being no fan of it herself, she understood. However, getting the series noticed mattered, and if the early stats were anything to go by then Iz's strategy, whatever it actually was, seemed to be working very much in their favour.

Connor would cheer up as soon as he forced himself to come on board with that.

Turning in her chair to study the whiteboard, it was a moment before she realized she was seeing past the shots of Janina and Lukas, now added to those of Sadie and her aunts, to how very different the board had looked during their last investigation – and to how conflicted and challenged she'd felt as it had unfolded. David's headshot had dominated then, along with those of his murdered wife, mother-in-law and a family friend. He'd unnerved her a lot during that time, long before they'd even met. What she'd heard about him, all that she came to learn, had made looking at him an almost interactive experience, as though his piercingly watchful eyes were actually seeing right into her, and following her every move. It had been deeply discomfiting to find herself so affected by a total stranger, especially when she'd fully believed in his guilt for most of the series – in fact right up until she had proven his innocence.

She felt sure that his case, its complexities and its success, were the reasons she was finding it so hard to let go of him now. Living and breathing the triple murders day in, day out, and for so long, had all but taken over her life, but it wasn't just the series, she knew that in her heart. She'd been deeply attracted to him from the moment they'd actually met, and he was the first man she'd lowered her defences for since Matthew. It hurt a lot to know that she'd got it so wrong.

*It doesn't matter*, she told herself sharply. *It's over, already fading into history and sitting here dwelling on it isn't going to change a thing.*

Refocusing on the headshots of today, most particularly Mia's, she was soon wondering, again, what she'd been protecting Sadie from for all these years. They already knew that a crime had been committed through the abduction, but if Sadie's fake identity was taken into consideration, and added to the possibility that Janina had been trafficked into the country and had since disappeared, they were looking at a lot more than one crime. In fact, the most troubling issue for Cristy right now was how very hard she was finding it to believe that they were going to find Janina alive after all these years. The same went for

Lukas who seemed to have disappeared around the same time as his sister.

If they were they'd surely have come back for Sadie long before now.

Unless they had and . . .

Quickly going to the transcript of the latest extract, spoken by Sadie, she scrolled almost to the end and hit play.

*Everything you have, Edwin, everything you are, is in our control. Never forget that. We could, if necessary, discredit you to a point where you'd make yourself disappear without a trace to save us the trouble.*

Had Lottie written those words simply for effect, or had she actually said them? Was she the kind of woman who'd do whatever it took to 'disappear' someone who stood in her way? Perhaps more relevantly right now, was she someone who'd pay for a child to be taken from its mother in order to make it her own?

But who would she have paid? A trafficker? It begged the question, how would she have known such a person? Although, who knew what contacts anyone had if you delved deeply enough. Even Cristy's own address book contained some very murky characters, and Lottie's work with various charities would have opened her up to a whole world of immorality and corruption. But how had she known about Janina and Sadie? Had they been 'introduced' by a third party and that was the real reason Mia and Lottie had taken a house on Exmoor that year?

If the story about finding Sadie on the beach was true, then there had been no illegal transaction of that sort, but it still didn't rule out the possibility of it being some kind of a set-up. Something that the sisters had 'spent many years protecting' her from.

Thinking again of how the pages were being 'discovered' more or less in order, Cristy wondered if, in fact, Sadie might have found them some time ago and put them together to build the story they had so far. If that was the case then she'd presumably decided to feed them an extract at a time, maybe as a way of keeping Cristy's interest alive?

'If you're right about that,' Connor said when he and the others returned and she shared her thoughts for discussion, 'then there's a high probability that she's already got more extracts lined up and is working out the best time to hand them over.'

'I can buy into that,' Clover said.

'Me too,' Jacks agreed.

'And for what it's worth,' Clove continued, 'here's what I've been thinking about Sadie being sold to the sisters. Why would they choose her when Lottie had access to any number of kids in need of parents? The answer is Sadie's white, while the others would have been of a much darker hue, and if the child was for Mia, which I'm getting the impression it was . . . Do you agree with that . . .?'

Though neither Cristy nor Connor had actually articulated this suspicion, they both nodded.

'Then maybe Mia has a bit of a race problem?' Clove finished.

Wrinkling his nose, Jacks said, 'OK, I get all that, but what's your actual point?'

'There isn't one yet. I'm just doing what we always do and putting it out there.'

Cristy was still mulling it as a video call came up on her screen. 'What timing,' she murmured. Clicking straight to speaker so the others could hear while remaining out of shot, she said, 'Sadie. How are things there?'

'Sorry, I meant to call earlier,' Sadie replied breathlessly, 'it's been a horrible day, the worst. I crashed my car first thing – nothing serious – then I got to the villa and Mia bloody well locked me in Lottie's rooms. Can you believe it? She's only just let me out.'

Clocking everyone's astonishment, Cristy simply allowed the girl to run on.

'She's trying to say it was a mistake, that she had no idea I was in there, but she knew. If I hadn't left my phone in the kitchen I could have rung Anna or Jasper to come and get me out, but I didn't have it with me. Then it turned out the WiFi was down in the whole house, including Lottie's office, so I couldn't reach anyone that way either.'

'Has your aunt ever done anything like that before?' Cristy asked, recalling what a steep and treacherous drop it was from Lottie's balconies, so no escape route there.

'I'm afraid so. It's her thing, locking people up. She used to do it to Lottie if she was angry with her, or wanted to be the one in control. She's nuts at times, honestly. Harmless, but definitely nuts. Anyway, I'm back at the lodge now and I wanted to let you know that she's heard the first episode. It'll be why she locked me up, as a punishment, I'm sure of it . . .'

'She rang me last night,' Cristy interrupted, 'so I know she's heard it. We'll get into the details of the call in a minute, but I think you should know that she's accused you of writing the extracts . . .'

'*What!* You can't be serious. She is so . . . I swear I *did not* write them. I found them, like I told you, in amongst Lottie's other stories and travel pieces . . . Oh my God! She thinks it'll make you stop helping me, that's why she said it. She comes out with such horrible lies sometimes. She's done it all my life. Please tell me you don't believe her.'

'I don't,' Cristy admitted, 'but there is something I'd like you to clear up.'

'Yes, of course. Anything.'

Sadie looked so eager to comply and fearful of not being believed that Cristy could feel herself starting to soften. 'The extracts you've given us so far seem to be telling the story in order, so am I right in thinking you found them all before you and Anna approached me with the first one?'

The girl's dismay was so apparent that it was admission enough.

'Talk me through it,' Cristy encouraged.

Sadie took a breath, lowered her head and looked so guilty and ashamed as she met the camera lens again that it was hard not to feel sorry for her. Depending, of course, on what she had to say next.

'I came across the third one first, during the pandemic,' she said quietly. 'That's the single page where the envelope turns up and they get all worried about what's inside. I found it a bit weird that Lottie had used our names for a story like that, but it was so short and seemed to go nowhere that I decided it was just an idea that she'd jotted down to work on later and never went back to. I forgot about it even, until I found the box with the toys and a note. Seeing that note – *Her name is Sasha, she will be two years old* . . . Well, you know what it said, and I . . . I felt sick inside, because I just knew that it was about me, and whoever had written it had meant to come back for me but somehow, for some reason, they hadn't.'

'Did you find the photographs of your mother and uncle at the same time as the note?' Cristy prompted, recalling that they'd been in the box Sadie had brought to Bradford-on-Avon.

'No, they came later . . . I can't remember now if it was before, or after, the chapter where Edwin turns up at the house, I only knew that when I saw them I felt certain I was looking at my parents. I swear I wasn't making it up when I said I remembered a man in a hat . . . I know we think now that he was my uncle, but at the time I was sure he must be my father.'

'So exactly how long have you had everything you've shown us so far?'

Sadie was shamefaced all over again. 'I found the latest extract, the one that ends with Lottie having an idea, a few months ago.'

Recalling how shaken she'd appeared after reading it aloud, and her initial claim that she'd only come across it four days before, Cristy said, 'I'm not sure whether to admire your acting skills or simply to call this all to a halt right now . . .'

'No, no, please don't do that,' Sadie jumped in. 'I'm sorry, I really am.'

'But how can we trust you, Sadie, when you've misled us . . .'

'But only about when I found things. Everything else is true, and please remember that when I read out the last one I'd only just heard Robert and Gita Brinkley's interviews. That's why I was so emotional . . .'

'But why the hell didn't you hand it all over as soon as we met?'

Colouring, Sadie said, 'I was afraid you might just dismiss it, or think I was some sort of fantasist. And as the pages don't prove anything, I thought . . . Oh God, I thought if I drew it out, gave them to you bit by bit, it would give me some time to find more, if there is more, but I still don't know if there is.'

As a tear dropped onto her cheek, Cristy sighed and said, 'I want you to know, Sadie, that if we hadn't already posted the first episode I really would be calling everything off right now. This level of duplicity and manipulation is unforgivable, and not one of us sitting in this room now takes kindly to being made a fool of . . .'

'That wasn't my intention,' Sadie cried desperately, 'and I'm sorry, I really am . . .'

'How long were you intending to continue with the charade?'

'I – I didn't have a plan, exactly, but I knew I'd have to tell you if I didn't find any more . . .'

'And apparently you haven't. So what now?'

Sadie regarded her helplessly, her face a picture of guilt and despair.

Cristy looked from Connor to the others and back to the screen. 'If we do carry on,' she said, 'I want your solemn word that there will be no more deception, and if there is anything else you're holding back, I need to know now.'

'There isn't, I swear, but I'm still looking. You've seen for yourself how much there is to go through . . .'

'OK,' Cristy cut in, needing to move things along, 'when you come over to talk to Robert Brinkley maybe you could drive and bring some boxes with you so that we can help with the search.'

Sadie was already eagerly nodding. 'I'll get Jasper to rent a van, we'll be able to fit more in that way and if it's too much we can always bring it back again. Oh God, thank you for not giving up on me. I know I've handled it all wrong, I just . . . It's hard to express how much it means to me, having your support . . .'

Cristy's hand went up. 'Your apology is accepted, so let's deal with other things. We're considering coming to interview your old housekeeper, Corny, unless you think we'll be treated to a Mia-inspired account of your life on the island.'

Sadie grimaced. 'It might be best if you could arrange things so that neither she nor Mia know you're coming. I'd be there, obviously, to introduce you to Corny – it might scare her otherwise, if you just turned up – but at least that way we'd know that she hasn't been told what to say by Mia.'

'OK, we'll talk some more about it after you've met with the Brinkleys. Have you arranged a time and date with Robert yet?'

'Yes, we're coming over the day after tomorrow, and meeting in Minehead.'

'How are you feeling about that?'

Sadie's eyes closed as she inhaled deeply. 'Nervous, a little bit excited . . . I know, obviously, that they can't tell me where my mother is now, or my uncle, but the fact that Robert met her, actually spoke to her . . .' She broke off, took a moment and started again. 'He sounds like a nice man in his interviews, and when I spoke to him on the phone.'

'He is and you'll love his mother. Clover and Jacks will be there to record your chat, but only if you're comfortable with it.'

'I'm sure that's fine. Are Clover and Jacks listening now?'

Cristy nodded for Connor to switch everyone into the call. Moments later they were all on the screen with Clove and Jacks waving a friendly hello.

'I'm sorry I've messed you all around,' Sadie told them earnestly. 'Thank you so much for giving me a second chance.'

Before she could get into any more apologies, Cristy said, 'There's something else your aunt told me during our FaceTime chat and, frankly, it's what's really keeping us all on board.'

Sadie frowned.

'She said she's been protecting you from something all these years, and she's not going to stop now.'

Sadie's frown deepened as bright spots of colour flared in her cheeks. 'Did she say what it was?'

'No, but feel free to ask her and if she'll tell you . . .'

'She won't.'

'I suspect you're right, but whatever she says, we'll be interested to hear it.'

'Of course. I'll let you know right away, provided she hasn't locked me up again. But don't worry, I'll be on my guard next time I'm there and, anyway, Jasper will be with me to help load the van.'

*

Two hours later, as Cristy walked home in the dark, the call she'd been waiting for finally arrived.

'Dad's furious with me,' Anna confided, sounding stressed and sorry. 'He said I had to call right away to explain myself and to make sure you don't think Sadie is entirely to blame.'

Having suspected Anna had played a bigger role than Sadie had let on, Cristy said, 'I'd find your apology easier to accept if your father hadn't pushed you into it.'

'Oh, he didn't. I mean, I was going to call you anyway, and I would have right after Sadie rang me, but then Ludo, Rosie's boyfriend, had a melt down and no one knew how to handle it. Dad had to hold him down while I rang Ursula, that's Ludo's mum, and she took forever to come . . . It was a nightmare; I think he wanted to kill us . . . Ludo, I mean, not Dad.'

Reminded of how life went on regardless, Cristy said, 'What set Ludo off?'

'A bat, would you believe? He's got this collection, baseball, tennis, golf, cricket – I know they're not all technically bats, but it's what he calls them and he's super proud of them. He won't let anyone touch them, even his mother, but he brought them over to show us today, and Laurent and Rosie used one to play rounders and the next thing we knew Ludo was going off on one and trying to attack them. So, that's the reason I've taken a while to call, I've been trying to comfort Rosie with Dad doing is best with Ludo and Ursula.'

'And how's Rosie now?'

'Much calmer and apparently she isn't going to marry him if he behaves like that again.'

Smiling, Cristy said, 'Does that mean he's proposed?'

'No, I think she did, but anyway, I can't see Dad or Ursula allowing it, especially after this.' Barely pausing for breath, she said, 'Back to Sadie and our stupid plan to eke out the extracts and stuff. I don't think she'd have done it if I hadn't put it into her mind, and I only did because I was afraid if we gave it to you all in one go you'd turn us down.'

'Then you were wrong on both counts, first for not being completely honest, second for assuming it wouldn't be enough to interest us. It's an intriguing case with some pretty serious crimes at its heart.'

'Really? What crimes exactly?'

'We're still working on that.' It would be crazy, not to mention unfeeling, to tell Anna at this stage how strongly she suspected they were going to uncover at least one murder – probably Janina's. Anna would be sure to confide in Sadie and until they had more to go on there was absolutely nothing to be gained from shattering a young girl's dream of one day finding her mother alive.

# CHAPTER FIFTEEN

Cristy was driving as Connor read aloud the email she'd typed into her laptop.

'*Dear Marley, My apologies for not getting back to you sooner, and huge congratulations on the safe arrival of the baby.*'

He turned to her, confused. 'Is that it?' he asked incredulously. 'After the two-page cry-from-the-heart she wrote you, this is all you're sending back?'

Wincing, Cristy said, 'I haven't finished it yet.'

He remained incredulous. 'Remind me how long it's been since she emailed you?'

'Will you just stop! I was hoping for some support over this. I mean, what am I supposed to say when I kind of wish the child had never been born, and I wouldn't mind never seeing her again in my life? Please don't quote me on any of that.'

'Well, at least it would be honest – and even go a bit further towards filling up a page.'

She rolled her eyes and indicated to join the A38 heading out of Bristol. 'Matthew would never forgive me if I was that cruel,' she pointed out. 'Not that I care what he thinks, but then I'd have to deal with him as well as her and I'm already struggling with that, thank you very much.'

'Have you seen him since he turned up for the drop-party?'

'You mean since he *gatecrashed* the party. No, thank God. He's gone suspiciously quiet on me, and how wonderful if it would stay that way, but I'm not fooled. He'll be planning some sort of ambush, I'm sure of it, or something will happen that he'll need to share with me, or get me to sort out . . . Honestly, it's like having another child and I'm not even married to him any more.'

'So feeling needed isn't really working for you?'

She laughed, and came to a stop at a red light. 'He has to deal with the situation in LA: whether he's going to stay married to Marley, be a father to Baby Bear, work out some kind of long-distance relationship if she decides to stay put over there . . .'

'Do you think she will?'

'God knows. And frankly, I don't care. He chose the path he's on, and contrary to what both he and Marley seem to think it has nothing to do with me. I can't even get my head around why they want me as part of their world. I'm the ex-wife, for God's sake . . .'

'You're also *you*, so I get why they want you in their lives. I wouldn't want to let you go either if I was Matthew . . .'

'But he did . . .'

'And he's regretting it. And Marley can see how wonderful it would be if you two were friends. And she's right, because we all love having you as a friend . . .'

'Stop winding me up. I need some help deciding how to answer Marley's email and you are proving about as useful as . . .' She struggled. 'I'll come up with something and it won't be good.'

Grinning, he closed her laptop and hit the car's display screen to take a call from Clover and Jacks. 'Hey, guys!' he cried. 'How's your day at the beach going?'

'Just got here,' Clover replied. 'Pissing down with rain and blowing a hooley so good job we brought the sunscreen. Anyway, just wanted to let you know that Sadie and Jasper are running late, ferry was delayed, but they should arrive in the next half an hour. Robert's here, and his mother, obvs, given we're in her residential village, and what a doll she is. If my flat was bigger I'd try to take her home with me.

'So, is there anything in particular you'd like us to try to get from this?' Clover continued. 'I know we've been over everything already and we're just here to eavesdrop, so to speak, but Jacks had a thought in the night—'

'. . . that we ought to capture some video of the reunion,' Jacks interrupted. 'Provided everyone's happy to go along with it, natch.'

'Great idea,' Cristy told him. 'It could be quite an emotional moment for the old lady seeing Sadie all grown up and still bearing a sweet resemblance to the child she once was. Have you checked it with her and Robert?'

'Yeah, they're cool with it. He wants me to tell you he's just nipping out to buy popcorn and Kleenex.'

Laughing, Cristy said, 'Please thank him again for doing this and make sure he knows he can call any time if he's worried about anything.'

'Will do.'

'See,' Connor said, as they rang off, 'you're even a good friend to people you don't really know. Although I've got to admire how neatly you worked that in. Tell him to call any time . . .'

'You're starting to get on my nerves,' Cristy interrupted, and pressed her foot down to speed away from the lights. 'Where are we heading, again?'

'Chew Magna, and as we've already missed the turn to go up over Dundry, take the next to go through Winford. We could, of course, have gone via Hartcliffe . . .'

'What did I just say about getting on my nerves? I take it you've got Catherine Shilling's actual address with you?'

He went silent. 'Maybe we need to call Clover back.'

Cristy glanced at him.

'Joke!' he cried. 'Of course I've got it, and if you don't slow down right now we're going to end up at the airport.'

Hitting the brakes she indicated to make a sharp left turn onto Barrow Lane, narrowly missing a van waiting to exit onto the main road.

'No offence,' Connor said, as she straightened the car, 'but would you like me to take over the driving?'

'I'm fine,' she assured him, 'just a little . . .' She could have said distracted, but if she did he'd be sure to ask what was on her mind and she wasn't keen to tell him.

Keen or not, it came out anyway. 'I had a text from David last night,' she said, keeping her eyes straight ahead.

Connor turned to look at her. 'And?'

She shrugged. 'No big deal. He was just adding his apology to Anna's for what happened with Sadie.'

'OK. That's good.'

'I guess he was just being a concerned father, taking responsibility for the actions of his daughter. Parents do that. You'll find out soon enough.'

He returned to his scrutiny of the road ahead. 'Did he say anything else?' he asked after a while.

'No, that was it.'

'So you told him it was all forgiven and forgotten and you didn't blame him for anything so there was no need for him . . .'

'I didn't reply.'

He looked at her again. 'So he's someone else who's getting your silent treatment? Marley, Matthew, David . . . I'm sensing a theme here.'

'Well, what was I supposed to say?' Cristy cried irritably. The truth was she really hadn't known what to write back that felt right, and she hadn't wanted it to seem as though she was using Anna's mistake as a way for them to stay in touch. 'I will reply,' she said, meaning it, 'but FYI I'm still feeling a bit raw over the way things ended between us, so cut me a break, OK?'

His hands went up. 'No more from me about your love life, but just saying, wouldn't a fling with Robert Brinkley be . . .'

'For God's sake!' she cried, banging the steering wheel. 'Apart from anything else he's married! And you can't seriously think I'd do to another woman what was done to me.'

'No, no, engaged mouth before brain. Sorry. Change of subject coming . . . Actually, saved by the bell!' And clicking on quickly he said, 'Hey, Jacks. Great timing!'

'Cool,' Jacks responded. 'Also great news. Just heard from my new best friend at Butlin's HR, she's only come through with a surname for Lukas. It's Andris. I'll put it in an email, but spelled the way it sounds. She can't give me any more than that, such as an address for where Lukas was before Butlin's, or after – not sure if that's data protection or she just doesn't know. But she did give me the name of an assistant manager who was Lukas's boss for the time he was working at the Minehead camp. Hilary Stokes. Could be male or female. No contact details, but I'll get onto it as soon as we're back at the office.'

'Genius,' Connor declared. 'And whatever charm you used to

get your Butlin's babe talking, send some this way to help me with Cristy, because I'm *really* getting on her nerves.'

*

Half an hour later they were all set up in the cosy living room of ex-Detective Sergeant Catherine Shilling's quirky house in Chew Magna, an eclectic sort of village at the heart of the Chew Valley, with pubs and cafés, lots of narrow streets and a reputation for being a great place to live. Their knees were pressed up against a bamboo coffee table where a small pile of old files was sitting beside a tray of hot tea and scrumptious-looking biscuits. Catherine Shilling herself, who had to be in her early sixties, was her own kind of ex-detective, with a mauve spiky hair-do, nose and eyebrow piercings and a fluorescent pink crushed velvet kaftan that, either by design or chance, matched the cushions behind her.

Wondering if she did some sort of readings these days, given all the crystals and candles dotted about the place, Cristy said, 'What you've just outlined for us is extremely interesting and is going to be a valuable addition to our series. So thanks for agreeing to record before we go any further.'

'No problem,' Catherine smiled, her pearly teeth making her as pleasing to look at as her slight lisp was entrancing to listen to. 'I did some digging around after Clover got in touch, more to refresh my memory than to find answers to your questions – although they're one and the same, I suppose. I just want to be clear from the start that anything I say for your podcast can't be categorized as an official statement from Avon and Somerset Police. I mean, they know I'm talking to you and that I'm giving you sight of these files. They just want it understood that I am fifteen years retired from the force and while I was involved in certain investigations concerning the presence of Eastern European gangs in our area back in 1998 through 2001, the overall operation was being conducted by the Met Police. The Serious Organized Crime Agency as it's known today.'

Nodding her understanding, Cristy noted this down and, receiving a thumbs up from Connor, asked Catherine to identify herself for the recording and to add what she'd just told them about the SOCA.

With the formalities out of the way the interview began.

CRISTY: 'So what can you tell us about gang activity in the Minehead area at the time Janina and Lukas Andris were known to be there?'

CATHERINE: 'Well, it first came to our attention via social services. They were concerned about the occupants of a house near Kylve. Do you know the beach there? It's famous for its fossils. Anyway, the house in question, Mannycott Farm, turned out to belong to a distant relative of a prominent aristocrat and landowner – think Gloucestershire, Worcestershire and Wiltshire rather than Somerset. Not that said highfalutin' aristo had any involvement in what was happening at the house, or none that I ever knew about. I simply tell you that as part of the background we had on the main resident.'

CRISTY: 'And what was happening at the house?'

CATHERINE: 'If you'd listened to the neighbours you'd have thought all sorts of terrible things – slavery, trafficking, prostitution, drugs . . . All on the edge of this sleepy west Somerset village. They claimed he – George Symmonds-Browne, Lord Mannycott as some called him – had a constant procession of Russian brides being supplied by his very dubious foreign cohorts. They had it – the locals – that these "brides" were tested out by Symmonds-Browne and his cronies before being passed on to the highest bidder.'

CRISTY: 'You're sounding sceptical?'

CATHERINE: 'No, I think in part that bit might have been true, but our surveillance of the property soon told us that local reports were . . . exaggerated. Girls were living there, no doubt about that, but not in numbers. In fact there only ever appeared to be three or four there at any given time, and whoever they were they seemed free to come and go as they pleased. Sometimes they went out with men, other times on their own.'

CRISTY: 'So you don't think they were being held against their will?'

CATHERINE: 'It didn't look like it, but I'm sure you know as well as I do, trafficking gangs hold leverage over their victims by threatening to harm the families they've left behind. So running away wouldn't have been an option for those girls.'

CRISTY: 'Did you ever speak with any of them?'

CATHERINE: 'No, our instructions were simply to observe and report back.'

CRISTY: 'Do you know what nationality they were?'

CATHERINE: 'Not specifically, but I'm not sure they were actually Russian, the way the locals claimed. Definitely not English though.'

CRISTY: 'How long did they stay at the farm before being moved on?'

CATHERINE: 'That's hard to answer, because the surveillance wasn't constant, no twenty-four-seven or anything like that. More a couple of times a month for a two-to-three-day period. We soon learned that our little stake-out was small fry in comparison to what was going on with the op in the rest of the country. The big boys in London weren't particularly interested in what we had going in Kylve unless we could report sightings of certain individuals, or vehicles, they had a special interest in.'

CRISTY: 'And could you?'

CATHERINE: 'Not at first, no. You'll find more details in those files there on the table, along with the identities of some of the key gang members. Not people to be messed with, that's for sure, and I can tell you we wouldn't have wanted to give it a go. More than one officer lost his life during that particular op. None of ours, the unlucky were London- or Midlands-based, but none of us was keen to add to the number.

'Anyway, the risk of that was removed as soon as we reported the sighting of one Matis Albescu. That would have been late 1999, I think. We'd been on the case for a good year by then, and he'd been one of their top POIs – persons of interest – long before we were brought into the picture. Then, suddenly one night, there he was, right in front of us. A tall, wiry bloke with a lot of facial hair, and a gammy left leg – meaning he walked with a limp. We knew it was him right away, and got plenty of shots of him entering the house, and coming out again a couple of hours later. That's when the London boys took over and we, of course, were mushroomed . . . Kept in the dark about whatever went down from there. However, I can tell you that Albescu is no longer with us. He was shot and killed during a dawn raid in Birmingham a year or more after we laid eyes on him.'

CRISTY: 'So that would have been sometime in 2001?'

CATHERINE: 'Could have been early 2002. It'll be in the file.'

CRISTY: 'And what happened to the resident of Mannycott Farm?'

CATHERINE: 'Symmonds-Browne? Nothing as far as we knew. Everything calmed down after the sighting of Albescu in late '99 – at least for us it did. There were still the occasional reports from neighbours of girls at the farm, but nothing that got anyone excited enough to send us back there. Then one day, I guess it was in the late spring/early summer of 2000, we got a call from a local vicar expressing concern about the disappearance of a young woman. He referred to her as "one of the Russian brides" who, he said, had been living at the farm for the past couple of years. *Years.* Not months, which was how long most of them seemed to stay. This one, apparently, had been there the whole time since the surveillance was called off, maybe even longer. Obviously the vicar didn't know anything about the Met operation that had targeted the house, but he was able to tell us that the young woman – he didn't know her name – had a child and no one had seen them for the past several weeks.'

CRISTY: 'Did he say why he was concerned about her?'

CATHERINE: 'I think mainly because of the child, and how long the young woman had been there – and then suddenly she wasn't.'

CRISTY: 'So what happened after you received the vicar's call?'

CATHERINE: 'We went to have a chat with Symmonds-Browne, asked about the mother and child and, would you believe it, he started to cry. Proper threw us, that did. Sobbed and blubbered like a great big kid saying she'd gone back to wherever she'd come from and she'd never got in touch with him again. It was all an act, of course, but it worked, because it got rid of us well enough.'

CRISTY: 'Was any follow-up done on it? No, first, did he tell you the names of the woman and child?'

CATHERINE: 'I wouldn't have remembered, but it's in the file. She was Janina Andris and the child was Sasha.'

Cristy broke off for a moment, the surprise of hearing the names resonating deeply and almost electrifyingly through her. She glanced at Connor and saw it had affected him too. It was all real, this confirmed it, not that they'd seriously doubted it – Robert and Gita's interviews didn't allow for that – but even if they'd continued to have concerns they were dispelled by this. Janina and Sasha had lived at Mannycott Farm in Kylve. She had almost definitely been a so-called Russian bride, even if it wasn't her true nationality. Sasha's father . . . could have been anyone.

After making several quick notes for herself, she continued.

CRISTY: 'Was the mother and child's disappearance investigated?'

CATHERINE: 'Not that I ever knew about. Our higher-ups got in touch with the Met and we were told no further action was necessary. Whether that was because the mother and child really had returned to their homeland, or because they didn't want to waste resources trying to find illegals, I can't say.'

CRISTY: 'And you knew they were illegals?'

CATHERINE: 'They would have been then, if they were from one of the Eastern European countries, and the vicar seemed to think they were.'

Cristy turned to Connor to see if there was anything he wanted to add.

CONNOR: 'Do you have any idea where George Symmonds-Browne could be now?'

CATHERINE: 'For all I know he's still at the same address. If not, you'll find the names of his blue-blood family in the file, maybe they can put you in touch with him.'

CONNOR: 'Does the name Lukas Andris ring any bells for you?'

CATHERINE: 'No, I don't think so. What was he, a relative of the mother and child?'

CONNOR: 'Brother and uncle.'

After the recording was over and Connor was packing up the equipment, Catherine said to Cristy, 'I heard the first episode of your new series, so I'm going to assume that Sadie Winters is the Sasha I just mentioned?'

'It's looking very likely,' Cristy replied. Then, 'Do you happen to recall anything about the Winters sisters being on Exmoor back in 2000?'

Catherine wrinkled her nose as she thought. 'I'm not sure I've ever heard of them. Who are they? Oh, hang on, were they a couple of wealthy Londoners who holidayed at Hilltop Lodge . . . That's right, I remember them getting a few tongues wagging for a while, something to do with them being there one day and gone the next.' Her eyes narrowed suspiciously. 'If I'm reading this correctly, you're thinking they took the child with them when they left?'

Meeting the direct question with a slightly less direct answer, Cristy said, 'It's looking that way.'

'And now what you're trying to find out is if they had some sort of arrangement with Symmonds-Browne or one of his . . . suppliers, to make the child theirs?'

'Do you think it's possible?' Connor asked.

The detective gave a mirthless laugh. 'I never put anything past anyone, not after the things I saw when I was with the police. In this instance . . . Well, let's say, there's certainly a coincidence of events and times that warrants further enquiries, which is of course what you're doing.' She went further. 'My best guess is that someone made your girl Janina disappear so your sisters could have the child they wanted.'

Wishing they could have got that on tape, while also knowing they'd be unable to air it, or certainly not at this stage, Cristy thanked her warmly and followed Connor out to the car.

As they drove away, she said, 'So where do you think Janina's knowledge of the sisters fits in with this? I'm thinking of Robert's interview now.'

'God knows,' Connor replied. 'But it's looking increasingly likely that Lottie's beach story is nonsense. And if that is, what about everything else?'

As neither of them had an answer several minutes passed with the Chew Valley and its winter-sunlit lakes falling away behind them until a sprawling vista of Bristol opened up ahead. 'Let's call Clove and Jacks,' Cristy said, taking out her phone. 'If they're still in Minehead they can swing by Kylve on their way back to find out if Symmonds-Browne is still at Mannycott Farm.'

'And if he is?'

'They should leave it to us to go talk to him. If he's no longer there, maybe they can start work on where he might be now. Also, we need to check the files Catherine Shilling just gave us for the vicar's name. If he's still around he could be worth a few words. They can handle that themselves once we've briefed them.'

Fifteen minutes later, with Clove and Jacks on their way to Kylve, and all sorts of scenarios still flashing through their minds, Connor said pensively, 'I can't stop wondering, given the suddenness of Lottie's death and the fact that no more extracts have yet come to light . . . I'm asking myself, did someone get to her before she could write any more?'

Cristy frowned. 'Talk me through that.'

'Frankly, I don't know where to go with it, apart from the obvious place.'

She glanced at him, her hands tightening on the wheel. 'You mean Mia?'

He nodded soberly.

'That doesn't make any sense when the story is designed to cast them as rescuers of a child from social services, rather than anything more . . . sinister. She surely wouldn't have had a problem with that.'

'It was still illegal to hold onto the child, and maybe Mia found the rest of the story and . . . destroyed it? She wouldn't want any of it getting out for the very reason she's facing now: Sadie is looking into it and wants to know more.'

Slowing as they reached the Ashton Gate traffic lights, Cristy said, 'And we know that Lottie's computers were disposed of quite soon after her death. Was that Mia's way of making sure nothing more came to light?'

'Seems a reasonable conclusion to me.'

'There must have been a post mortem following Lottie's death. We'll get Jacks onto it.' She thought about it some more and added, 'I think we should keep this to ourselves for now, at least until we've got something a bit more substantial to work with.'

'Clove and Jacks?'

'Obviously we'll share with them, but at this stage it's absolutely not something to share with Sadie.'

# CHAPTER SIXTEEN

'Sadie was very upset about the way she deceived you,' Robert was telling Cristy the next morning as they enjoyed a coffee together at Côte Brasserie in Clifton. He'd rung late yesterday, after returning to Bristol following the reunion between his mother and Sadie, and his suggestion that they meet today had raised Cristy's spirits in a way she didn't care to examine too closely. She was just glad to see him.

'She feels foolish and ashamed,' he continued, 'and says she acted immaturely when she should have trusted you from the start.'

'And you said?' Cristy prompted, liking the avuncular amusement in his eyes.

'I told her she was right, that she should feel all those things and that perhaps she should go out and shoot herself to show proper remorse.'

Cristy choked on a laugh. 'I know you didn't say that, but I hope you didn't let her off the hook too readily.'

He smiled. 'From where I was sitting she looked a lonely, mixed-up kid who's desperate not to be hurt while knowing she's probably going to be.'

Impressed and touched by his insight, she said, 'I think you're right about that. How did she react to seeing your mother?'

'She wept, quite a lot, and Gita was wonderful with her, as she is with most people. Have you seen the video?'

'Not yet, but it's ready for me to view when I get to the office.'

'You're working today? It's Saturday.'

'We're prepping the next episode ready for Tuesday. Music,

sound effects, last-minute edits. You remember it features your interviews?'

'I do, and I'm ready to embrace the fame. Will you use any of the reunion?'

'I'm sure of it, given how pumped-up Clove and Jacks are about it. Incidentally, they're looking into ways of adopting your mother – and from what I can tell Gita is looking into ways of adopting Sadie?'

Laughing, he said, 'It had quite an effect on her seeing the small child she remembers from so long ago all grown-up and quite lovely now. When you watch you'll see how she kept touching her face and gazing at her as if she was some sort of angel come back to life. I can't recall her ever looking at me that way.'

Amused and liking his evident love for his mother, Cristy said, 'How was Sadie with you?'

He gave it a moment's thought before answering. 'A little shy at first, but she warmed up when we went through the photos together. She really is astonishingly like her mother . . . There was no mention of her father. Have you made any progress with that?'

'Not on who he was, exactly, but we do know now where Janina was living at the time you met her.'

He raised an eyebrow with interest.

'It was in a farmhouse, near Kylve, that was under police surveillance for a while . . . I'm afraid it was all gang- and trafficking-related, and part of a much bigger organized crime network. Anyway, the man who lived at the farm – one George Symmonds-Browne – is no longer there, so before we go knocking on the Met's door for whatever they're prepared to give us, we're working on tracking him down.'

'Are you thinking he's Sadie's father?'

'There were so many men coming and going from that place back then, traffickers, punters . . . It might well end up proving impossible to find out who the real father is. We're hoping to have more luck with the uncle, now we have his name and something that resembles a lead.' She sipped her coffee and continued. 'Our detective told us that the girls had seemed to have a certain amount of freedom while they were at the farm, which would tie in with Janina's visits to Minehead to see her brother.'

As Robert took this in he leaned forward to pick up his cup, his large, olive-skinned hand closing around it and making her think of what he did for a living. It was both easy and hard to see him as a surgeon. Certainly he'd be one with a good bedside manner, while the thought of such strong, masculine fingers working on such a delicate and vital part of the human body made her feel oddly light-headed.

'What I'm thinking about now,' he said, seeming unaware of her scrutiny, 'is the day I came across Janina in the woods, when she was so upset. She never did tell me what was wrong, but if she was planning to give Sadie up, or to leave her for a while . . . The note said—'

'I should probably tell you,' Cristy interrupted, 'strictly between us of course, that we've begun asking ourselves if the beach scene was real. If it wasn't, it obviously calls into question the note's authenticity.'

His eyebrows rose in apparent surprise.

'It could have been written by one of the aunts as part of an elaborate plan to explain why they kept the child. In other words to throw any future investigation off the scent by carefully constructing a plausible alternative to how Sadie came to them – if you can describe it as plausible, and I'm not entirely sure about that. We're considering the possibility that they actually "arranged" to have the child brought to them while they were in Somerset.'

He frowned. 'By whom?'

'A singularly unpleasant individual called Matis Albescu, or one of his thugs, and initial research shows that there were plenty of them from all over Eastern Europe. Albescu himself was Romanian, and is known to have brought girls to George Symmonds-Browne at Mannycott Farm around the time Janina was there. We're thinking he could have been behind her trafficking and that one of his operatives, or maybe Symmonds-Browne himself, made a deal with Lottie for the child.'

Robert's expression was solemn as he shook his head in dismay. 'To think she could have been going through all that when I met her,' he murmured. 'Hardly surprising that she didn't mention it, she'd have been too afraid to if they were threatening her family back home. Were they?' he asked, looking at Cristy again.

‘It seems likely, although we know her brother was in Minehead at the same time as she was. Obviously that doesn’t mean there weren’t others back in Romania, or wherever they were from, and it still could have been anywhere. The good news is that we now know the brother’s name, largely thanks to you. And according to one long-time resident of Kylve who used to be the vicar there – our researchers interviewed him while they were down that way – a young man in a “rakish sort of trilby hat” was a regular visitor to the farm. He – the vicar – remembers Janina and the “hatted man” combing the beach for fossils that the little girl collected in a bucket. Unfortunately, no one knows at this point exactly what Lukas’s role might have been in Albescu’s set-up, but he clearly wasn’t making a secret of his association with Symmonds-Browne. As we know, he seems to have left the area around the same time as his sister, and the vicar thinks it was sometime in May 2000, which is when Lottie claims they “found” Sadie on the beach.’

‘Did the vicar ever see “the hatted man” with just the child and no Janina?’

‘A very good question. Let me know if you’re ever in need of a job. Fortunately Clove thought to ask it, and he thinks it’s possible, but it was so long ago he can’t be certain. I guess you’re wondering if Lukas delivered his niece to the sisters, and maybe picked up the money?’

He nodded.

‘A horrible thought, but where men like that are concerned nothing can be ruled out. On the other hand, he might have taken her there, because he knew what happened to the children of girls in captivity, and so this was his way of saving his niece from a life of servitude or worse.’

‘In which case he’s more of a hero than a villain. I can see that sitting a lot better with Sadie than the alternative.’

‘Of course, but whichever way we look at it, I’m afraid that finding either him or Janina is not going to prove at all straightforward.’

‘And could end in terrible disappointment.’

‘Indeed.’

Robert checked the time and said, ‘I hate to say this, but I need to be going. Am I allowed to ask for a repeat get-together?’

She smiled. 'I don't see a problem with that. And if, by any chance, you should be interested in helping us to go through some of the boxes Sadie and Jasper brought with them . . .'

'What do they contain?'

'Lottie's papers, journals, photographs, short stories . . . Decades of the stuff apparently, and in no particular order. If nothing else they might help us to gain a better insight into the woman herself and whether or not she was as scheming and cold-blooded as we've currently cast her.'

'But don't you get the impression the aunts cared for Sadie?'

'Yes, I do, they just don't appear to have provided her with any real sort of anchor. In a material sense, yes, without question. But a true understanding of a child's needs, of her cultural heritage and what it might mean to her . . . You have to say that was missing.'

He glanced at the time again, and rose to his feet, gesturing for Cristy to stay where she was. 'I'm sorry to dash – I'll get this – but do count me in for some box searching, probably not this week though. I'm going to be in Geneva until Thursday, back here sometime on Friday. Obviously I'm contactable if you feel I can help with anything at a distance.'

'And maybe next time we have coffee,' she said, 'you can tell me more about you?'

He grinned. 'It's a deal. Sorry to bail on you now, but it's been great to see you.'

After he'd gone Cristy remained where she was, her thoughts seeming to follow him as she wondered where he was going, who he was meeting . . . Maybe his daughter, a colleague, an old friend . . . There was no denying that he intrigued her quite a lot more than many people had of late. He'd also, bizarrely, left her feeling glad she'd messaged David last night, instead of worrying if she did so she might not hear back.

*There was no need for you to apologize, but thanks anyway. No harm done. Anna told me about what happened with Ludo. I hope Rosie is feeling better by now. Please send her my love. Just wondering how you're getting on re the Winters sisters' financial situation? Cx*

No word from him so far this morning, and she wished she

could stop checking just in case. Fortunately, the past hour with Robert had been a very welcome distraction, and there was such a lot to get through today regarding the next pod that there was a good chance she'd go for hours without thinking about him again today.

'I thought it was you.'

She looked up and her heart immediately somersaulted. 'Matthew,' she declared, as if one of them might have forgotten his name. 'I wasn't expecting to see you.'

'No, I guess you weren't,' he said, pulling out a chair to join her. 'So who was the guy who just left? You seemed to be getting along very well. Don't tell me you've joined Tinder already. Didn't think it would be your style.'

Keeping her voice low, she said, 'Could you please fuck off.'

He laughed, and his smile immediately reminded her of why so many people were drawn to him. 'I know you don't mean that . . .'

'I do.'

'. . . so I've taken the liberty of ordering you another coffee.'

She would have got up and left, but they were already attracting attention thanks to who he was. The last thing she wanted was to find herself back in the press as an object of pitying speculation.

'So have you?' he asked.

'Have I what?'

'Joined a dating site now that Mr Guernsey is no longer on the scene.'

'There are times,' she told him quietly, 'when I'd like to smash your face in and this is one of them.'

He laughed again. 'I love that I can still inspire such passion in you,' he told her cheerily.

Her look was deadly.

'OK, so not a date?' he ventured.

'Not that it's any of your business,' she retorted, 'but he's helping with the new series. How're Marley and Bear?'

He seemed to sink a little at that. 'They're doing OK, I think. She asked me to tell you that she understands you might be finding it difficult to know what to say to her now she's had my baby, but maybe it would help if you could think of him as yours too.'

Cristy stared at him, dumbfounded.

He shrugged.

'That woman is certifiable,' she stated. 'She surely doesn't think . . . Actually she does think I want to be part of your family, so please can you disabuse her of that idea?'

'I'm doing my best, but it's not easy when I want you to be involved too.'

Her eyes closed in despair. She couldn't allow herself to get drawn into this or she'd end up as crazy as they were. Changing the subject she said, 'Where's Aiden?'

'Cardiff, checking out a new band, back tonight or tomorrow. Haven't you heard from him?'

'Not for a couple of days. Has Hayley told you about her relationship issues?'

He grimaced. 'Do you think I should call her?'

'For God's sake, Matthew, why are you asking me? You never used to be like this . . .'

'Like what?'

'I don't know, pathetic, unable to make decisions for yourself. I'm not your mother, any more than I'm your wife, so please stop asking me what you should do in any given situation. Especially where Marley is concerned.' She glanced up as a server put two steaming Americanos on the table. 'I really don't want that,' she said when they were alone again.

He came over so helpless at the prospect of her leaving, so ridiculously at a loss, that she grudgingly set aside the urge to abandon him. It might be satisfying for her to have everyone think she'd walked out on him, but it would be embarrassing for him. So, for the next ten minutes or so, she chatted with him about his work, how busy he'd been lately which, apparently, was why he hadn't been in touch, until inevitably they came back to Marley.

'Would you think the worst of me if I cut all ties?' he asked, staring at a sugar pack as he emptied it into a saucer. 'Not financially, obviously, I'll pay what I have to towards Bear's upkeep . . .'

'Upkeep! He's not a car . . .'

'You know what I mean. I'll do the child maintenance thing and set up a savings account for him. I'll even have him for holidays if she wants me to, but I just can't be married to her any more.'

'You need to tell her that, not me.'

'I intend to, the next time I'm there. I'd do it via FaceTime, just to get it over with, but Aiden called me a disgusting name for even considering it.'

Proud of her son, Cristy said, 'When are you planning to go?'

'In a couple of weeks, I guess. Or I could delay until you've finished this series and maybe you'd consider coming with me. We could go on to Hawaii after or . . . OK, you're not on board for it.'

Shaking her head in disbelief, she said, 'You know, sometimes with you I feel as though I've gone right through the looking glass and there'll never be a way back. I used to understand you, I could even guess what you were thinking, but now . . . I have to put it down to Marley's influence because you're clearly as delusional as she is.'

'That's a no then?'

In spite of herself she laughed. 'Come on, finish that coffee and we'll leave together. Then I have to get to the office.'

'Any chance of meeting up later?' he asked, once they were out on the street.

'Zero,' she smiled, and planting a quick kiss on his cheek she hurried off towards the Downs to find her car.

*

*Anna tells me you might be coming to Guernsey soon. You know you're welcome to stay here. We'd all love to see you. Sending info re Winters financial affairs via email. Sorry it took a while. Hope it's OK to say this, but I miss you. David x*

Jodi looked up from the message, eyes shining with delight. 'I always said it wasn't over between you,' she declared.

'The point,' Cristy responded, hefting the baby onto her other shoulder, 'is that his relationship with Juliette isn't over. And saying he misses me doesn't actually mean anything.'

'He's invited you to stay with him,' Connor pointed out, coming to refill her wine glass.

'That'll be his mother's doing, but even if he wants me there what good can come of it? Actually, don't answer that. It's been a long day thanks to digging into all the Albescu stuff this afternoon –

God I felt like I needed a shower by the time we'd finished. Time to relax now, and talking about David, or Matthew . . .'

'Or Robert,' Connor quickly put in. 'You still haven't told us about this morning . . .'

'Because there's nothing to tell,' Cristy cried with a laugh. 'It was just coffee and we talked about Sadie and the series the entire time. So, will you please stop trying to create a drama out of a void and talk me through the email David sent about the Winters sisters' finances.'

With a roll of his eyes, Connor sank back down on the sofa with Jodi and, slipping an arm around her, he said, 'They're basically stinking rich, have got wealth managers working for them all over the planet, directed from London, and have a strong preference for so-called ethical investments and biomedical research. Everything's run by their trusty advisers at Crosswell Haigh in the City who liaise with bankers, lawyers and finance analysts, all appointed by CH and approved by the sisters' chief lawyer, Victor Dubois. Apparently, Dubois has divulged something interesting in his report, but David is still waiting to hear if he can share.'

'Did he give any sense of what it might be?'

'No, and I haven't been back to ask. I figured he'll get in touch himself as soon as he has an answer. Anyway, I think we can safely say we won't be receiving any historical bank statements or records of dubious investments circa 2000–2001, which is what we'd really like to see.'

'Do you honestly think,' Jodi said, 'that there would be an official record of a trafficking transaction? I've no idea how these things work, but I'd say much more likely is that the payment was made by a third – or forty-third – party. So, in other words, in a way that could never be traced to them. That's even if such a payment was actually made, though I know we're assuming for the moment that it was.'

Knowing she was right, Cristy rested a cheek against Aurora's downy head and thought, fleetingly, of Matthew's baby son in LA. He'd probably smell and feel much the same and would be every bit as vulnerable and adorable and scrumptious as the dear little soul she was holding now.

'Well,' she said, 'it's going to be interesting to find out what this Victor Dubois has told David, presuming he's willing for us to know. Seems odd that he'd mention it if he wasn't. Is he Guernsey-based, do we know?'

'I'm sure we can find out,' Connor replied, stifling a yawn. 'So what's your current thinking on a trip to the island?'

Wishing she had better control of her heart flips, Cristy said, 'You mean to speak to Corny the housekeeper? It'll have to wait until Sadie's back there. I think she and Jasper are leaving on Tuesday so maybe the end of next week. Are you going to come?'

Looking at Jodi, Connor said, 'How would you feel about that?'

'I think I'll cope. Will you take up David's offer to stay at *Papillon*?' she asked Cristy.

Sighing over her nerves, Cristy said, 'I'm not sure. Maybe it would be best for us to check into the Cobo Bay Hotel, Con. It's close to where Corny lives and as nowhere is that far away on the island we'll be fairly well placed for any other interviews we can fit in. Anyway, a lot will depend on what happens between now and then. If we can trace George Symmonds-Browne, or Hilary Stokes, the ex-bar manager at Butlin's, they could be a priority. And we're still keen to speak to the elusive Edwin Prosser.'

'Frustrating that Jacks isn't making any headway with him,' Jodi commented. 'Do you think he's deliberately avoiding you?'

'Highly possible,' Cristy replied. 'But is he likely to know where Janina is? There's nothing to say he even knew she existed.' She sighed and resettled the baby. 'If someone, anyone, could steer us in the direction of where Janina might be, or even to a place that might ultimately lead to her, we'd be right there. I just can't see it happening with the way things are right now.'

'However, we know from experience,' Connor said, stretching out his legs and exposing his hairy midriff, 'that anything can change at any time and the next thing we know we'll be charging off down avenues we never even knew existed, never mind didn't see coming.'

# CHAPTER SEVENTEEN

CRISTY: '. . . You have just been listening to our interviews with Robert and Gita Brinkley, followed by Gita's reunion with Sadie Winters after twenty-three years. I think you'll agree that it was very moving, and if we put ourselves in Sadie's shoes for a moment, perhaps we can imagine how it must have felt to have this contact with Robert, who knew her mother.'

CONNOR: 'It goes without saying that if any of you happen to know Janina Andris, or her brother Lukas, either from that time or later, we'd love to hear from you. There are photographs of them on our website, but do bear in mind that they were taken over two decades ago.

'It's possible Janina and Lukas returned to their homeland sometime in 2000 or maybe later, so this is a particular shout out to our overseas followers. If you guys have any information you think might help Sadie to reconnect with her family please get in touch through the usual channels.'

CRISTY: 'We're also keen to speak to Edwin Prosser, Mia Winters' ex-husband – you'll be hearing more about him in our next episode when Sadie reads out another chapter of her aunt's story.'

CONNOR: 'Someone else we're trying to reach is Hilary Stokes who worked at Butlin's in Minehead during the time Lukas Andris was there. As a reminder that was sometime in the late Nineties, early 2000s.'

CRISTY: 'We also want to mention George Symmonds-Browne, who is thought to have been a key figure in Janina's life back at that time. I'm sure someone out there must know him, and if so, please be in touch.'

CONNOR: 'We'd like to thank everyone involved in the making of this podcast, our sponsors . . .'

Fading out the sound Connor looked across the room to Meena who was comfortably ensconced on the leather Chesterfield with Jodi and Aurora. Harry was perched on one arm, Clover on the other, while Cristy and Jacks were at their desks and Iz was busying herself filling glasses with champagne.

'Terrific episode,' Iz declared excitedly. 'Everyone's going to be looking for the missing people now so you're bound to find them.'

'The challenge,' Jacks quickly put in, 'will be sorting the nutters from the normal, and even the normals can be time-wasters or, worst of all, publicity seekers.'

Clearly taking this on board, Iz said decisively, 'I think we need to bring someone in to help with the social media feedback. I know it takes up a lot of your time which I'm sure is better spent on following leads rather than trying to find them.'

Cristy was impressed. This was probably the first sensible suggestion she'd heard from Iz, her PR strategy notwithstanding.

'Can we leave you to set that up?' Cristy asked, smiling as Iz handed her a drink.

'Indeed you can. There are specialists in the field who SLD have used in the past to great effect. I'll get onto it first thing tomorrow.'

'Cristy and Connor will still want to read their fan mail,' Clover informed her dryly. 'It's what keeps them going, knowing all about the sexual fantasies they're whipping up on a global level.'

'You're so funny,' Cristy retorted. 'Although I think it works for Connor.'

'Yeah right,' he grunted, 'live for it, I do. Thanks,' he said to Iz, almost smiling as she placed a glass on his desk and curtsied.

Glancing up from her adoration of the baby, Meena said,

'You didn't mention anything about trafficking in this episode. I thought you might.'

'We will, when the time is right,' Cristy replied, 'but there's no way Symmonds-Browne will be in touch if he thinks we're going to expose his connections to Albescu, which is why we haven't run the interview with Catherine Shilling yet either.'

'Who's Catherine Shilling?' Iz asked.

'The ex-detective sergeant we interviewed last week. We need to find Symmonds-Browne before we put it out there that he was involved in bringing girls into the country illegally or we don't stand a hope in hell of ever getting him to talk.'

'We know,' Connor continued, 'that he's related to aristocracy and we also know how they protect their own when scandal comes calling.'

'What level of aristocracy are we talking?' Harry asked.

'Near the top,' Cristy replied, 'but Symmonds-Browne is a distant cousin with no direct claim on the title himself.'

'Shame,' Harry retorted. 'That really would have been a killing if you could pin a duke-in-waiting or lowly prince to forced prostitution.'

'What does Sadie know about Symmonds-Browne and Albescu?' Meena asked. 'Have you told her anything yet?'

'Only that Symmonds-Browne lived at the farm while her mother was there,' Cristy answered. 'She leapt to the obvious conclusion that he might be her father, but now accepts how unlikely that actually is.'

'Because she knows her mother was probably trafficked into the country and forced into prostitution?'

Cristy nodded. 'Understandably it's made her feel very protective towards Janina who'd have been more or less the same age as Sadie is now when she came here.'

Iz said, 'If you can tell me what you know about Symmonds-Browne I'll see if SLD can help you get to him. We have a huge network of contacts, and a couple of our members are titled.'

Appreciative of the suggestion, Cristy quickly sent her an email with Symmonds-Browne's known details and said, 'Jacks! Are you still with us? What's happening on your screen that's so fascinating?'

Jacks looked up, shook his head and sat back in his chair. 'Just checking initial feedback,' he said, 'but nothing doing so far. I mean, good reviews, in the main, but no one offering leads to the mispers.'

'Mispers?' Iz queried.

'It's what the police call missing persons,' Clove explained.

Colouring, Iz said, 'Of course. Silly me. Anyone ready for a top-up?'

Harry got to his feet, saying, 'Time for me to go. I have a hot date tonight with your ex, Cristy. I told him to join us here for the party, but he thinks he's not welcome.'

'He isn't,' she assured him.

Laughing, Meena said, 'If those two are gallivanting about the town, maybe the rest of us can treat ourselves to a meal somewhere very expensive?'

'Count us in, wherever it is,' Jodi piped up. 'Little French? Though we might struggle to get in.'

'Leave it to me,' Iz instructed, and taking out her phone she made a few quick calls and said, 'OK, we can't get in.' As everyone laughed she said, 'But there's bound to be somewhere that'll take us at short notice on a Tuesday evening. It's your city, any more suggestions?'

In the end they opted for a Deliveroo from one of the best Indian restaurants outside of Mumbai according to Meena, and had it brought to Jodi and Connor's Southville town house so Aurora could be got ready for bed.

They were in the process of sorting out their chosen dishes when Jacks suddenly cried, 'Result! Or it looks like one anyway. I'll have to check it out, but it's from someone called James Prosser claiming to be the son of Edwin. He's just listened to the pod and found our email asking his dad to be in touch with us.'

'And?' Connor prompted when Jacks stopped. 'Please don't tell me the old guy's snuffed it.'

'No, he's not saying that . . . What he's actually saying is that his father wants nothing to do with us so can we please not mention his name again in relation to our podcast about the Winters sisters.'

Cristy and Connor exchanged glances. 'I'm guessing he doesn't go into why,' Cristy ventured.

'He doesn't,' Jacks confirmed.

Taking a quick decision, Cristy said, 'Send him the story extract where his father appears at the Exmoor house. Tell him it's due to be aired next week and this is us giving him the right to respond. Maybe that will change Prosser senior's mind about speaking to us.'

'On it,' Jacks said, 'but actually, Prosser junior is saying he'll consider talking to us in his father's place. Anyway, I'll suggest a Zoom, shall I? We don't want to be travelling all the way to the Outer Hebrides or furthest Scilly to find out he's not really going to tell us much anyway.'

'Good idea,' Cristy said, and checked her phone as it rang. Her eyebrows rose and, putting the call on speaker, she said, 'Sadie! Good to hear you. How was the drive back to Guernsey?'

'Pretty straightforward,' Sadie replied. 'We got in a couple of hours ago. I thought I should tell you that Mia's heard the latest pod and she's saying that the Brinkleys are liars, and that I'm an interfering little fool for being so easily taken in by charlatans.'

'OK,' Cristy responded, drawing out the word. 'And what did you say to that?'

'I reminded her that *she'd* told *you* she was protecting me from the past, so if the Brinkleys weren't part of it, maybe she'd like to tell me who was.'

'But you do believe Gita worked for them . . .'

'Of course, and that Robert met my mother. But there's no point arguing with my aunt when she's decided to go off on a rant about people trying to get money out of her and she's convinced that's what all this is about. Anyway, she said she was going to call you, I just wondered if she had.'

'Not yet,' Cristy replied, 'but I hope she does.'

'Where are you now?' Connor asked.

'I've just come up to the lodge. I hate leaving her when we've fallen out, but there was no getting through to her, so I'll try talking to her again in the morning.'

Silently wishing her good luck with that, Cristy said, 'Connor and I will probably be in Guernsey at the end of the week to speak to Corny. Are you still OK with setting that up?'

'Of course. And who knows, Mia might be up for talking to

you too. I wouldn't take any bets on it, but she's so unpredictable there's no knowing what she might do. Of course, there's always the possibility you'll hear from her lawyers threatening to sue you if you don't stop the podcasts.'

'We're kind of expecting it,' Cristy told her, 'but don't worry, we've got lawyers too and she can't shut us down as easily as she might think. I'll let you know if she gets in touch. Meantime, we've heard from Edwin Prosser's son who's said he might talk to us in his father's place. And, hang on . . .' she said, as Clover put a screenshot in front of her showing a tall, well-built man with a shock of dark hair and eyes shielded by sunglasses, looking over his shoulder as he walked through a grand-looking doorway. 'Is that . . .?'

'George Symmonds-Browne,' Clover finished. 'Catherine Shilling just sent it.'

Cristy studied the shot more closely, feeling something decidedly strange coming over her as she took in the way he seemed to be staring right at the camera as if threatening whoever was behind it. There was a woman next to him, short with fair hair, but in profile so it wasn't possible to make out her features. She didn't appear particularly young, probably mid-forties, and the same went for the other man in the shot, although his back was turned completely so there was no knowing what he looked like.

Clover was saying, 'Apparently Catherine Shilling asked someone, presumably still active in the force, to do some more digging on our behalf and they came up with this. She thinks it was taken in 2016, in a place called Vence, north of Nice, and could be connected to an investigation that was going on at the time into an organized crime network operating on the French Riviera.'

'Oh my God,' Sadie murmured.

'I'll give Catherine Shilling a call,' Cristy said, 'and get back to you if she can tell me any more.'

After ringing off she checked the time and decided it wasn't too late to call Shilling now.

'Hi, I was expecting to hear from you,' Shilling said, as soon as she answered. 'I don't have anything else yet, hopefully tomorrow or the next day, but I expect you already know that the Côte d'Azur is as synonymous with criminal gangs as it is with the disgustingly rich.'

'How did you come by the photo?' Cristy asked.

'Apparently it turned up on the UK national database back in 2016, probably due to Symmonds-Browne's connection to the undercover operation in the late Nineties and early 2000s. It was most likely sent the Met's way for cross-referencing of some kind and got entered into the system. Anyway, I'm assured it's him, and I've already given you the location, so I'll get in touch again if I manage to find out more.'

As she ended the call, Cristy said, 'Better send the picture to Sadie.'

'We've got other shots of him,' Clover reminded her. 'Mainly from an old Facebook page that hasn't been touched since 2014, and nothing connecting him to anyone or anything much apart from a horse and a couple of dogs.'

'Have you got them there?' Cristy asked. 'We could run a comparison with this shot from the police files.'

'Easier done at the office,' Jacks informed her. 'I'll get onto it first thing.'

'And now we should eat,' Jodi and Meena declared in unison, surprising themselves and making the others laugh.

A couple of hours later, home at last and ready to crash, Cristy checked her phone as it rang and felt a thud in her heart when she saw it was David. Did she want to speak to him now? Yes, of course she did, why was she even asking herself the question?

'Hi,' she said, clicking on, 'this is a surprise.'

'I hope a welcome one,' he responded, 'and not too late?'

Assuming he meant the time of night, not a point in their relationship, she said, 'It's fine. By the way, thanks for sending the info about the finances. I'm not sure where it takes us—'

'It's a very broad overview,' he interrupted, 'and I'm afraid it probably won't get much better than that. Their dealings are extremely well protected, as is the case with most individuals of similar net worth. The managers at Crosswell Haigh wouldn't be doing their jobs if something dodgy could be sniffed out that easily.'

Sinking down on the edge of the bed, she said, 'You're a wealth manager. Do you break the rules for your clients?'

'You can't ask me that and expect a straight answer when there are so many ways of interpreting said rules, particularly in the finance world. Incidentally, this isn't why I'm calling, but I'm happy to carry on discussing it if it's something that interests you.'

The dryness of his tone made her smile and remember how much she enjoyed his irony. 'So why are you calling?' she asked, knowing what she wanted to hear, while dismayed with herself for hoping.

'I said in the email I sent with the finance report that Victor Dubois, the Winters sisters' lawyer, told me something interesting that I couldn't share until he cleared it.'

Disappointed and intrigued, she said, 'Has he given the go-ahead?'

'I'm afraid not. I'm bound by my word not to reveal what he said, but I don't have a problem with advising you to ask Sadie about Lottie's will.'

Giving that a moment, she said, 'OK, thanks. I guess you're not going to tell me whether or not it will change things.'

'I'll let you make up your mind about that once Sadie's given you an answer.'

There was a pause, an awkward silence that they suddenly tried to fill at the same time.

'You first,' he said.

'No, you. I was just going to thank you for the call.'

'You're welcome. And I was about to ask if you've made an arrangement to come to Guernsey yet?'

'We'll probably be there at the end of the week. I'm not sure at this stage how long we might stay.'

'We being you and Connor?'

'Yes. Oh, and thanks for offering to let us stay at *Papillon*. It's really kind of you, but it's probably best if we check into the Cobo Bay Hotel.'

'I think you'll find it's closed at this time of year.'

'Oh, well, there are other hotels, obviously. I don't want to offend your mother, or Rosie, I'd love to see them, but under the circumstances it wouldn't feel right for me to stay at the house. I'm sure your mum understands that.'

'OK, if that's your decision. Will you consider seeing me while you're here, just the two of us?'

'I . . .' What was the best way to answer that? 'Can I think about it?' she said. 'I just feel that we've . . .' What was she trying to say? Why weren't the words coming?

'Let me know when you're ready to talk,' he said, and the line went dead.

# CHAPTER EIGHTEEN

CRISTY: 'It's two days after our last drop, and while Clover and Jackson are back at the office digging through the boxes Sadie brought with her from Guernsey, Connor and I are in the car on our way to Malmesbury in Wiltshire to have a chat with Mia Winters' ex-husband, Edwin Prosser.'

CONNOR: 'Interestingly, when Mr Prosser's son first made contact with us, it was to say that his father wanted nothing to do with the pod. However, we got a message last night saying that Edwin was prepared to be interviewed after all.'

CRISTY: 'It could be you'll never hear any of what we're recording now if the interview turns out to be a waste of time, but if Mr Prosser is willing to discuss his marriage to Mia Winters, and what Lottie's written about him, we'll certainly be interested to hear it.'

Connor hit the stop button and said, 'What sort of a link was that?'

Cristy sighed. 'Not a very good one. Sorry. Shall we try it again?'

With a quick check of the satnav he said, 'Maybe let's wait until we know what the guy has to say. We're nearly there now.'

He indicated to leave the M4 at junction 17, and slowed at the exit roundabout to turn north towards Malmesbury. 'Is it the looming trip to Guernsey that's getting to you?' he asked, coming straight to the point.

She glanced at him, sighed again and said, 'Yes, but not entirely for the reasons you're thinking. I'm concerned that we haven't heard from Sadie since yesterday morning when she messaged to say she'd received the picture of Symmonds-Browne.'

'Were you expecting her to say something in particular about it?'

'I'm not sure, but I emailed our flight details last night and asked her to confirm she had things set up with Corny, but no reply to that either. You don't think Mia's locked her up again, do you?'

'Why not give Anna a quick call and ask if she knows what's going on over there?'

'I've already sent a text. She can't get hold of Sadie either, so she's calling back as soon as she's been to the villa. That was just before we started out so . . .' Cristy checked the time, 'about forty minutes ago. Too soon to chase her. I'll do it when we've finished with Prosser.'

They drove on in silence for a while, each with their own thoughts about the series and its many tangled threads, where they were going to lead, how they should be unravelled – until Cristy found herself reflecting on the message she'd received from Robert Brinkley.

*Listened to the latest pod last night. I hope our interviews have helped move things on a way for you, and Sadie, maybe too soon to tell. Wish there was more Mum and I could do, but I fear our roles in the past were more incidental than informative. Still, at least we were able to provide names and share a few memories with Sadie. I think they mattered to her.*

*Returning from Geneva late tomorrow. There's a fundraiser for MSF at Merchant's House on Saturday evening, yours truly one of the speakers. Wondered if you'd consider being my guest?*

At a fancy dinner in a super-smart location for many of Bristol's elite? Him in black tie, her in a sparkly dress with her hair pinned up in a chic-messy-style, and their eyes meeting over glasses of champagne. An evening full of easy laughter and who knew what else . . .

She couldn't go, of course, and not only because he was married and she might be going to Guernsey. Matthew had already asked her to be his plus-one at the very same event. The coincidence, coupled with the sheer absurdity of it . . . She was sure if she told Connor he'd laugh out loud.

She was right, he did.

'I swear to God,' he cried, slapping the steering wheel, 'if we did a series about your love life we'd triple the ratings.'

'You're so funny,' she told him darkly.

'I'm glad you think so. Does Meena know about this?'

'Of course not, and please don't tell her. I'm having a hard enough time trying to sort things out in my head . . . Not that there's anything to sort out. I'm obviously not going to the dinner with Matthew so he can get everyone speculating on us being back together, but if I turn him down I can't go with Robert either. Not that I would, it feels too much like a date for me to consider it, and even if it's not, it'll look like one and that would just be a slap in the face for Matthew. For Robert's wife as well, who he's probably not planning to cheat on. I just don't want anyone thinking that's what's happening and everyone will, because he's so gorgeous why wouldn't I want to flaunt him in Matthew's face after what Matthew did to me?'

Still entertained, Connor said, 'Who knew life could get so complicated for a singleton approaching fifty? I reckon most women your age would kill to have just one man interested in them, and you have *three*.'

'If you're including David in that . . .'

'Of course I am, and you should see him on your own when we go. What harm can it do?'

'The same sort of harm I might do you if you make one more jibe about my age.'

He let the silence run for a moment, then glancing at her said, 'You're keen to go really, aren't you? I mean with Robert.'

Having to admit it, she said, 'If the circumstances were different, then maybe. He's great company and I imagine he's a really good speaker.'

'Then go. He hasn't said it's a date and has he done anything else to make you think he'd like to . . . you know, get you into some horizontal dancing?'

Wrinkling her nose, she said, 'What kind of an expression is that?'

He shrugged. 'I think it's commonly called a euphemism, but if you'd like me to spell it out . . .'

'No thanks. And the answer's no, he has not made any overtures of that sort, I'm just . . . Well, let's leave it that he's married, OK? Shall we change the subject now and concentrate on where we're going?'

'No probs, but just tell me this, what would you say if David was inviting you?'

Trying not to be annoyed, she said, 'As Matthew's going to be there, the answer would be the same. Now, it's saying to take the next left just up here and then we should probably be more or less there. Remind me again who we're going to see?'

Clearly amused Connor followed directions to the address they'd been given and a few minutes later they were pulling up outside a double-fronted detached house, one of five in a small cul-de-sac, all with private driveways and fenced-off gardens.

'Is this where Edwin lives, or his son?' Cristy asked, as they got out of the car.

'Him, apparently. The son's got a place in town, but he's going to be here.'

'If he's from a second marriage he could be younger than Sadie.'

'If this is him coming to meet us I'd say he's about your age.'

Seeing a wiry man in his late thirties heading down the garden path, she had to smile. Connor was so droll.

'Cristy! Connor!' James Prosser cried warmly, as they got out of the car. 'Good to meet you. I hope it's all right to use your first names.'

'Of course,' Cristy responded, as they shook hands. He seemed quite a nice man all told, kindly eyes, good smile, a little grey at the temples, and was apparently a bit of a toff given his jaunty cravat and plummy voice.

As he greeted Connor she tried to figure out where he might actually fit into Edwin's pantheon of past-players. He clearly predated Mia's marriage to his father, which was twenty-odd years ago, so maybe Edwin had had several wives along the way, or just several children with various mothers. It hardly mattered, they were only interested in his relationship with Mia, or, more pertinently, in what had happened after he'd stumbled across Sadie and been given his marching orders.

'Dad's waiting inside,' James told them jovially. 'I've made coffee, but tea's just as easy if you prefer.'

'Coffee's fine,' Connor assured him, going first along the garden path.

Cristy stopped at the gate, checking her phone. 'If you'll excuse me a moment,' she said, 'I need to take this,' and receiving a pleasant smile from James Prosser, she turned back towards the car.

'Anna? Is everything OK?' she asked.

'Yeah, it's all cool,' Anna assured her. 'Sadie's right here, just back from the hospital . . .'

'What?'

'They thought Mia had a stroke last night, but turns out it wasn't that serious, just a weird sort of turn or something. Here, I'll put Sades on . . .'

'Hey, Cristy,' Sadie said, coming onto the line. 'Sorry I'm only just getting back to you. It's been a bit frantic. We thought we were going to lose her, but false alarm and she's home again now. She has to go back for more tests later, but Corny's just turned up to make a fuss of her, which'll probably drive her mad. And if Corny ends up staying it could screw things up a bit for you coming tomorrow.'

Closing her eyes with frustration, Cristy said, 'OK, well, keep me posted and if we have to change our flights . . .'

'No probs, but I was hoping to catch you before you speak to Edwin Prosser. Are you there yet?'

'Just arrived. Why? Has Mia told you something about him?'

'No. I haven't even mentioned you're going to see him, or that I found a letter from him before she keeled over last night. It was written to Lottie and I think you should read it before you talk to him. Jasper's scanning it now ready to send.'

'Give me the bullet points,' Cristy urged.

'OK, well, he addresses her as bitch-sister, so definitely no love lost between them, and he goes on to say that if she doesn't meet the terms he laid out in his last letter she knows what will happen. Nothing to say what the terms were, or what they're about, just the threat of doing something if she doesn't agree to whatever he's asking for.'

'Is there a date on the letter?'

'July ninth, 2000. Now listen to this, Lottie – I presume it was her anyway – has scrawled across it, *Non-negotiable.* Whether she wrote back to him to that effect, I've no idea, but I thought you should know about it before you go in.'

'OK, thanks. Get Jasper to send it, and I'll pick it up on the phone. Let me know how things go with your aunt and Corny.'

'Will do. By the way, she told the doctor I'm trying to kill her, and now she's banned me from Lottie's rooms.'

Wondering how Sadie was managing to sound so unfazed by the chaos, Cristy said, 'Well, we've got a lot of stuff at the office, and I'm sure you'll find a way around it.'

'Oh, I will. Don't worry.'

'I need to go now. I'll call when we're on our way back to Bristol.'

As she rang off Cristy forced herself past the disappointment of having to delay the trip to Guernsey and only recalled David's suggestion that she should ask Sadie about Lottie's will as she was walking towards the house. It was too late now, and anyway it wasn't the time while everything was going on with Mia.

'Ah, there you are,' James Prosser smiled, as she entered the hall. 'We're just getting comfortable in here.' He directed her towards a set of double doors to the left and as she walked into a spacious drawing room she felt her phone vibrate. Presumably the email Sadie had promised.

'Thanks,' she said, as James Prosser took her coat. She looked around the room, taking in a faux log burner at the heart of a red-brick fireplace and various lamps switched on to help brighten the gloomy day. Rising from a comfy chair to greet her was an older man with sparse white hair and a similar cravat to his son's.

'Edwin Prosser,' he said, reaching for her hand. 'Thank you for coming all this way. I was just saying to Connor, I don't get many visitors these days, apart from James and my grandchildren, so new faces are always welcome.'

He was nothing like the runtish or weaselly individual she'd imagined, thanks to Lottie. To the contrary, in fact. Though he had to be in his late seventies, maybe even early eighties, it was easy to see how handsome and dapper he'd been in his day. His eyes, like his son's, were kind and welcoming, as was his smile, and in spite of his apparently frail physique, he stood quite tall. She wondered what he'd thought of Lottie's description of him when he'd read it, if it had angered or upset him, or not surprised him at all.

'It's good to meet you,' she said. 'Thanks for agreeing to talk to us.'

He nodded and gestured for her to sit in a wing-back armchair next to his, while James poured the coffee and Connor began unpacking the equipment.

'Can I ask,' Cristy said, 'why you changed your mind about being interviewed?'

Edwin's eyes went down as he bunched his gnarled hands together. 'Those years, when I was with Mia,' he said, 'I'm not proud of what happened back then, of who I was and the things I did. For over two decades it's been behind me and I've chosen not to think of it, or to talk to anyone about it.' He reached for a framed photograph on the table beside him and stared down at it for a moment before passing it to Cristy. 'This is my wife, Yolanda, James's mother. She died six years ago . . . She knew all about Mia, of course, and she forgave me when I really didn't deserve forgiveness at all.'

Looking at the sweet, open face of a woman in her prime who seemed to be flirting with the photographer, Cristy said, 'She's lovely.'

'Yes, she was. We still miss her and I don't think it'll change, at least not for me. Will you take milk or sugar?'

Glancing to the coffee James was holding out, she took the mug, saying, 'Black is fine, thanks.'

She watched as James stirred two lumps into his father's World's Best Grandpa mug and passed it over.

'I'm going to tell you what I know,' Edwin said, 'for the girl's sake – Sadie? Is that her name? – and for no other reason. I'm afraid it will cast me in a very poor light, and to be honest I'd rather my grandchildren didn't know anything about how I behaved towards their dear grandma during those shameful times.'

'We've already agreed,' James came in gently, 'that we'll talk to them before this goes out. And they're quite grown-up now, at least they like to think they are,' he added wryly to Cristy, 'so I'm sure they'll be able to handle it.'

'How old are they?' she asked carefully. They weren't in the business of destroying someone's cred with their grandchildren – unless they deserved it of course.

'Fifteen and twelve,' James replied.

'They'll look at me differently,' Edwin said, 'and that'll be hard. On the other hand, they've had a very loving and stable upbringing, while Sadie . . . I've no idea what it's been like for her growing up with those sisters, but I do know that she deserves to get to the truth of who she really is.'

*

A few minutes later, carefully hiding her excitement and having received Edwin's permission to record, Cristy began by asking Edwin how he'd first met the sisters. Yes, they were keen to get to the crux of things, but backgrounds had a funny habit of throwing all sorts of unexpected and intriguing information into the mix.

> EDWIN: 'I used to own a wine shop on Kensington Church Street. The sisters were regular customers and we always enjoyed some banter when they came in. Lottie was especially flirtatious, while Mia was . . . quieter, not shy exactly, just not as extrovert as her sister. I, on the other hand, was a foolish and arrogant dupe who should have been able to see through what was going on, but I'm afraid I didn't, not at first anyway. All I saw was two rich women who seemed to like me, and then were prepared to share some of what they had with me. I was too stupid, too greedy to realize that I already had what really mattered – a woman, a wife, actually, who truly loved me, a son who needed me . . . but I was dazzled by those sisters. I'd never known anyone like them, especially Lottie. She was captivating, exciting, reckless, irresistible

and I was ready to do anything she asked of me. Including marry her sister.'

Cristy allowed a moment for the bombshell to drop for her and the listener before picking up again.

CRISTY: 'But you were already married?'

EDWIN: 'Indeed I was.'

Silence fell over the room as Edwin's rheumy eyes stared into the past, perhaps seeing all that he'd done, the people he'd clearly hurt and betrayed, and those who'd apparently done the same to him.

CRISTY: 'We'll get into the illegality of it in a minute, but tell me first, why did Lottie want you to marry Mia?'

Edwin nodded slowly, staring at the fire as he considered his response.

EDWIN: 'Mia wasn't a beauty. She didn't sweep people off their feet or even particularly interest them the way Lottie did. She existed in Lottie's shadow and was so terrified of losing her sister and being left all alone that Lottie thought it would be a good idea to make her a gift of me. That way Mia would have someone to call her own, and Lottie would be free to live the life she wanted.'

CRISTY: 'But surely they knew you were already married?'

EDWIN: 'Lottie did, but not Mia, and apparently she'd – to quote Lottie – developed a passion for me. I'm sure Mia wouldn't have gone through with anything if she'd known about Yolanda, but *inconveniences* such as an existing wife didn't matter to Lottie. If something stood in her way she simply removed whatever it was and carried on with no regard for what she might be leaving in her wake. Keen though I was to take her money, I made it clear that I didn't want to divorce Yolanda; but even that wasn't an obstacle for Lottie. She simply said that it would take too long anyway, so I should just go through a ceremony with Mia and we'd sort out the finer detail later. Oh, and of course I wasn't to mention anything to Mia about my wife. It would upset her, she said.'

Edwin gave a mirthless laugh, clearly still incredulous at the comment even now.

EDWIN: 'You're no doubt asking yourselves why on earth I agreed to it and the answer is Lottie was very persuasive, and very clear about the difference she was prepared to make to my life, financially.'

CRISTY: 'But how did you get away with it? Weren't the sisters quite well known in society circles?'

EDWIN: 'I don't know what they told their friends, it's possible they knew nothing about Yolanda anyway so no questions were asked.'

CRISTY: 'Did you tell Yolanda?'

EDWIN: 'Oh yes, she knew, and I can tell you she wasn't happy about it. Well, of course she wasn't. But I explained what Lottie's investment could do for us, how it would grow my business beyond our wildest dreams and make us comfortable for the rest of our lives. I assured her I'd pull out of the fake marriage once everything was in place, and she mustn't think I had any feelings for Mia because I didn't. It still hurts me terribly to remember what I put her through, and how much she suffered when she finally agreed to go along with it. The only surprise is that she didn't end up despising me as much as I despised myself.'

Edwin fell silent again and put a shaky hand to his mouth. It was clear that his emotions were getting the better of him. Cristy glanced at James expecting him to ask them to stop now, but he was staring at his father, not with disgust or condemnation, merely as though he pitied him for the weakness that had caused him to behave the way he had all those years ago.

Edwin's voice was hoarse as he continued to speak.

EDWIN: 'The whole time I was "married" to Mia I continued seeing Yolanda and James, regularly, and I was soon able to move them to a very nice house in Hammersmith. My official address, of course, was in Kensington, with Mia and Lottie, when Lottie was there, but she travelled a lot. I never liked being alone with Mia, and I certainly didn't treat her well. Looking back I was cruel to her and I'm not proud of that either. Of course, we were pawns in one of Lottie's grand schemes, not that I ever knew, or found out, what she was trying to achieve. It just seemed it was more than getting a husband for her sister so she could be free of her . . . I thought there might have been a man, but she never mentioned one and no one ever came to the house. In fact, I'm not sure she ever had any real feelings for anyone, apart from Mia, I guess. And I can't even swear to that.

'I'll come on to Sadie now and the first, the only time I saw her. To be honest my only real surprise when I found they had a child in the house was that she wasn't black or brown. I'd long suspected something like it would happen, that they'd somehow smuggle a child out of Africa or Asia and sort the legalities of it later. It was never going to be difficult for someone with Lottie's contacts and their resources. And it would be someone for Mia to call her own. It didn't occur to me until after I saw Sadie that of course they'd choose a white child, it would be so much easier to pass her off as a relative, a niece, the child of a distant cousin – that's what they tried to tell me – but I knew very well that the child was no relative of theirs.'

CRISTY: 'At this point we'll edit in some of what Lottie wrote about the day you went to the house on Exmoor, just to remind listeners of what happened. Is there anything about it you'd like to correct, or challenge . . . We can play it back for you if you like?'

EDWIN: 'No, it's fine. I don't need to hear it again. It happened more or less as she described. An ugly scene, that's for sure, there again nothing about my association with them was pretty.'

CRISTY: 'So what did you do after you left?'

EDWIN: 'I drove back to London with all sorts of madness going on in my head. Obviously I had no idea who the child really was, and to be honest I'm not sure I was of a mind to find out, only perhaps to use her to get myself out of their lives. Before I could come up with a plan Lottie was in touch to remind me that bigamy was an imprisonable offence and that would be just the beginning if I didn't take the offer she was about to make. Get out of Mia's life for good, never talk to anyone about my bigamous marriage, least of all Mia, and no mention should ever be made of the child. In return for my silence – I think she called it co-operation – I would become even wealthier than she'd already made me and my legitimate family would always be taken care of, should anything "untoward" ever happen to me.

'Of course I understood the threat, and I knew very well that she had ways of making things go her way that I wouldn't be able to stand up to. She told me once, "Never underestimate my reach, Edwin. I can become a dangerous enemy for someone like you." And I didn't doubt it. Beautiful, vivacious, wildly exotic and generous as she was, there was something very dark in her soul.'

CRISTY: 'So you agreed to her terms?'

EDWIN: 'Actually, not right away. I guess you could say greed got the better of me again, so there was a lot of back and forth over the next few weeks, me trying to get even more out of her than she was offering by threatening to tell Mia about Yolanda, or call social services about the child, but Lottie had all the cards and she knew it. I was never going to beat her and, to be honest, I was starting to become afraid of her. She kept bringing Yolanda and James into conversations or letters, never in an outright threatening way, she was too subtle for that, but I knew she wouldn't hold back on hurting them if I ever did anything to try and hurt her.'

Edwin sighed wearily and pressed his gnarled fingers to his eyes.

EDWIN: 'And that more or less concludes my association with the Winters sisters. A grim and reprehensible period of my life that feels now as though it happened to a stranger who has nothing to do with me . . . I only wish that were true.'

JAMES: 'I'd like to point out here that Dad has led a totally blameless life since, and has always been completely loyal to his family, as well as an engaged and respected member of his community. So I hope it's not too much to ask that he isn't judged on the very bad decisions he made more than a quarter of a century ago.'

Knowing it wasn't in her power to prevent that once his story was out there, and clearly he knew it too, Cristy turned back to Edwin. It made her sad to think of what his earlier crimes were likely to cost him at this late stage of his life. He might have deserved it once, but not any more. She'd discuss it with Connor, and see if there was a way to limit the damage. Meantime, she decided not to show him the letter Sadie had just brought to light. He'd addressed his attempt at blackmail, there was nothing to be gained from going over it again.

'Anything you want to add?' she asked Connor.

CONNOR: 'When you listened to the most recent podcast you'll have heard us talk about Janina and Lukas Andris. Do those names ring any bells for you?'

EDWIN: 'I'm afraid not.'

CONNOR: 'Were you ever aware of Lottie being in contact with, or having any dealings with Eastern European "businessmen", aka traffickers?'

EDWIN: 'I can't say I was, but who knew what she was doing during her overseas trips? I know what she wanted us to think, and I've every reason to believe she was involved in a lot of good work, but where Lottie's concerned I'd say almost anything is possible.'

Taking that as a perfect out, Cristy was about to thank Edwin for his honesty and insights when he spoke again.

EDWIN: 'What she wrote about finding the child on the beach . . . I don't believe it for a minute and I'd be surprised if you do.'

CRISTY: 'So how do you think they came by the child?'

EDWIN: 'That I don't know. I wish you luck in trying to find out.'

# CHAPTER NINETEEN

As they drove away from the cul-de-sac with James Prosser waving them off from the garden gate, Cristy said, 'It would have been inappropriate to ask what sort of pay-off was involved, wouldn't it?'

Checking the road was clear to pull out, Connor said, 'Probably, but I wouldn't mind knowing. Do you reckon it was in the millions?'

'I'd have thought so.'

'But he's not exactly living the high life now, is he?'

'I'd say he's comfortable enough. I mean, not everyone can afford a house like that, and maybe the bulk of what's left is squirrelled away for James and the grandkids. Anyway, he's given us a fascinating insight into Lottie's character which, interestingly, paints her in no more flattering a light than she painted him. Although he wasn't quite as spiteful in his descriptions as she was.'

'Do you believe what he told us?'

'I'm sure he wouldn't have outed himself as a bigamist if it weren't true.'

Nodding agreement, Connor said, 'I'm not sure we need to make a big deal of that. In fact, I think we should try to edit around it the best we can. It doesn't serve the series and would only diminish him in his grandchildren's eyes. That's not what we're about.'

'Exactly what I was thinking.'

'I can't help wondering,' he continued after a moment, 'if Mia ever discovered the role Lottie played in the marriage. That it was actually a sham.'

As she considered it Cristy's frown deepened. 'Are you sensing a theme here?' she said. 'Lottie buys her sister a husband, then a child . . . Apparently to get some freedom for herself, and yet she never seems to have left.'

'Something for Corny when we go over there?' he suggested.

Remembering that she hadn't had a chance to tell him about Mia's turn last night she filled him in and took out her phone. 'I promised to call Sadie when we left Edwin's. Keep your fingers crossed that Corny hasn't decided to stay on with Mia.'

'I'm really sorry,' Sadie groaned when Cristy asked. 'She's kind of planted herself, so I'm not sure coming now is going to be the best use of your time.'

Biting down on her frustration, and disappointment, Cristy said, 'So how is Mia?'

'She's up and about, ticking us off for making a fuss over nothing. "I'm not ready to join Lottie yet," she keeps saying, "so don't even think it." Fortunately, she seems to have forgotten about banning me from Lottie's rooms because it's where I am now and she sent Corny in with some tea ten minutes ago. In case you're wondering, I haven't come across anything else of interest today. Was Edwin Prosser able to shed any light on the letter I sent you?'

'He was. We'll put the details in an email when we get back, but as we suspected he doesn't know anything about Janina and Lukas.'

Sounding fed up, Sadie said, 'No surprise there, I guess. Did he tell you anything interesting at all?'

'A few things, but most significantly, he confirmed that the scene in the hall at the Exmoor house happened more or less as Lottie described it. So, at least some of her writings are based in reality. It remains to be seen whether anything else is.'

'Well, it's much harder for photographs to lie, and today I've set myself the happy task of ploughing through boxes and boxes of them that predate the digital age. Most seem to be of people I have no way of identifying – a lot of children in refugee camps, or makeshift schools and in clothes that have clearly come from donations. There are various dignitaries in all sorts of uniforms and traditional dress . . . Plenty of cocktail parties in glorious sunsets, swimming off yachts, flying about in small planes . . .

Lottie definitely didn't slum it while she was out there doing her good deeds.'

'Have you come across anyone who might have been significant in some way?'

'Not really, but I'm not very far in yet. Are you thinking about someone she might have been romantically involved with?'

'Amongst other things. Do you actually know of anyone she was involved with in that sense?'

'She never talked about anyone specifically, but I don't have a problem believing she had an active sex life when she travelled. She never brought anyone home for us to meet though.'

'What about Mia? Did she have any relationships after Edwin?'

'Not that I know of. It was like neither of them ever wanted to expose me to men, so Lottie played away, so to speak, and Mia, well, she didn't play at all.'

Speaking up, Connor said, 'Didn't they have a lot of friends on the island? People they socialized with?'

'Yes, quite a lot, actually, but no significant others, so to speak. Or, if there were, they were both very discreet. Am I allowed to ask now if anyone's been in touch since Tuesday's drop claiming to know Janina or Lukas?'

'It's still only Thursday,' Cristy reminded her gently, 'and listeners are contacting us all the time. Obviously, if anything comes up that we think is worth pursuing we'll let you know right away.'

'OK, thanks. And sorry again about the Corny thing.'

After assuring her it wasn't a problem, Cristy rang off and waited until Connor had parked the car in front of the office before saying, 'I keep coming back to the same thing with Lottie . . . She clearly had some sort of agenda going when she paid Edwin to "marry" Mia, and when she "found Sadie" . . . So why, when they took Sadie to Guernsey and Mia had a child to care for, didn't she leave?'

'Because she became attached to Sadie too?' Connor ventured, without much conviction.

Certain it wasn't that, Cristy got out of the car saying, 'We need to find George Symmonds-Browne. I'm sure he's key to it all.'

'And wouldn't it be great if someone in that high-pedigree, inbred family of his answered emails,' Connor stated, leading the way inside. 'Even Iz's contacts don't seem to be breaking down those hallowed doors.'

Cristy was right behind and almost collided with him as he came to a sudden stop.

Stepping around him to see what was wrong she cried, 'What the hell?'

'We found it like this when we got back from lunch,' Clover declared from the floor, where it appeared the entire contents of Lottie's boxes had been upended and unceremoniously dumped. 'We're trying to sort through it now and put it all back. The trouble is, we haven't got a clue if anything's missing, or which box any of it came from.'

'Did anyone in the building see someone coming in or out?' Connor asked, as he and Cristy trod carefully over the strewn contents to their desks.

'Not that we know of,' Jacks replied, 'although there are a couple of dirty great footprints on some of the paperwork . . . We've put them to one side in case we need to show the police. Not that they'll be interested in helping us. With the doors always being open, we can't even claim it was a break-in.'

Looking at Connor, Cristy said, 'Who the hell would do this? And what were they looking for?'

'Have any of the computers been touched?' he asked, checking his screen.

'Cristy's was unplugged,' Jacks replied, 'as if someone was about to make off with it, but I'm guessing they were interrupted, or changed their mind, because it's still there. And up and running. I've checked the latest activity and it's all ours, so no interference, or copying, or bugs as far as I can tell, but I'll definitely give it another going over.'

Cristy turned to the whiteboard to see if a message had been left there, but it was exactly as they'd left it earlier. 'This is bizarre,' she said, dropping into her chair. 'Who even knew the boxes were here apart from us and Sadie?'

'Gita and Robert Brinkley?' Clover reminded her.

Cristy almost laughed. 'Well it obviously wasn't Gita in her wheelchair, and Robert's currently in Geneva so I think we can safely rule them out.'

'In my opinion,' Jacks said, 'this with the boxes, is the kind of vandalism morons go in for, for fun, or to let you know they've come calling. A kind of intimidation tactic.'

Frowning, Cristy cast her mind back over their most recent podcast. 'We haven't mentioned anything yet about Matis Albescu or Eastern European gangs,' she said, 'but we did ask George Symmonds-Browne to be in touch.'

'And this is how he does it?' Clove cried incredulously.

'If it was him,' Connor put in.

'Do you have any other suggestions?' Cristy asked.

No one did.

'OK, let's work this back,' Connor said, settling into it. 'The last known sighting of Symmonds-Browne seems to have been in France circa 2016. Sure he could be anywhere by now, even in clink, but everyone knows that the Riviera is run by mobs, so it could be he was there . . .'

'I'll get onto a journalist contact of mine on the *Nice-Matin*,' Cristy said. 'She might be able to give us something with Vence being in her neck of the woods.'

'We should also try Interpol,' Connor suggested, 'to find out what they might have on him, presuming they're prepared to share it.'

Cristy grimaced. 'The only person I know who has a good contact there is Matthew. Unless one of you can suggest someone?' She looked at them all hopefully, and sank. 'No, I thought not, but if you do think of someone please let me know before I get myself indebted to him.'

*

'Hi, Mum, are you OK?' Hayley cried over WhatsApp video. 'What are you doing?'

'Making chicken soup with dumplings for Aiden, if he shows up,' Cristy replied, propping her phone against the toaster and reaching for her wine. She still had a mountain of research to get through for the series, but rather than stay at the office she'd decided to do it at home given that Aiden was supposed to be staying with her tonight.

'He's got a new girlfriend,' Hayley said. 'Did he tell you about her?'

'No. Anyone we know?'

'Her name's Pearl and she's cool. That's all he's told me. Unless it's changed since Tuesday, you know what he's like. Anyway, I wanted to check you're OK since the last time we spoke.'

'Remind me when that was and why I wouldn't be OK?'

With a laugh, Hayley flicked back her hair as she said, 'Guess what, I can't remember, but I know I've told you about maybe breaking up with Hugo . . .'

'Yes, and I think it's a shame when you seem so well suited. Have you done it now?'

'Actually, not quite. I mean, Stefan's really cool and everything, but he's not . . . I guess he's not Hugo and . . . Well, I'm just not sure what to do. I'm really attracted to Stef, you know, in a physical way, but what if we sleep together and it turns out I'd rather be with Hugo?'

Not much liking the sound of that, Cristy said, 'Is this you asking if you should cheat on Hugo to find out which one you feel you want to be with?'

'No, that's not what I'm saying. Not at all, but . . . Well, should I? Actually, you're totally the wrong person to ask after what you went through with Dad, so forget the cheating bit. Just please tell me you're free this weekend so I can come and talk it through with you. I really need to clear my head, and I thought it would be great if we could hang out, just the two of us. I mean, if you're going to be around, obvs.'

Thinking of her aborted trip to Guernsey, Cristy tried to sound upbeat as she said, 'As a matter of fact I am. When are you thinking of coming?'

'Tomorrow night? I've looked into flights and one gets in about six, so would you be able to pick me up?'

What a treat, a drive to the airport during the Friday rush hour. 'Of course,' she said. 'It'll be lovely to see you.'

'We've got so much to catch up on,' Hayley ran on excitedly. 'It's ages since I last saw you and I really miss you. If the weather's bad we can stay in our jammies all day and say to hell with the rest of the world. I'll bring chocolate.'

Laughing, Cristy blew her a kiss, and clicked off just as Aiden clattered in through the front door.

'Hey, Mum!' he shouted from the hall. 'Something smells good. Piers and Richie are with me. Hope there's enough for us all.'

Having expected him to turn up with at least one other monster appetite in tow, Cristy said, 'There's plenty and if you want to take some out to the homeless after, I've got flasks.'

'We're your men,' Aiden declared, coming into the kitchen and making straight for the fridge.

'Hi, Piers, Richie,' she said, as they traipsed in after him, just as tall, spottier in Richie's case, lots of facial hair in Piers's, all three of them more manly in their growing bodies than they were in their minds.

'Hey, Cristy,' they responded, in unison. 'We're starving,' Piers informed her.

'Hope it's OK to have a shower?' Richie said. 'The hot water's down at home so Aiden said I could jump in here.'

'That was kind of him. Off you go and don't leave wet towels all over the floor.'

'Just listened to the latest pod today,' Aiden told her, tossing a protein bar to Piers and tearing one open for himself.

'They are supposed to be *my* snacks,' Cristy informed him.

'I'll get some more,' he promised. 'Anyway, pod seems to be going well. Have you managed to find out where Sadie's mother is yet? We all reckon she's dead and the brother sold the child.'

Cristy frowned. 'The brother? Why him?'

He shrugged. 'He had access to her, didn't he? She'd have trusted him, and it kind of makes sense that someone close delivered her to the creepy aunts. She'd have kicked off otherwise. Any idea where he is now?'

'Not yet, no.'

'I reckon she was trafficked, same as her mother,' Piers put in.

Lowering the heat under the soup, Cristy said, 'Would someone like to set the table?'

'On it,' Aiden responded, showering her with chocolate and

peanut crumbs. 'Sorry. Didn't mean to share. Is Dad coming for supper?'

'No, why would he be?'

'Just asking, you've got so much there. Have you emailed Marley back yet?'

Stung by the reminder, Cristy said, 'I'll definitely do it this weekend. Hayley's coming so we can work on it together.'

'Cool. She's great at stuff like that. I'm in Yeovil on Saturday, don't forget. Back on Sunday.'

'What's in Yeovil?'

'Duh! Playing rugger for the school. We've got a party after, so staying over. OK, table's ready, feel free to bring it on any time you like.'

'You can serve yourselves,' she told him sharply. 'I've got work to do, so I'll take it into the bedroom.'

'Awesome. Love you.'

'Thanks for the soup, Cristy,' Piers added, as she packed up her things. 'Love you too.'

Laughing, Cristy carried her laptop, wine and phone into the bedroom where she'd dumped a couple of Lottie's boxes on her way in, and closed the door. The last thing she wanted was to be distracted by the boys' inane chat, or their awful music, or some kind of farting contest, which they always seemed to find so hilarious. It was why she'd set up a small desk in here right after moving in. She loved her son, adored him, but there were limits to her tolerance of teenage-boy wit and wisdom.

Opening up her laptop she took another sip of wine and sat down to read the message she'd started to Robert.

*Sorry for late reply, thanks so much for inviting me to the dinner on Saturday night. I wish I was in a position to accept as I'd love to hear your speech, but I'm afraid it won't be possible.*

That was as far as she'd got and she still wasn't sure whether to come right out and admit she couldn't go because he was married. Or maybe she should explain that her ex-husband was also invited and she had a morbid dread of gossips . . . Did she really need to give a reason at all? After all, the late notice presumably meant his first choice had let him down, and she did have a life, even if it didn't always feel like it.

Sighing, she picked up her wine again. It would be so much easier if she were going to Guernsey tomorrow, a bona fide excuse that would require no further explanation and that might, just might, lead to her seeing David.

In the end she wrote, *I truly am sorry to be missing out, but perhaps we could meet for a drink one evening next week so you can tell me all about what I missed. Cristy.*

She pressed send, listened for the whoosh and went to sit on the bed as if to distance herself from the fact that she'd just asked a married man on a date.

She thought of David again. She'd far rather be seeing him this weekend, no offence to Robert, or disloyalty meant to her daughter. However, continuing to have feelings for David when Juliette was still in the picture was something she really had to get over.

*So put him out of your mind and get on with sending an email to Camille Jardine on the* Nice-Matin. It might not lead them to where Symmonds-Browne was today, but at least it could give them a start.

*

The following evening Cristy was almost at the airport to collect Hayley when David rang.

'Hi, I hope this isn't a bad time,' he said.

'No, it's fine,' she replied, trying not to be thrown. 'I'm driving and it's . . . good to hear you.'

'OK. I'm a bit late to this,' he said, 'but I've only just heard you're not going to be here this weekend. Something about Corny staying with Mia?'

'That's right. We'd hoped to interview her without Mia knowing until after, but that's obviously not going to be possible while she's at the villa.' It really never had been a good enough reason to go all that way when they had no idea what Corny could tell them, she just hoped David hadn't seen through it.

'Well, I'm sorry you've had to cancel,' he said, 'because I'm really keen to see you. So I was wondering, if you're not doing anything else this weekend, how about I fly over there?'

She was so startled that she actually hit the brakes. 'That,' she said, quickly speeding up and waving an apology to the driver behind, 'would have been lovely' – *way beyond lovely* – 'but as we speak I'm on my way to collect Hayley. She's having boyfriend issues, so she's decided to come home for a couple of days.'

'Girl chat?'

'I'm afraid so. Oh God, I'm really sorry. If I'd known you wanted to . . .'

'It's OK, I have kids,' he reminded her. 'I get that you need to be there for them, even when you might prefer to be doing other things. I'm not saying you'd prefer to be seeing me . . .'

'I would actually, but her plane will already have landed.'

'Then say hi to her from me, and if there's anything I can do for you here . . . I'm not suggesting I interview anyone, but if there's any more background stuff . . . Have you asked Sadie about Lottie's will yet?'

'Actually, I missed an opportunity today . . . You heard about Mia being taken to hospital last night?'

'I did, and she's fine now, I think?'

'Apparently. Anyway, I'd rather talk to Sadie about the will face-to-face, or at least when she's at the lodge out of Mia's earshot.'

'Probably wise.'

'That sounds like you know what was in it.' When he didn't respond right away, she said, 'Sorry, you don't have to answer that, but if you're serious about more background stuff, we'd love to know something about the time Lottie and Mia moved to Guernsey.'

'You mean like where they lived when they first arrived?'

'I think they rented somewhere until the villa was ready, but was there anyone on the island they already knew? Someone who might have helped them get set up?'

'I wasn't here myself back then, as you know, but a lot of my family were, so I'll start with them and report back.'

'Fantastic, thanks.' Deciding to push on, Cristy braced herself and said, 'I was also wondering if there was any . . .?' How should she put this? 'Any confusion around the cause of Lottie's death?'

It took him a moment to catch on to why she might be asking.

'She had a heart attack, on the tennis court,' David reminded her. 'Are you saying . . .? What exactly are you saying?'

'We're just wondering if it really was that, or if there was some . . . Well, from what we hear it was very sudden, and I get the impression she was in good health during the days and weeks leading up to it . . . Maybe she had a heart condition we don't know about?' Starting to feel foolish, she said, 'Actually, please forget I asked . . .'

'No, no. It's fine. I think I understand where you're coming from, so leave it with me. And when you have Sadie's answer about the will I'll be happy to talk through what you make of it.'

'OK. Thanks.'

'I'll let you go now. Have a good time with Hayley and we'll speak soon.'

*

'Mum? Are you listening?' Hayley demanded, glancing up from her phone to check she had Cristy's attention.

'Absolutely,' Cristy smiled, still focused on her laptop screen.

Moments passed until she registered the silence and looked up to find Hayley watching her through narrowed eyes.

'So what did I just say?' Hayley challenged.

Cristy thought fast. 'That you're about to make a cup of tea?' she suggested hopefully.

Rolling her eyes, Hayley unwound her long legs and stalked over to the kettle. 'You are so bad, do you know that?' she declared. 'Anyone would think my love life meant nothing to you.'

'It means everything, but you've got to admit, my darling, we've been going round and round in circles ever since we got up this morning, and it's now . . .' she checked, 'almost four o'clock.'

Unembarrassed, Hayley said, 'I just need to talk things through, and sometimes saying things out loud makes them clearer. And did you just kind of call me boring?'

Cristy feigned shock. 'The thought never entered my head, but I would say that if you're having doubts about Hugo then maybe he isn't the one for you.'

'So I should end it?'

'Your decision, not mine. Remind me when we've agreed to FaceTime with Marley?'

'Seven our time. You're not backing out, are you?'

'If only. No, I just need to send some emails first . . .'

'You never stop working. I bet you can't even remember the name of the other guy I've been talking about.'

'Stefan and he's messaged you at least fifty times today . . .'

'Exactly, and Hugo's only been in touch once.'

'Clever Hugo, I say.'

'Why?'

Stifling a scream, Cristy said, 'Let me finish this and then I think we should go for a walk.'

'Great idea, if it weren't chucking it down out there, but it's OK, I get the hint. Do we have any cake to go with the tea?'

'There should be some hot-cross buns in the top cupboard.'

'It's not even February yet – well, just! Do you want one?'

'Sure. Toasted, if you don't mind,' and going back to the message from Camille Jardine at *Nice-Matin* Cristy forwarded it to Connor and read through it again.

*Great to hear from you, Cristy. Hope you're doing well. I was really sorry to hear about you and Matthew, you guys were always so great together, definitely his loss. Hope you've met someone more worthy of you by now.*

*Regarding Symmonds-Browne. Sorry, no idea where he is these days, didn't even know he was working out of the Riviera, tbh. Hadn't seen the photo from UK database before you sent it. If he is/was in this area he'll have been mixing with some seriously hardcore types back in 2016 (see list below for names that might interest you – advise you to stay clear of them all). Definitely something unusual about S-B because it seems every time he's taken in for questioning he's just let go again. So, is he an informer? Or does he have something on someone that buys him a get-out-of-jail card?*

Cristy scanned the list of names. They didn't mean anything to her, she couldn't even pronounce half of them, but she did recognize the countries of origin that Camille had assigned to each one. Three were Serbs, two Albanian . . . and now she was seeing one that she had come across before. How the heck had she missed it first time around?

*Matis Albescu – Romanian.*

There were plenty of men with the same name in the same line of business, so clearly it couldn't be the same Albescu as the one who'd been killed in a police raid back in 2002. Nevertheless, it was quite the coincidence. Worth exploring further?

Anyway, Camille was right about one thing, no one on this list was likely to be the kind of character she, Cristy, would want to run up against. She couldn't even see herself trying, at least not at this stage, which didn't mean they wouldn't send someone to make contact with her if Symmonds-Browne got another mention on *Hindsight*.

Putting her laptop aside she heard her stomach rumble as Hayley set down two mugs of their favourite raspberry infusion and a plate of toasted buns.

For the next hour, having apparently exhausted even herself with the dilemma over Hugo and Stefan, Hayley helped go through some of the letters from Lottie's box. They were all from children Lottie had sponsored over the years, some unbearably sweet and simplistic, others difficult to decipher, while some – most in fact – were begging her to visit them, or to let them come and live with her.

Interestingly, they all addressed her as *Dear Carlotta*, or *Dear Carla*.

Yawning and stretching as she set aside a postcard, Cristy jumped as Hayley suddenly cried, 'Oh my God! Is that the time already? I need to go.'

'What?' Cristy asked, confused.

'I told Dad I'd be there by six. Can you give me a lift?'

Cristy blinked as Hayley flew off the sofa and disappeared into the hall. 'Can I borrow your silver dress?' she shouted from the bedroom. 'The one with the drop back? And the shoes?'

'Where are you going?' Cristy shouted back.

'Dad's invited me to this amazing dinner tonight at Merchant's House.'

As the words reached her Cristy stared disbelievingly at the door. Hayley was going to the MSF event? Hayley, who'd come to spend the weekend with her, was right now, this minute, ransacking *her* wardrobe to go and be her father's plus-one at a gala dinner where Robert was the speaker, while she, Cristy, having turned Robert down and put David off from coming, was apparently being left at home to FaceTime Marley on her own.

# CHAPTER TWENTY

'Now this is interesting,' Jacks declared as he absorbed the information he'd just downloaded onto his screen. 'Seems Iz's social media team is up to the task after all.'

Cristy put aside the lawyer's letter they'd just received from Symmonds-Browne's father – second cousin to the actual duke – informing them that their client had no wish to participate in their series and would appreciate not being contacted again. 'We're all listening,' she told Jacks.

'There's a voicemail,' Jacks explained, 'from someone claiming to be Hilary Stokes.'

He had everyone's attention now. 'You mean, the Butlin's bar manager who worked with Lukas Andris?' Clover asked for clarity. 'What does she say?'

'Here, have a listen,' and removing his earpods, he set the message to replay on speaker.

'*Hi, I'm Hilary Stokes and I think you might be looking for me – or more specifically for Lukas Andris. It's been a long time since Lukas and I were in touch and I'm afraid I have no idea where he is now, but there is someone who might be able to help. Her name is Natalie Irwin. She worked at Butlin's at the same time as me and Lukas, and they were always quite close. She knew his sister, Janina, as well, and the little girl. The last time I heard from Talia she was in Canada, as far as I know she's still there. If you like I'll try to get in touch and ask if she can throw any light on things. Or feel free to call me if there's anything you'd like to discuss.*'

'OK, she sounds on the level,' Connor declared, 'so make your next task to contact her while Cristy and I go do this promo for

Iz's Rapid Retail guys. Natalie Whatsit's details are paramount so we can reach out to her ourselves, so make sure Hilary Stokes understands we'd like her to act sooner rather than later. Clove? You're looking worried.'

'Just googling the list of lowlifes Cristy passed on from *Nice-Matin*,' Clover explained. 'I've got to tell you, I'm not up for going anywhere near one of this lot . . .'

'You won't have to,' Cristy assured her. 'None of us will. It's too dangerous.'

'What are we thinking about this Matis Albescu?' Clover asked. 'It obviously can't be the guy who got killed back in 2002, but it sure as hell looks like him – although this one seems younger . . . Maybe father and son?'

'Could well bc,' Cristy agreed, 'but don't let's get hung up on him. He's never going to lead us to Symmonds-Browne, none of them will, there wouldn't be anything in it for them. Luckily, there are other ways.'

'All ears,' Jacks piped up.

Resigning herself to the inevitable, she said, 'Give Matthew a call and ask if he'll sound out his contact at Interpol for us – presuming the guy's still alive and functioning.' After a beat she added, 'If Matthew wants to know what he gets in return tell him I spent over an hour on FaceTime with his wife and son on Saturday evening while he was schmoozing with the rich and famous at a black-tie charity dinner, so *he* owes *me*.'

Clearly amused, Connor waited until they were walking through to the studio before asking, 'So how did that go for you?'

'With Marley? It was horrible and cringey, I hated every minute, but at least I didn't have to do much talking. She was too busy gushing over Boo Boo Bear – yeah, that's really what she called him – and telling me all about the auditions she's got lined up, the supernanny she's about to hire, some new-fangled fitness regime to get herself back into shape, and how worried she is about Matthew.'

'Why's she worried about him?'

'She's afraid he's feeling left out, and that I am too, but we are welcome to visit any time we like, for as long as we like, oh and will I agree to being Boo Boo Bear's legal guardian should anything happen to her?'

Barking out a laugh, Connor urged her to continue.

'I said we could discuss it some more the next time we speak,' she told him, pushing open the studio door. 'Honest to God, there's no shaking that girl, I don't know how Matthew stands it.'

'By being here in England?' Connor suggested, giving a wave to the technicians in their glass box. 'When's he planning to go over there again?'

'No idea, and no interest. Now, let's get this playacting over with so we can focus on last-minute edits for tomorrow's drop. And we still need to make a decision as to whether we're going to say more about Symmonds-Browne.'

'You mean so we can get turned over again? Or worse? Great! Let's do it.'

*

Much later in the day Cristy was in the office alone when Iz bounced in, all smiles and yogi bows as she declared the latest promo so convincing and effective it was sure to win awards.

Not asking which awards in particular, Cristy said, 'I'm glad everyone's happy with it, and I swear we won't let on that we've never shopped in a Rapid Retail outlet in our lives.'

Iz laughed delightedly, bowed again and then, to Cristy's surprise, went to close the door.

'Is everything OK?' Cristy asked, seeing how serious Iz suddenly looked.

Iz shook her head and pulled up a chair to sit close to Cristy. 'I don't know how you're going to take this,' she said quietly, 'but you might remember I was going to find out if certain SLD directors with high-flying connections could open some doors to George Symmonds-Browne?'

Cristy nodded cautiously. She hadn't actually expected Iz to come through, however if she had something to share . . .

'One of them has got back to me,' Iz whispered, 'and he has been advised to advise me to advise you that Mr Symmonds-

Browne – that's what he called him, Mr Symmonds-Browne – cannot be a person of interest for you at this time.'

Cristy blinked. 'Cannot?' she repeated.

Iz shrugged. 'That's what he said.'

Cristy looked up as Connor came in, appearing startled to find the two of them in a huddle. 'Something I should know about?' he asked, going to his desk.

'You'll want to hear this,' Cristy told him.

He listened as Iz repeated the message, his eyes widening with surprise. 'And that was it?' he asked when she'd finished. 'That he *cannot* be a person of interest. Remind me, how they get to decide any of this?'

'I have no idea,' Iz replied miserably. To Cristy she said, 'I'm afraid I've upset Connor again.'

'It's not about upsetting me,' he growled. 'I just want to know how someone with as many connections to the criminal underworld as he has to the British establishment *can't* be a person of interest at any time, never mind this one?' He looked at Cristy. 'I think we just ignore it.'

Cristy had to agree. 'I might just run it past Frances Rush, our friendly DSI who heads up Gloucestershire's Organized Crime Unit,' she said. 'She couldn't tell us Symmonds-Browne's whereabouts the last time I was in touch, but maybe she'll have something to say about this. Meantime, we need to continue being vigilant about locking up when no one's here, and make sure everything's regularly backed up to the cloud.'

Apparently approving of that, Iz said, 'Do you think it had something to do with this Symmonds-Browne guy?'

Mindful of how keen Iz might be to put the answer in some sort of press package, Cristy said, 'We have no idea what it was about. Probably just a random burglary attempt – and a wake-up call to us to take security more seriously. Jacks!' she exclaimed as he came in the door carrying a giant takeout coffee and sticky bun. 'We're waiting for news on Natalie Irwin and if she knows where to find Lukas. Anything doing?'

'Absolutely,' he replied, returning to his desk. 'I missed lunch,' he explained, taking a bite from the bun.

Cristy waited, watching him chew as Iz signalled the need to catch a train and left.

Swallowing, Jacks said, 'So, I contacted Hilary Stokes and she typed out a message to Natalie Irwin while I was talking to her. She also gave me Natalie's email address and landline number, which could be out of date because they haven't been in touch for ten years or more. Anyway, the phone number rang out when I tried it, and as yet Hilary hasn't had a reply to her iMessage, however, it has been "seen".'

'So she's read it,' Cristy stated, 'and knows we want to be in touch, but isn't responding?'

'She'd only have got the message an hour ago,' he pointed out, 'so give her a chance.'

Curbing her impatience, which actually had more to do with wanting things sorted in time to meet Robert for drinks later than it did with any real urgency regarding Natalie Irwin, Cristy said, 'Did Hilary Stokes tell you anything useful about Natalie, other than the fact that she was friends with Lukas while they were at Butlin's? Is she still in Canada, by the way?'

'I can't be sure of that yet. But apparently she's from Sheffield, worked in several holiday camps back in the day, until she met her now husband, Clive, while she was on a ski trip in Austria and ended up moving to Toronto. By Hilary's reckoning she'll be in her late forties by now.'

'Have you tried the email address yourself?' Connor asked.

'Yes, and it hasn't bounced back. Yet. So could still be current.'

Checking her mobile as it rang it took Cristy a moment to recognize the caller's name. 'It's Lottie's publisher, Felicity Green,' she announced, and clicked the call to speaker. 'Hi, Felicity,' she said warmly. 'It's good to hear you. Are you back from your travels?'

'A couple of days ago,' came the reply, 'and horribly jetlagged, but I thought I'd get in touch just in case you'd still like to talk to me.'

'We would,' Cristy assured her, making a quick shift of focus to Lottie Winters' aborted literary career, 'especially if you can throw any light on the reason Lottie decided to stop being published.'

'I'm not sure I ever received a straight answer to that,' Felicity Green responded, 'but since you got me thinking about it I remembered an email she sent me a year or so before she died. I hadn't heard from her in so long, it was quite a surprise and I was thrilled to see her name in my inbox. I've managed to track it down, so I can read it out to you if you like.'

'Please,' Cristy encouraged.

'I can't imagine,' Felicity said, 'how it managed to slip my mind, although it arrived during a very difficult time in my personal life and I suppose, when Lottie never followed it up . . . Anyway, here's what she said: "Flissy, I've been mulling the idea of writing a kind of memoir, part fact, part fiction. It would be about two middle-aged sisters and a little girl they find on the beach near their home. I've already made a start, mainly notes and the odd chapter or two, and for the time being I'm using our names – Mia, Sadie and me. *Why?* I hear you ask. Because, say I, this way I won't have to conjure any up until I'm ready to. I think you'll like the way it progresses to include some very colourful characters, many of the sort you might not expect from me. Lottie, of course, will have the most tremendous love story . . . I believe you might be smiling at that. Oh, how I miss him still. I wonder if he ever thinks of me. I am planning a truly shocking denouement to my story. Hard to write, but I feel it has to be done for the sake of . . . well, everything. More soon, Lottie."'

Cristy was looking at Connor in expectation and bafflement. 'Did she ever send you anything?' she asked, watching Connor start to scribble a note.

'I'm afraid not, but I know I replied encouraging her to continue.'

'What about the love story? She refers to it as though you knew who she was talking about.'

'I did, and I didn't,' Felicity replied. 'She never mentioned him by name, but there was someone who, let's say, stood out from the others. We're going back a while, mid-Nineties, I'd say, perhaps into the Noughties. She took to sending me postcards from exotic places telling me she was with him and having a marvellous time and felt she might die from sheer happiness.'

'Was he involved in the charities she supported?'

'She never said, but she met so many people from so many walks of life.'

*Some very colourful characters, many of the sort you might not expect from me.*

'Do you know what happened to the man she mentions?' Cristy asked.

'I don't, I'm afraid,' Felicity responded. 'I'm not even sure how long the relationship went on for, but I do remember wondering at times how much of it was actually real. It wasn't always easy to tell with Lottie.'

Cristy glanced at the note Connor put in front of her and nodded. He was right, they needed to record this, which meant her six o'clock rendezvous would have to wait. Unless Felicity was willing to do it tomorrow.

Quickly reminding herself that was unprofessional, she said, 'Felicity, would you be willing for me to interview you on Zoom, going over everything you've just told me? We can send you a link . . .'

'That will be fine.'

Jacks raised a thumb.

'It should be on its way now. So I'll speak to you again in a few minutes.'

After ringing off she sent a quick text to Robert saying, *Sorry, running late. Should be there by 6.30*, and said to Connor, 'What do you think about slotting this into tomorrow's episode?' If he agreed she was going to be a lot later than 6.30.

'It's not immediately obvious to me where it would go,' he said, 'although with the right links . . .'

'Hello, hello, look who we have here,' Jacks interrupted, as if a person of great import had entered the building, though he was actually peering at his screen. 'Natalie Irwin has just emailed,' he explained, 'and she's saying that yes, she remembers Lukas and Janina. No idea where they are now, but apparently Lukas went back to Vilnius after he left Butlin's . . .' He looked up. 'So Lithuanian.'

Not sure why she was surprised by that Cristy said, 'What else does she say?'

'That she's been worried about Lukas ever since he was last in touch with her . . .'

'Which was when?' Connor interrupted.

'She doesn't say, but apparently she's happy to talk and share what she knows, will Wednesday work for us?'

'Set it up,' Connor replied, 'and send her copies of the first two pods just in case she hasn't already heard them.' To Cristy, he said, 'Why do you keep checking the time? Do you need to be somewhere?'

'It's OK,' she assured him. 'I'm just . . .' She broke off as Robert texted back.

*Taking part in an online seminar at eight, so let's reschedule. Same time, same place on Wednesday?*

Hoping it wasn't going to clash with the Natalie Irwin interview she texted back, *See you then*, and was about to put the phone away when Matthew's name came up on the screen. Ordinarily she'd have hit reject; however, they'd asked a favour of him and it might be about that.

'Before you ask, no word yet from my Interpol guy,' he told her when she answered.

'Then why are you calling?'

'Nice to hear you too. I was hoping we might get together . . .'

'It's not a good time, Matthew. I'm about to do an interview . . .'

'So will you let me know when is?'

She didn't answer.

'No, of course you won't. By the way, everyone was asking about you on Saturday night.'

Unable to imagine why, when everyone knew she was no longer his wife, she said, 'I really do have to go . . .'

'You know, I thought I recognized the main speaker, and then it came to me. He was your Tinder date . . .'

'I'm not on Tinder,' she said, through her teeth.

'But it was him, wasn't it? Nice guy. Hayley was smitten at first sight.'

'She told me.' Cristy also knew, from Robert, that he thought she had a very beautiful daughter and he'd been charmed to meet her ex-husband (no irony there). 'I'm ringing off now,' she told Matthew, 'but thanks for trying to help with this Symmonds-Browne character.'

'You know he's distantly related to the Duke of . . .?'

'Yes, I do. Is that a problem?'

'No idea yet, I guess we'll find out. OK, off you go, but thanks for FaceTiming with Marley at the weekend. It meant the world to her.'

Having no idea how to respond to that, Cristy simply ended the call and turned to her screen where Felicity Green was ready and waiting.

*

'Sorry. It's late. Did I wake you?' Sadie asked.

Keeping her eyes closed as she spoke into her mobile, Cristy took a moment to register that she was at home and said, 'It's fine. I was just dozing. Is everything OK?'

'I'm not sure,' Sadie replied. 'I mean, yes is the short answer, but I've found a portable safe at the back of one of Lottie's closets. I've tried opening it, but I don't know if I'm even close to guessing the combination, and I don't want to ask Mia in case she just spirits it away, or throws another scene.'

Swinging her feet to the floor, Cristy said, 'Why not take it to David? He might know someone who can help.'

'That's what I thought. There's probably nothing important inside, just cash or some jewellery, that sort of thing, but it'll be interesting to know, because I haven't found anything else that's as securely locked.'

'Where is it now?'

'Jasper helped me bring it up to the lodge, so it's right in front of me.'

Seizing the moment, and hoping she wasn't going to be too clumsy about it, Cristy said, 'Maybe there's a copy of her will in there. I know it's been read and presumably everything's sorted . . .'

'Yes, that happened not long after she died. She left everything to Mia.'

Cristy blinked. 'Everything? What about her charities? What about you?'

With a soft sigh, Sadie said, 'Mia will take care of the charities when she goes, I'm sure, and Lottie gave me so much when she was alive, but I have to admit I was a bit disappointed. I thought maybe she'd set something aside for me, a special ring or necklace, a memento of a time we'd shared, a letter even, admitting I wasn't her actual niece and explaining where I really came from. I can't help thinking that something like it might be in this safe, that's why I don't want to show it to Mia in case she tries to take whatever it is.'

Understanding that, Cristy said, 'Well, I'm sure we'll get it open one way or another.' She was staring down at a message from Clover now that had apparently come in about an hour ago. *You need to take a look at this.*

She clicked the attachment and when she saw the image that filled the screen her heart contracted so hard with shock that it took a moment for a surge of adrenalin to kick through.

# CHAPTER TWENTY-ONE

Cristy and the others were watching their screens fill with the shots Clover had taken of five original photographs and uploaded onto *Hindsight*'s main clipboard. They'd come to the office early to discuss this unexpected breakthrough – bombshell Connor was calling it – before making a decision about whether or not to change the episode due to drop tonight.

'Where the heck did you find them?' Cristy asked, as they came into full focus.

'They were in this,' Clover replied, holding up a crumpled, bright yellow Kodak envelope with Quality Photos stamped on the front. 'It fell out of a notebook I was going through and the minute I saw the first one I knew I had to send it straight to you.'

'Anything in the notebook explaining them?' Connor asked, studying them closely.

'Not that I've found so far.'

All five of the shots showed a much younger Lottie seated on one side of a table with George Symmonds-Browne and Janina Andris facing her. Both Lottie and Janina appeared animated, unsmiling, as if arguing about something, while Symmonds-Browne's position hardly changed as he sat watching them. In one photo his hand was over Janina's, in another Janina's head was in her hands. The last showed all three of them leaving the café, Symmonds-Browne very close behind Janina, Lottie ahead, already turning away.

'What are they telling us?' Connor demanded. 'What was going on at that meeting?'

'The shots were taken with a long lens,' Jacks mumbled, almost to himself.

'They're obviously in a café, or coffee shop,' Clover observed, 'but nothing to say what the place is called or where it is.'

'We need to know *when* they were taken,' Cristy stated. 'Is there any way of finding that out?'

'It's got to have been sometime around 2000,' Connor said, 'you only have to look at Janina to know that. She looks the same as she does in the other shots we have of her.'

'Is there a date stamp on the backs of the originals?' Jacks asked Clover.

She shook her head. 'Already checked and there isn't.'

Articulating what was on everyone's mind, Cristy said, 'Are we looking at photographic evidence of Lottie negotiating for Sadie?'

'Not possible to say for certain,' Connor answered, 'but we could be.'

'What I'd like to know,' Jacks came in, 'is who took the shots, and why.'

'And how did they end up with Lottie?' Cristy added. It wasn't hard to work out. 'It's smacking of blackmail to me,' she said. 'Symmonds-Browne set Lottie up for this and made sure it was on record. Which makes it possible, likely even, that these photos are what turned up in the envelope just after the sisters took Sadie in.'

Sitting back in his chair, Connor said, 'We can end tonight's pod with it. It's a great cliff-hanger – *photographs have just come to light of Lottie Winters meeting with Janina and suspected trafficker George Symmonds-Browne. We'll bring you more in the coming episodes.*'

Cristy wasn't sure. 'Do we actually want to out him as a trafficker yet?'

'I say we do,' Connor replied. 'We can run all of Catherine Shilling's interview, with an emphasis on the parts where she talks about Symmonds-Browne. Then it'll have a proper impact.'

'OK,' Cristy agreed, 'but before we do anything that dramatic we need to let Sadie see the photos. It'll be pretty devastating for her if they're painting the picture we fear, but I guess she's more than half-expecting it, and we can't let her learn about them through the pod.'

'If you want to warn her they're coming,' Jacks said, 'I'll package them up and send when you're ready.'

Cristy was checking the time. 'She's going to be with David at some point today – she's found some sort of safe that needs opening and we're hoping he'll be able to help her. So let's send them to him first. That way he and Anna can be with her when she sees the shots of her mother with Symmonds-Browne, quite possibly trying to extract the highest price for her.' Even saying the words made her feel sick. It wasn't how any of them wanted to view Janina, but who knew what kind of pressure she'd been under at the time, what dark forces had been at work in her life, so it wasn't a good idea to rush to judgement.

'I'll get everything lined up ready for the edit,' Connor said, 'and I guess we'd better check with Sadie before adding anything to the website.'

Cristy reached for her mobile and pushed right on past the flutterings inside as she clicked to call David's number.

'Hi,' he said when he answered, 'this is a nice surprise so early in the morning.'

She smiled. 'I'm glad you think so, but please tell me you're not still in bed.'

He laughed. 'Actually, I've just dropped Laurent at school, and believe it or not I was about to call you.'

Pleased, she said, 'Really?' Then, 'Oh, does that mean Sadie's already been in touch with you?'

'No, but from the sound of it she's going to be?'

'I'm sure she will,' and after explaining about the safe and then the photos, she said, 'So is it OK if we send them to you first?'

'It's fine,' he assured her. 'You're right, she shouldn't be alone when she sees them for the first time, although I think my mother and Anna will be her best support with that. I'll be around if she needs me, obviously, and meantime I'll be happy to see what can be done about the safe.'

'Thanks,' she said warmly. 'I really appreciate it. Oh, I've asked Sadie about the will, by the way. You can probably imagine my surprise when she told me that Lottie hadn't left her anything.'

'I can tell you now,' David said, 'that it was a surprise to Victor Dubois, the lawyer, as well. She didn't explain her decision when she made the change. Apparently she simply told him it would be easier for Mia to sort everything when the time came, should she live the longest, and if she didn't then she, Lottie, would adjust accordingly.'

Unsure what to make of that, Cristy said, 'Have you managed to find anything out about Lottie's cause of death?'

'It's why I was about to call you,' he replied. 'Nothing suspicious according to the records. She suffered a massive heart attack, and apparently it wasn't her first.'

Blinking with surprise, Cristy said, 'So she had a pre-existing condition?'

'And was taking medication for it. Apparently the first attack happened when she was in her early forties, and there was a smaller one about ten years ago.'

Cristy nodded slowly as she considered this, not entirely sure whether she felt more relieved or baffled by the verdict of natural causes.

'Does this help or hinder your investigation?' David asked.

'I'm not sure it changes anything,' she replied, 'but it's good to have it cleared up. Have you managed to talk to anyone about the time the sisters came to Guernsey?'

'I have, but so far nothing particularly interesting to report. I'm trying to track down the agent who sold them their house, he'll probably remember them pretty well. He doesn't live on the island any more, but someone's getting back to me once they've found out where he is now.'

'OK, thanks, and for taking care of Sadie today. I'm glad for her sake that she has your family to lean on, because heaven knows what Mia's up to these days.'

'Or any day, but I'm told she's back to normal health and is planning to reinvent herself as a Sixties Bond girl the next time you visit.'

Cristy choked on a laugh. 'Tell me you're not serious.'

'I'm not, although it wouldn't surprise me. Anyway, I've just arrived home and Sadie is at the front door waiting for me. I'll call later to let you know how things go.'

As Cristy rang off, feeling uplifted by how relaxed they'd been with one another, she spotted Connor playing an air violin and scowled menacingly at him before giving Jacks the all-clear to send the photos to David now.

*

It was just after seven in the evening by the time they finally uploaded the latest episode – unusually late, but they were more concerned about getting things right, especially where the outing of George Symmonds-Browne was concerned, than hitting their self-imposed deadline. By then they'd recorded Sadie's response to the photos so were able to include it at the end of the episode, before the closing comments.

SADIE: 'To be honest they made me feel horrible inside. I mean, obviously we have no idea what was being discussed around that table, but the fact that Lottie was meeting with Janina and George Symmonds-Browne . . . Well, it kind of speaks for itself, doesn't it?'

CRISTY: 'Once this goes live your aunt Mia will know about the photos. What do you think she'll have to say about them?'

SADIE: 'I've no idea, but frankly I'm more concerned about what was being done to my mother at the time they were taken.'

CRISTY: 'That was a very sombre and sad-sounding Sadie earlier today. My heart goes out to her, and I'm sure you all feel the same. Imagine how it must feel to learn that your mother was being controlled by a criminal gang to the point she was forced to give you up. If that's what these photos are telling us, and as Sadie herself says, it's hard to see them any other way.'

CONNOR: 'We know from our interview with ex-Detective Sergeant Catherine Shilling, who was part of the surveillance team watching Symmonds-Browne's farm at the time

Janina was there, that she, and many young women like her, were lured from their homes with promises of good jobs and better lives only to be *forced* into prostitution and probable slavery.'

CRISTY: 'We don't know how many more children might have been born to those young women, at this time we only know about Sadie. I think, I hope, that, like us, you care deeply about helping her to find the truth of who she really is. And what happened to her mother, Janina Andris, who we now believe to be Lithuanian.'

CONNOR: 'It's almost certain George Symmonds-Browne will have the answers, so if you know where he is, or how we can get hold of him, please contact us through the usual channels and be assured that any information you can give us will be treated in the strictest confidence.'

CRISTY: 'That's it from us for now. Thank you for listening and if you'd like to see the photographs referred to in this episode you'll find them on our website.'

As the recording of Connor reeling off the closing credits began he faded the sound out and checked the time. 'If that doesn't set the cat amongst the pigeons,' he said, starting to pack up for the day, 'then I don't know what will.'

'We're going to be flooded with sightings,' Clover groaned. 'I'll lay money that everyone and their granny will know where Symmonds-Browne is. And his posh family aren't going to like it one bit.'

Not doubting that for a minute, Cristy said, 'It had to be done, and let's try to stay optimistic that someone, somewhere, who knows the truth will decide to come forward.'

'You mean before or after the criminal gang?' CloveR queried.

As they had no plans for their usual after-party this evening – Meena and Harry were in Italy skiing, Iz was in London doing Iz-things and Connor wanted to hurry home because the baby was unwell – Cristy decided to send CloveR and Jacks off into the night on expenses to make up for no party, while she made a final check of her messages before setting off for home herself.

She guessed only time would tell if they were prepared for what this latest episode might bring down on them. However, the email she found from Frances Rush of the Organized Crime Unit threw a different sort of light on things.

*My interpretation of you being told that Symmonds-Browne 'cannot be a person of interest for you at this time' is that you're either being subtly warned off, or there's a chance he's in witness protection. I can try to look into it, but it's notoriously difficult to get info out of UKPPS and that's presuming he's in this jurisdiction. If he's overseas, say Europe or the US, I can't help you at all. Frances.*

After forwarding the message to the rest of the team, Cristy turned to the whiteboard where printouts of the photos of Symmonds-Browne, Lottie and Janina were now posted. She tried to imagine again what they could have been discussing, where they'd been at the time, had gone after, and what had happened in the days and weeks that had followed. Had Symmonds-Browne used the shots to force more money out of Lottie? Why else would he have wanted them taken? How else would they have ended up with her?

Sighing with exasperation, she began stuffing everything into her capacious tote bag and checked her phone as a text arrived.

*Aiden and I at Clifton Sausage. Would love you to join us.*

In spite of feeling tempted, she'd have to call an Uber to get there and actually she was keen to go home. *Maybe next time. Any news from your guy at Interpol?*

*Strangely no. He's usually pretty quick at getting back to me. I'll give it another day and chase him. Aiden's talking about a pancake-party next week (Shrove Tuesday). Everyone invited after the drop. We can do it at the house if you like.*

Cristy stiffened. She hadn't set foot in their family home since leaving it five years ago and she had no intention of going there again. Those days, those cherished memories of how happy they'd once been were behind them, and she sure as hell wasn't interested in seeing what changes Marley might have made during the time she'd been there.

A text arrived from Aiden. *Dad is chief tosser, which has nothing to do with pancakes and everything to do with what a knob he is for getting everything wrong. Can we do it at yours?*

Cristy texted back, *Of course. I'll let everyone know.*

Dropping the phone into her bag, she followed her usual route down to the waterfront and turned away from the SS *Great Britain* towards the M Shed. As she went, stepping around puddles and avoiding other late commuters, her mind was so full of Symmonds-Browne and where he might be now that it took her a while to pick up on the sense of being followed. She turned quickly, half-expecting someone to bump into her, or duck into the shadows, but no one was there – or no one who seemed interested in her.

She walked on, alert for the sound of footsteps or the feel of someone closing in. On Prince Street Bridge a couple of joggers overtook her, and a cyclist barely missed her arm as he sped by. She crossed the cobbled street to pass the Mud Dock and headed along The Grove towards her end of the harbourside. She wasn't sure about being followed now, couldn't make up her mind if she was freaking herself out, or if someone really did have her in their sights.

At the Riverstation she took a quick decision to go inside rather than risk leading someone right to her door.

Finding the downstairs bar unusually quiet, she accepted the offer of a window booth overlooking the water and ordered herself a gin and tonic. From here she could see who was coming and going, and if anyone suspicious did appear she could always call Matthew and Aiden and ask them to meet her when they'd finished their meal. She might not relish the idea of having to explain herself, but better that than try to deal with some sort of stalker alone.

*

'I'm not sure I'm liking the sound of this,' David commented when he rang later to ask what sort of feedback they'd had so far to the latest episode. She was home now, safely inside with doors and windows locked. The kindly neighbour who'd found her at the Riverstation and walked her back was on standby upstairs if she needed him. 'Did you actually see anyone?'

'Without really knowing who I was looking for, other than Symmonds-Browne,' she replied, 'it's hard to answer that – and I don't actually think he'd be following me in person if he did have anything to do with it. Anyway, it could have all been in my head. It was dark, and I guess I was feeling spooked by the attempted burglary . . .'

'Have you contacted the police about that?'

'There's nothing they can do, so we'll just have to be extra careful about who could be watching us, or who gets in touch with possible leads.' Going to refill her wine glass, she said, 'It's been suggested by a reliable source that Symmonds-Browne could be in witness protection. If that's the case then it's possible others are looking for him.'

'And now, thanks to the pod, they're hoping you might lead them to him?'

'Maybe, but surely no one thinks I'm hiding him at home or in the office.'

'No, but I'm thinking you could consider getting yourselves some sort of security,' he said gravely.

She smiled as she sank down onto the sofa and rested her feet on the coffee table. 'I survived quite a lot of intimidation when I was working on your story,' she reminded him. 'In fact, even you sent me anonymous emails at the beginning.'

'To try and protect you,' he pointed out, 'but OK, you didn't know that at the time. Hang on, are you suggesting this stalker might actually be looking out for you?'

She laughed. 'If there is such a person, it's a nice thought, but I don't think I'll put too much trust in it. Anyway, let's move on and talk about Sadie. Is she still with you, or has she gone home now?'

'Anna took her a couple of hours ago and is staying over because Jasper's away.'

'Is she still feeling shaken up by the photos?'

'Let's say she seemed calmer by the time she left, helped I think by everyone reminding her that she didn't really know what was happening in them. Anna has a theory that Janina was trying to get Sadie back, but Lottie was refusing to let her go.'

Cristy's eyebrows rose. 'That would put a different slant on things. What about Symmonds-Browne? Did she have any thoughts on what he might have been doing there?'

'Not that she shared with me. I'd say it's a question for Mia.'

'Yes, and good luck with that. I wonder if she's listened to the pod yet.'

'If she has no one's heard from her so maybe not.'

As frustrated as ever by Mia's intransigence and capriciousness, she said, 'And the safe? Any luck with it yet?'

'It's still here, and I'm sure we'll get it open once the guy I have in mind is back from wherever he is. His wife says Jersey, I'm wondering if it's a little more secure than that, i.e. a Crown facility. However, she assures me she's expecting him any day now. We'll see and I'll let you know, but if he's not here by the weekend I'll make enquiries elsewhere. Now, I'm interested to know if you have any thoughts of when you might be coming this way again?'

Checking the lift in her heart with a reminder of Juliette, she said, 'Is Corny still with Mia?'

'As far as I know, but maybe I should put it another way, I'm keen to see you.'

Unable not to feel pleased by that, she said, 'You could always come here.' Before he could react she added, 'But I'm not sure it's a good idea, under the circumstances . . .'

'What circumstances?'

Not willing to spell it out, and suddenly annoyed that he seemed to be making her, she said, 'Shall we leave it for now? It's late and I've had a busy day.'

'OK, but we do need to talk.'

'If you say so.'

'I do and I would fly over there this weekend if I knew you were free – and if I wasn't hosting an event at the yacht club on Saturday night. I was hoping you might come with me, but it's sounding as though you'd prefer not to.'

'That's not what I said, but given the way things are with the series right now I think I need to be here, or ready to go at short notice if something comes up.'

There was a moment before David said, 'I get that, just don't shut me out altogether, OK? At least not until we've properly straightened things out between us.'

# CHAPTER TWENTY-TWO

The following afternoon, as arranged, Cristy and Connor were ready to connect to Natalie Irwin in Toronto while Clove and Jacks continued ploughing through Lottie's jumble of boxes. No more incriminating photographs as yet, and still no explanation for those now posted on their website.

They'd spent the morning combing through early feedback reports from Iz's supersleuths, as they were calling the social media back-up team, while discussing Cristy's concern that she'd been followed home last night.

'If it was someone hoping we – you – might lead them to Symmonds-Browne,' Connor said, 'then they surely have to know from the last episode that we have no idea where he is.'

'And if the guy turns out to be in some sort of protection scheme,' Jacks added, 'then we're never likely to find him.'

'Frances Rush also suggested,' Cristy reminded them, 'that being told he can't be a person of interest at this time could be a subtle way of warning us off. Exactly which one of the SLD directors is doing the warning, and who exactly primed him, or her, for it, is anyone's guess, but I'm expecting things could become a little less subtle in the coming days.'

'If the lowlifes the *Nice-Matin* sent us are involved,' Clover said, 'then I can't see them bothering with subtle at all, but hey, what do I know about how gangsters operate? I just don't want to be face-to-face with any of them on a dark night. Are we thinking they're behind the trashing of this office?'

Having no idea, Cristy shrugged as she checked an incoming text.

*Can I take a rain-check for this evening? Flying to Paris later, hope to be back on Saturday. Robert.*

Disappointed, although relieved she wasn't the one having to call off their drinks this time, she texted back, *No problem. Just let me know when works for you. C.*

'There's an iMessage here released by one of the supersleuths,' Jacks said, reading from the feedback reports. 'It could – at a stretch – lend some credence to Symmonds-Browne being in witness protection. It says, "Dear Hindsight Team, I believe George Symmonds-Browne is my neighbour here in Naples living under another name. He isn't alone. If you want to know more please message me back."' He glanced up to find everyone looking at him.

'Naples?' Connor echoed. 'Not the most obvious place to go if you're trying to avoid mafia types. On the other hand, if you're in bed with them, so to speak . . .'

'"He isn't alone" is another stand-out for me,' Cristy said. 'Message this person back, Jacks, and say we'd love to know more. Then get in touch with the supersleuths to find out what in particular made them release this one to us, and are there any more like it?'

By mid-afternoon they were still awaiting replies. However, Natalie Irwin had just connected, a sweet-faced woman in her late forties, with shiny black hair and large brown eyes, so all focus was now on her.

After introducing herself and Connor, and thanking her for agreeing to chat with them, Cristy said, 'Would you mind if we start recording right away?'

'Sure, I was expecting it,' Natalie replied with a smile that revealed a pierced tongue and small white teeth. She had retained her native Yorkshire accent, albeit slightly uplifted by a Canadian twang. 'Sorry I couldn't do this sooner, kids and commitments, you know how it goes. Anyhow, I've had time to do some digging to remind myself of dates and places, that sort of thing, so with any luck I'll be able to help you in some way. I know I couldn't find Lukas when I tried, so I'm hoping you'll be better at it than I am.'

Receiving a nod from Connor, Cristy asked Natalie to identify herself for the recording, and began by taking her back to how she and Lukas had first met.

NATALIE: 'Oh that's easy, it were in Minehead. I was working at Butlin's, the holiday camp, and I ran into him a couple of times on the beach or in town. We got talking, he told me he was looking for his sister who he thought was in the area. When I found out he had no money and was sleeping rough I started smuggling him into my quarters so he could get some decent sleep while I was working. I'd take him food as well, and then we managed to get him some shifts, and before too long he had his own room and a proper job. He was a great guy. He had a way with him that kind of cheered you up, if you know what I mean. Always positive, up for a laugh and joke, interested in what you had to say. I remember when he found his sister and how much he cried with happiness. He wanted me to meet her, and I was up for that, so we made it happen, only a few times, it has to be said. I saw her little girl more because Lukas would bring her into the camp. A proper little cutie, she were. And his sister, wow, she were a real looker, she were.

'I always thought she had a housekeeping job further along the coast – I didn't know about any of the "Russian bride" stuff until way later when it came out in the local paper. They was all long gone by then, but before that, whenever I saw her, I can't say she ever seemed, you know, scared or anything, but then, like, one day she was, and so was he. I don't know what happened, all he ever told me was that she was going to be moving on, and then a few weeks later, just like that, he'd gone too. I was proper upset, I can tell you. I never dreamt he'd take off without saying a word when we'd been such good friends, but that's what happened.'

CRISTY: 'During the times you saw Janina did she ever talk about having to leave Sasha, or being forced to give her up? Did Lukas ever mention anything like that?'

NATALIE: 'Sasha – that was her name, I've been trying

to remember. Anyway, no way can I see Janina leaving her, they was bonded at the hip, and Sasha adored her uncle . . . You should have seen the pair of them together. He was like a big kid himself when he brought her into the camp, dead proud of her he was. No, if Janina ever gave her up – and I guess what you're saying in your pods is that Sadie Winters is Sasha – I'd lay money that someone forced her to.'

CRISTY: 'We posted some shots on our website last night of Lottie Winters with Janina and the man she was working for. Have you seen them?'

NATALIE: 'I have, and if you're asking do I recognize the other two, I can tell you I don't remember seeing either of them before.'

CRISTY: 'OK, going back to when Lukas disappeared, was that the last you heard from him?'

NATALIE: 'No, actually. I got a postcard about six months later from somewhere in Lithuania – I can't find it I'm afraid, chances are I didn't keep it – but in it he said he was sorry about bailing the way he did, apparently the authorities caught up with him and he'd been deported. He was staying with his sister now until he could get back to England.'

CRISTY: 'His sister being Janina?'

NATALIE: 'That's what I thought until he turned up in London one day a few years later, three or four, could even have been a bit longer than that. I was working front-of-house in a theatre at the time, so yeah, it would have been around 2005. It turned out he'd been with his older sister, Audra, since being shipped out, but now his country had joined the EU it was possible for him to get to England legally. So he was back to find Janina because they hadn't heard from her since she'd left Minehead.'

CRISTY: 'Did he tell you then why Janina had left Minehead?'

NATALIE: 'Not that I recall. And I didn't say anything about what I'd read in the paper. You just wouldn't, would you, over something like that?'

CRISTY: 'Do you know if he ever found her?'

NATALIE: 'Not that I ever knew of. He went everywhere searching for her, and the bloke whose house she'd been staying at in Kylve, but he couldn't find a trace of either of them anywhere. I remember him saying something about a couple of women who lived, or were staying on Exmoor, but he never knew their names and when he went to the house he thought was theirs they weren't there any more. To be honest, I didn't really know what that was about, but I could see he was ready to grasp at any straw. It was a horrible time for him. He was proper scared about what might have happened to his sister and niece, but it was like no one knew anything and the police, typically, weren't interested. I reckon it was because he was foreign, they don't admit that sort of thing, do they? They just said they had no record of his relatives ever being in the country so had no way of knowing if they were still there, or if they'd left again.'

CRISTY: 'Do you know if he told them about George Symmonds-Browne?'

NATALIE: 'I don't, I'm afraid, although I guess he must have. I mean, why wouldn't he? Even so nothing ever came of it. Lukas was drawing blanks everywhere and it carried on like that way after I left and moved here, to Canada. I felt really bad for him and wished there was more I could do, but I'd met Ian by then, my husband, and we had our own lives to be getting on with. I mean, I stayed in touch with Lukas, I didn't just drop him. He'd write me a line – and then an email when we started sending them – a couple of times a year to ask how I was doing and to say where he was living and what he was doing. He was still in England, and had all sorts of jobs, delivery driver, hotel porter, builder, plumber's mate, you name it, and he lived all over. I think he had a couple of long-term girlfriends, but the one who stands out for me was Evie. He was obviously really keen on her, and as far as I know he was still with her the last time I heard from him.'

CRISTY: 'When was that?'

NATALIE: 'August 2015. I've been trying to find the email, but I've changed provider since then, and moved house, but I remember he told me that he'd been contacted by George Symmonds-Browne. It took me a while to work out who that was. When I did I felt kind of excited for him, and worried, obviously, given what I knew about the bloke. Anyway, maybe it meant he was going to find out something about his sister at last, but then I read on and it was really weird, because it turned out this GSB had offered him an amazing job and he was going to take it.

'And that was that. Nothing since. Obviously I emailed straight back to ask what was going on and what the hell sort of job was he talking about given GSB's rep, but to this day he's never answered.'

Needing a moment to assimilate, Cristy nodded for Connor to take over.

CONNOR: 'Do you still have the address he emailed from?'

NATALIE: 'Sure, I'll send it to you, but it's defunct now, just bounces back, and same goes for the old mobile number I had for him.'

CONNOR: 'What about his sister, Audra? Do you have any contact details for her?'

NATALIE: 'I wish. I tried finding her, but none of the Audra Andrises I got in touch with knew him. That's if they spoke English at all, and not many of them did so I didn't hear back from all of them. I think she was married, so she probably had a different name.'

CRISTY: 'Did Lukas ever send you any photographs when you were still in touch that might indicate where he was when he took them?'

NATALIE: 'Oh yeah, Lukas at Blackpool Tower; Lukas and Evie paddleboating on a lake somewhere; Evie with a Beefeater; both of them outside Buckingham Palace . . . He used to send snaps more regularly than he did messages, I guess as a way of keeping in touch and letting me know he was still alive. That's why I've been so worried since everything suddenly stopped.'

CRISTY: 'OK. Can I take you back to the time you were all in Minehead for a moment? Did you ever meet any of the other so-called "Russian brides"?'

NATALIE: 'No, like I said I didn't even know about them until way after it was all over.'

CRISTY: 'Did either Janina or Lukas ever talk about Sasha's father?'

NATALIE: 'Never got a mention. I presumed he was someone she'd left back in her own country, or later, I thought he was probably one of the scumbags who trafficked her. Could have been just a random punter. I never liked to ask.'

CRISTY: 'Is there anything you'd like to say to Lukas, in case he listens to this podcast?'

NATALIE: 'Yeah, sure, be in touch you crazy bastard! I need to know you're OK. Same goes for you Janina, wherever you are. I really cared about you guys, still do, so give me a break here and call or message. You know how to find me, Lukas, the mobile number hasn't changed.'

Cristy looked around to see if anyone had anything else to add. They all shook their heads, so Connor stopped the recording and Cristy said, 'I can't thank you enough for this, Natalie. You've added something very special to the series by bringing Lukas and Janina to life in a way no one else has been able to so far, apart from Robert, the doctor Janina met a couple of times.'

'Yeah, I heard his interview. Sounds like an interesting guy, his mother came over well too. I guess you still don't know what really happened with those sisters? Myself, I reckon that finding a child on the beach stuff is bullshit, and I especially do now you've posted those shots of one of them with Symmonds-Browne and Janina. What the heck was all that about, is what I'd like to know?'

'So would we,' Cristy responded. 'I'll let you go now, but if anything else comes to mind you think might help us, you know where we are. Your interview should be in the next episode, so please let us know if Lukas, or anyone, gets in touch after that. Or before.'

'Let's hope it happens. I'll sleep a lot easier if I could be sure he's not out there somewhere, six feet under.'

As she disappeared from their screens, Jacks gave it a moment and said, 'In case anyone's interested, I've heard from the supersleuths. Apparently the "Naples" message got forwarded because we didn't mention anything about the theory of witness protection, or identity switch, in the pod, so it was decided this one could have some cred.'

'Someone on that team is doing their job,' Connor commented approvingly.

Agreeing, Jacks said, 'I've also heard back from the anonymous sender. I'll put it up for you all to read, but here's what it says if you want to record it for a drop in.'

Receiving a thumbs up from Connor, he continued,

JACKS: '"Sorry, my mistake. Please ignore last message. Good luck."'

Cristy regarded him thoughtfully. 'That was a fast about-turn,' she commented. 'Any way of tracing the sender?'

'I'm on it,' Jacks replied, 'and I've tried messaging again, but so far being blanked. Interesting aside, the English, what little there is of it, is pretty damn perfect. Which isn't to say Italians can't speak our language fluently, just making the point, is all.'

'And Brits do live in Naples,' Cristy reminded him. 'OK, let's see how you get on trying to track our Napoleon friend down. That's not what you call natives of Naples, is it?'

'Neapolitan or Napolitano,' Connor provided.

Grinning, Cristy turned back to Jacks as Clover asked if there was anything else from the supersleuths worthy of follow-up.

'Nah, only stuff we'd have rejected out of hand if we were doing the job,' he replied. 'A lot of fan mail apparently, especially for you, Connor.'

Connor started. 'Me?' he protested. 'Tell them to bin it, right now.'

'I think it all goes into folders in case we need to refer to it. Anyway, sounds like you haven't looked at your profile page on the website in the last twenty-four hours. Iz has posted some of the "at home" shots of you with Jodi and Aurora, and now there are lots of women out there wanting to have your babies.'

Cristy gave a snort of laughter as Connor groaned and sank his head into his hands.

'If it makes you feel any better,' Clover said, 'they're pretty good. All very tastefully done – *and*,' she added, meaningfully, 'they're going to appear in one of the upmarket colour supplements at the weekend. So I think Iz has done you proud.'

Clearly not ready for any sort of Iz praise yet, Connor said, 'OK, can we get back to what we're supposed to be doing here . . .'

'Oh my God!' Cristy suddenly cried, seeing who was calling her. 'It's Mia. Quick, set up to record . . . We'll worry about permissions after.'

'Is it video?' Connor asked, hitting the keys.

'Yes. OK, I'm clicking on now.' It took the usual few seconds for the connection to stabilize, but as Cristy started to speak she was stopped by the sight of Mia. The older woman's face was taut and stark white, her eyes seemed to blaze, and her hair was backcombed so haphazardly she surely couldn't have used a mirror to prep it.

MIA: 'You're a wicked, wicked woman, Cristy Whatever-your-name-is. I don't know how you live with yourself doing the things you do, interfering in other people's lives, making wildly offensive accusations, speaking to people who know *nothing*, and now you've gone too far. Those photographs are *fake* and you know it. You've doctored them, used them to sensationalize and scandalize, because that's what you people in the media do. What I want to know is why you're tormenting my niece this way? She doesn't deserve your cruelty. She's a good girl – misguided, and angry with me, but safe from things that will only hurt her. The way you're exploiting her is disgusting and shameful. So please leave us alone and stop this evil persecution.'

CRISTY: 'I'm sorry you feel this way, Mia, but I can assure you Sadie's welfare and the truth of her life matter a great deal to us. And the photographs aren't fake. We have the originals along with the negatives, so I'm afraid your sister *did* meet with George Symmonds-Browne and Janina Andris. Did you know about it?'

MIA: 'I don't have to answer your questions, nor do I have to believe a word you say. I'm telling you those photographs are forgeries . . .'

CRISTY: 'Perhaps I can bring them to you so you can see for yourself . . .'

MIA: 'I don't want you in my home, and I don't want you near my niece again. If you don't heed my wishes there will be terrible consequences for you.'

Cristy watched her on the screen, expecting her to ring off now, probably to call her lawyer, if she hadn't already. However, she simply looked around the room she was in, almost as if tracking a fly, or perhaps no longer sure about where she was.

CRISTY: 'Are you OK?'

Mia's eyes came back to the camera and peered in fiercely.

MIA: 'You are besmirching my beloved sister's reputation, and mine, with all your lies. She is very unhappy with you and it's never been wise to get on the wrong side of Lottie.'

This time the screen did go dark and Cristy sat back in her chair, inhaling deeply as the final words continued to land. 'Wow!' she murmured. 'So what do we make of that?'

'She's clearly nuts,' Clover offered, 'but at least she didn't threaten any sort of legal action. It's what I was waiting for.'

'Me too,' Connor said, 'although we should still brace ourselves for it and make sure our lawyers are up to speed with everything. What do you think about using it in a pod?'

Cristy shook her head doubtfully. 'Even if we got clearance, given her mental instability it's likely we'd be accused of gross insensitivity, or worse – and frankly, I don't want to get bogged down in proving the photos' authenticity to the world at large. We know they're genuine, so I say no to using Mia's weirdness against her, at this time. Let's think about whether we want to show the video to Sadie.'

After deliberating it Clover said, 'How about we just send the audio? The woman looked such a fright it actually feels wrong to share it, even with her niece.'

*

It didn't take Sadie long to get back to them.

'She's said it all to me already,' she told them, sounding tired and upset, 'and I quickly gave up trying to reason with her. She doesn't want to hear it, so she won't. As far as she's concerned – or maybe as far as Lottie's concerned, I can't be entirely sure who she thinks she is today – the photographs are fake and that's that.'

'How would you feel about using it in a pod?' Cristy asked. 'I don't think the video would be a good idea . . .'

'God no! I saw what she was like after she called you, so let's at least spare her the indignity of the world seeing her like that. As for what she said, if you think it's appropriate to use it, then why not?'

Surprised, Cristy added it to the clipboard for future use and looked up again as Sadie said, 'Can I ask if anyone's come forward about the photos yet?'

Knowing how hopeful she remained in spite of everything, Cristy's heart went out to her. 'As soon as anyone does we'll let you know,' she assured her, 'but I can't help worrying about how prepared you are for a . . . difficult outcome.'

Sadie's laugh was tired and humourless. 'Probably not

prepared at all,' she admitted, 'but it doesn't matter. We have to keep going.'

Not arguing, only worrying more, Cristy said, 'I take it you haven't found anything else of interest in Lottie's rooms?'

'No, but here's some good news. David's heard from the safe-cracker. Apparently, he's in Ireland at the moment, due back here on Friday, and he's saying that going by the images David sent him he shouldn't have any problem getting us access.'

Concerned now about what Sadie might find inside, Cristy said, 'Maybe you shouldn't be alone when you open it.'

Sounding anxious too, Sadie said, 'I must admit I am quite nervous about it, probably because nothing else has been locked away. So I'll ask Anna to be with me for the great unveiling.'

Cristy smiled at the attempted humour, and almost hated herself as she said, 'How would you feel about recording it as it happens? Or would that seem too intrusive until you actually know what's in there?'

'You mean you'd come over and be with me?'

'If you like.'

After a moment, Sadie said, 'I don't know. Can I think about it?'

'Of course.'

'I'm probably getting worked up over nothing, but instinctively it's feeling as though I should find out what's in there before I decide whether or not I want to share it.'

*

'That makes sense to me,' David said later when they spoke on the phone. Cristy was taking a different route home this evening, along Cumberland Road to the top of Bathurst Parade where the Louisiana pub loomed like an old-fashioned steamboat next to the basin. 'There's no knowing what dark secrets Lottie could have stored in that safe, and there's no doubt she had them.'

Grimacing, Cristy said, 'I'm actually starting to feel nervous about it myself, so I'm glad Anna, at least, is going to be there once the safe-cracker has done his job.'

'Indeed. And speaking of Chas – that's the bloke's name by the way – he told me something else when I was on the phone to him earlier. It turns out he knew the estate agent who sold Mia and Lottie the house. He doesn't think he'll be of as much interest to us as a "good mate" of his who did some work for the sisters back in the day.'

'What sort of work?'

'He doesn't know, or won't reveal details, but said mate, who apparently has a very respectable printworks based in the Home Counties, is also known in certain circles for being a master penman. I believe that's an insider's term for a forger.'

Cristy blinked. 'Talk me through this,' she said quietly.

'I don't know any more than that, but what I'm thinking, and I just know you're on the same page, is birth certificates, passports, photographs of fake parents . . . It could be this guy fixed it all.'

'Do we know where to find him?'

'Chas, who's actually a very good farrier in case you're interested, isn't prepared to go public with a name, or an exact location. However, he's agreed to tell you himself as much as he told me.'

'Of course we want to speak to him, it's a dynamite piece of information even without the mate's input. It kind of backs up what we've always known, that the sisters bought Sadie's identity in order to pass her off as their niece.'

'Exactly. I think I'm going to owe Chas a drink or two after this.'

Taking the iron footbridge over to the Ostrich pub, Cristy said, 'You can put it on expenses if you like, given you're practically one of the team now.'

He laughed. 'I might just hold you to that. Now, before you ring off, I want to know if anyone's been following you again, or tried to remove things from your office.'

'Nothing to report on that front,' she replied, deciding not to mention the text she'd received earlier advising her not to be afraid. It didn't mean anything, she was certain of that. It was simply the sort of messing trolls went in for to unnerve or destabilize their victims, and God knew it was a whole lot better than the vicious or depraved sort of fantasies some sickos inflicted on her. Thankfully, they were mostly blocked by the supersleuths these days, with death threats being sent straight to the police. It was a shame, for the whole team, not just her, that one or two wise-guys still managed to get hold of their personal numbers, but they simply did as they'd been advised back in their TV days. They stored the messages in a designated file just in case they were ever needed for further investigation, then got on with their day.

*

It was Friday afternoon and everyone was working quietly on their computers – Jacks still trying to trace the Naples messenger, Clover reaching out to a Vilnius-based journalist to see if he could help find Audra, Cristy and Connor pulling together sound effects and a structure for the next episode. The rain outside was so heavy and persistent it was making them reluctant to leave for the day, so they were all still there just after six when Sadie FaceTimed.

Guessing the safe-cracker had done his job, Cristy alerted the others and quickly clicked on. The instant Sadie's expression came into focus her insides tightened with unease.

'What is it?' Cristy asked. 'What's happened?'

Clearly agitated, Sadie said, 'It's full of cards and letters . . . I thought . . . They seemed sweet at first . . . They *are* sweet and passionate and not like anything I've read . . . He clearly loved her one hell of a lot and in her journals . . . Almost everything in them is about him. You need to read them. She was besotted with him; she talks about leaving me and Mia to be with him.'

'Who is it?' Cristy urged, already knowing it must be Symmonds-Browne.

'She doesn't call him by name, just says he's her darling, her one true love, and that's how he signs himself, but then I found photos of them together . . . Oh God, Cristy!' she sobbed. 'Anna's just sent one for you to see . . .'

As it came up on the screen the others murmured their shock.

'Shit!' Connor swore. 'This can't be right.'

'That's what I thought,' Sadie told him, her eyes desperate as they went to him. 'It can't, can it?'

They all looked to Cristy, but she was still staring at the screen, her heart contracted in disbelief and something close to horror. 'How the hell didn't we see this coming?' she muttered, and reached for the phone.

# CHAPTER TWENTY-THREE

Cristy was so angry with herself that she'd only narrowly avoided an accident while driving. It wasn't as if she hadn't considered the possibility of Robert Brinkley knowing Lottie Winters through their overseas work because she had. It had occurred to her more than once, so why in God's name had she never asked the question? The answer was because she'd assumed – and who wouldn't – that if he did know her he'd have said so, but he hadn't.

She wanted to know why.

More than that, she wanted a full explanation of what the hell was going on.

By now she was seated at a corner table of the White Lion pub, part of the Avon Gorge Hotel in Bristol's upscale area of Clifton. It was unusually quiet for a Saturday evening, most of the long bench tables were empty and only one server at the bar, but it was only just past six-thirty so it would probably start filling up quite soon. She wasn't interested in who was coming or going, only in Robert Brinkley who was seated opposite her, scrolling through the photos on her phone. As she watched him she felt so much anger, and on so many levels, that she was finding it hard to keep it to herself.

As his head was down she had no way of telling how he was reacting to the shock of her finding out about his relationship with Lottie, apart from the tightness gathering around his mouth. No matter that things had ended between them a long time ago – if Lottie's letters were anything to go by and actually they were everything – what Cristy needed to know was what the heck he was doing here, now, messing with Sadie, and with her?

When he eventually looked up she was momentarily thrown

by his expression. He seemed both stunned and confused, as if *she* were playing some unfathomable trick on *him*. There was none of the guilt or embarrassment or defensiveness she'd expected.

His voice was hoarse as he said, 'Where . . .? How did you get these?'

'Sadie found them,' she replied coolly, 'in her aunt Lottie's safe along with your letters, the cards you sent, the journals she wrote about you . . .'

'I don't understand,' he interrupted. 'They're . . . This is . . . *Lottie?*'

'You must know . . .'

'Oh God,' he groaned, clasping a hand to his head as though sinking into an unimaginable horror. 'If this is Lottie . . . Oh Christ, what can I tell you? How the hell is this even possible?'

'I'm waiting for you to answer that very question,' she told him tightly.

He regarded her helplessly, clearly not sure what to say, and looked at the photos again almost as if they weren't real, or they were of someone he didn't know, which couldn't be the case because he was in them.

Warily, she said, 'Have you never looked at our website?'

He shook his head. 'No, I haven't, but it seems if I had . . .'

'You'd have known right away that Lottie – *Sadie's aunt Lottie* – was the woman you had an intimate relationship with for . . . God knows how many years?' Her tone was every bit as sarcastic as she intended.

He scrolled through the photos again. 'Seeing these . . .' He paused, took a breath and she noticed his hand shake slightly as he said, quietly, 'So she's dead?'

Cristy became very still. *Did he really not know that? Was this truly how he was finding out that the woman he'd written so many beautiful letters to, who he'd apparently loved with a near blinding passion, was no longer alive?*

She watched him inhale deeply, softly, and take a while to let the breath go.

'We haven't been in touch for years,' he said quietly. His eyes were captured by a photo of Lottie laughing and looking as beautiful as Cristy had ever seen her. Had he taken it? He was in the next one, and the next, in fact most of the others Sadie had found in a small wallet inside the safe.

'I was never sure why she . . .' He took a moment and started again. 'The last time I saw her . . . We were in Nairobi. We'd stolen some time to be together . . . We often did that. She'd meet me a few days before I joined the medical team I'd been assigned to, or when I was on my way out . . . Sometimes we were at the same camp, or conference, or we were invited . . .'

'Please just tell me this,' Cristy interrupted. 'When you met Sadie, did you already know who she was?'

He looked up at her, clearly aghast. 'Of course I didn't,' he replied. 'You can't seriously think . . . Jesus Christ, what *do* you think? That I'm somehow involved in all this . . .?'

'Persuade me you aren't.'

He threw out his hands. 'How am I supposed to do that when I apparently know even less about Lottie Winters than you do? She was Carla to me, Carla Andrews. She lived in London, was the daughter of some wealthy banker, a free spirit, had no children of her own, was devoted to those she helped.'

Was this the truth, or did Cristy just want it to be because she didn't want to be wrong about him? 'If you were that close,' she said, 'and your correspondence shows that you were . . . Did she never talk about her sister and her niece?'

'Yes, often. Emilia and Sophie. I assumed they were mother and daughter . . . She was very close to them, but there were times when she needed to get away . . . She said they were . . . that sometimes she felt she couldn't breathe when she was with them . . . If you've read the letters you'll know all this.'

'We don't have the ones she wrote to you,' Cristy pointed out. 'When exactly did you meet her?'

Robert inhaled again, and took some time to roll back through the years, unlocking memories he seemed not to have visited for a very long time. 'It was 1998 in Tierkidi, one of the Sudanese refugee camps. She was brought to me as an emergency. She'd suffered a major cardiac event while helping to process new arrivals and . . . It was severe, we almost lost her . . .' He broke off, drew an unsteady hand across his mouth, the memory of it seeming to have the power to affect him even now. 'She always liked to say that I gave her a reason to go on living . . .' He tried to laugh as if to lighten the weight of it, but it came out as more of a groan. 'That was how it started between us. She was a patient; I was the surgeon who . . . wanted, more than anything, to save her.'

A touching picture that Cristy was finding it very easy to believe in . . . perhaps too easy? 'I'm guessing you were married at the time?' she said, seeing little choice but to go with his story, at least for now.

He nodded. 'And not in the habit of cheating. It was just with her . . . Christ, Cristy, you have to believe I'd have told you right away if I'd realized Sadie was in any way connected to her. It never even entered my head . . .'

Still angry with herself for not having explored the possibility when she'd known they moved in the same world, she said, 'You have to see that this . . . *revelation* . . . calls everything into question about you, and seriously jeopardizes our credibility for not having known something so important about you sooner. It seems pretty obvious now, having read your letters, that you were the reason Lottie was so keen to break free of her sister. She got her a husband, and then a child . . . And the fact that you just happened to stumble across that child's mother on a hillside close to the house where Lottie and her sister were staying, and then you turn up all these years later just as the same child goes public with her suspicions . . . Everyone's going to be asking who the hell you really are. *I* am asking who the hell are you?'

His eyes were solemn and dark with sincerity as he said, 'I am exactly who you think I am, Cristy, and the main reason I took an interest in helping Sadie is because it matters to my mother.'

'But the sisters were in Somerset at the same time you were back in 2000,' she cried. 'By your own admission you knew Lottie – Carla – then. Janina even talked to you about her . . . That's what you said.'

'She did, but I had no reason to think that one of the women she was referring to was Carla. There are hundreds, thousands, of women from all over the world who get involved in the camps. And as far as I can remember Carla was in Malawi around the time I was in Somerset, or I thought she was . . . For God's sake,

Cristy, coincidences can be real even if they seem unlikely, or convenient, or flat out unbelievable. You must know that.'

Though she did, she remained very uncomfortable with this one. Opening up the *Hindsight* website on her phone she found the shots of George Symmonds-Browne with Lottie and Janina, and thrust the phone at him. 'Do you know who he is?' she asked.

Looking at it Robert frowned and shook his head. 'I've never seen him before.'

'But you do recognize Lottie?'

He nodded.

'So can you explain what's happening there, where this is . . .?'

'I have no idea, I'm sorry.' He put the phone down on the table. 'I know you won't want to hear this, why would you, but finding out that Carla is dead . . .'

'Lottie. Her name was Lottie, and I think we've already established that she really wasn't the woman you thought she was.'

His eyes hardened slightly as he said, 'Maybe not, but we're all capable of being different people at different times, and if, as you say, you've read my letters you'll know how much she meant to me. I saw nothing bad in her, only good . . .'

'If you loved her so much, why didn't you leave your wife to be with her? You told her in one letter it was too soon, your children were still too young . . .'

'They were, and they're the only reason I wouldn't end my marriage. When you've seen the kind of suffering I have, that Carla saw too, children, babies, orphaned and maimed . . . Losing parents to a divorce doesn't equate, of course it doesn't, mine would still have had a mother and father who loved them, a proper home to live in . . . Even so, I didn't want to hurt them, to see that same look of bewilderment and fear in their eyes as I was seeing in the field and know I had caused it.'

'Did your wife know about Lottie?'

'Yes, she did.' He gazed down at the phone, its screen dark now, masking Lottie's image, and Cristy couldn't help wondering how much he wanted to feast his eyes on her again.

'Here's the thing about my marriage,' he said, circling a hand around his empty glass as if to stop himself reaching for the phone.

'I know you'll see my affair with Carla as cheating, a betrayal of my family, my principles, of everything really, but Jenny, my wife . . . We came to an agreement after our second child was born, which – here's another coincidence you're probably not going to like – was the year I met Carla, and yes my wife and I went on to have another child after that, in 2000. But the decision Jenny and I took in '98 to have an open marriage was actually nothing to do with Carla. It was so that Jenny could be true to herself and stop pretending she was someone she wasn't.'

*True to herself? Pretending?* Regarding him sceptically, Cristy said, 'Are you about to tell me your wife is gay?'

'She is bisexual,' he confirmed. 'The children know that now and have long accepted it. What they find slightly more *unusual*, or used to anyway, is that Jenny and I have chosen to stay together.' He seemed to expect her to find it unusual too, even scorn it, but she said nothing.

'It suits us both,' he explained. 'We like one another, enjoy each other's company – I guess you could say we're each other's best friend, and yes there have been times – still are – when we're intimate. She's always been there for me when I've needed someone, and I like to think I'm always there for her. Certainly she helped me over the break-up with Carla. I might have gone mad otherwise. I simply couldn't understand why she'd decided we shouldn't continue our relationship. I could see, when she told me, that it was tearing her apart too, but nothing I said or did was enough to make her change her mind. She kept saying we had to move on, to stop the dependency on one another that was only going to hurt us more in the end.'

'Did she know you were in an open marriage by then?'

'Yes, and she'd always sworn she was happy with the way we were, that she could wait until I was ready to be with her completely, just as long as we kept seeing one another. Then suddenly it changed.'

'When exactly did it change?'

'In 2005. We were in Nairobi, as I said. She told me she couldn't see a future for us even if I left my wife, so it was best that we let one another go right then.'

'Did you see her again after that?'

He shook his head. 'I wrote to her, of course, many times, but she never responded to my letters or emails and the number I had for her was disconnected. Obviously, I could have made contact through other people, but it clearly wasn't what she wanted, and so in the end I . . . I was going to say I gave up, but I never consciously did that. I guess what I did was carry on hoping that eventually she'd change her mind and contact me.'

Realizing that the hope, on some level, had still been alive until a few minutes ago, when he'd learned of her death, Cristy's tone was a little gentler as she said, 'Why don't you get us another drink and we'll try to work out how we handle this now, with Sadie.'

Picking up their glasses, he said, 'What is she actually thinking . . .?'

'I'm afraid that you're a liar, a cheat, someone who knows George Symmonds-Browne and who might have been involved in getting her to her aunts, even in harming Janina or Lukas, or both.'

'Jesus Christ,' he murmured, clearly appalled. 'You have to tell her . . . Please tell me it's not what you think too?'

She simply stared at him.

He swallowed dryly, but said no more as he went to the bar to order another beer and glass of wine.

As she waited she turned everything over in her mind, trying to get a sense of what her instincts were telling her about the affair, and deception, intended or not. Robert was right about coincidences, of course, they really did happen and sometimes they could stretch credulity to breaking point. So maybe he hadn't known Carla and Lottie were one and the same person. Maybe he really hadn't looked at the *Hindsight* website before today.

When he returned to the table and sat down again, Cristy said, 'If I'm prepared to believe what you've told me then, the way I see it, we have two choices going forward: we either make a big deal of Sadie finding out about the love affair between you and Lottie and put your current involvement in Sadie's search down to spectacular coincidence . . .' She stopped, shaking her head. 'It's not going to fly,' she said helplessly.

'I think what matters is whether or not Sadie believes it,' he said.

Agreeing with that, she picked up her drink and continued to think. 'The alternative is that we pretend it hasn't happened and carry on with no mention of it . . . But it's bound to come out sooner or later, and if the public realize we've deliberately held back, duped them even . . . No, we have to run it, take a proactive stance rather than risk having our reputation trashed by what could easily be viewed as duplicity on our part to the point of outright deceit.'

He reached for his glass, made to drink, but put it down again. 'Can I remind you that my mother and my children listen to your podcasts?' he said quietly. 'If you're intending to use the letters, the cards . . . They're very personal and from another time . . .'

'I realize that,' she said, 'and I'm sorry if you think your family will be upset by it, but they're adults, I'm sure they can cope with the exposure of an affair that ended twenty-odd years ago. And you have to understand that Sadie is my concern. Obviously, your secret will be safe if she doesn't want us to reveal it, but we have to let her make the decision, and I'm afraid I will be doing my best to persuade her to let us dedicate time to it.'

When he didn't protest further, she continued.

'I think she might find it easier to accept if you were to go over there and talk to her in person.'

Though he seemed startled by the suggestion, and reluctant, he then began to nod slowly, until finally he said, 'Yes, I should see her, but if you're . . . If you intend to be there I hope you'll consider it enough to have my letters broadcast around the world without having to add a very difficult conversation with Sadie to my humiliation.'

Recalling the letters, their tenderness and intimacy, and how genuinely upset Robert had clearly been on learning of Lottie's death, Cristy said, 'I can't make any promises yet, but I can tell you that it will not be our intention to exacerbate or sensationalize either your, or Sadie's, grief.'

*

After leaving Robert to walk back to his rented flat, Cristy drove out of Clifton, updating Connor by phone as she went. 'It'll be interesting to see what happens when he and Sadie do get together,' she was saying as she edged between the parked cars on Granby Hill.

'Even more interesting,' he responded, 'will be Mia's reaction when she finds out about the affair. Presuming she doesn't know already, and personally I reckon she does.'

'I agree, but what I'd really like the answer to is *why* Lottie ended the affair when she did in 2005. They were still, according to Robert, very much in love, and he got the impression it wasn't something she wanted to do, but she did it anyway, and never went back.'

'And it was sometime in the same year that Lottie decided she didn't want to be published any more.'

Cristy was frowning so hard by now it almost hurt. 'What the heck happened?' she murmured, forgetting to indicate as she turned onto Hotwells Road. 'Sadie would have been seven at the time. They were in Guernsey, she was at school, but I can't think of anything else that might be significant from around that time. Can you?'

'Not off the top, but that's why we need to speak to Corny. Where are you now?'

'I'll be driving past Spike Island in the next few minutes. Are you at the office?'

'It's Saturday night and I have a life. Also, you surely don't need me to remind you that *you've* got other things to do this evening.'

As her heart fluttered, she said, 'You're right, I have, but we should meet tomorrow to discuss next week's episode . . .'

The line dropped for a moment; when Connor came back he was saying, '. . . idea when Robert's intending to go to Guernsey?'

'He says he'll reach out to Sadie tonight, and if she agrees to see him he hopes to go as soon as Monday. One of us needs to be there when it happens.'

'A trip to the Channel Islands? Let me see, who should that be? Oh, hang on, that's right, David's already here, that's why you're in a hurry to get home. Jodi's asking if you'd like to come for Sunday lunch tomorrow.'

'Sounds great. I'll ask and get back to you. He should be at the flat by now.'

'Tell him we'd love to see him, and if you two haven't straightened things out by then, bring yourselves here for a shot of Connor and Jodi counselling.'

'That'll sort everything once and for all,' she commented dryly, and after assuring him she'd be happy to fly back to Guernsey with David on Monday, if necessary – provided all went well between them this evening, of course – she sped up along Cumberland Road, daring to hope that he really was there.

It seemed unbelievable in a way, and yet he really had rung this morning to tell her he was on his way and if she didn't want to see him he'd wait until she did. How was that for assertive? And how could she resist when she wanted to see him more than anything? Given how insistent he was being she was ready to believe that she might, somehow, have got it wrong about him and Juliette.

*Just please don't let me be fooling myself and he's about to tell me, in person, why we can't continue seeing one another.*

*That doesn't make any sense. Why would he want to do that when we've already stopped seeing one another?*

*So there's nothing wrong with hoping this evening is going to turn out well.*

Cristy was ready to believe that right up until the moment she pulled into the leafy courtyard outside her building to find Matthew's car in her parking space. What the hell was he doing here? She was expecting Aiden to be inside the flat; he'd agreed to come and let David in, so she could only presume that some other pressing engagement had arisen for her son and he'd asked his father to step in for him.

She was going to brain the boy, she really was, but before that she had to work out how the heck she was going to get rid of Matthew. What if he decided to stay and screw things up for her while making an ass of himself?

As her neighbour was in Manchester tonight, she backed into his space, somehow resisting the urge to kick Matthew's car as she passed. God only knew what was going on inside the flat by now, she just hoped David didn't think she'd set this up, or worse that she was making some sort of childish point along the lines of: if you're still involved with Juliette, don't forget Matthew is very keen to get back with me . . .

*For God's sake, Cristy. Pull yourself together.*

'Hey, Mum!' Aiden shouted, as she closed the front door. 'We're in here.'

Wondering where the hell else they'd be other than the sitting room, while relieved to know that her son hadn't completely let her down, she shrugged off her coat and scarf and kicked off her shoes. Were those David's loafers sitting comfortably between Matthew's Timberlands and Aiden's Nikes? Christ, this was starting to feel like some bizarre kind of alt-world where all the footwear got along while the owners – didn't.

'There you are,' Aiden said, coming out of the sitting room to greet her. 'Wasn't my idea,' he muttered under his breath. 'Tried to stop him, but you know what he's like . . .'

'Don't keep us waiting,' Matthew called out. 'There's a lovely white Rioja here, and we're keen to open it.'

Wondering if there was such a thing as ex-mariticide – or was that just plain murder? – Cristy braced herself and followed Aiden into the sitting room. There she found Matthew ensconced on one sofa, as if he actually lived here, while David was in one of the armchairs, appearing perfectly relaxed and highly amused by the unexpected welcome he'd received.

'Hello, darling,' Matthew gushed, not bothering to get up. (Just as well or she might have knocked him down again.) 'David and I have been having a lovely chat about deep sea fishing and how it's a bit of a hobby of mine. I get the impression he's way more experienced than I am, but too modest to admit it . . . Here, come and sit down,' he said, patting the sofa cushion next to his own.

Suspecting he'd manoeuvred things to make sure she couldn't sit with David, Cristy pulled out a dining chair and plonked herself on it. She was aware she hadn't actually spoken to David yet, but she couldn't think what to say with Matthew earwigging from three feet away. 'Good flight?' she managed in the end.

'Easy,' he assured her. 'Everything on time, and Aiden was waiting outside when I got here.'

'Dad drove me,' Aiden confessed. 'He was supposed to drop me off, but . . . here he is.'

Matthew laughed. 'Here I am,' he agreed, cheerily, 'in the bosom of my family, and I must say, it's a great pleasure to meet you, David. Sorry, repeating myself, but I've heard so much about you from Hayley and Aiden and what a wonderful time you gave them at Christmas . . .'

'While you were in LA getting arrested,' Aiden reminded him.

Matthew grimaced good-naturedly. 'That happened *after* Christmas,' he said, 'but I admit it was an unfortunate incident for which I was entirely to blame. I haven't been quite myself since Cristy and I . . .'

'Are you going to pour the wine?' Cristy cut in, noticing that Aiden was starting to see the funny side of this.

'Of course, of course,' Matthew declared, sitting forward.

'And then you can go,' Cristy told him.

He gave a hearty laugh as if she'd just cracked the most hilarious joke. 'Don't worry, no offence taken,' he assured her, as if she'd apologized for it.

Deciding he'd lost his mind, she said to David, 'I've made dinner reservations . . .'

'Oh, that's a shame,' Matthew interrupted. 'I've managed to secure us a table at Casa and you know how hard it is to get in there. My treat. I'd be at a loose end otherwise.'

'What a shame,' Cristy retorted, sarcastically.

'I think we should accept Matthew's invitation,' David told her, and she felt she might like to kick him too, given the unmistakable laughter in his eyes.

'Yeah, I think you should,' Aiden agreed, clearly lapping it up.

She glared at the glass Matthew was passing her, and clocked the moment he realized it might be safer if he just put it down.

'I think I've heard about the restaurant you've chosen,' David said, as he and Matthew settled back into a friendly chat. 'Doesn't it have an award-winning chef?'

'Peter Sanchez-Iglesias,' Matthew confirmed, delightedly. 'I know him quite well. It's how we got the table. Aiden, you're going to join us I hope.'

'Actually, I've got to be somewhere,' Aiden grimaced.

'No you haven't,' Cristy informed him.

'I have . . .'

'You have not,' she insisted.

Getting the message, Aiden choked back a laugh and said, 'OK, I'll clear the decks. Just making a few calls,' and he disappeared into his bedroom.

Deciding to do the same, after all she needed to change, Cristy made her excuses and took her wine and phone with her.

As soon as she'd closed the door, she texted David, *Sorry. I know he's excruciating, but he wasn't always like this.*

A moment later a message came back, *I kind of like him.*

*I don't believe you.*

*He's taking me out to dinner, what's not to like?*

*

In the end it was gone eleven by the time Matthew was persuaded that no one else wanted a nightcap; it was time for him to go home and take Aiden with him. Of course, he'd had too much to drink to drive, so he'd have to come back in the morning to pick up his car.

'I'll bring breakfast,' he promised, as he got into an Uber.

'Croissants are good for me,' David told him. 'Let us know when you're on your way, I'll put the coffee on.'

'You might be even worse than he is,' Cristy told him, as they went inside.

'At least I didn't bring Juliette,' he retorted.

Laughing in spite of herself, she led the way through to the sitting room and feeling suddenly absurdly teenagerish – thrilled that David was here, excited by the prospect of him staying, anxious about the talk they needed to have – she said, 'I actually wouldn't mind a nightcap, if you're up for one too?'

'Count me in,' and he began collecting up the glasses they hadn't bothered to carry into the kitchen earlier.

A few minutes later, as they sat down with their brandies, he said, 'I know we're both tired, and we've had a few drinks, but I still want to get this off my chest tonight. And I hope that by the time I'm done this gulf,' he gestured to the space on the sofa between them, 'might have closed a little.'

Very much hoping the same, she said, 'I need you to understand that I . . .'

His hand went up. 'I think I can guess what you're going to say so please let me speak first.'

Her eyes stayed on his, her anticipation building as she thought, *God he's gorgeous.* Then, *Just don't let yourself be swayed by it, or drawn into anything until you know what he's going to say.*

'First of all,' he said, 'I am not involved with Juliette in the way you seem to think. In the way I confess I probably allowed you to think . . . It wasn't a conscious decision to hurt you, far from it, but when I realized what was happening I was angry that you didn't trust me.'

She started to speak, but his hand went up again.

'Obviously, she and I are close,' he continued, 'and I won't apologize for that. She's my son's mother and it means a lot to Laurent that his parents don't only get along, but that we feel at least a little bit like a family to him.'

She held her silence, as he took a sip of his drink.

'The last time Juliette and I were intimate,' he continued, 'was back in August, in Paris . . . It's not the only time it's happened since we split up, but I can promise you that it doesn't happen often, and it certainly hasn't since you and I got together.'

Knowing she was far too eager to believe that, Cristy countered it with a reminder of Juliette emerging from the gazebo on New Year's Eve, and how closely they'd danced together after. 'I think she still has very strong feelings for you,' she said, 'and whether you return them or not, you disappeared with her on New Year's Day, and no one saw you for the next couple of hours.'

He frowned, as though trying to recall it, until his expression cleared and he said, 'Laurent was sick. Actually he was hungover, but that's another story . . . He wanted us both to sit with him, to feel sorry for him, I guess, so we did.'

'But I saw you take wine with you . . .'

'I came back for it because Juliette thought the smell might help Laurent to throw up. It worked, and after we'd cleaned him up all three of us fell asleep on the bed. That's why I was gone for so long.'

Although it was believable, and David certainly seemed sincere, she had to point out how cold he'd been with her after, right up until she'd left.

'Because that's how you were being with me,' he told her. 'I knew you were worried about Matthew and I could see you wanted to get away . . . I didn't blame you, I understood, but at the same time I was angry, jealous, I guess . . . And you were behaving as though I was holding you back, or standing in the way . . . Obviously, I should have done the grown-up thing and tried to get you to talk, but in my stubbornness, arrogance if you like, I decided that if you couldn't come out and say what was on your mind then I wasn't going to ask.'

Having to accept that she probably had gone into some sort of passive-aggressive routine, Cristy started to speak, but he said, 'There's more. It's my guess, well, it was my mother's actually and I saw right away that she was probably right . . . She thinks that because of your experience with Matthew, what you went through after the break-up, it's made it difficult for you to trust someone again. She also said that if I want you in my life, I need to be mindful of your past and make sure I don't give you cause to doubt me or my feelings. And that was exactly what I'd done over New Year, whether I realized it or not.'

Having to swallow a lump in her throat, Cristy said, 'I've always loved your mother, since the day we first met.'

He smiled. 'You probably know the feeling's mutual.' Then after a pause, 'So this is me apologizing for not being sensitive to your feelings, and for not coming here sooner to try to make things right between us.'

The gulf was definitely closing, almost faster than she could keep up with. 'I realize I didn't make it easy for you,' she said, 'I know I can be very defensive. I'm so afraid, probably too afraid, of being hurt like that again . . . It's almost like I keep expecting it, and because we still don't know one another that well, I guess it's inevitable that we – that *I* – will get some things wrong. I just wish I'd faced down my demons . . .' She stopped as he got up from the sofa and held out a hand.

She allowed him to pull her up into his arms, and said dryly, 'I guess that's the gulf dealt with then.'

He laughed and brought the length of her body against his. 'I was just thinking,' he murmured against her lips, 'maybe that's enough talking for tonight?'

Mmm, she thought as their embrace deepened, he was right, it probably was.

# CHAPTER TWENTY-FOUR

CRISTY: 'Hi, it's Cristy, it's Tuesday morning and I am on my way to Florida.

'Yes, I really am on a non-stop flight to Miami. All will be revealed in a later episode, but for now I'm sorry to tell you that we're unable to bring you a podcast at our usual time this evening. Never fear, there will be an episode coming your way at the end of the week that will contain surprises all of its own. Nothing to do with Florida.' (And everything to do with Robert Brinkley, she didn't add.)

'It's funny how life throws things at you, swerves you off in directions you'd never have dreamt were coming only days, maybe hours before. That is certainly happening with this series. So, I hope you'll be patient and bear with us. Connor will be your host on Friday and I hope to be sharing the reasons for my unexpected trip Stateside by next Tuesday.'

After connecting to the plane's WiFi and uploading the recording to the team, Cristy stretched out her long legs and sighed luxuriously as she settled deeper into the business-class seat. She truly had *not* seen this coming, had only learned yesterday that instead of flying to Guernsey that day, she'd be heading for the US in the morning to meet none other than George Symmonds-Browne, or so she'd been told. Or, as he was known these days, Gabriel Bailey.

Apparently, he was not in witness protection, or under any other kind of state protection. In fact, according to Evie Baker, who Cristy had been in regular email contact with since Sunday, he was living a quiet life in a safe and comfortable community on Florida's Gulf coast. He'd changed his name, said Evie, partly out of respect for his family, but also to avoid some old business associates. He was willing to talk to *Hindsight*, but only in person – in other words not over Zoom, and nor was he coming to the UK.

Whether or not Evie Baker was the same Evie Natalie Irwin had talked about in her interview had not yet been established. However, she'd been the subject of much debate since Jacks had found the first email from her at eight-thirty on Sunday morning and alerted the whole team to its existence.

A video conference was almost immediately under way.

True, there had to be a million or more Evies out there. This particular message, spotted and forwarded by an insomniac supersleuth, had once again claimed that George Symmonds-Browne was in Naples.

In the end, it was Matthew who'd redirected their assumptions from southern Italy when he'd turned up at the flat around ten o'clock not only with croissants and pastries, but with information from his late-responding Interpol contact. *Last known location of Symmonds-Browne: Naples, Florida. No longer person of interest to international law enforcement agencies.* Nothing about protection, or turning state's witness, or even that Symmonds-Browne might be living under another name. However, it had been enough to convince Cristy and team that a trip to Florida was worth committing to.

'But not alone,' Connor had declared firmly. 'We've got no idea what you might be walking into and I, for one, am uncomfortable with the fact that neither this woman, nor Symmonds-Browne – Bailey, whatever we're supposed to call him – will connect online.'

They'd all been at Cristy's flat by then with Matthew, showing no inclination to leave, taking charge of food deliveries, while David sat watching and listening in what appeared to be growing fascination with the delegation and decision-making process.

Finally, when it became clear that Connor needed to take on the Guernsey trip – they still wanted to interview Corny the ex-housekeeper, and possibly record Robert's meeting with Sadie – it was decided that Clove and Jacks should fly to Vilnius to talk to the journalist who was helping to locate Lukas and Janina's older sister while Cristy went to Florida. When David volunteered himself as Cristy's 'bag-carrier' she turned to him in amazement.

She was thrilled, of course, but really? Did he mean it? The nonchalance of his shrug told her that he did.

'Why wouldn't I want to go to the sunshine state in February?' he'd asked, not adding, *with you*, but she'd known from the way he was looking at her that it was what he was thinking.

'Darn! Beat me to it,' Matthew declared, clearly nowhere near as thrilled as he'd tried to sound, and looking, for one truly alarming moment, as though he might offer to go too.

Shuddering at the memory of that now, and just how horrendous it would be if the three of them actually were on this plane, Cristy turned to David and smiled to find him watching her.

'OK?' he asked, reaching for her hand.

She nodded and felt grateful to Iz all over again for the way she'd swung into action yesterday, getting their sponsor Open Destiny on board to arrange this flight to Miami where they were due to spend the night before a hire car was delivered in the morning for them to drive across the state to Naples.

Closing her eyes, she sat quietly wondering what might lie ahead, if there was danger lurking, maybe answers to questions they hadn't even thought to ask. Would Evie Baker turn out to be the same Evie who'd been Lukas's girlfriend back in 2015 when Natalie had last heard from him? If so, and she was with Symmonds-Browne in Florida, how on earth had that come about? Perhaps more to the point, what had happened to Lukas?

*

'OK, all aboard for Alligator Alley!' David declared the next morning as he started the engine to their rented SUV.

Cristy turned to look at him.

He shrugged. 'It's what they call the highway between Miami and Naples,' he explained.

'But we're not likely to see any?'

'Who knows. We'll be going right through the Everglades and

last I heard it's where a lot of them hang out. So, do you have the address?'

Pulling up the latest email from Evie Baker, Cristy programmed in 4456 Verbena Circle, Naples, FL, and hit go. It was true, their journey was going to take them right through the heart of the swamp and as far as she knew there was only the one road, but if people were doing it all day, every day . . . Anyway, she should probably record a description of the drive in order to set the scene and maybe share some of her feelings about what might or might not be about to happen as a result of this unexpected swerve into territory unknown. What she wouldn't do was mention David. Given his central role in their last podcast, it would seem beyond weird that he was figuring in this one, especially on a transatlantic trip to the sunshine in the middle of an English winter.

Glancing over at him, taking in his profile and letting her eyes fall to his hands on the wheel, she felt amazed all over again to think of how only a few days ago they'd been caught up in a ludicrous misunderstanding of how their relationship was going. And now, here they were, in sunny Florida, almost like a honeymoon couple with, perhaps, as much to look forward to from one another as they had from the real reason for being here.

'Are you going to tell?' he asked, indicating to overtake a slow-moving truck.

Realizing he meant her thoughts, Cristy said, 'I'm trying to make myself believe you're really here.'

He glanced at her in surprise. 'Last night wasn't enough for you?' he said dryly.

Smiling as the reminder lit through her, she said softly, 'We should probably try harder.'

With a laugh, David reached for her hand and brought it to his mouth for a kiss. 'We could have a priority issue facing us,' he said, 'so I'll put it out there now that I'm OK with being second fiddle while you're working. I've brought my bikini.'

She started to laugh.

'Just the bottom half,' he added, 'and happy to share.'

Still laughing, she said, 'Do you realize Iz – or Open Destiny – have booked us into the Ritz-Carlton, which is apparently right on the coast and starts at around fifteen hundred dollars per night? All I have to do in return is mention it in the podcast.' She looked down at her phone as it started to ring, 'Ah ha! Evie Baker,' she declared, and quickly clicked on.

'Hi, have I reached Cristy?' The voice was female, cheery and sounded both American and . . . There was something else, but it was too soon yet to tell what it was.

'You have,' Cristy told her, hitting record in case the conversation proved useful later. 'Good morning, Evie. How are you?'

'Oh me, I'm fine. We're excited to see you. Have you set off yet?'

'About half an hour ago so already on Alligator Alley.'

Evie laughed. 'You watch out for them naughty little critters now, they're not to be messed with. We've got a big old boy in our pond here, snappy as fuck he is.'

Startled as much by the language as the pet, Cristy said, 'Please tell me you're not serious.'

'I could have been, once, but he got taken off to the marshes a while ago. We're not even sure how he came to be where we found him, but we've got some *interesting* neighbours in this community with their own kind of humour. By the way, when I say pond, in British terms it would be a lake, like Windermere or Ullswater – probably not that big actually, never was good on size. Just not the kind we Brits keep our goldfish in.'

'Can I ask where you're from?' Cristy said, as they pulled up to pay a toll.

'Liverpool, born and bred,' Evie answered, exaggerating her Scouse accent. 'Been a long time since I was there though. Now, I'm calling to redirect you to our country club. We've booked a table poolside for lunch and that's about the time you should arrive. It seemed easier than getting our cook in on her day off. I'll pop the address into an email so you can just click on. It's only about fifteen minutes from the house . . . You're staying at the Ritz-Carlton, is that right?'

Having sent the information yesterday, Cristy said, 'Correct. Is it far from the club?'

'Twenty to thirty minutes, depending on traffic. It's a cool place, great beachside café, but you have to get there early, they don't take reservations. How long are you staying?'

'I'm not sure yet,' Cristy replied, taking in the endless expanse of tropical foliage either side of the highway and trying not to imagine too much of what lurked in the depths. 'I guess a lot will depend on you and what George – Gabriel – is willing to tell us.'

'Sure, good. He's up for this, just . . . just don't push him too hard, OK?'

With a glance at David, Cristy said, 'Is he joining us for lunch?'

'I hope so. He said he would, and he doesn't have any other commitments today so I expect he'll be there. Now, you're heading for the Royal Poinciana Golf Club – don't ask me why it's royal, I've never figured that out – but it's not hard to find. We'll head over there early to make sure we're waiting when you arrive. Remember, we're going to be poolside and there's parking right out front.'

As she rang off, David said, 'Given her Liverpool roots it's seeming more likely that she's Lukas's old girlfriend?'

Cristy nodded thoughtfully. 'I'm dying to find out how she ended up here with Symmonds-Browne,' she said, all manner of scenarios dancing through her head, none of them good, especially not for Lukas.

'Gabriel Bailey,' David corrected quietly. 'Has Evie mentioned Janina or Sadie at all in her emails?'

Cristy shook her head. 'Not once. I mean, she knows it's why we're here, obviously, but she hasn't volunteered a single thing about them so far.'

Speeding up to pass a U-Haul truck, he said, 'I wonder why she asked you not to push Bailey too hard. Does that signal a short fuse that could have him walking out at the merest hint of a difficult question?'

Taking out her recorder Cristy clicked on and started to speak.

CRISTY: 'Not far from Naples now and you'll have heard the phone conversation I just had with Evie Baker. So I'm wondering, will Gabriel Bailey decide to join us for lunch, or have I come all this way just to be ghosted?'

She paused, lowering the device to her lap as she thought. After a while she continued.

CRISTY: 'You know, I can't help feeling like a pawn in some sort of a game I don't know the rules for, which is . . . kind of sinister, and making me glad I didn't come alone. On the other hand, I could be overthinking things, getting too caught up in my own imagination. So maybe I just keep moving forward, follow directions and hope, when I finally manage to talk to Symmonds-Browne – aka Gabriel Bailey – that I don't find myself sorely wishing I hadn't come.'

*

Half an hour later they were merging from one of the many wide, palm-lined boulevards they'd followed since entering the outskirts of town to begin a slow, meandering crawl through the Royal Poinciana's extensive grounds.

CRISTY: 'It's so green and manicured, sun-drenched and fragrant, I feel as though I'm floating off into the Elysian Fields. To give you an idea of its size there are, apparently, two Audubon International Certified golf courses here – I'm sure that will hugely impress the aficionados amongst you – seven HydroGrid soft tennis courts, and seven pickleball courts (whatever that is). We know there's a pool, because Evie's already told us, but what she didn't mention was the dress code that apparently requires "acceptable attire" throughout the club. I guess I'll just have to hope that the knee-shorts and floaty blouse I'm wearing are suitable. If not, well, the luggage is in the boot – or trunk, depending on which version of English we're speaking.

'Anyway, from what we've seen of Naples so far it's hard to describe what a striking contrast it makes to its Italian counterpart. All they seem to have in common is sunshine and blue skies; one so grungy and cluttered with history, the other so *new* and clean and *rich.* Ah, I'm guessing this is Evie, waving out to us, unless everyone's ridiculously friendly around here . . .'

As David swung the car into a space, Cristy continued to

record, lowering her window and smiling expectantly at the woman coming to meet them.

EVIE: 'Cristy! You made it. So lovely to see you. And you're . . .'

DAVID: 'David. Good to meet you.'

EVIE: 'You too. You can leave the car right here, the pool's just through that gate. Gabe's already at the table, and very keen to meet you.'

As Evie stepped back to check her phone, Cristy continued recording.

CRISTY: 'Evie's a very attractive woman of around fifty, I'd say – to be honest it's not easy to tell when various enhancements have been brought into play. Maybe edit out that last bit, I don't want to offend her, but honestly, those lips . . .? Anyway, she's petite, lots of jewellery, a cloud of fair hair, a winning smile and merry blue eyes.'

Turning off the engine, David said, 'OK, are you ready for this?'

Cristy started as Evie reappeared at her window. Quickly lowering it again, she said, 'Are we properly dressed?'

Laughing, Evie said, 'We're quite casual at the pool. If you've brought a suit you can take a swim after we've eaten. Or you can wait until we get to the house and take a dip there. Of course there's an excellent facility at the Ritz-Carlton, but obviously it's shared with other guests. Ah! Here's Lukas. He didn't think he'd make it in time, but luckily he has. Come say hi.'

Still blinking, Cristy watched Evie hurry over to a smart white Lexus where an impeccably dressed, athletic-looking man of around fifty was already stepping out – and as he enveloped her in a tender, almost intimate hug it seemed only polite to look away.

'Well, there's a turn-up,' David muttered wryly.

Cristy turned to look at him. 'Please tell me I'm still recording,' she said, holding up the device.

'You are,' he confirmed.

Speaking into it, she continued.

CRISTY: 'So they're all together, George, Lukas and Evie. Is it too much to hope that Janina might also be here in Shangri-La?'

*

Cristy and David were out of the car by the time Lukas came loping across the car park to greet them, all smiles and outstretched hands. She felt, oddly, as if she already knew him – she did from photos, though of course he was older and greyer – and there was an air of easy sophistication about him that he almost certainly wouldn't have had twenty years ago. (No sign of the hat!) Maybe it was the expensive cut of his clothes and his natural tan that made him appear so comfortable in these surroundings; he really did seem to belong.

'Thank you, thank you for coming all this way,' he said, grasping Cristy's hand in both of his, his Lithuanian accent making his words somehow warmer and friendlier. 'I was worried I might miss you and I want to hear all about Sasha. How is she? Will she come too? Can we meet her?'

As Cristy struggled for an answer, David said, 'We call her Sadie, but if you prefer Sasha . . .'

'Sasha, Sadie . . . We don't mind just as long as she's safe and happy. That's all we've ever wanted for her. Oh, but to see her, to hold her dear face in my hands . . . I'm sorry,' he said. 'Lukas Andris, pleased to meet you.'

'David Gaudion,' David replied, shaking hands. 'And likewise.'

Turning back to Cristy, Lukas said, 'When we were told about your podcast it was like being blessed by God above. After all these years . . . Of course Evie got in touch right away, and now here you are . . .'

'Honey,' Evie said gently, 'Gabe is at the table alone. We should go in or . . . Well, let's go in.'

Cristy glanced at David and caught the arch of an eyebrow as they linked hands and fell into step behind the others. Keeping her voice low, she said, 'This is so not what I expected . . .'

'On the same page for that,' he told her. 'And there's so much money around here you can almost smell the laundry.'

Realizing he'd be far more attuned to that than she would, she said, 'Are you serious?'

'I could be.'

'It's beautiful, though, isn't it? Helped by the weather, of course. But what about Lukas being here? I'm still struggling to get my head around that.'

'Me too.'

Smiling and waving as Evie turned to check they were coming, Cristy said, 'I wonder how open and honest they're going to be, how *real* they actually are. I mean, they haven't gone out of their way to find Sadie in all these years, and yet now they want us to believe that they can't wait to see her and we're a gift from God.'

'Whatever their story, I feel it's going to be an interesting one. I guess it'll just be a question of whether or not we believe it, which makes me doubly glad we didn't bring Sadie with us.'

Sadie had wanted to come, had virtually begged to be included, but Cristy had been adamant that she and David should check everything out first. 'We only have this Evie's word that she has a link to George Symmonds-Browne. And even if she does, we still don't know exactly *why* he's willing to see us, or, more importantly for you, if he'll be able to tell us where your mother is.'

Seeming to accept that, Sadie had said, 'Will you keep in touch, let me know what's happening?'

'Of course. And if we feel it's the right thing to do maybe you and Jasper can fly out to join us.'

Wondering if that was now more likely to happen than not, Cristy went ahead through an arched gateway to a spacious pool area filled with loungers and palm trees, although not many people. An array of large, circular tables was set out on a shady terrace overlooking the water and as they approached a tall, slender man of around sixty with thick silver hair and dark glasses stood to greet them. For a strangely disorientating moment Cristy felt she was watching him morphing from his younger, almost shadowy self into this older, markedly less sinister reality.

'Cristy, David,' Evie said eagerly, 'this is Gabe. He's very pleased to meet you.'

As Cristy shook his hand, which was lean and bony, he said in a decidedly plummy British voice, 'I'm very pleased to meet you. I hope you'll excuse me for not removing my glasses.'

'He's photophobic,' Evie jumped in. 'Ultra-sensitive to light.'

'You're from England?' he asked Cristy.

'We are,' she confirmed, and stood aside for him to greet David.

'What part?' he asked, addressing David now.

'Originally Gloucestershire,' David replied. 'These days, Guernsey. And you?'

Evie said, 'Gabe was also born in Gloucestershire, close to the Oxfordshire border.'

'Shall we?' Lukas suggested, holding out a chair for Cristy to sit next to Gabe.

David took the other side and immediately a server was there ready to take orders for drinks. Arnold Palmers all round. As the server departed Evie began extolling the club's many virtues, gamely backed up by Lukas, while Gabe sat quietly in his chair, smiling benignly and gently tapping his fingers on the table. Other diners began to appear, filling nearby tables, some waving a hello to Evie, while Lukas discreetly provided names and status. High flying lawyers, real estate agents, CEOs of multi-nationals . . .

The list went on and Cristy couldn't help wondering how he'd describe Gabe were he giving a commentary to someone else. *Gabriel Bailey, old English aristocracy, ex-human trafficker no longer sought by law enforcement?*

Seizing a pause in Evie's lengthy plaudits (was she nervous, or always as chatty as this?) and Lukas's asides, Cristy said, 'I have to confess we weren't expecting to see you, Lukas. You're a very welcome surprise.'

He smiled in a way that made him appear both apologetic and pleased by the compliment. 'We weren't sure until this morning,' he said, 'that I was going to make it back in time to see you. I've been in New York, on business, but here I am now, and delighted to meet you.'

Still trying to get a through line on things, Cristy said, 'Can I ask, before we go any further . . . Two colleagues of mine are in Vilnius searching for your sister Audra . . .'

'Ah, yes. Am I able to help with this? I can let you have her phone number and email and I'll make sure she knows it's all right to speak to them. I'll need their names, of course.' He was already poised to tap into his mobile.

After providing Clove and Jacks's details, Cristy waited for him to relay them to Audra, while Evie and Gabe smiled on and David looked as amazed as he did amused. Cristy recalled Natalie Irwin saying that Lukas had a way with him that 'kind of cheered you up', and it didn't seem he'd changed, for she had to admit he really was likeable.

Lukas looked up from his phone, grinned and saluted them: *mission accomplished.* 'I've been listening to your podcast since we found out about it,' he told her. 'I've got so much to ask . . . We'll come on to it, of course, but I want to apologize for being so difficult to find. It's just that when Evie and I took this job, with Gabe, one of the conditions at the time was that we didn't let anyone know where we were. There were some very good reasons for it, but things have changed over the years . . .'

'Not completely,' Gabe put in.

'No, not completely,' Lukas agreed, 'but there's no harm in us talking to Cristy and David now.'

Cristy half-expected Gabe to object, but he only nodded absently, so she said, 'Just before coming here I spoke to an old friend of yours, Natalie . . .'

Lukas nodded. 'Ah yes, Nat. How is she? I've always felt terrible about cutting contact with her. She was such a very good friend to me when I needed one most.'

'You should be in touch,' Evie told him. 'At least let her know you're still alive.'

'I think she'd appreciate that,' Cristy said.

Clearly glad she thought so, Lukas said, 'I should do it before she has chance to hear the interview we give you. It seems only fair for her to find things out before everyone else, don't you think?'

'Absolutely,' Evie agreed.

'I'll arrange for her interview to be sent to you,' Cristy said, 'so you can hear her in advance as well.'

'Thank you,' he smiled. 'I'm already looking forward to hearing her lovely voice. I used to try to mimic her Yorkshire accent, and the way she laughed at my efforts . . .' He laughed himself and gave a sigh of nostalgia.

When no one seemed inclined to say anything else, Cristy said tentatively, 'Will it be OK to record here?'

'Oh, I'm sorry,' Evie jumped in, 'I should have explained right away. No phones, or anything of that sort, are allowed in public areas. I hope you don't mind. And we thought that rather than dive right in, this would be a nice, relaxed get-to-know-you lunch before we go back to the house. We can talk about anything you like there. Is that OK with you?'

'Of course,' Cristy replied, embarrassed that she'd rushed into asking when it should have been obvious that a recording device would be close to offensive in a place like this.

'We're happy to talk to you,' Gabe told her. 'And we want to hear all about Sasha.'

'I'm sure they'll tell us everything,' Lukas said. 'After all, we want a two-way exchange here, don't we?' He was looking at Cristy, apparently seeking assurance that she wasn't going to hold back on them.

'Of course, we'll tell you about her,' she promised, 'but I hope you'll explain things to us first.'

Lukas's eyes crinkled at the corners as he smiled. 'A very reasonable request,' he agreed, 'but please keep in mind that no one here intends her any harm – if that's what you're afraid of.'

'No one ever did,' Gabe put in.

Lukas grimaced. 'Well, that's not exactly true, but let's leave it until later.'

Gabe nodded and let the subject drop as easily as if they'd been discussing the weather. 'What would you like to eat, Cristy?' he asked. 'Can I recommend the Cobb salad? Or perhaps you'd prefer lobster? It's always very well prepared here.'

As Cristy scanned the menu Evie said, 'I think I'll have the snow crab,' and smiled up at the server, as he brought the drinks.

Lukas and David decided on lobster, Cristy went for the seared tuna while Gabe ordered shrimp pappardelle.

The menus were taken, and toasts of welcome were made – and next thing, almost as if they were picking up on a recently abandoned conversation, Lukas and David were engrossed in a detailed discussion of the financial markets. Evie smiled on happily, clearly proud of her man, while Gabe tilted his head to one side seeming to listen, although he had nothing to add. Apparently realizing she was watching him he turned to her and said, 'Are you a golfer, Cristy?'

'Uh, no, I'm not,' she replied, feeling absurdly as though she might be letting him down. 'Are you?'

'Mm, I play most days. Did you know that they call Naples the golfing capital of the world? Some say it's Myrtle Beach in South Carolina, but for me it's right here. What about tennis, is that your game?'

Caught by the suddenness of the question, she replaced her glass on the table and said, 'It was, some years ago. I haven't played in a while.'

'Pity. How about pickleball?'

'I don't actually know what that is.'

'Very noisy. Evie's quite good at it.'

'It's kind of like badminton, but not,' Evie explained. 'There are courts here. I can show you if you like.'

Cristy smiled back at her and felt once again as if she were in some sort of parallel universe where the real world was something that happened a long way from here.

'We're not Trump supporters,' Lukas was telling David. 'The man is fiscally and judicially ignorant, although he likes to think he's king of all he surveys. Of course, everyone around these parts has Republicanism running through their veins, so it's best not to get into a conversation about politics. Not the done thing, old boy,' he added, affecting an accent almost as British as Gabe's.

'We have some very interesting wildlife here,' Gabe announced. 'Especially the birds.'

Cristy turned to him uncomprehendingly.

'Gabe conducts bird tours,' Evie explained. 'He's very knowledgeable. They call him an avian consultant.'

'Amongst other things,' Gabe chortled. 'If you're interested I'll be happy to show you around while you're here. We have a pair of ospreys on Pines 9 that you ought to see. I'm very keen on the American Kestrel, myself – you'll know that as a sparrow hawk, I expect.'

'Tell us about the Florida Wood Storks,' Evie urged. 'I know they're one of your favourites and you speak so poetically about them.'

And so, bizarrely, for the next hour or so, they listened to George Symmonds-Browne waxing lyrical on his specialist subjects (which also included wildflowers and turtles' mating habits) while tucking into some delicious food and becoming, in Cristy's case, increasingly fascinated by the dynamic between these three. How on earth had they ended up here together, and who in the heck was paying for it all? It surely wasn't coming from the proceeds of Gabe's earlier career, or maybe it was. She was, of course, dying to ask, but clearly this wasn't the time or place, and she wasn't sure she could anyway, when there seemed no way in through the shiny, happy carapace they exuded, not a single crack nor a shadow of an opening.

Finally, they were walking back to the cars, David side by side with his new best friend, Lukas, and Cristy between Evie and Gabe who'd very gently taken her arm.

'Were you followed here?' Gabe asked quietly.

Startled, she said, 'No, I don't think so.'

He nodded and Evie said, 'There's nothing to worry about, Gabe. We'll be home soon, safe and sound.'

*

Barely waiting until David started to drive out of the club's grounds behind Evie's car, Lukas following in his, Cristy said, 'What is it with Gabe? He doesn't seem . . . He's so . . . not what I expected.'

'I know what you mean,' David responded, 'but if you ask me none of them are.'

'You appeared to get along very well with Lukas.'

'Sure, he comes over as a regular guy, very knowledgeable about the world of finance . . . Wasn't he a builder, a plumber, a delivery driver, back in the UK?'

'That's what Natalie Irwin told us, but that was ten or more years ago. He's obviously upped his game since coming to work for Gabe.'

'And has in that time amassed himself – or Gabe – a small fortune.'

'Did he tell you that?'

'He didn't have to. No one who knows the stock market the way he does isn't playing it and winning. So I'd say, they're pretty well covered financially speaking.'

After considering that for a moment, while clocking one exclusive gated-community after another as they drove the glossy eight- or ten-lane boulevards, still behind Evie's Mercedes, Cristy said, 'Gabe asked me if we were followed here. Do you think we might have been?'

David frowned. 'I can't say I noticed anyone, although we haven't exactly been looking. Anyway, he surely wouldn't be hard to find in a place like this, so who'd need to track us to get to him?'

'He's changed his name,' she reminded him thoughtfully. 'So I'm asking myself, is he still running scared of the gangs? I guess he must be, given he's no longer a person of interest to Interpol, so it can't be law enforcement he's hiding from.'

'If he really is hiding.'

She glanced at him quizzically.

He shrugged. 'Something's off – or at least odd – about the set-up here,' he commented.

Knowing exactly what he meant, Cristy watched Evie turn into a private development with exquisitely tended flower beds and clusters of succulents on the sloping lawns each side of the entrance. They slowed to a stop in front of two towering electronic gates with the community's name, Floral Grove, in gold lettering on each one, and a uniformed guard ambled out of a whitewashed, red-roofed booth to greet Evie and Gabe.

'There seems to be a lot of security around here,' she remarked to David, noting a handsomely groomed German Shepherd eyeing the apparently friendly exchange between his handler and the recent arrivals. 'What do you say to that?'

'What I'm thinking is, once this particular episode airs the whole world is going to know where they are, so why have you been invited here?'

'I'm going to guess that part of the deal of telling us what we want to know is going to include not revealing their whereabouts. Which will make the intro I did on the plane redundant along with most of what I've recorded since. However, this is about Sadie, not location – so what really matters is finding out how she ended up with the Winters sisters back in 2000, and what the heck happened to her mother?'

# CHAPTER TWENTY-FIVE

Feeling she could get used to hanging out poolside in Florida, this time at Gabe's intriguing Floral Grove residence where a small forest of climbing plants and huge, colourful pots filled the deck, Cristy watched Evie pour tea over five large glasses of ice, while Lukas settled himself next to Gabe at a mosaic-topped table. An assortment of delicious chocolate-chip cookies, taken from the club, was laid out centre stage and managing to look almost as irresistible as the gently lapping blue water beside them. Beyond the exclusive garden the sprawling pond that was actually a lake shimmered and rippled in the glorious afternoon sun.

The whole place was, without a doubt, a little piece of heaven set amongst the development's many other secluded homesteads, some vast, others discreet, all in their own grounds, while this one, occupying the end of a leafy cul-de-sac seemed to have a charm all of its own. The exterior was whitewashed and gleaming behind its shining, exotic foliage, while the interior was airy and light, filled with unusual and beautiful paintings – apparently many done by Gabe – and various treasures collected during their travels around the world.

'Have you ever been to the South of France?' Cristy had thought to ask.

'Oh yes, several times,' Evie assured her, 'but not for a few years. I think the last time was when we visited an old friend of Gabe's in a small town called Vence. Do you know it?'

'Not really,' Cristy replied. 'And do you all live here, in this house?' she'd asked, as Evie showed them through to the garden.

'We do,' Evie had confirmed with a smile. 'Gabe has his studio and private rooms upstairs, and Lukas and I have a lovely suite in the West Wing.' She giggled. 'The place isn't big enough to have wings,' she added quietly, 'but it's what we like to call it. Mostly though we're here, in the kitchen and sitting room, or out on the deck – when we're not going about our busy days, of course. We enjoy one another's company, which is lucky or this little arrangement would never have worked.'

*Arrangement?*

'Are you here all year round?' David was asking Lukas now, as Cristy admired a vividly coloured sculpture, apparently from Sicily. 'I'm just thinking of how hot Florida gets in summer,' he added.

'Oh boy does it,' Lukas agreed. 'No, we close the place up in April and drive to Wisconsin where we generally stay until just before Thanksgiving.'

'What's in Wisconsin?' Cristy wondered as Evie passed around the iced tea.

'Lake Geneva,' Evie replied. 'Gabe's cousin, Salina, has two cottages on the shore. We always take the smaller one and very often Verity and her family are in the other. We were hoping you'd meet her while you're here – she and her husband have a place at Port Royal, that's the really fancy neighbourhood of Naples – but they're in Brazil right now and we're not sure when they're back.'

Unable to imagine – at least for the moment – anything much fancier than where they were, Cristy said, 'So how did you all come to be here?'

Evie twinkled. 'It's all down to Verity,' she replied, as if sharing a secret. 'If it weren't for her heaven knows where any of us would have ended up, especially Gabe. Howeeeever,' she drew out the word, 'we thought we'd start at the beginning – or Lukas will, and Gabe will fill things in as we go.' Lowering her voice she added, 'You've probably already gathered that he's not much of a talker, but rest assured he takes everything in and he feels things very deeply even if he doesn't always show it.'

Wondering, not for the first time, if Gabe, apart from being photophobic, might have other issues, Cristy discreetly set up to record. Perhaps he'd suffered some sort of damage from drug abuse over the years? Certainly his reticence was marked, and the way he occasionally veered off subject could be both disconcerting and puzzling.

'So, are we all ready?' Evie asked, rubbing her hands excitedly.

'Bring it on,' Lukas encouraged, while Gabe managed a half-smile and next to Cristy David stretched out his long legs preparing simply to listen and, later, be a helpful sounding board as they went through it all.

After checking everything was working, Cristy said, 'Let's just treat it as a chat, OK? We don't have to be formal, or even chronological with events – that can always be sorted in an edit. But as you seem to have discussed how you want to tell the story I'm guessing you're going to start us off at the beginning, Lukas?'

He nodded and beamed. He really did have the most engaging way with him, seeming so full of warmth and good humour. However, his expression sobered as he prepared to share his memories, and his dark eyes appeared to lose focus, conveying a more serious and reflective side of his nature.

LUKAS: 'You have probably learned by now that Janina and I are originally from Georgia – county, not state – but our father was Lithuanian so we moved to Vilnius when we were still quite young. This became a very fortuitous move in later years, but I will come on to that.

'We have another sister, Audra. She is older and was already married to her husband, Yuri, when Janina took the decision to leave Lithuania. She, Janina, was nineteen at the time, headstrong, beautiful, eager to explore the world . . . She had many qualities – and failings – but they only made her, in my opinion, even easier to love. We always believed she'd grow up to achieve great things, not only because of her beauty and lively spirit, but because she was intelligent and compassionate, interested in people, and oh boy was she daring. She was definitely the risk taker in our family, the one who showed us how to be brave in the face of our many adversities. We were very poor, you see, and our adopted country was still suffering from the after-effects of the Soviet occupation. So few opportunities for us, and so often very little food to eat.'

CRISTY: 'Can you tell us a little about your parents?'

LUKAS: 'We barely knew our father, he died soon after we moved to Vilnius, and our mother passed away the year before Janina left. Looking back, as I often do, I believe Janina was not seeing things clearly because of grief, and out of fear of what would happen to her now that she no longer had our mother to advise her. I told her I would always take care of her – we were very close, we always had been. I wouldn't say I was a father figure to her, I was too young for that, but by the time we are talking about I was working very hard to keep us in our mother's apartment and to make sure we could eat. Janina wanted to help, of course, but the path she chose was not one that either I or Audra approved of.

'We didn't know about it at first, only found out later that she'd been introduced to an overseas employment agency by a co-worker at the hotel where she helped in the kitchen . . . I am sure you know many stories like this, of young girls who are promised better lives in faraway lands by unscrupulous men . . . It is tragic how many fall for it and I'm afraid Janina was one of them.

'It was through these *traffickers*, because that's what they were, that she came to meet Gabe. They – the agency in Vilnius – were acting for clients, usually men, in search of "housekeepers", "companions", "secretaries", "nannies for their children" . . . There were all sorts of opportunities, and there was, of course, no mention of sex work or dance clubs or worse, but even if there had been I think some girls were so keen to get to the West that they'd have gone anyway. Janina wasn't one of them. She truly believed she was going to keep house for a man with aristocratic connections and a lot of money. She was even shown a photograph of him and, in spite of him being a clear twenty years older and having no name yet, she insisted she already trusted him. He had kind eyes and a lovely smile, she said.'

GABE: 'I was also shown a photograph of her and I knew right away that I wanted to meet her.'

Cristy's eyes moved between the two, picturing the scenario Lukas was painting and reflecting on how romantic they were making things sound. Love at first sight by photograph, organized by a criminal gang? An instant connection with a stranger who Janina must surely have feared was far more likely to be a tyrant than a saviour?

LUKAS: 'Neither Audra nor I were aware of the arrangements to smuggle Janina out of our country until they were already made. As soon as I knew of them I tried to stop Nina, of course, but by then she had built up such a rosy picture of how her life was going to be, working for this aristocrat, living in a big house with plenty to eat and always warm, that she refused to listen. Audra was very angry and afraid, we both were, but then suddenly one day Nina had gone and there was no more we could do, other than wait for her to be in touch to say she was safe.'

GABE: 'She was safe with me.'

LUKAS: 'But we didn't know that. She was still very young and she'd allowed herself to be transported out of her country by evil strangers in order to be delivered to someone who might not even exist.'

CRISTY: 'When exactly was this?'

LUKAS: 'The end of '96 – before Lithuania was a part of the EU, so Janina would have been an illegal immigrant in the UK, if that was in fact where she'd been taken. As far as we knew she could have been anywhere. I tried to find out from the agency where she might be. I was desperate, but I had nothing to offer that they wanted in exchange for information, and each time I confronted them they had me beaten up.

'It was a terrible time, full of fear for Nina and for ourselves. We knew what could happen to families if the trafficked person didn't comply with demands. Audra had two children by then and I had already been hospitalized twice. Worse though, was not knowing what Janina was enduring and if we would ever hear from her again. No money came, though she'd expected to be able to send some, and no letters or phone calls either.

'A whole year went by, maybe longer, but then one day, out of the blue, a postcard turned up at the apartment telling me not to worry, that she was fine and would be in touch again as soon as she could. Of course I had no way of knowing if she'd sent it herself, or if it was true that she was all right, but at least it was something. A postcard showing a forlorn beach at a place called Minehead in Somerset, England. Audra and I decided that this small contact was Janina's way of letting us know where she was and that we should try to rescue her.

'It took all our savings to buy my passage into the UK, and it was several months before I could actually get one. But I did in the end – I won't go into the details of my journey, they are not relevant here, but it took many weeks to finally get across the Channel and eventually to this small town in Somerset. Once there, I lived in doorways and bus shelters, ate from dustbins and washed in the local facilities, all the time searching the streets and coastline for Janina. People didn't want to talk to me, I was dirty and smelly and, although I already spoke English well because we'd learned it at school, my accent was thick.

'Then I met Natalie and she was kind to me in a way no one else had been. She snuck me into where she worked, at the local holiday camp, let me use her room to wash and sleep and brought me food. I'm not sure how she managed to fix me up with a job – I think they were desperate for staff at the time – so I then had somewhere to stay, two good meals a day and on my days off I continued to search for Janina. The internet wasn't really a thing back then, not like it is today, so it was mostly showing people photographs and asking if they'd seen her. No one had. At one stage I contacted a private investigator, but even though I could very well explain the situation and my concerns, I couldn't afford his fees so he was unwilling to help. I considered going to the police, but of course, if I did, I'd have been deported right away.

'In the end it was like a miracle happened. I had been in Minehead for more than six months and I had started going to church to ask God to help me mainly because there was no one else. Then one day, maybe less than two hours after I had said my usual prayers, I was leaving a café on the high street and there she was, right in front of me. I couldn't believe it, and nor could she. We stared at one another, needing to be sure, then we laughed and threw our arms around one another and jumped up and down with joy. It wasn't so easy for her, she was quite heavily pregnant, but we clutched onto one another anyway and people passing by looked at us strangely, or laughed and shared in our happiness.

'We went back into the café and she told me all about what had happened to her since she'd been brought to Somerset. She was living with Gabe – George as she called him – some way further along the coast and he was the father of her child.'

Cristy's heart jolted, not only with surprise, and God knew it was that, but at the way Lukas had come out with it so simply, as if assuming they already knew. Her eyes moved to Gabe, as her thoughts went to Sadie and what this was going to mean to her.

LUKAS: 'What Janina told me that day was very upsetting, but also a big relief. Gabe treated her very well, she said, and she loved him, and was happy to be having his child. But there was a darker side, as I knew there must be. Gabe – George – was being used, exploited is probably a better word, by the traffickers who would only allow him to keep Janina if he agreed to them using his farm as a kind of holding place for girls from all over the continent. When they came, having been made all sorts of promises, they soon found themselves being auctioned to the highest bidder. Anyone could "try them out" and if they were chosen they were taken away to act as sex workers in other parts of the country. Nina told me how George allowed the girls a lot of freedom when no one else was around, but very few of them ran away, they were too afraid of what would happen to their families if they did.

'Janina assured me she was always left unmolested in return for the traffickers' use of Gabe's home, but she was warned that if she ever tried to contact her own family, or did anything at all to disrupt their business, she would never see George again. This is why she took such a long time to reach out to us. She knew, because she'd seen it, just how brutal these men could be. She'd even experienced the trauma of witnessing girls being beaten to death, and there were no consequences because no one cared about girls who didn't officially exist.'

GABE: 'We never knew what happened to the bodies. It would have been foolish and dangerous to ask.'

LUKAS: 'All that mattered to Gabe, and Janina, was that she and their unborn baby were left unharmed. They talked all the time about finding somewhere to hide, a refuge far away from the evil all around them, but George's family wouldn't help him, and they were too afraid of what would happen if they were caught. Then Sasha was born and so began the most terrifying time of all. Janina was in fear that her daughter would be taken away and sold or simply disposed of and left to die. But it didn't happen. Time went on, Sasha grew and was loved by her parents, and by the girls who came to stay. And as long as she was nowhere to be seen when the traffickers were around they carried on as if she wasn't there.

'Then a new man took over. His name was Matis Albescu. He was Romanian, from Budapest, and everyone was afraid of him, even his own men. He had no kindness, only hate in his soul. I should say here, that by the time his reign of terror began, I had come to know my niece well. Janina used to bring her to Minehead and I'd take her into the camp to play on the rides, and with other children. George would stay at the farm with the "guests" – this was how they referred to the girls. He was expected to be there in case the traffickers turned up unannounced.'

CRISTY: 'Did you meet George while Janina was with him?'

LUKAS: 'Yes, a few times, walking on Kylve beach. He would be with Nina and Sasha, and I'd wander past as if we were strangers stopping to talk about the weather. It never felt safe for me to visit the farm – but these brief encounters assured me of his feelings towards my sister and niece.

'I need to tell you more about Albescu. Janina had felt him watching her for some time, and then she was told that the next time he came to the farm he was going to take her as a gift for his son who bore his name and was like his father in every way. This meant Nina would be taken away from George, and no one had any idea what would happen to Sasha once Nina had gone.

'She didn't discuss her plans with me or with Gabe. I'm not even sure how well formed they were when she carried them out . . . She was acting out of panic and love and a desperate need to keep Sasha safe from Albescu. Gabe didn't even know when she returned to the farm one day without Sasha what she'd done with her. She would only say that it was best he didn't know but Sasha was safe. She told him nothing at the time about the Winters sisters, but we learned later that she had read about them in the local paper and had decided they would take care of Sasha until she could come back for her. It was a big risk, of course. If the sisters went to the authorities Sasha would be taken into care and she, Janina, would be found and deported, but even that would be better than whatever fate Albescu and his son had planned for them.'

As Lukas's voice died away Cristy was caught in the moment of learning that Sadie had not been stolen, that Lottie's story was real. It had always been possible, of course, but she'd doubted it for so long . . . Her eyes moved to Evie as she began to refresh the drinks. For his part Gabe remained motionless, head averted, but then his mouth trembled slightly and as he put a hand to his head she saw that it was shaky too. She watched him get up and walk to the fence, his back turned as he stared out across the lake, and she found herself imagining the times he might have gazed out over an altogether different body of water, the Severn Estuary, with Janina and their daughter, Sasha.

It felt oddly surreal, and displacing as she watched him now and wondered about the truth of what she'd heard so far. Moving and credible though the story sounded, something about it wasn't adding up and she knew what it was. She could even see it in her mind's eye – the photograph of George and Janina with Lottie, the three of them captured on film at a café table, engaged in what appeared to be a heated exchange. So the claim that Janina returned one day without Sasha, and neither George nor her brother knew where she'd left her, simply couldn't be true.

Deciding not to mention it yet – she wanted to find out first where the story was going next – Cristy smiled a thanks to Evie and glanced at David. He appeared pensive and worried, as if he too was mulling over the veracity of Lukas's account of giving up Sasha.

'There's a turtle,' Gabe said quietly, pointing down at the water.

Cristy watched the reptilian head bob up and down on the silky surface, its mottled shell glinting silver in the sunlight.

She glanced at Lukas and saw that he probably hadn't even heard Gabe speak. Maybe he was focusing on how to continue lacing his story with enough truth for the falsehoods to sound more credible.

Evie said quietly, 'Everything's OK, Lukey. Just keep going.'

Lukas looked up and seemed to brighten a little as he said, 'Do you have any questions? You must have some by now. Maybe I've left things out . . . It was more than twenty years ago, you understand.'

Since they were still recording, Cristy said, 'Tell me more about Sasha and what happened to her. You said Janina didn't tell you at first, but she did later?'

Lukas nodded and continued to nod as Gabe returned to the table and sat down quietly. In the end he was the first to speak.

GABE: 'Janina didn't tell us then. There was no time to. She was taken from me by Albescu.'

Though Cristy couldn't see his eyes, she heard the emotion in his voice.

LUKAS: 'We had no way to find out where she was. Sasha was gone, so was Nina. Our world was . . . empty, shattered, more frightening than ever. None of Albescu's men would speak to us about it, it was possible they didn't even know where Nina had been taken. There were no leads, nothing at all to guide us. Our only hope was that she would find a way to contact us.'

GABE: 'When we heard on the news, a long time later, that Albescu Senior had been killed in a police raid we waited and waited, but she still didn't come.'

LUKAS: 'And we still had no idea what she'd done with Sasha. It was a hellish time. We even feared for a while that she'd killed Sasha rather than see her fall into Albescu's hands. Then one day the police turned up at the farm asking about Janina and Sasha.'

GABE: 'The vicar had reported them missing.'

Recalling ex-detective Catherine Shilling telling how Gabe – George – had wept when they'd questioned him, Cristy regarded him closely now and wondered if he too was remembering his show of emotion.

LUKAS: 'Gabe was afraid to tell the police anything in case he made things worse for Janina, so he said she'd gone back to Lithuania and taken Sasha with her. It probably wasn't the right thing to do, but neither of us knew what was. Then I was stopped one day on the street and taken into custody. After that I was deported without being able to speak to anyone first.

'I couldn't get back to the UK until a very long time later, after my country became a part of the EU. That was in 2004, but it took me a while to sort out a passport, having been born in Georgia. So it was in 2005 that I returned. I hadn't heard from Janina in all that time, and by then I'd also lost contact with Gabe. What I didn't know until many, many years later, when I next saw him, was that Janina had managed to make her way back to him in the middle of 2005 and they'd fled the farm soon after. So they'd gone by the time I managed to get there. We worked out later that I missed them by only a few days.'

Cristy watched Lukas look at Gabe as though waiting for him to speak, but Gabe simply nodded, as if to confirm what had been said.

LUKAS: 'Gabe still finds it difficult to talk about Janina and Sasha, so we've agreed that even though this next part of the story is his, I will tell you what happened and if I make any mistakes he will step in to correct me.'

Lukas paused as Evie put a comforting hand on Gabe's arm and for several moments there was nothing more than the sound of birdsong threading and flaring through the hum of the pool pump. Then Cristy became aware of a beautiful scent, like peonies but sweeter and more pungent, and she glanced around to see where it might be coming from. There was no obvious source, but there never was when she picked up this unexpected drift of fragrance. It came out of nowhere, often when she was thinking about her mother, and it made her feel as though she was close by now. She asked Evie where the scent was coming from and Evie seemed puzzled, as if she hadn't noticed anything out of the ordinary.

LUKAS: 'After I was returned to Lithuania Gabe was left alone at the farm. The traffickers had stopped using it after they took Janina and he had very few visitors . . .

'He didn't answer the door if anyone knocked. He'd look out first to see who it was and if it was someone he didn't know he stayed quiet until they left. He went out only to buy food and to walk the beach; he read, listened to music and started to paint . . . He waited and counted the days, the months and then the years, always believing that Janina would come back to him and then . . . then . . . she did.'

Evie's hand tightened on Gabe's arm.

LUKAS: 'For almost five long years Janina had been enslaved to Matis Albescu's son, a man with the same name as his father and whose depravity was perhaps even worse. She wouldn't tell Gabe what had been done to her, only that she would have killed herself if it weren't for the need to see Sasha again. It was what had kept her alive after the many cruel beatings she received for trying to escape. Finally she managed it and made her way to the farm, in spite of knowing that Albescu would expect her to go there. But she had no other way of finding Gabe, the farm was all she knew and when she got there . . .'

GABE: 'She was terrified and dirty, so thin that I hardly recognized her . . .'

Gabe's voice failed and Cristy saw how pale he'd become.

GABE: 'She was cold. So cold.'

Lukas waited a moment in case Gabe wanted to say more.

LUKAS: 'He cleaned her up, bathed and fed her and then he took her to a hotel before Albescu could find them. They kept moving, one small hotel after another, all the time heading to Gloucestershire where Gabe's parents gave them shelter, but only for a few days. They were ashamed of the kind of person he'd become – they believed he was involved in the trafficking and that he'd fallen in love with one of his victims. They wanted no part of his world, or his crimes, so they made him leave.'

GABE: 'They are not kind people. There was very little love when I was growing up. I think they despised me for being the way I am. Not quick and clever like the rest of my family. I am sometimes slow to understand or to react . . .'

LUKAS: 'Gabe's only happiness in childhood was with his cousin Verity. She always cared for him and he cared for her, but then her parents moved to the States and eventually she married Sylvan . . .'

GABE: 'I'm sure she'd have helped me with Janina and Sasha, but I was afraid of bringing her to the attention of the gangs. She would have despised me for that.'

LUKAS: 'So after being expelled from Gabe's parents' home they continued to move from place to place, and it was a month, maybe more, before Janina was finally able to find out where the Winters sisters had gone after they'd left Exmoor. By this time she'd told Gabe all about how she'd left Sasha on the beach below the sisters' home and had watched from a short distance as one of them had come down from the house and taken Sasha in. She truly believed the sisters would be kind to Sasha. Everything she'd read about them had told her they would be, and when nothing was reported on the news about a missing child she took heart and went to the house early one morning. She didn't knock, she simply delivered photographs and some of Sasha's favourite toys. It was her way of letting the sisters know that Sasha had a family who loved her but who couldn't take care of her right now. She had no idea as she made her way back to the farm that day that Matis Albescu was already there waiting to take her away.'

Gabe started to speak, but his voice was barely audible. Cristy leaned in and gently eased the recorder closer to him.

GABE: 'I wanted to kill him. I would have. I had a knife, but he had men with guns. They locked me up . . . There was nothing I could do . . . I heard Janina screaming for me, and I shouted for her, but then they were gone and I still couldn't break free.'

LUKAS: 'She'd had no time to tell him where Sasha was. She was helpless, they both were . . . I was the one who released Gabe from the cellar a couple of days later when I went to the farm to find out why I hadn't seen Nina. We were frantic and powerless to act. We knew no one and nothing that could help us. At that point girls were still being brought to the farm, but the men who escorted them only laughed at us or beat us. I am sure it was one of them who tipped off the authorities and that is how I came to be deported.'

Needing to move things along, Cristy gently brought them back to when Janina and Gabe had finally found out where the Winters sisters were.

LUKAS: 'Yes, they were in Guernsey, so Gabe and Nina went there, not to cause a scene, or to do anything to disrupt Sasha's life, they simply wanted to find out if she really was there.'

CRISTY: 'What age would Sasha have been by then?'

GABE: 'She was seven and beautiful and lively, just like her mother. We watched her being taken to school and driven home again . . . We could see that she was happy, and healthy, but we wanted her so much. She was our daughter, she belonged to us, but we had no home; we were still running from Albescu . . .'

LUKAS: 'It was an impossible situation, they had very little hope, but Janina needed to let the sisters know how grateful she was that they'd taken Sasha in and treated her as their own. She was very eager to explain how desperately she and Gabe wanted to be a part of Sasha's life, if they would allow it. So they went to the house and left a note in the mailbox addressed to Emilia and Carlotta Winters saying who they were and asking if they would meet them at a café in St Peter Port.'

So that was when the photographs had been taken, Cristy

realized, long after Sadie had gone to live with the sisters, not before. Hadn't Anna suggested that, and Cristy had just dismissed it? In any event, it seemed that what the photographer had captured wasn't some sort of transaction in which Sadie was being bought and sold, it was her parents begging to be allowed to see her.

LUKAS: 'They went to the café at the same time every day for over a week until eventually one of the sisters came. She listened to their story, sympathized with them even and understood how much it would mean to them to be a part of Sasha's world. At the same time she explained how disruptive that would be for Sasha, and confusing. They were only going to bring sadness and even danger to Sasha and she couldn't allow that.

'Janina begged and pleaded with her, saying Sasha didn't have to know who they were, they'd pretend to be old friends, or new neighbours, anything if they could just have some contact with their child. She became so desperate that she threatened to go to the authorities to report the sisters for abduction. Of course she couldn't do that, they would all suffer if she did, Sasha most of all if she was removed from the home she'd come to know and love.

'In the end the sister agreed to think things over and to meet them again in a couple of weeks. She said perhaps something could be worked out, she just couldn't see what it was yet. She asked where they were staying and promised to be in touch soon. Eventually she did contact them and asked if Janina could meet her at one of the sisters' other properties, further south on the island. She wanted Janina to come alone while Sasha was at school.'

CRISTY: 'Why another property, and why alone?'

LUKAS: 'She said it was because she didn't want her sister, Mia, to know anything yet, and she didn't want Gabe there because she was afraid he might try to harm her.'

Cristy glanced at Gabe. He didn't appear at all intimidating now, but she couldn't deny she'd considered him sinister in the photos she'd seen of him from that era.

LUKAS: 'So Janina took the little car she and Gabe had bought to get around the island, while he waited at their rented apartment for her to come back with news. When she left he had no idea that was the last time he'd see her.'

Cristy's heart clenched. This wasn't what she'd expected to hear, although she had no clear sense of what she'd been thinking, where she'd imagined this would go.

GABE: 'Have you seen her? Do you know where she is?'

Cristy stared at him helplessly, having no idea whether Gabe believed she could answer that, or if he simply couldn't let go of what was surely a vain and desperate hope.

CRISTY: 'You must have gone to the sisters' house to find out what had happened to her?'

LUKAS: 'Yes, he did, but Lottie told him she'd waited all day at the other property and Janina hadn't turned up. He began searching the island, desperate to find her, and in the end Lottie said they should go to the police, as long as he swore not to mention anything about Sadie.

'The car was found the next day, at the bottom of a ravine not far from the address where Lottie had waited. It was a dangerous stretch of road, there had been accidents there before, people who didn't know the island . . . Nina wasn't in the car, and they never recovered her body.'

Realizing that must be why Gabe was unable to give up hope of finding Janina alive, Cristy allowed several moments to pass before continuing.

CRISTY: 'Do you think Lottie is responsible for whatever happened to Janina?'

Lukas looked at Gabe and more hushed seconds passed, filled only by the twitter and song of birds and, strangely, another drift of the exquisite, unidentifiable perfume.

GABE: 'I did think that for a while, I was certain of it, but now I believe that Albescu Junior's people managed to find us and they . . . they took her away.'

Cristy thought of the café photographs and wondered again who had taken them. Whoever it was, they'd ended up with Lottie, so did that mean Albescu had not only found Janina, but a way to extract money from the women who had the child?

# CHAPTER TWENTY-SIX

'So what did you make of it?' Cristy asked, as she and David finished listening to the playback later. They were at the Ritz-Carlton now, in a penthouse suite that could probably swallow up her entire apartment, with glorious Gulf views from the wraparound terrace and such sumptuous soft furnishings it would be easy to sink into them and never come up. Completely over the top, in her opinion, although as far as she could tell just about everything in Naples was, with its glossy white mansions, toweringly exotic palms and its perfectly turned-out residents with their luxury cars. A sun-baked playground for the super-rich and overprivileged if ever there was one.

David reached for his champagne flute – there was so much Krug in their personal bar it would have seemed rude not to open at least one bottle. 'Do you mean the whole thing,' he asked, 'or specifically Janina's disappearance?'

'Both, but overall, did it strike you as a true retelling of what happened all those years ago?'

He didn't take long to answer. 'Actually, it did,' he replied. 'I had a couple of issues here and there, but they kind of got ironed out the deeper in we went. How about you? Are you having a problem with it?'

She shook her head. 'Like you, I did once or twice, but it came clear.'

'And Albescu Junior being involved in Janina's disappearance?'

She sipped her drink, and gazed out at the sea spreading like a ground swell of starlight before them just as a pelican dipped down into the waves. 'I think it's possible,' she replied, 'but it's also easier for Gabe to believe that than it is to accept she might have gone off the road and will never be coming back.'

'Would Albescu really still have her, over twenty years later?'

'Josef Fritzl,' she responded, referring to the Austrian who'd kept his daughter in a cellar for almost a quarter of a century, raping her thousands of times and fathering seven children on her.

Conceding the point, distasteful as it was, he said, 'So the next step has to be finding out where Albescu is these days?'

'Indeed.' Cristy checked her laptop as it signalled a call, and clicked on to let Connor join the conversation. 'You're up late,' she commented, as he appeared on the screen, tousle-haired and unshaven.

'Just gone ten,' he replied. 'Looks as though you're living the good life over there.'

'We're doing our best,' she smiled, saluting him with her glass. 'So, have you listened to the interview with Lukas?'

'Just finished, and by the way, I'm recording this. So, here's my answer.'

CONNOR: 'What he told you is pretty sobering, that's for sure, but one of the big takeaways for me, apart from having paternity confirmed – that's major, obvs, and we need to talk about breaking it to Sadie . . . But it seems Lottie's story about finding Sadie on the beach *is* rooted in truth.'

CRISTY: 'Yes, that was a standout for me too, so a case of truth being stranger than fiction. Must keep that in mind. What are your thoughts on Janina's disappearance?'

CONNOR: 'I guess it's my one difficulty. Not that I don't believe Albescu caught up with them, there's a chance he did, but that it happened right when Janina was on her way to see the sisters . . .?'

Cristy let that hang as she glanced at David.

DAVID: 'Am I allowed to speak?'

CONNOR: 'Go ahead, we can always edit around if necessary.'

DAVID: 'Are you thinking that Lottie might have found a way to contact Albescu while she was supposed to be considering the possibility of Janina seeing her daughter?'

CRISTY: 'She knew about Albescu because Janina had told her.'

CONNOR: 'Exactly, and now we know that there was no earlier contact with Janina's child being the object of some ungodly transaction, we have to come at it differently. So, we're agreed that Lottie had time to find Albescu before making contact with Janina again?'

CRISTY: 'It's possible. Keep going.'

CONNOR: 'OK, Gabe said he suspected Lottie for a while, so what happened to convince him that it could have been Albescu?'

CRISTY: 'Didn't you see the link I sent with the rest of the interview?'

CONNOR: 'No, I . . . Oh shit, here it is. I'll listen and get back to you. Or no, give it to me now.'

CRISTY: 'OK, apparently Gabe and Janina's landlady in St Peter Port had a visit from a man with a foreign accent who didn't leave his name, but he was asking for Janina. This was a day or two prior to Janina's car going off the road.'

CONNOR: 'So this guy turns up out of the blue, finds the landlady and what? Gets confirmation they're staying there?'

CRISTY: 'I guess so.'

CONNOR: 'So he watches the place until Janina shows up then he follows her when she drives to meet Lottie – that's what we're being asked to believe?'

CRISTY: 'It's what Lukas and Gabe believe.'

CONNOR: 'Then answer me this: why would Albescu want her dead instead of back where he could control her?'

CRISTY: 'Because Lottie made it worth his while to abandon his own plans and adopt hers? But, remember, there was no body, so maybe he got hold of Janina and took her off the island.'

CONNOR: 'And no one saw it happen? Finding that hard to swallow, but I guess it's possible. Did anyone see this guy again, after he turned up at the landlady's door?'

CRISTY: 'We don't know, but the assumption has to be that he left the island as soon as the job was done.'

CONNOR: 'OK, what did Gabe do after the search for Janina was abandoned?'

CRISTY: 'He eventually went back to the farm in Somerset hoping she'd manage to escape again and come to find him there.'

CONNOR: 'But she never did. How long did he wait?'

CRISTY: 'A few years, apparently. His cousin Verity, whose insanely rich husband seems to have bankrolled a new start for Gabe, turned up one day in 2010 and persuaded him to return to the States with her. I think he was pretty destitute and desperate by then, and she promised to pay someone to keep a watch on the farm in case Janina did turn up. So he went with her. The someone who was keeping an eye out was in fact a private detective by the name of Sean Littleday, who found Lukas in 2015. That's when Lukas and Evie were hired by cousin Verity to take care of Gabe. He's . . . I'm not sure how to describe him . . .'

Cristy looked at David.

DAVID: 'To quote Gabe himself, he's not quick and clever like the rest of his family, and frankly you can see how easily exploitable he must have been back then. Probably still is, actually. He's the type who would have been bullied at school; definitely shunned by his parents. Fast forward to him as a lonely forty-something when he answered an ad he found in a newspaper offering to connect the right clients with companions or housekeepers, and the rest, as they say, is history.'

CRISTY: 'So let's get back to Janina's disappearance. Did she go off the road in a tragic accident, or was Albescu, possibly hired by Lottie, making sure she wouldn't be able to come back for her daughter again?'

DAVID: 'Why would Lottie only target Janina when she knew that Gabe was also on the island?'

CONNOR: 'If, as you say, he's not the fastest on the uptake, maybe she decided that he wasn't going to be as much of a problem. And if she could persuade him Albescu had made a return . . . Plus, Gabe was – is – very well connected. There could have been a hell of a lot more fuss about him disappearing, estranged from his family or not.'

CRISTY: 'You're quite good at this.'

CONNOR: 'Which is why you pay me the big bucks – not. Anyway, we need to talk to that landlady, find out what she remembers. Lucky I'm in Guernsey now, so if you can get me a name, or an address, or both, I'll see if I can track her down.'

CRISTY: 'OK. Meantime, let's listen to the whole interview again and then we should probably send it to Sadie. As you're there, perhaps you and Anna can break the news about Gabe being her father so it doesn't just come at her the way it did for us.'

CONNOR: 'Got you. OK, this is me ending the recording.'

As the red light disappeared on their screens, Connor said, 'How do we feel about recording Sadie's reaction to the news? To the whole interview, in fact. Do you think she'll be up for it?'

'The fact that we now know Gabe was very much more victim than villain,' Cristy replied, 'definitely makes it worth asking.

Especially as he seems to have really loved Janina. That'll mean a lot, I'm sure. Where are you staying?'

'Chez David. Your mother and Anna insisted.'

David laughed. 'I hope they're taking good care of you.'

'The best.'

'Have you interviewed Corny, the housekeeper, yet?' Cristy asked.

'This morning,' Connor replied. 'I'll send it over, but she hasn't added anything we don't already know, so she's either been briefed by Mia, or she really was in the dark about Sadie. Needless to say I can't get near Mia herself. How have you left things with the ex-pat trio?'

'We're meeting for dinner at their club tomorrow evening,' Cristy told him, 'which means we now have the onerous ordeal of trying to fill our time in this rich man's paradise.'

'Hard. I guess you must be feeling quite at home there, David, being one of them and all that.'

'Already got my eye on a property or two,' David assured him dryly.

'After Sadie's listened to the interview,' Cristy said, 'or even before, make sure you tell her that her father and uncle are very keen to meet her.'

'Will do. Something that just occurred to me, do we ask Gabe to prove paternity? I mean, we can tell her it's possible he's her father, in fact highly likely, but . . .'

'It's already in hand,' Cristy assured him, 'and Lukas is doing the same. You're right to think of it, because we'll need the cover once we go live with this and the army of cynics get stuck into it.'

'But we're not foreseeing a problem?'

'No, but if there is and they turn out to be fakes . . . Actually I can't go there, it's already making me feel faint, although I guess it'll make a fantastic twist in the series if they are.'

*

'Are you OK?' David asked the following morning as he and Cristy strolled barefoot along the soft, white-sand beach in front of their hotel.

Cristy's fingers tightened around his, as though to reassure him. She wasn't going to mention the nuisance, nonsense texts she'd been receiving before, and since they'd arrived, and maybe spoil what little time they had here. It was the same crazy who, for some reason, had advised her not to be afraid in his first message. This time he'd just spewed out all his random fan-stuff, nothing threatening, or even standout really, so she couldn't think why it was bothering her.

'I might be a little jetlagged,' she said. 'And I'm concerned about the way things are going with the series.'

'In what way?'

'Something's not feeling right.'

'You mean with Gabe and Lukas?'

'No, I believe what they told us and I know you do . . .'

'As does Connor . . .'

'I just keep getting the sense that we're still missing something . . . Like it's there in front of me, something I should be seeing, but I'm not.'

Pulling her down next to him on the sand, David slipped an arm around her shoulders and rested his head on hers as they stared out to the shimmering horizon while inky blue waves lapped gently, coolly, over their feet.

'Whatever it is,' he said, 'I'm sure it'll come clear—'

'Shall we put it aside for now?' Cristy interrupted, loving the feeling of being with him and deciding she wanted nothing more than to lose herself in it while she could.

'Your call,' he said, and pressed a kiss to her hair.

Moments later they both murmured in surprised appreciation as a dolphin appeared, only a few feet away, and began to circle and dive, skim and leap, as if putting on a show just for them. It was so early in the morning that there was no one else around, only the attendants quietly setting out loungers and raising parasols.

David started to speak, then stopped as his mobile rang. Seeing it was Rosie on FaceTime, he clicked to answer it. 'Hi, sweetheart,' he said, holding the phone so she could see Cristy too.

'Hi Dad – and Cristy. It's Rosie here.'

'We can see,' David responded dryly.

'How are you?' Cristy smiled.

'Have you run away to get married?' Rosie asked and giggled as they laughed.

'Not the plan right now,' David told her. 'How are things with you?'

'I'm OK, but I think Ludo's made me pregnant.'

Feeling him stiffen, Cristy quickly said, 'Why do you say that, sweetie? What did he do?'

'He put his tongue in my mouth when he kissed me and said that was how babies are made. I told him it's not, because I know it's not, but he keeps saying it is.'

'Have you talked to Grandma?' David asked.

'Yes and she said I'm right, but I thought I should ask you as well just in case she doesn't know.'

Stifling a laugh, Cristy said, 'So I'm guessing it's all back on with Ludo since he made a scene a couple of weeks ago?'

'Yes, I forgave him, because he has mental health issues and that's the kind thing to do. When are you coming home?'

'Why? Are you missing me?' her father asked.

'No!' Rosie cried, and laughed delightedly. 'Connor's staying here,' she told them. 'He's much nicer-looking than Ludo. Shame he's married or I would ask him to be my boyfriend. I'm going to the doctor today for my regular check-up.'

'Good girl,' David told her. 'Is Grandma taking you?'

'I think so. Anna's going somewhere with Connor. Oh, that's right, they've already gone to Sadie's. I wanted to go, but I have a lot to do here so I'll see them later. Cristy, are you in love with Dad again?'

As Cristy hesitated, David said, 'Of course she is. How could she not be?'

'So are *you* making babies?'

David's first answer was lost in a laugh. 'That's not a very polite question to ask,' he scolded gently.

Leaving him to explain why, Cristy got up to take a call from Connor. 'Hey,' she said, moving a little further down the beach.

'Jesus, it's all kicking off here,' he told her, sounding tense and hurried.

'Why? What's happening? Where are you?'

'At the lodge. Sadie listened to the interview, spoke not a word, just took off down to the villa to confront her aunt, I'm guessing about Lottie meeting Janina and no one telling her. God knows what's been said down there, but it obviously got pretty heated because she's just rung Jasper to let him know she's locked Mia up.'

'You're kidding!'

'No. She's locked Mia in a downstairs cupboard and is refusing to let her out until Mia tells her the truth. Jasper's gone to investigate. Anna and I are waiting here on his advice, but if we don't hear anything in the next ten minutes we're going down. Meantime, I'm recording an account of events as they unfold in the hope of using it, because this is pretty dramatic stuff.'

'You're telling me,' Cristy agreed. 'Keep me updated, and if you think we should come back . . .'

'Actually, I do. Sorry, but it seems you've got what you went there for and right now this is where it's happening.'

'OK. I'll call again as soon as I've got Iz to organize the flights,' and ringing off Cristy turned back to David, pausing as she realized he was talking to his mother now. In spite of the hour she texted Evie to ask if she and David could come over this morning, probably in about an hour, then she emailed Iz with their flight requirements.

Iz came back so fast Cristy almost blinked. *Leave it with me. How many tickets?*

*Just the two. We need to end up in Guernsey.*

*All is possible.*

With a smile Cristy checked Evie's message. *We're here. Come whenever suits you. Is everything OK?*

Deciding not to answer that for the moment, Cristy made a quick check of her other texts, and felt a surge of distaste as she came across another from the crazy. Very short this time, saying, *He doesn't love you as much as I do.*

In spite of it being a Matthew kind of line, she knew instinctively that it wasn't him, not only because the sender's ID was withheld, but because her ex, for all his faults, just wasn't that creepy.

Quickly scrolling back through the thread she saw, to her alarm, that there were even more messages than she'd realized and whoever was behind them appeared to have been following her every move.

*You didn't see me tonight, did you, Cristy? I saw you walking through the rain.*

*Sorry about the mess at your office. Got frustrated when you weren't there.*

*Don't go back to him. He's a liar and a cheat.*

He – and she presumed it was he – even seemed to know she was in the States. *I waved you off at the airport, but you didn't wave back. How's Miami?*

And now this – *He doesn't love you as much as I do.*

Deciding again that she wasn't going to let it distract her, she dumped the messages into a folder and shut down the thread just as David finished his call.

'We're going to Floral Grove for breakfast,' she told him as he stood up. 'I'll explain on the way.'

*

Evie had coffee and pastries waiting when they arrived. Lukas was at his computer, checking the markets apparently, although he joined them moments after they'd sat down in the kitchen. Gabe was standing almost statue-like with his back to the glass doors onto the deck, a dark, indistinguishable silhouette against the early morning sunlight – until he too came to the table and sat down. He wasn't wearing his dark glasses this morning and his eyes, Cristy noticed right away, were blue and clear, and so filled with anguish that she instantly regretted blurting out Sadie's predicament the way she had.

'They lock one another up?' he said in confusion. 'Why would they do that?'

'I'm not sure I understand it myself,' Cristy confessed, 'although I think this might be the first time Sadie has done it to her aunt. Usually it's the other way around.'

'What the . . .?' Evie muttered under her breath.

'She locked her aunt up . . .' Gabe repeated.

'She's not her aunt,' Lukas reminded him.

Flummoxed, Gabe said, 'What does she hope to gain from this?'

Cristy glanced at David, not quite sure how to answer that.

'Probably more of the truth,' David suggested. 'Now Sadie knows—'

'She's Sasha,' Lukas interrupted. 'Our Sasha. I think we must call her by her name.'

Going with it, David said, 'Now Sasha knows that at least one of her aunts met her mother and lied about it, she understandably wants to know what else they've kept from her.'

'Like how Janina died,' Lukas put in tightly. 'I'm sorry, Gabe, I've never liked to say this to you, but I'm sure those women know more than they ever let on.'

Gabe's eyes were full of uncertainty as he looked at David. 'Is Sasha in danger?' he asked.

'I don't think so,' David replied, 'but clearly things are getting out of hand which is why we need to get back there.'

'We should come too,' Lukas stated, getting to his feet. 'We have to be sure she's safe. We can't lose her again.'

'She'll be OK,' Evie assured him gently. 'Won't she?' she asked Cristy.

Deciding not to remind them that, as things stood, Mia was the prisoner, not Sadie, Cristy said, 'It's probable that the worst is already over and things have calmed down. I'll check with Connor, my colleague, who's there, at the house, and call you as soon as I have an update.'

'We – are – coming,' Lukas insisted. 'Gabe is her father. She needs him now, and I'm her uncle . . .'

Seeming to read the situation more clearly than he did, Evie said, 'Let's wait until we know that she wants to see you, sweetie. She hasn't said anything about it yet . . . Has she?' she asked Cristy.

Feeling for Lukas and Gabe who were looking increasingly afraid, Cristy said, 'Not as far as I know, but I'm sure she will, once we've got things straightened out over there.'

'It won't help to walk into the middle of everything,' Evie cautioned Lukas. 'She has people there to help her sort that out, then we can meet her and let her know how very much we want her to be a part of our lives.'

Lukas looked at Cristy, clearly torn, unsure of the right thing to say. 'We'll be on the next plane if she wants us to be,' he told her. 'Or she can come here. Whatever works best for her.'

Impulsively squeezing his hand, Cristy said, 'We're going straight to Guernsey from Miami – one change – but my phone will be on the whole time. I'll be in touch the minute I know more.'

Going to shake Gabe's hand, David said, 'I have no doubt she'll want to meet you, and when it happens you'll be very proud of her.'

Gabe stared back at him, tears welling in his eyes. 'Is she like her mother?' he asked hoarsely. 'The photos say she is.'

David smiled. 'You'll probably be surprised by just how much.'

'I wish,' Gabe began and faltered.

Placing a comforting hand on his shoulder, David said, 'It's OK, my friend, I get it.'

A few minutes later, as they drove away from the house, Cristy said, 'What do you get?'

Waving a thanks to the security guard who opened the gates, David said, 'He wishes we could find Janina.'

Cristy nodded, impressed that he'd intuited that, while wishing the same thing for them all – and what a coup it would be for *Hindsight*.

'Clove and Jacks have already started a search for Albescu,' she said, as they headed for I-75, 'but my gut is telling me that whether he was involved in the disappearance or not, the answers are all with the sisters. Either written down, or, more likely, stored inside Mia's head.'

*

Cristy and David had already checked in at Miami International when Connor rang.

'Has Mia been released yet?' Cristy asked right away.

CONNOR: 'FYI, I'm recording this. The answer is yes, Mia's free and Sadie's back at the lodge. Anna and I have just left.'

CRISTY: 'Is Sadie OK?'

CONNOR: 'I think so. Not as angry as she was, anyway, but she's obviously still shaken up and now she's totally focused on reading Lottie's journals. The ones that were in the safe. Apparently, Mia told her it's where she's going to find the truth.'

CRISTY: 'Why the heck can't Mia just tell her?'

CONNOR: 'She says she doesn't know all of it.'

CRISTY: 'So she's not read the journals herself, but claims it's where Sadie will find the truth? How does that work?'

CONNOR: 'I've no idea, but it's what's happening right now. Sadie's got the journals and has promised to call if she finds anything. Have you spoken to Clove and Jacks?'

CRISTY: 'Not yet, have you?'

CONNOR: 'They're still in Vilnius, and they've interviewed the older sister. All it's really adding is more background to Janina and Lukas's childhoods – an expansion of what he's already told you. They're heading back this afternoon, and I'm on my way to St Peter Port to interview the landlady who's already told me on the phone that she doesn't remember renting her flat to anyone with the names I gave her.'

CRISTY: 'But it was a long time ago, maybe photographs will jog her memory?'

CONNOR: 'That's what I'm hoping. Where are you now?'

CRISTY: 'Waiting to board a flight to Dublin. Changing there for Guernsey, so I'll call as soon as we land. Before you go, how did Sadie take the fact that George Symmonds-Browne is her father?'

CONNOR: 'She didn't actually say much at first, I think she was in shock, needed time to process, then she heard Lukas speak and started to cry, sobbed when Gabe came in. It was hearing about Lottie directing Janina to some random house that really got to her . . . Incidentally, she didn't know that the sisters ever had any other properties on the island. Anyway, that's when she took off to the villa.'

Anna's voice came down the line. 'If it helps, she told me while Connor was on the phone that she's really excited to meet her father and uncle, and nervous, but she wants to find out what happened to her mother first. Then she thinks she'll probably want to go there rather than them come here, because it'll punish Mia for lying to her all these years if she just ups and leaves.'

Cristy checked her phone as a text arrived. It was from Matthew so she let it go for now. 'Does she understand that her father has a slightly impaired cognitive ability?' she asked Anna. Was that the best way to put it; right now she couldn't think of another.

'Yes, she does and she says it just makes her feel more protective of him.'

Cristy smiled. 'Much like her mother did, by the sound of it. I'll let him and her uncle know that she *is* keen to meet them. This being the States with practically everything on same-day delivery if you can pay, we should have their DNA results pretty quickly so we can be certain they match with Sadie's.'

'Are you doubting it?'

'No, I'm not.'

After speaking briefly with Connor again, she rang off and, seeing David was on his phone, she checked Matthew's text.

*How's it going over there? Am I allowed to say I'm missing you? OK, not what you want to hear. He's a lucky guy, but he'll never love you as much as I do. Mx*

As the final words jarred, Cristy looked up, almost as if expecting to find someone watching her, messing with her. No one was, and of course, the echo in Matthew's text of what the weirdo had said in his latest was nothing more than an unfortunate coincidence, because Matthew *really wasn't that creepy*. He simply wouldn't send anonymous messages designed to unnerve and annoy her. He had no reason to when he was pretty good at that anyway.

Messaging him back, she said, *How's Aiden?*

*Accusing me of being 'de-lulu' for thinking you'll marry me again. I'm guessing that means delusional. Shall we prove him wrong?*

Did he never give up?

*How's Baby Bear?*

There was no reply to that until she and David were settled into their seats for the flight and a photograph of a wide-eyed, cute-as-a-bear-cub baby came through. Finding no accompanying message she typed in, *Sweet, you must be very proud. When are you going to see him?*

*We're both invited to LA any time we want to go. Fancy it?*

Irritated, she switched from the thread and sent a quick message to Evie. *Thanks to you all for your hospitality and for your frankness. I have it on good authority that Sasha is very keen to meet Gabe and Lukas.* She read it through quickly, and pressed send.

# CHAPTER TWENTY-SEVEN

After a heart-stoppingly bumpy flight from Dublin to Guernsey, Cristy and David walked into the vaulted kitchen of his incredible home in the wooded heights of the island to be greeted by his mother, Cynthia, and the heavenly aroma of freshly baked cookies. To Cristy it felt like coming home, and simply seeing Cynthia's dear, crinkled face before being hauled in for a hug made her once again think of her own late mother and how alike the two were. Sweet-natured, mischievous, sharp-eyed behind the scattiness, and somehow managing to exude warmth without even trying.

'Where is everyone?' David asked, going to fill two mugs with coffee and helping himself to a biscuit on the way.

'Rosie's at rehearsals for a new play,' Cynthia replied, 'and Anna's . . . Ah, here they are,' she said, as the back door opened and Henry the golden retriever burst joyously through and made a beeline for David.

Connor and Anna followed, Connor unravelling his scarf as he said, 'Good flight? Great! We have news, only we're not entirely sure what it is yet.'

Amused, Cristy sank down on a sofa saying, 'OK, that sounds promising. Just tell me, has anyone locked up anyone else in the past few hours?'

'Not that we know of,' Connor replied, grunting as Henry jumped at his groin.

Dragging the dog away, Anna said, 'Bad boy! Go say hi to Cristy.'

Immediately Henry bounded onto the sofa and launched into a hearty lick of Cristy's travel-weary face.

'Basket!' Cynthia commanded.

Henry apparently enjoyed the taste of Cristy.

'Basket,' David commanded.

Henry cocked his head as though puzzled by the word, before promptly doing as he was told.

'So what's the news you're not sure about?' Cristy asked, sipping her coffee as Connor brought his to the opposite sofa. 'Well, before we get to the big stuff, the landlady in St Peter Port was no help. She was too hazy on everything and who can blame her, considering how long ago it was, and how many people must have rented from her since.'

Clearly unable to wait any longer, Anna dived straight into the main news. 'Sadie's found something in Lottie's journals,' she declared. 'She won't tell us what it is until after she's shown it to Mia and as far as we know that's where she is now. I offered to go with her – Jasper flew to London this morning – but she told me she could handle it and she'll call as soon as she's done.'

Concerned, Cristy said to Connor, 'Did you speak to her before she went off on this mission?'

'I did and frankly she sounded kind of manic. I told her to wait, that we could be there in twenty, but she was determined to go alone. Obviously we went anyway, but we can't get past the gates without a code.'

'I'll call the security company,' David said, opening up his phone. 'If I say it's an emergency they'll do an override and let us in.'

'We're waiting for Jasper to call back,' Anna ran on, 'but he's in a meeting and can't be interrupted. Obvs he has the code.'

Only half aware of David talking in the background, Cristy was envisaging all sorts of scenarios unfolding at the villa, none of them good. Nor was the thought of Gabe, Lukas and Evie waiting patiently, trustingly, to hear when they could meet their precious Sasha.

'OK, thanks, Jeff,' David said into his phone. 'We'll head over there now.'

Cristy and Connor were on their feet, and already half out the door when Anna suddenly cried, 'It's Sadie!' and quickly clicked to take the call. 'Hey! Are you OK? We've been worried.' She paused, glanced up at Cristy and said to Sadie, 'Where are you now?'

'Put her on speaker,' Cristy instructed.

'. . . still at the villa,' Sadie was saying. 'She's a mess, but she deserved it.'

'What do you mean, a mess?' Anna cried, turning frightened eyes to her father.

'I recorded it all,' Sadie answered, her voice sounding shredded by exhaustion.

'Jesus, we need to get over there,' Connor muttered.

Snatching Anna's phone, David said, 'Sadie, we're on our way. You need to open the gates.'

When Sadie didn't answer, Anna cried, 'What did you find in the journals, babe?'

'You need to come,' Sadie said weakly. 'Please come. I'll go up to the lodge and see you there.'

*

Less than half an hour later Cristy and Connor were in the lodge's small sitting room, all pale oak beams and cosy furniture, with Sadie hunched into a capacious armchair looking both dazed and beaten, as though she'd just fought her way through some sort of storm. Anna was on the floor next to her, while David was outside dealing with the security guard who'd just turned up. Cristy didn't know yet whether they were going to head down to the villa to check on Mia, or wait until Sadie had explained what had happened during the past hour.

'You can listen to it all,' Sadie said quietly, half-throwing her mobile onto the coffee table between them. 'I told her I was recording, but I'm not sure it went in. She's . . . I don't know what she is . . . Crazy, cruel . . .' Her breath caught on a dry sob and Anna reached up to take her hand.

'I'm OK,' Sadie assured her. 'Just a bit . . .' Her eyes went to Cristy, and for a fleeting moment Cristy thought she sensed something horribly dark inside her.

'Did they come back with you?' Sadie asked, suddenly seeming so much more vulnerable than she had a moment ago.

Knowing who she was referring to, and understanding how bewildered and conflicted she must be feeling, Cristy said, 'They were very keen to, but you said you wanted to sort things out with your aunt first so they're waiting . . .'

'I'm glad they're not here,' Sadie interrupted, seeming to mean it, then her voice faltered as she said, 'but I really . . . I really want to see my dad.'

Feeling her heart swelling with empathy, Cristy said, 'What would you like me to do?'

Sadie shook her head. 'I don't know. I . . . It's all so messed up . . .' She looked at her phone and said, 'You'll find it in voice notes. I want to listen to it too just in case . . .' She gulped as she swallowed another sob, and pressed her hands to her face.

Still amazed that she'd recorded everything, Cristy found the file and after hitting play she placed the mobile back on the table and kept her eyes on it as it began to reveal why Sadie was in such an emotional state.

SADIE: 'I've read the truth, Mia. I know everything . . .'

MIA: 'What are you talking about? I don't understand you.'

SADIE: 'I've got it all here, in this journal . . .'

MIA: 'All what, for heaven's sake?'

SADIE: 'Everything you did to my mother.'

There was a lengthy silence, broken only by the sound of muted voices, too indistinct to decipher.

'This is where I'm telling her I'm recording,' Sadie explained.

'Did she object?' Cristy asked.

'She accused me of being in thrall to you "people" and that I'd end up regretting it.'

'Is she saying anything,' Connor asked, 'about *what* had been done to your mother?'

Sadie shook her head. 'Not really, only that I was a fool to believe everything I read, especially if it was written by Lottie.' She stopped as her voice became clearer on the recording.

SADIE: 'So here it is, are you listening? I *said*, are you listening?'

MIA: 'I don't feel I have a choice. If I don't you'll lock me in a cupboard again.'

SADIE: 'You're right, I will, until the police get here.'

MIA: 'What are you doing?'

SADIE: 'I've decided you should go into the cupboard anyway. I don't want you running away before I've finished.'

MIA: 'There's no need of that . . . Let me go, please. I promise I'll sit here and listen.'

SADIE: 'If you move from that chair you know I'll catch you and this time I'll put you in there without a light on.'

Mia's next words were indistinguishable as she muttered angrily, or helplessly, probably both.

SADIE: 'This entry in Lottie's journal is dated Tuesday eighth of March, 2005. *2005.* Do you remember that year?'

MIA: 'You don't have to shout. I can hear you perfectly well.'

SADIE: (reading) '"We received a note today from someone claiming to be Sadie's mother. It was a terrible shock, coming out of the blue like that. Maybe we should have been better prepared, but how do you prepare for something so earth-shattering? She wants to see her child, she says, and we have to believe she's who she's claiming to be because she goes on to describe how she left 'Sasha' on the beach five years ago.

'"We can't let it happen, of course, for any number of reasons, although most of all it will be far too disruptive for dear Sadie when she's so settled with us now and such a happy little child. She's about to have her seventh birthday and she's doing well at school, at sports, at just about everything she sets her mind to. We are tremendously proud of her, I guess you could say we're like satellites revolving around her sweet little world. It would be very hard for me to give her up, but it would devastate Mia and I can't have that. Mia needs Sadie in a way I don't, although I defy her to love her any more than I do. I have a life elsewhere with my darling Robert who I plan to go to soon, when the time is right for us both. Mia's whole existence revolves around Sadie – insofar as it revolves around anyone apart from herself. Such a needy and selfish woman, I actively detest her at times, but of course I love her too.

"'I debated for a long time over whether I should tell her about the note from Sadie's mother, and in the end decided I had to. I need to ensure that we are protected from blackmail, because that's what this could be about. After all, why would the woman suddenly turn up now asking for contact, when she could have come any time over the past five years? We're both certain she can be paid to go away, so I'm considering meeting her in the café she's suggested. Apparently she's going to be there every morning this week so I can choose my day. If I go I have to make sure we're in a window seat so that Mia can take photographs from across the street. This will give us a record of the meeting – blackmail attempt – should we need it later. Mia's idea, not mine, but no point arguing.

"'Thursday tenth of March, 2005: I still haven't been to the café. Mia is as frightened as I knew she would be. She's angry too. Apart from valuing her freedom and good name, she truly believes no one has a right to take Sadie away. This attributes a depth of feeling to my sister that I'm not entirely sure she possesses. She's all about ownership and control, and can't bear the idea of anyone challenging her. I believe that sometimes she despises me simply for being an equal partner in our fortune, but worse than that, she's jealous of Robert. Not that she knows his name. I've told her nothing about him, it's best that way, but she's not a fool, she knows there's someone and I'm sure she'd do anything, *anything* to make him go away, mostly out of fear of me leaving her. She'll probably fall apart if I do. I feel sorry about that, but I'm afraid he means more to me than she does. I'm already wracked with guilt about leaving the child with only Mia to take care of her, she'll be damaged for life and the dear little thing doesn't deserve that. Will I actually be able to make myself go when the time comes?

"'Friday eleventh of March, 2005: I still haven't gone into the café, but I've seen Sadie's mother there waiting in case I show up. A man is always with her and I want to find out who he is before I go in. Unfortunately we have no idea how to do that as we have no contact details for the woman who calls herself Janina. Mia is certain he's a thug who's going to force us to give Sadie up. She could be right, but he surely can't do that in a public place, so I've decided I'll go tomorrow. If they're not there, all well and good; if they are I guess I'll just listen to what they have to say. If it is about blackmail we'll go straight to the police. Or maybe not. It's a very complicated situation, especially after all we've done to make our girl officially ours. If our crimes are revealed it will be an end to everything and there will be nothing we can do to stop Sadie being taken away. It could even mean prison and I don't think Mia would survive that. I'm not sure I would either.'"

There was a pause in the recording leaving Cristy to imagine Sadie looking at her aunt, perhaps to be sure she was paying attention, or hoping for some sort of response. It was impossible to know what was going on in those moments, only that there was a silence before Sadie started reading again.

SADIE: (reading) "'Saturday twelfth of March, 2005. I met with the mother this morning and it turns out the man is Sadie's father. I have no idea if that's true, but it's what they claimed. He said almost nothing, only watched me, as though keen for me to listen and understand what was being said. They called Sadie 'Sasha,' of course, but I stuck with Sadie, wanting to press it home that the child they'd abandoned was someone else now. A happy, rounded little girl, who was loved and cared for, and who had every advantage in life – and no memories of them. I added that part and saw the mother flinch, but why not? I'm sure it's true. I asked why they would want to deprive Sadie of so much (feeling certain they couldn't equal it) and why they were only coming to find her now when there had surely been many opportunities to reclaim her since they'd abandoned her. The mother flinched again and the father looked as though he might cry. Strange man.

'"As I listened to Janina's reasons for leaving Sadie in our care I have to admit to being profoundly shocked – and moved. She claims she was trafficked to the UK back in '97 and though poorly treated by the men who brought her, she was taken to the man who'd paid a large sum for her to become his 'companion.' This was George, Sadie's father. He's apparently a man of some means and standing, although you wouldn't know it to look at him. Handsome, yes, and strongly built, just not assertive or even confident enough to speak up for his wife (are they married?) or his child. When they got onto how he'd been used, exploited, by a criminal gang I began to see him in a different light and of course I felt sorry for him. Apparently the leader of this gang, someone by the name of Matis Albescu, or his son (some confusion there), has been holding Janina captive for the past five years. She didn't go into detail of what she'd been subjected to during that time, but she didn't have to, I am familiar enough with these kinds of stories to know what happens to girls in her position. And actually, I could see the trauma of it in her eyes. Naturally, I'm deeply upset by the experiences she's suffered, no one deserves such a fate, but in my opinion – and Mia agrees – it makes her an even less suitable parent for Sadie.

'"Monday fourteenth of March, 2005. The question that's been plaguing me since meeting Sadie's mother is whether or not I'll be able to live with myself if I deny her access to her own child? Mia keeps ranting on about it being madness to allow the woman into our lives, and of course it would be. We might never be rid of her, and sooner or later Sadie will find out who she really is and what then? So how can we make her go away? I'm really not sure money will do it. It wasn't mentioned while I was at the café and if the father's as comfortably off as they claim, they don't need it. So now I am considering Mia's idea of tracing this Albescu character and telling him where he can find his missing sex worker."'

MIA: 'It was not my idea! It was hers.'

SADIE: 'Did you try to stop her?'

MIA: 'Yes, of course, it was a monstrous idea that only someone like Lottie could think up. You never really knew her, Sadie. All she wanted was to be with some doctor she'd met in Africa who she always claimed had saved her life. She wanted to keep you here, with me, so I wouldn't be alone when she left to be with him. She thought I didn't know that, but I did. She told herself it would stop me from going after her, from falling apart, from exposing the fact that we'd taken a child – *you* – and made you our own . . .'

Sadie's voice was emotionless as she continued.

SADIE: (reading) '"Wednesday sixteenth of March, 2005. I have contacted Janina and invited her to meet me at the Sark View house so we can talk some more. I'd rather Mia wasn't around, but she's insisting that she has to be. It's a shame she doesn't trust me, her own sister, to do what's best for us all."'

MIA: 'Sadie! Listen to me—'

SADIE: 'No, Mia, you are listening to me.'

MIA: 'Yes, yes, of course, but you have to understand—'

SADIE: (reading) '"Friday eighteenth of March, 2005. Janina has agreed to meet me at Sark View. I asked her to come alone in the hope she'll feel more intimidated – acquiescent might be a better word – if she's outnumbered. Mia has found herself a gun, heaven only knows where from. It doesn't work, I've made sure of that . . ."'

MIA: 'I never had a gun. Never!'

SADIE: (reading) '"I don't anticipate anyone being hurt, unless, of course, Mia has managed over the past few days to make contact with this Matis Albescu character. Then, obviously, things won't go well for Janina. Him taking custody again is an answer, of course, just not the one I'd have preferred.

'"Saturday nineteenth of March, 2005. I waited at Sark View all day yesterday but Janina didn't come. Sadie seems fretful this morning, I'm not sure why. Mia thinks we're being watched and that something terrible is going to happen. I asked what she imagines that might be, but she seems not to have any idea.

'"Sunday twentieth of March, 2005. I know why Janina didn't come now and I'm so horrified I've started to have palpitations. How could Mia have done this?"'

MIA: 'What? No! No!'

SADIE: (reading) '"She confessed about an hour ago. I've had to come here to my rooms to get away from her. She is even crazier than I realized . . ."'

MIA: 'I don't understand. Why has she written this? My own sister . . .'

SADIE: (reading) '"She says no one will know that Janina was coming to see us. She must have forgotten about 'the father.' He will know, and he's sure to come looking. What are we going to tell him? Not the truth, we can't do that or we'll lose Sadie for sure along with everything else. How could she have done this? I'm so angry I could strangle her."'

MIA: 'I didn't do anything. I don't know what this is about.'

SADIE: (reading) '"Monday twenty-first of March, 2005. The father came earlier, as we knew he would. We told him that Janina didn't show up – that at least was the truth. He was distraught, poor man. We mentioned Albescu, and it was clearly his greatest fear. Nevertheless, he wanted to search for Janina, so I went with him and eventually, as I knew we would, we came to the spot where Janina's car had gone off the road – *where Mia had forced it off the road* – down onto the rocks below. There was simply no way anyone could have survived such a fall . . .'"

Sadie stopped reading as her aunt screamed her denial. It was painful to hear, wrenching gulps of fear and desperate pleas to be believed. Cristy was watching Sadie as she listened, her face ashen, her eyes so large and tortured it was as if she was seeing the crumpled car for real and could register nothing beyond it.

SADIE: (reading) "'Tuesday twenty-second of March, 2005. The car has gone. The police must have taken it away. They are as certain as I am that it would be impossible for anyone to survive such a fall, but as yet no body has washed up on any of the nearby shores. Sometimes they never do. Everyone is wondering about the driver – they're certain it was a woman because of the bag found inside. It's a notoriously dangerous spot, but still they wonder, was it suicide or a tragic accident? Maybe she was drunk or high on drugs. Who was she? What happened to the body and why has no one come forward to say they're missing a loved one?

"'The poor 'father' is distraught, hardly knows what to do. Should he go to the police, tell them what he knows, but if he does will his involvement with the traffickers, or his and Janina's abandonment of Sadie, end up making things worse? I don't try to answer his questions, what matters is that he seems to understand we must do everything in our power to keep Sadie safe and out of the news. He's terrified now that if Albescu does have Janina, he might come back for Sadie. He is right to be so afraid, because there's no knowing what a man of Albescu's character would do with a child.

"'Tuesday nineteenth of April, 2005. Mia's terror seems

to be subsiding. She was certain for a while that the police were going to come for her, that someone had seen her using her car to force Janina's over the edge.

'"Luckily for Mia the 'disposing' of Janina seems to have gone very well. That's how she refers to it, the disposing of a problem; she doesn't refer to Janina by name. I am shocked, and I admit partly fascinated, to see my sister starting to show pride in the fact that she sustained no damage to her Golf when she swerved at Janina's Fiesta. There wasn't even the slightest collision, she tells me. Janina reacted so fast, maybe hit the accelerator instead of the brake and the next thing she'd gone and Mia simply drove on. I don't think Mia is losing any sleep over this, if anything she's becoming more buoyant by the day, and keeps making such a fuss of Sadie that I'm sure the poor child is feeling smothered.

'"We're not sure where 'the father' is now, if he's left the island or still combing the shores hoping Janina's body will turn up. Even if it does we have no need to feel concerned, there can be nothing to tie it to Mia's murderous act, nothing at all. 'I took care of it,' she said to me earlier. 'You should be grateful instead of sitting there looking at me like that.'"'

MIA: 'I never said that. I didn't take care of anything. It was all her.'

SADIE: (reading) '"Friday twenty-second of April, 2005. I need to get away from here, from *her*. I detest her more as each day passes and am only saved from doing something rash by the need to protect Sadie. I don't think Mia will harm her, physically, but I know now what she'll do if I try to leave. She has guessed how important Robert is to me, and she has told me that if I see him again, or try to leave the island without her permission, she will make sure that he knows what I did. Not only the abduction, for that's what it was no matter how gentle or well-meaning we were at the time, but how I – *I* – forced Janina's car off the road to make sure she could never take Sadie away from us."'

Mia was clearly beside herself as she started shouting.

MIA: 'It's not true, Sadie. You have to believe me. It was all her. Lottie's the one who ran your mother off the road, who tricked your father into believing Albescu had returned, who kept the police from our door. She's twisted it all round . . . Sadie, don't go, please . . . Oh God, oh God . . . No, Sadie! Please, don't do that . . . *Nooo!*'

Cristy looked at Sadie, certain she was going to explain what all the thudding and crashing about was, why Mia was screaming so hard, but Sadie didn't speak, simply let the recording come to an end.

Finding herself assessing Sadie for bloodstains, scratches, bruises, ripped clothing even, Cristy said, very gently, 'Sadie? Is your aunt OK?'

Sadie continued staring at the phone as if still trapped in the violence of those final moments. She gave a small shudder, but still didn't speak.

'I've spoken to Mia,' David said quietly.

Cristy turned, unaware that he'd come into the room.

'Is she all right?' Connor asked.

'I haven't seen her,' David replied. 'She wouldn't come out, but she told us she was fine and that we had to go away while she dealt with a private family matter.'

# CHAPTER TWENTY-EIGHT

Over the next twenty-four or so hours Cristy and Connor waited for something, anything to break. It felt almost surreal, as if they'd all entered a peculiar sort of holding state with no idea when they might land, or what would happen when they did. Had Mia been injured during the scene with Sadie? Why wouldn't she answer that question? Why wouldn't Mia show herself at the door?

Sadie stayed shut up in the lodge with Anna until Jasper returned on Friday morning, while Mia wouldn't see anyone unless Sadie was with them. Sadie refused to go near her.

Needing to honour the promise to drop an episode of *Hindsight* before the weekend, they set up a small studio in David's portside office and connected with Clove and Jacks who were now back in Bristol. The recordings with Lukas's old friend, Natalie Irwin, and Lottie's publisher, Felicity Green, were already edited, so ready to drop into the start of the interview with Lukas and Gabe. This they decided to run in its entirety and end with the cliff-hanger of Cristy being told by Connor that it was all kicking off in Guernsey so she needed to return pdq.

Mia's lawyers had already slapped down an injunction – no surprise there, although very fast work. Sadie, as it turned out, was supportive of the ban, having now decided that she didn't want her aunt to be named and shamed, and a whole lot worse, at least not yet.

'It's all happening so fast,' she'd said during her last conversation with Cristy. 'I know it's terrible what she did, unforgivable, but maybe Lottie did twist things around to make Mia the guilty party when really, it was all her.'

Unable to argue with that, Cristy had simply listened as Sadie continued. 'I feel so awful about things now, the way I . . . I shouldn't have forced her . . . I didn't mean to frighten her . . . I was just so angry and . . . Well, I think we need to take a breath before making any more big decisions.'

On Friday evening, after the Gabe and Lukas pod had been uploaded, Cristy, Connor and David took themselves off to Le Nautique, overlooking the port, for dinner.

'What we're no closer to knowing for certain,' Cristy remarked, wondering if she'd ever had such good oysters before, 'is which one of the sisters was actually responsible for Janina's death. Mia has only denied that it was her who forced the car off the road, not that it didn't happen, and obviously Lottie isn't around to speak for herself.'

'Does it actually matter which of them was responsible?' Connor asked. 'If we can't air it anyway . . .'

Cristy grimaced. 'I'm sure it matters to Sadie, and it will to the police if we ever do get it out there.' For no particular reason she felt a clench of unease as her mind flashed on the anonymous text she'd received earlier: *You're back, but you keep failing to notice me. I hope you know how hurtful that is.*

Connor said, 'I guess we could have a great debate-pod on our hands at some point in the future. Did Lottie twist the tale to make her sister the villain? Or is Mia putting on a good show of being framed for something she didn't do? The amateur sleuths and armchair psychs will lap it up.' He seemed to slump. 'You know, we have to get the crucial parts of the journal past the lawyers or the final episode is going to be all about Sadie reuniting with her father and uncle – and heart-warming as that is, everyone will want to know what really happened to her mother.'

Cristy checked her phone as a new text arrived. Relieved to see it was Lukas she clicked to open it.

*We're in London staying at the Savoy. No pressure, we just wanted to be nearby – or at least in the same time zone – in case Sadie needs us. You don't even have to tell her we're here if you think it won't be helpful. How is she? Can you tell us what's been happening since you got to Guernsey? Lukas*

Sighing, she looked at the others. 'How do I answer that?' she asked, after they'd read the message. 'Do I tell them to give up all hope of Janina being alive? That one of the sisters – we don't know which – murdered the big love of Gabe's life in order to hold onto his daughter? That Sadie has very probably beaten her aunt up and is now seriously conflicted over what she wants to do next? I'm just wondering how to spin this so they don't come jetting over here with their own lawyers in tow.'

David said, tentatively, 'Would it be such a bad thing for Sadie to see her father right now? Maybe he's who she really needs even if she doesn't quite realize it.'

Cristy glanced at Connor as he said, 'You two have met the guy, so would you say he's up to it? I mean, this is pretty traumatic stuff that's going on here and he's not . . . Well, you know what I'm saying.'

Cristy was trying to think it through, to figure out how it might work if Gabe and Lukas did come over, but her instincts didn't seem to be directing her one way or the other. 'We need to sleep on it,' she said in the end, 'and maybe I'll talk to Evie in the morning so she can help with the decision. For now I'll just say that Sadie's still working through a few things, but it's good that they're nearby and I'll let Sadie know they're ready to come as soon as the time is right.'

*

As it turned out Cristy didn't get the chance to speak to Evie the next morning. She, David and Connor were in the kitchen with Cynthia and Lawrence and only partway through breakfast when a message arrived from Sadie.

*Mia wants to see you. Please call when you get this.*

'Wow,' Cristy murmured, showing the text to the others. 'Can't say I saw that coming,' and she quickly connected to Sadie's number. Finding herself pushed to voicemail, she said, 'Hey, it's me, Cristy, calling back. What's happening over there? Are you OK? Tell Mia we're happy to see her whenever suits.'

'At least you'll find out if she's been injured,' Cynthia observed, tapping Laurent's fingers away from the butter.

'I don't know where my knife is,' he complained.

Handing him one, David said, 'Where's Rosie?'

'Putting her make-up on,' Anna replied. 'She's got a new boyfriend, apparently, and he's going to be at rehearsals today.'

'What's happened to change Mia's mind about seeing us?' Connor said to Cristy.

'Maybe the fact that we know either she or her sister committed a murder?' she suggested ironically.

'Sure, but why does she want to talk when she obviously knows her lawyers are shutting us down?'

Cristy shrugged as Laurent said, 'Who's been murdered?'

'No one you know,' David told him, 'and it was a long time ago. Now, you need to go and clean your teeth . . . Are you taking him to sailing club?' he asked his mother, 'or am I?'

'I will,' Cynthia replied. 'I have errands to run in town and I can drop Rosie off at the rehearsal rooms on my way through.' To Cristy and Connor, she said, 'Will you be staying over the weekend? You're very welcome, of course, I just need to know how many to shop for.'

'We're both booked onto a flight later today,' Connor replied, 'but now this has come up . . .' He stopped as Cristy's phone rang, waiting to see if it was Sadie.

'Matthew, I'll have to call you back,' Cristy told her ex as soon as she answered the phone, gesturing helplessly at the others.

'OK,' Matthew replied, 'but make sure you do. I have some important news you'll want to hear.'

'I spoke to the children first thing,' she said. 'Tell me nothing's happened since.'

'Nothing's happened since,' he echoed obediently, and satisfied with that she rang off as Sadie's call came in.

'Hi, Cristy. Sorry, I was in the shower.'

'Do you know why Mia's suddenly willing to see us?' Cristy asked.

'She says she wants to tell you her side of the story.'

Cristy's eyes widened as she looked at Connor. 'Will her lawyers be there?' she asked, sensing something off about this, but there again, wasn't everything off where Mia was concerned?

'She didn't mention them,' Sadie replied.

'Do you know if she's listened to the latest podcast yet? The one that dropped last night featuring the interview with Lukas . . .'

'Oh yes, she has, and she says you're using actors to tell the story you want to hear, rather than bothering to find out the truth.' Then after a pause, 'They're not actors, are they?'

'No, of course not,' Cristy assured her. 'You can't really believe we'd do that to you. In fact your father and uncle are in London ready to fly here the minute you give the word. It'll mean the world to them if you do.'

Stifling a sob, Sadie said, 'I want to see them, I really do.'

'So shall I tell them to get on a plane?'

'Yes, no. I don't know. They can't come here, it's crazyville . . . Maybe I should go to them? I'm just not sure about leaving Mia.'

'Have you actually seen her since you read her the journals?'

'I went down there earlier, but she wouldn't let me in. She shouted at me from behind the door, calling me treacherous, spiteful, a liar, a viper in her nest . . . So I think we can safely say that she's still mad at me for forcing her to listen to them.'

Looking at the others, Cristy said, 'Are you going to tell us now what all the noise was about at the end of the recording?'

Sadie's voice was wretched as she said, 'It's hard to explain. Something just came over me . . . Well, you'll see for yourself when you get there.'

Cristy looked at David as he said, 'I can have your father and uncle picked up at the airport and brought here, to *Papillon*, if you like . . .'

'I'll come and get you,' Anna offered. 'And then I can wait with you.'

Sobbing, Sadie said, 'OK, if you don't mind. Oh my God, I can't believe I'm going to see them, that they really exist, that we share actual genes and DNA and blood and everything else. They're my family, Anna. I mean, my *real* family. I just . . . Oh God, I can't describe how it feels . . .'

Glad to have the DNA results announced like this – presuming Connor's attempt to record the call on his phone was working – Cristy said, 'Before Anna comes will you ask Mia what time she'd like us to be there? Or would you prefer me to call her myself?'

'It's OK, I'll do it and text you the time. Actually, Jasper's saying he'll drive me over to *Papillon*, Anna, so you don't need to come.' There was a pause before she said, 'Cristy, will you tell my dad that I've listened to the interview and I . . . I'm really looking forward to meeting him. And my uncle. Is Evie with them?'

'Yes, she is,' Cristy replied gently. 'This is going to be a very special day for them, but most of all for you, so if you decide you'd rather see them privately, without us there . . .'

'No, I want you to be there,' Sadie told her. 'I think it matters that you are, and then we'll always have a record of just how special it was to see one another for the first time since I was two years old.'

CRISTY: 'Connor and I have just arrived at the Villa des Roches. Sadie sent us a code for the gates, so we're already through and winding down the hillside towards the main house. The sun is glorious, splashing all over the immaculate gardens, and the views out to sea are spectacular. It's all so tranquil and perfect, it's hard to imagine that some very dramatic scenes have recently played out at the heart of it all.'

CONNOR: 'I guess we're about to find out if another is waiting for us when we get to the villa. Apparently Mia's lawyers know she's meeting with us – we're not sure if they'll be there – but we keep asking ourselves, how is she going to convince us that it was Lottie who organized Janina's death and the journals are all a lie? Presuming that's what this is going to be about.'

To Cristy he said, 'I hope we'll be able to use that at some point.'

'As do I,' she replied, 'and it's good we have it in case something does shift to clear the way.'

CRISTY: 'We're here now, just pulling up outside the villa . . . No sign of any other vehicles . . .'

CONNOR: 'God, this is a stunning place. I know Cristy's already described it in an earlier episode, and there are photos on the website, but seeing it for real . . . It's kind of blowing my mind.'

Ending the recording Cristy looked around the quiet courtyard with its sculpted bushes and neatly raked gravel, not sure what she was expecting to see, only knowing that a sense of unease was starting to come over her. 'Are you feeling as creeped out as I am, all of a sudden?' she quietly asked Connor.

He turned off the engine. 'Let's just say I'm not exactly inside my comfort zone,' he replied. 'Are we early or late?'

She checked the time. 'A couple of minutes late.' Neither of them moved, until she said suddenly, 'Come on, we can do this,' and pushing open the car door she stepped out into a swift, chill breeze.

'What if Mia's got a gun?' Connor murmured, coming to join her a few steps back from the arched front door.

Cristy frowned. 'You're asking me that now?'

'Thought it was better than when we're already facing it.'

'Why would she want to harm us?'

He scoffed incredulously. 'Maybe because we're planning to spill her crimes all over the airwaves and destroy her family?'

'But how would offing us help prevent that?'

'She's got to know she's beyond help so why would she care?'

Glancing at him, she said, 'Do you want to turn back?'

'No way. I'm just pointing a few things out. So, you go first.'

Unable not to laugh, she went to the door and as she knocked it creaked slightly open.

'Fuck,' Connor murmured.

Slanting him a look, Cristy pushed the door wider and stepped into the entrance hall. 'Hello!' she called out. 'It's Cristy and Connor!'

Nothing but the arrhythmic ticking of clocks.

She looked around taking in the paintings and pottery, exquisite formal furnishings, the original Arts-and-Crafts staircase and all the closed doors leading to other parts of the house. All that had changed since her last visit was the posting of a sign outside Lottie's rooms saying, Private, Keep Out.

'Hello! Mia?' Cristy shouted. 'We're here.'

Still nothing.

Starting to fear what they were about to walk into, she led the way through to the kitchen, all the time praying that her suspicions were wrong. Please don't let Mia have called them here to find her dead body. Was that her plan, to spare Sadie the horror of it? Would there be a note, blaming them for shattering her world, for trashing her and her sister's reputations, for the corruption of her niece, for the relentless persecution of lies, all lies, all in the name of entertainment?

'Mia?' she called, gingerly opening the kitchen door.

'Come in.'

The response was so unexpected that Cristy's heart leapt.

She entered the room and her eyes immediately rounded in horror. 'Jesus Christ,' she choked. It wasn't so much the chaos of upturned furniture and smashed everything, or even the bizarre sight of Mia herself – all pasty-faced and wild hair. It was the noose dangling from a beam right above her head.

'What the fuck?' Connor muttered under his breath.

'Come in,' Mia said again, and she gestured for them to sit down even though there was nowhere, unless they righted some chairs.

Trying to keep her eyes from the rope, Cristy said, 'You don't look well, Mia. Can we call someone?'

Mia stared at her unblinkingly, her eyes burning like two small fires inside her chalky mask. 'This won't take long,' she said, 'but I'd prefer you not to record, thank you. Your intrusion into my life and family has gone far enough. It's my intention now to bring it to an end.' She watched Connor as he stepped in closer to Cristy, presumably readying himself to stop Mia going for her.

Continuing, Mia said, 'I want you to know that if you make my sister's journals public I will hang myself and make sure the world is aware that my blood is all over your hands.'

Cristy stared at her in disbelief.

Beside her, Connor said, 'Don't you want to refute anything your sister said? This is your chance.'

Mia looked at him. 'What is the point?' she asked. 'Regardless of what I say, everyone will believe her. What reason would she have to write such an account, they'd ask, if she didn't want to set the record straight? Tell me this,' she continued, sitting forward slightly, 'has it occurred to you that she didn't write it in 2005, that she might actually have written it much later than that, say in 2012, or 2018?'

Knowing from Sadie that the dates had been entered by hand, Cristy said, 'What we do know is that she stopped seeing Robert in 2005, after you threatened to tell him about Sadie and Janina.'

Mia drew back. 'Ah yes, you have me there,' she conceded and glanced away. 'So maybe she did write them at the time, but that still doesn't make them true. In fact, just so you know, the real truth is that I had no idea Sadie's mother had ever made contact until two days ago. Everything in those journals is a lie . . .' She broke off suddenly and, apparently reassessing, said, 'I suppose the part about forcing the car off the road is true, there certainly was one at the bottom of the cliff around that time, and yes, the police did come to find out if we knew who it might belong to. I think Lottie might even have involved herself in the search for a body, but at no point did I even suspect it might have been Sadie's mother. And I certainly didn't know that the man who came to speak to her was Sadie's father.'

Although she sounded convincing, Cristy knew it couldn't be the truth. Mia had to have known at some stage that Janina had been in touch, why else would she have threatened to expose Lottie to Robert?

'What would you have done if you had known Sadie's mother was trying to see her daughter?' Connor asked.

Mia glanced down at her clutched hands and allowed a few moments to pass. 'I'm not sure. I was never asked, and now it doesn't really matter anyway, does it?'

Thinking that it did, that in fact it could go a long way towards telling them what sort of person she was, or had been then, Cristy said, 'I'm intrigued to know why you think your sister would twist things around to make you the guilty party?'

Mia's answering laugh was bitter. 'Because that's the sort of person she was. She hated me, despised me for being a burden she only ever wanted to shed.'

'So why didn't she? Shed you?'

'You'd have to ask her that.'

'You know we can't, so why don't you tell us?'

With a sigh, Mia said, 'Lottie wasn't satisfied with being our parents' favourite, or with being the beautiful one, or the most popular in any room, she wanted to be the *only* one. I stood in the way of that, I was always there, the other Winters sister, as if I was diluting her dazzling existence. She especially detested me when it came time to inherit our parents' fortune. She wanted it all – of course she did. Not that she ever said that, but I knew. She deeply resented the fact that she had to share everything with me, whereas I was always happy to share with her.'

'And yet,' Connor said, 'when she died she left everything to you and cut Sadie out of her will. Why would she have done that?'

Mia's eyes darkened and Cristy could see that the question had rattled her. 'How would you know that?' she asked. 'Did Sadie tell you?'

'Yes, she did,' Cristy replied.

'Was she upset about it?'

'I think she was hurt.'

Mia nodded as though understanding that.

'So why did Lottie name you as her sole beneficiary?' Connor prompted.

Mia's head poked forward again as she said, 'And why do you think it's any of your business?'

Sensing they weren't going to get any further with that, at least for now, Cristy said, 'Do you realize that Sadie's father will be able to tell us whether or not he met you back in 2005?'

'He's not her father,' Mia spat angrily. 'You're tricking Sadie into believing things that simply aren't true. Her father died when she was a baby, and you should be ashamed of yourselves for bringing these *imposters* into her life the way you have.'

Quietly, Cristy said, 'We know that he is her father.'

Mia twitched and huffed and started to scratch her arms. 'They're not real,' she blurted, 'they can't be. None of it is. You're in cahoots with Lottie, aren't you? I know she's not dead. I've always known. I'm the one who died and she's taken over my body. That's what she does . . . She takes you over and uses you like a puppet. She makes you think and say things that she wants to be true even when they're lies. I keep trying to fight her, but she's here, inside me, and she won't let me go.'

Having no idea how much she believed of what she was saying,

Cristy said, 'We want to help you, Mia, we really do, but you have to realize that what you're telling us . . . None of it makes any sense . . .'

'And Lottie's story does?' she cried angrily. 'Except she didn't write it, *I did*. She found my journals and changed around the names to make it look as though I am the devil incarnate and she was just an innocent bystander in it all.'

'Except she didn't paint herself that way,' Connor pointed out. 'She's also blaming herself – for the abduction, the lies, the deception . . .'

'But she doesn't blame herself for what happened to Sadie's mother, does she? Oh no, she's laid that monstrous act at my door, but the way *I* wrote it proves that it was all her.'

'How does it prove that?' Cristy asked carefully.

Mia swallowed and let her eyes hunt around the room. 'It's not possible to *prove* it,' she finally admitted, 'but it's what happened.'

'Do you have your journals from that time?' Connor asked.

'No, of course not,' she snapped. 'Lottie burned them. She used them first then made a bonfire out of them. She used to do that with my things, it's why I had to lock her up, to keep her from destroying what was mine. She did the same to Sadie when she was growing up . . .' She began jabbing a finger towards them. 'And here's something else you've never considered,' she spat, as if addressing imbeciles. 'It's been staring you in the face all along, me too, but I saw it because I *see*.' She poked hard at the skin beside her right eye. 'I *seeeee* – and you, *you*, only know what suits you, what's the easiest to know, and to hell with the truth because it doesn't have a place in your rotten, interfering, made-up world.'

Having no idea what she was talking about, Cristy was about to ask when Mia rasped, 'Sadie wrote those journals. That's what I see. She's tricked you all along, led you by the nose to do her bidding, feeding you bits of a story that weaves and dodges around the truth, picking it up like stitches and casting it off again. She's painted herself as the victim of two wicked women who killed her mother so they could keep her like a prisoner, and all we ever did was love her.'

Stunned by the depths of Mia's craziness, by how desperate

she was to cling to invisible lifelines that were only drawing her further into her own fraught delusions, Cristy said, 'You told us just now that Lottie killed Janina and *you* wrote the journals.'

'That's what Sadie wants you to think, that *I* ran that car off the road, that *I* deprived her of her mother, but I'm telling you it was Lottie. It was my sister who wanted *me* to keep Sadie so she could be free to go off with *that man*. She thought to make me the guardian of the child *she* had taken from the beach, who *she* had falsified passports and birth certificates for, who *she* lied to all her life and who *she* had no idea would kill her in the end.'

Cristy blinked, as her head spun. What the hell was she saying now?

'It was Sadie who changed the pills in Lottie's bottles,' Mia ran on savagely. 'Who replaced them with placebos, sweets, and tiny white mints. It was the medication that kept Lottie alive, that allowed her to live the best life she could without *him*, until one day, out of the blue, Sadie challenged her over her parentage. She wanted to know the truth, but Lottie wouldn't tell her. Sadie wouldn't let it go, so Lottie said if she didn't shut up she'd change her will and Sadie would get nothing for being such an ungrateful little bitch. The next thing we knew Lottie was dead on the tennis court and before anyone could check the bottles they'd been refilled with the real medication.'

'Why on earth would Sadie want to do that to her aunt?' Cristy asked.

Mia gave a nasty laugh. 'I've just told you. Lottie threatened to cut her off, so Sadie made sure she couldn't. Except it took longer than she expected and in the end she got *nothing*.'

'While you,' Connor said quietly, 'got everything.'

Mia smiled. 'Of course. I told Lottie, I said, "Sadie's grown now, so if you still want to leave us and be sure I never tell what happened to Sadie's mother, you will make me your sole beneficiary." So that's what she did. She made everything over to me in the event of her death and so when Sadie began putting her plan into motion she was already too late.'

All too aware of the inconsistencies and conflicting claims, Cristy said, 'How do you know that Sadie did it?'

Mia's face twitched as she took her time to reply. 'I saw her,' she said in the end. 'I watched her doing it . . . Emptying the bottles into small packages she'd already labelled, then filling them again with the concoction she'd put together.'

'If you knew it was happening,' Connor said, 'why didn't you stop her?'

Mia seemed puzzled by the question. 'Why should I?' she asked. 'I had no reason to interfere.'

'Meaning you wanted your sister dead?' Cristy stated carefully.

Agitated, Mia said, 'You're putting words in my mouth. I didn't say that.'

Cristy shook her head. 'I can't think of why else you wouldn't stop her,' she said.

Mia blinked and tilted her head. 'Stop who?' she demanded. 'What are you talking about? I don't know why you're here. I want you to leave now. Go! *Go!*'

Realizing that no matter how long they stayed they were unlikely to get any closer to a believable, never mind provable truth – and even if they could there was still the injunction – Cristy said, 'Before we leave will you let us take that down?' She gestured to the noose.

Mia looked up, as if she'd forgotten it was there. 'No!' she snapped. 'It stays right where it is until I'm certain you will not publicize those journals.'

'Your lawyers are making sure of it,' Cristy reminded her.

Mia regarded her blankly, as if she had no idea what she was talking about.

'You instructed your lawyers,' Cristy said carefully, wondering now if she had. But she must have, the injunction had been issued by the court right here in Guernsey.

'Yes! I did,' Mia cried. 'And I'm going to call them right now to tell them you're harassing me.'

Cristy looked at Connor. Short of getting into a physical tussle with her over the rope there was no more they could do, so it was time to go. At the door she turned back to find Mia staring absently into the heart of the chaos around her, clearly so deep in thought that she no longer seemed to know they were still there. What was she seeing, Cristy wondered, what kind of madness was tearing through her now?

'Tell me,' she said gently, 'was it you who forced Janina's car off the road?'

Mia's eyes narrowed as she glared back at her. 'I guess you'll never know the answer to that,' she said tightly, and turned sharply away to stare out of the window.

*

'Jesus holy Christ, what the fuck?' Connor muttered, as they drove away from the villa.

'You keep saying that,' Cristy told him.

He glanced over at her. 'She is completely batshit,' he stated.

'But still clever enough to know that we don't have a definitive answer to anything,' she said. 'So I guess it's down to the lawyers whether or not we get to use anything from the journals in the final podcast now they're under injunction.'

Connor grimaced. 'Are we going to tell Sadie what her aunt just accused her of?' he asked, accelerating out of the gates.

'I don't see how we can avoid it.' She turned to him. 'How much of it did you believe?'

His breath expelled in a humourless laugh. 'I don't even know where to start with that,' he confessed. 'Sadie writing the journals? Sadie offing her aunt?' He shook his head incredulously. 'What are you thinking?'

Cristy gazed out at the passing landscape, wondering if they were anywhere near the spot where Janina had lost her life. 'I'll admit she's got me as confused as she no doubt intended,' she replied, 'which has to make her one of the most deviously manipulative, not to mention cunning and calculating individuals we've ever encountered.' The ghastly image of the noose came back to her. 'Do you think she really would hang herself if we got clearance to use the journals?' she asked. 'Or was it just an act?'

'She'd never do it,' Sadie declared when they returned to *Papillon* and put the question to her. 'It's the kind of crazy thing she does to get her way. Suicide threats, locking people up, acting insane . . . It sounds like she got really extreme today . . . I'm sorry . . .'

'It's not your fault,' Anna jumped in. 'You can't be responsible for the way she is.'

Smiling her thanks, Sadie said to Cristy, 'Did she let you record anything?'

Cristy shook her head and decided they could go no further until Sadie knew what she'd been accused of. As the girl's mouth fell open and tears flooded her eyes, Anna went to put an arm around her.

'I'm sorry,' Sadie choked. 'I – I had no idea . . . Oh my God! I've shown you the journals, you have copies, so you can see it's not my writing. I can give you samples of Lottie's that match . . . But why would she try to make out I interfered with Lottie's medication? I'd *never* do anything like that. I *loved* Lottie. I love them both, but this . . . It's a form of coercion, isn't it? If we keep going she'll accuse me of a murder I didn't commit, of forging Lottie's journals . . . She'd never be able to prove it, because none of it's true . . . Oh my God, this is terrible. First she kills my mother, then her own sister . . .'

'So you believe in Lottie's journals?' Cristy said gently.

Sadie nodded. 'Yes, I do. I think everything happened the way Lottie wrote it, maybe until the car was forced off the road. And that, maybe that's something they did together?'

Cristy nodded, suspecting the same. Seeing the way Sadie was trying so hard not to show how broken and betrayed she felt inside, Cristy's heart went out to her.

'What I'm asking myself now,' Connor said, 'is why would Lottie write it all down?'

Sadie swallowed hard. 'It must have been in case it did all come out. If it did, then she'd have a version that she could claim had more credibility because it was written at the time.'

'But pushing all the blame onto her sister,' Cynthia said. 'What a terrible thing to do, if she was involved too.'

'I'm sure Mia would have done the same if she'd thought of it first,' Sadie responded bleakly. 'It's only now that I'm really seeing just how *toxic* their relationship was.'

Holding firmly to one of Sadie's hands, Jasper said, 'We're going to have some big decisions to make in the next few weeks, such as do we want to stay on at the lodge after all this?'

Sadie looked lost, haunted, as she rested her head against his and said, 'Before that we'll need to do what we can to get the injunction lifted on the journals. I can see,' she said to Cristy, 'that it would totally screw up your series if you can't use the most . . . damning parts, and after everything you've done, all the research and moral support . . .' She sighed despairingly. 'I don't want to do it to Mia,' she said, 'but at the same time we can't let her hold us to ransom like this. I mean, I don't think for one minute that she's serious about using that noose, or about trying to blame me for something she knows I didn't do . . . But once I leave, if she feels she doesn't have anything left to live for . . . Maybe she will do her worst.'

'We need to talk it through with the lawyers before we go any further,' Cristy said. 'We know we can't use Lottie's record of the crucial day as it stands, but maybe there are ways around it?'

Sadie looked confused.

'Sorry, thinking aloud,' Cristy told her. 'But whatever we do, we have to be certain it doesn't fast track us straight into court.'

'Definitely not where you want to end up,' David declared, glancing up from his phone. 'Right now though Sadie has other things to think about.' His eyes were on her and his voice softened as he said, 'They're just coming in through the gates.'

As colour rushed to Sadie's cheeks Cristy felt a wrenching of nerves in her own heart. It was hard to imagine how momentous this was for Sadie when she, Cristy, like everyone else in the room, had always known exactly where she was from, and who her family was. Today, the next few minutes, were probably going to change everything for Sadie in ways too big and too subtle even to guess at, and Cristy could only wish she wasn't feeling so uneasy about it. Why was she so tense, so worried that something would go wrong, that it would all blow up in their faces, when she had no logical reason to feel that way?

Picking up on Sadie's nerves again, she said, gently, 'Are you sure you don't want to do this alone?'

Sadie shook her head unsteadily. 'No, I want you to be there,' she insisted. 'I think it helps that you've already met them, and like I said, I'd really love to have a record of it.'

'In which case,' Connor said, 'shall I video it for you?'

Sadie broke into a smile. 'Yes, please, that would be lovely.' Then to Jasper, 'Oh my God, I can't believe this is happening.'

He took her in his arms as David said, 'OK, unless we want to bring them straight into the kitchen, you guys should probably start making your way to the drawing room.'

'Can I come?' Anna whispered to Sadie.

'Of course,' Sadie replied, squeezing her hand. 'You all should,' she told David and Cynthia. 'Let's give them the biggest and warmest welcome we can.'

*

The drawing room was large and grand, with high, corniced ceilings, capacious furniture and an entire wall of towering sash windows overlooking an early blossoming copse just beyond Cynthia's rose garden. As they entered Anna crossed to the ornate limestone fireplace and lit the touch paper beneath a stack of knotted twigs, while Sadie, mindful of her father's photophobia, went to close the shutters and turn on the lamps.

A moment later she was standing in the midst of them all, hands bunched to her face as she listened to the voices outside, David greeting the guests and bringing them through to where everyone was waiting. Cristy watched the girl closely, never more beautiful, nor vulnerable or hopeful. As their eyes met Cristy felt her tension fleetingly increase, before she relaxed and willed inner strength Sadie's way.

It was going to be all right, it really was.

David came through the door first and held it wide for Evie to follow, and as Lukas and Gabe came in after them Cristy heard Sadie's breath catch on a sob.

'Sasha?' Gabe said, removing his dark glasses. 'Sasha, my girl?'

'Hello, Dad,' Sadie whispered, her mouth trembling on the words. 'Thanks – thanks for coming all this way.'

He broke into a smile and Cristy realized this was the first time she'd seen him look happy.

'I'm glad we did,' he said. 'I was very keen to see you,' and as tears dropped onto his cheeks Sadie ran to him, crying too.

'It's all right,' she soothed, holding him tight. 'Everything's going to be all right.'

He nodded, and his voice was muffled as he said, 'I missed you so much. I was always thinking of you . . .'

'Sssh,' she whispered brokenly, 'we've found one another now and that's what matters.'

Cristy glanced at Connor as he captured the moments with his phone.

Lukas came forward and cupped Sadie's face in his hands. 'I'm Lukas,' he told her, 'your uncle. I know you probably don't remember me . . .'

'I remember your hat,' she told him. 'You used to wear a hat.'

Laughing in surprise he said, 'I did. You're right. I can't believe . . . Imagine you remembering that when you were so small . . .' His voice faltered, but he pushed on, his accent a little more pronounced as he said, 'I can't tell you how happy we are to see you. We always hoped you'd come to find us one day . . .'

'I wish you'd come for me,' she said. 'If you knew where I was . . .'

'We thought you were safe, that you were getting everything you needed, but we wrote, many times . . . It seems clear now that our letters were intercepted. Oh, what mistakes we made . . . Can we ever forgive ourselves?'

'No, please don't say that. You're here now and we have so much to catch up on.' Sadie turned back to her father and Cristy suspected that only Janina had ever looked at him with so much tenderness.

'We have many stories to share with you,' Gabe said shakily, 'memories of when you were born and how precious you were . . .'

'I want to hear them all,' she said, gazing up into his eyes, 'but we should at least let you sit down first.'

He smiled again and let her lead him to a sofa where she sat between him and Lukas holding their hands. 'To think,' she said to Anna, 'I've only ever had women in my life, and now I only have men.'

'Hey, just a minute,' Evie cried, from where she'd been left at the door, 'you have me too and last time I looked . . .'

Sadie leapt up to embrace her. 'I'm sorry,' she gushed, 'so

stupid of me. You're Evie, obviously, and I couldn't be happier to meet you.'

'The feeling's mutual,' Evie assured her, patting her back. 'I've heard so much about you over the years, and now here you are, as beautiful as a summer's day and exactly as I always pictured your mother to be.'

'She is,' Gabe assured her. 'You're just like her, Sasha,' and as more tears pooled in his eyes Sadie went back to his side and wept with him.

# CHAPTER TWENTY-NINE

After an afternoon spent sharing memories of the small girl who'd once ruled Gabe and Lukas's world, David and Jasper brought in cocktails and Cynthia insisted everyone must stay for dinner. It turned into a lively affair with Gabe seeming as bemused as he did joyful, while everyone else indulged in a little too much wine and Sadie kept breaking into tears of relief and laughter.

The next morning, Cristy couldn't recall whose idea it had been to visit the place where Janina's car had left the road, only that it was David who'd contacted the police to find out the exact spot. When he'd received a call back the decision was made. It would happen this morning and act as a final farewell to Janina, someone had said, a memorial of sorts. Though the sentiment behind it was touching, by the time Cristy and David got up she wasn't feeling quite so sure about it. However, she didn't want to be the one to cast a shadow over the occasion by voicing doubts that she couldn't explain anyway, so she pushed past them and texted a yes to Connor when he messaged to ask if he should book their flights back to Bristol later that day.

Without actually meaning to she checked to see if there were any more anonymous texts, and thank God, there weren't. The latest had arrived last night and she'd already moved it to the folder. *He'll promise you the earth and end up letting you down. I will never do that.* She wondered if these missives were more responsible for unsettling her than what was happening here, then pushed them out of her mind too.

'So you're going home later?' David said, as he came into the bedroom to find her packing.

As she looked at him, standing in the misty rays of sunlight streaming through the windows, her heart swelled with feeling. 'I have to,' she smiled, 'but I'm not looking forward to leaving you.'

Taking her hand he pulled her to him and gazed searchingly into her eyes. 'Will you come back?' he asked, almost as if seeming to doubt it.

'Of course,' she whispered.

'When?'

She laughed and murmured softly as he kissed her.

'Maybe we should go away somewhere, just the two of us,' he suggested. 'I mean, when the series is finished.'

'I'd love that. Where are you thinking?'

'Somewhere warm and exotic, exclusive and . . . How about one of the Aman resorts?'

Her eyes widened in surprise. Though she'd never visited one she knew very well how luxurious and insanely expensive they were.

'Give it some thought,' he said, 'and let me know when you're ready for me to book. Or we can go somewhere else. Whatever works for you.'

*He'll promise you the earth and end up letting you down. I will never do that.*

'What?' he said, frowning.

Cristy shook her head, annoyed that the text had managed to push into her thoughts now. 'I hear the one in Morocco is exceptional,' she said.

'Amanjena,' he murmured. 'Have you been there?'

'I haven't.'

'Me neither. So maybe that's where we'll go.' His eyes rose to his hand as he ran it over her hair, and lowered back to hers as he said, 'I've loved spending the last week with you. I admit, when I flew over last Saturday I hadn't realized it would be quite so . . . hectic, or that we'd end up in Florida for forty-eight hours, but I've enjoyed the madness of it, and the experience of watching you work. I even got a kick out of being a small part of it.'

'Not so small,' she corrected. 'I might even say we couldn't have done it without you.'

He laughed. 'I'll take that, even though it's not true.'

'*Dad!*'

He groaned. 'Yes, we definitely need some time for us,' he said, and after kissing her again he picked up her bag to carry it down to the car.

'Have you heard from Sadie this morning?' Cristy asked, as Anna caught up with them on the stairs.

'Yes. She's already at the hotel with Gabe and the others. Apparently she went to see Mia first thing.'

Surprised and concerned, Cristy said, 'What happened?'

'Mia wouldn't let her in again, although she told her, through the door, that if she wants to be an "ungrateful bitch" – her words – and go off with strangers it's her choice, she won't stop her. But if she does she'll be out of the will.'

'Is she actually in it?' David asked wryly.

Anna shrugged. 'I think she's supposed to inherit everything when Mia goes, but as we know, nothing Mia says is to be trusted, and she's used her will for years to control everyone around her. Anyway, I don't think Sadie cares. It's not about money for her.'

'What was she hoping to gain from going down there?' Connor asked, coming out of the kitchen with a coffee and his holdall. 'After what she was accused of yesterday, why would she want any more to do with her aunt?'

Following Connor into the hall, David's mother said, 'Whatever we might think of that, Mia's clearly in the throes of some sort of breakdown, and Sadie will know that better than anyone. I grant you, finding out her aunts were involved in what happened to her mother will have changed things considerably for her, and will continue to as the reality of it sinks in further. Nevertheless, the Sadie I know isn't capable of simply turning her back on her aunt, especially when she's found so much happiness for herself.'

'You surely don't think she'll stay with Mia?' Connor said doubtfully.

Cynthia shook her head. 'I don't see how she can now, but she'll know already that if she decides to join her father in the States, it'll be really hard for Mia to cope with losing her.'

Dismally, Anna said, 'I want everything to work out for Sades, obvs, but I'll really miss her if she leaves. Trouble is, this island doesn't hold so many good memories for her now, and whatever you say, Granny, I can't see her ever being able to actually forgive what Lottie and Mia did to her mother.'

Knowing she wouldn't be able to if it were her, Cristy said, 'There's also Jasper. Would she leave him?'

Anna considered it. 'I reckon he'd go with her to the States. He doesn't always show it, but he's as besotted with her as Dad is with you.'

Startled into laughter, Cristy turned to David as he said, drolly, 'They're pretty serious then.'

'Is the right answer,' Anna told him, with a playful nudge. 'Now, come on, or we're going to be late and I don't want to miss this.'

'What about your mother?' Cristy asked David, as they started out to the cars.

'She's going to stay here with Rosie and Laurent,' he replied, dropping her bag into the boot of Connor's rented Captur. 'I'll take Anna in the Smart.'

'Give me a minute,' Cristy said, and running back inside she found Cynthia in the kitchen with Rosie, no sign of Laurent. 'I've come to say goodbye,' she said, hugging Cynthia first, then Rosie. 'Thanks for taking such great care of us – me and Connor. Any more of it and we'll be moving in.'

Laughing, Cynthia said, 'You're always welcome, you know that, and I'm glad you and David have sorted things out.'

'Me too,' Rosie told her, holding onto the dog. 'Dad was really grumpy when he thought you wouldn't be coming back. Now he's all smiley and happy like he's got sweets in his pockets and wind in his sails.'

Adoring her, Cristy pulled her in for another hug, saying, 'Good luck with the new boyfriend, and the new play, and don't forget to stay in touch. I love getting your emails.'

Beaming, Rosie watched her go while Cynthia said quietly, 'Something's not sitting right with her, I can feel it.'

'What did you say, Granny?' Rosie asked.

Cynthia smiled, 'Nothing for you to worry about, my angel, now, let's get you ready for rehearsals.'

*

CRISTY: 'We've just left the Fermain Valley Hotel where Sadie's father and uncle are staying, Evie too of course, and we're heading for the south east coast. There are three cars in our small convoy, with no one going very fast, staying within the island's speed limit of thirty-five miles an hour. The sun was shining gloriously earlier, making it the perfect sort of day for Sadie's farewell to her mother – if such a day can be perfect, and of course it can't. Clouds came rolling in about fifteen minutes ago though, and the wind is starting to pick up, let's just hope it doesn't rain.

'I can't help wondering how Sadie's feeling right now . . .'

To Connor Cristy said, 'We should have put a mic on her and tried to talk to her on the way.'

'It wouldn't have worked,' he told her. 'Too many trees to break the signal and look at the size of those boulders.'

Accepting that some were indeed almost mountainous, she continued.

CRISTY: 'This is a journey Sadie might well have done countless times over the years, but it must be feeling very different today, knowing where she's going and why. It won't be easy for her father either, or her uncle, but hopefully all three of them will be able to take comfort from the fact that they're together for this last goodbye.'

CONNOR: 'We're starting to catch our first glimpses of the sea through a heavily wooded hillside, sparkling and grey-blue, with the island of Sark on a close horizon . . .'

He broke off suddenly, narrowly missing a protruding rock as they rounded a bend.

CONNOR: 'The going is a bit hairy in places, definitely not for the faint-hearted, but thankfully there's not much traffic around so we're not having to stop to let someone pass. Let's hope it stays that way. Being a Sunday there's a chance it will, but I've got to tell you, it's starting to feel as though we're heading into some sort of nether world . . . If I could explain what I mean by that I would. How about you, Cristy, how's this working out for you?'

CRISTY: 'I agree there's an odd sort of feel to this road . . . Maybe because we know what happened towards the end of it . . .'

CONNOR: 'How far do you reckon we are from the villa?'

CRISTY: 'As the crow flies probably three or four miles.'

'I think I need to remind everyone that Janina was headed for Sark View House that day, a) to avoid confusion and b) to reemphasize the fact that she was directed to a place no one seems to have heard of before – or since.'

'Go for it.'

Once done, Cristy continued.

CRISTY: 'We'll hopefully see when we get there why that particular location was chosen, but I think we can assume it's going to be precipitous and remote.'

CONNOR: 'So what do you reckon Mia might be doing right now? Does she know what Sadie's doing this morning?'

CRISTY: 'I've no idea if Sadie told her, we can ask when we stop. As for what Mia's doing . . . The woman is such an enigma, and not entirely sane. (We'll never get away with that, but hey, what else am I supposed to say?) I wonder why she wouldn't let Sadie into the villa this morning?'

CONNOR: 'Maybe because she smashed the place up the last time she was there?'

CRISTY: 'Point taken. I wonder if Mia realizes that she could be facing a full-on police investigation into what happened to Janina? If it happens, and I can't see how it can be avoided if we can get the injunction lifted, the scandal, the loss of her reputation and even her freedom . . . Unless Sadie and Gabe decide they don't want revenge and keep the injunction in place. Making Mia pay won't bring Janina back, will it? And it'll probably only prolong the trauma of it all for Sadie.'

CONNOR: 'So you think Mia and Lottie should be allowed to get away with it?'

CRISTY: 'Not that they *should*, but I think there's a good chance they will.'

CONNOR: 'If that happens we're screwed for a proper end to the series. How the fuck have we managed to walk into that?'

CRISTY: 'Hang on, they're pulling over . . . Are we still recording?'

CONNOR: 'We are.'

CRISTY: 'We're coming to a stop on a scrubby patch of land – I'm guessing the road must have been rerouted sometime in the last twenty years. It runs along the back of this lookout area now, a good fifty metres from the cliff edge. There are picnic benches here, and public loos . . . Safety barriers and danger warnings all over the place, and the view of the other islands . . . Jersey in the distance, Herm and Sark nearby, would be spectacular, I'm sure, on a less grey day.'

As Cristy stepped out of the car she quickly grabbed the door as a sharp gust unsteadied her. She trapped her hair under a hat as she looked around, feeling the vulnerability of their smallness in the massive might of the landscape. She saw David and Anna battling the wind to get to where Sadie and Gabe were already standing as close to the cliff edge as the barriers would allow. Lukas and Evie joined them, huddled into their coats, and moments later Cristy and Connor were there too.

'Hell, I had no idea it was going to be so high, or so bleak up here,' Cristy murmured to Connor, feeling the terrifying thrill of it going up and down her spine. She was recalling what Lottie had written in her journal, that it simply wasn't possible for someone to survive such a fall, and she could only concur. It really wasn't. There was nothing to break the plunge, no way of avoiding the deadly rocks at the bottom or the gushing tide. She turned to look along the rugged coastline, searching for a spot where Mia, or maybe Lottie, possibly both, might have lain in wait, but none was evident. Too much would have changed since. Nevertheless, she could almost feel the horror of that morning when Janina came into view . . . She must have seen a car heading straight at her, would have braked with all her might, desperate to steer away from the cliff edge. She'd have known she couldn't make it, would probably have screamed, or prayed, or maybe covered her face as the car flew into the air, and dropped more than a hundred feet onto the rocks below.

It was sickening, heartrending, even now.

She turned back and saw that Evie was holding Sadie in a comforting embrace, while next to them Gabe and Lukas were staring down at the churning, angry waves, the brutal shoreline that had smashed Janina's car apart before the tide had carried her body away.

Aware of Connor unpacking his holdall, Cristy pointed towards a sprawling bungalow set back in the trees. 'I wonder if that's Sark View House,' she shouted over the wind. 'Do we need to find out if the sisters ever did own it?'

Apparently not hearing, Connor said, 'I've got the mics ready, but God knows how much we'll be able to pick up in this gale.'

Feeling David's arm going around her Cristy watched Connor fix lapel mics to Sadie, Gabe and Lukas, and wondered again if they should really be recording such an intensely private moment.

'It's what they all want,' Anna reminded her when she voiced her concern. The wind had miraculously dropped, at least for now, allowing them to communicate without having to shout. 'It's honouring Janina,' Anna continued, 'letting everyone know that she was loved and is still missed.' She looked at her friend and added, 'Janina mattered, even if the world carried on as though she didn't. This is Sadie's way of making amends for that, and you're helping her to do it.'

Admiring Anna's loyalty and support, Cristy turned to David and smiled into his eyes. She couldn't be sure where her feelings of apprehension were coming from, only that they were back, as though her instincts were trying to warn her of something – and then, mercifully, they were gone again.

Connor came to give her an earpiece and, as he clamped a headset over his own ears, Evie walked over to join them. This simple farewell was all about Sadie, Gabe and Lukas, the only ones who'd actually known Janina, and loved her still.

Cristy watched their silhouettes in a sudden blaze of sunlight that broke through the clouds, Sadie between her father and uncle, their arms around her and hands on one another's shoulders. Sadie started to speak, Cristy could hear in her earpiece and knew it was a prayer, but the connection kept dropping.

'. . . God bless . . . be with us . . . love you . . .'

Gabe said, '. . . I tried to find you, my darling . . . I never . . . up hope . . . Sasha and me, we found one another . . .'

Lukas said, '. . . love and take care of her . . .'

Sadie said, '*Ilsekis ramybeje, mamyte.*' Cristy knew this meant *Rest quietly, Mummy*, because Lukas had already told her.

'Do you feel she's here?' Sadie asked. 'I think . . . watching us?' Her head tilted back and as she gazed up at the turbulent sky Cristy heard her say, '. . . beautiful scent. Can you smell it? What is it?'

Gabe and Lukas shook their heads, but as the wind picked up again, Cristy caught the gentle fragrance as it passed by like a ribbon on the breeze, there and then gone. Peonies, but sweeter and more pungent. The scent of a mother, that could maybe only be recognized by a daughter.

*

Much later in the day, following a lunch at the hotel where they'd toasted Janina and the future for those who loved her, Cristy and Connor were at the airport waiting to board their flight.

'Are you OK?' he asked, bringing her a coffee. 'You've seemed . . . kind of edgy these past couple of days. Don't worry, I'm sure no one else noticed . . . Everything fine with David?'

She smiled and took the mug. 'Everything's great there,' she assured him. 'I just keep getting this . . . *feeling*, like a dread . . .? Is that the word I'm looking for?' She shook her head exasperatedly. 'I don't know what it is and it's not helped by the fact that some bloody stalker keeps sending me messages.'

Connor shot her a look.

'OK, nothing new there,' she said, 'we get them all the time, but these are . . . Actually, they're creeping me out a bit.'

'Can I see them?'

Opening up the folder she'd moved them to, she was about to hand her phone over when it rang. Seeing it was Matthew a pang of guilt hit her as she realized she'd forgotten to call him back. 'Hi,' she said, 'I'm sorry—'

'Have you seen it?' he snapped.

'Seen what?'

'The email I forwarded yesterday morning. Jesus Christ, Cristy, what's wrong with you? I told you I needed to speak to you, but apparently we all stop existing when you're with him . . .'

'I've been busy, working,' she interrupted.

'Where are you now?'

'At the airport on my way back.'

'Good. Read the email and I'll see you when you get here.'

As soon as he rang off she called up her emails. Opening the one he'd forwarded she took it in quickly and felt her heart starting to freeze. 'No!' she muttered, trying not to panic. 'No! No! No!'

'What?' Connor demanded. 'What the f . . .?'

She passed him the phone, and watched his face slacken with shock as he read the few lines Matthew had sent.

'*Shit*,' he swore under his breath. 'Holy fuck!' His eyes went to Cristy's. 'Is this for real?'

'It must be, he wouldn't have sent it otherwise.' Taking the phone back she sent a quick return message telling Matthew she'd text as soon as she landed and that he should meet her at the flat. *And bring Aiden*, she added before pressing send. Dropping her head in her hands she tried to work out if this was what the strange prescience had been all about. Nothing to do with the stalker, or Sadie, or anything other than some sort of mother's intuition working away on its own agenda waiting to be recognized.

*

Three hours later, feeling as though she'd stepped through some sort of looking glass very darkly, Cristy stood in her kitchen with hands on her hips, eyes blazing, as she glared at Aiden.

'What the hell were you thinking?' she shouted. 'How did you . . .? Jesus Christ, I can't believe you'd be this fucking stupid.'

'Chill, Mum,' he urged, 'there's no need to swear, it's going to be OK!'

'How the hell is it going to be that?' she raged, almost wanting to hit him. How could he sit there looking so unfazed by the fact that his life was never going to be the same again? 'According to this message *you* are the father of the child this girl is carrying,' she cried furiously, having to spell it out to try to make herself believe it, as if she wanted to, when obviously she didn't.

'Yeah, but . . .'

'You're sixteen, Aiden. *Sixteen!* And who the hell is she, for God's sake?'

'Her name's Pearl . . .'

'Yes, I can see that at the end of the message, but why is *she* sending emails to your father telling him what's going on when you should have told us this yourself?'

'Well, I kind of guessed you'd go off on one, and there's this . . .'

'This what? Baby? Is that the word you're looking for?'

'It wasn't, but hey . . .' He glanced at his father who was listening quietly, seeming to have nothing to say.

'For God's sake,' Cristy shouted. 'What's the matter with you two? First you,' she shot at Matthew, 'and now you . . .'

'Hey, hey!' Matthew interrupted. 'For the record, I'm married and I was *not* under age when . . .'

'Is *she*?' Cristy raged at Aiden as a whole world of other horrors suddenly rose up from the chaos.

'Is she what?' he asked.

'Under age?'

He screwed up his nose as he thought. 'I think she was sixteen a couple of weeks ago, so technically not any more.'

'But she was when you . . . Oh for God's sake, I don't even know what to call it.'

'Shagged?' he offered helpfully.

Certain Matthew smirked, she rounded on him again. 'So

this is the kind of parent you are, allowing your son, who's only fifteen . . .'

'Sixteen now,' Aiden reminded her.

'But fifteen when the child was conceived, if this girl is six months along.'

'No, sixteen,' he insisted. 'It happened last August.'

Finding herself dumbfounded she turned back to Matthew. 'Have you been allowing him to sleep with girls in your house?' she demanded. 'Knowing you, you encouraged it . . .'

'Hang on, hang on,' Matthew objected. 'I'm every bit as furious with him as you are, so I'm not the one you should be attacking here.'

'He's your son . . .'

'And yours. Maybe they got it together here, in this flat?'

Cristy glared at Aiden. 'Did you?' she demanded, desperately shutting out the image of it.

He shrugged. 'Maybe, once or twice, but it was no big deal . . .'

'*No big deal?*' she echoed incredulously. How the hell was she supposed to get through to him, when nothing ever seemed to faze him, not even the fact he could be guilty of statutory rape, and facing at least eighteen years of child maintenance, not to mention a lifetime of fatherhood, when he wasn't even an adult yet? 'Did it not occur to you to use a condom?' she demanded. Talk about horses and stable doors!

He grimaced. 'I kind of thought I did . . .'

'How can you not *know*?' He was beyond belief.

'Well it happened a few times,' he said, 'and maybe for one of them I just kind of forgot, or ran out . . .'

Not sure if Matthew was laughing again, she turned her wrath back on him, still wanting to blame him in spite of knowing it wouldn't make a blind bit of difference to anything. 'Have you met this girl?' she demanded.

He held up his hands defensively. 'The first I heard of her was when I got the email,' he assured her. 'I rang you straight off and *you* . . .' He stopped as her eyes narrowed – if he tried to blame her . . . 'And now we are where we are,' he finished lamely.

Aiden was texting.

'Put that damned thing down,' Cristy snapped at him.

Letting it drop into his lap he regarded her innocently.

'So who is she?' she asked. 'Are you still seeing her?'

He shrugged. 'You already know her name's Pearl. She joined our year when we started sixth form, and yeah, I still see her around, at school, obvs, and hanging out here and there . . .'

'So she's not actually your girlfriend?' Was that better or worse? Cristy had no idea.

'We saw each other a few times, but it was never, like, *official*.'

'Well you obviously had sex with her, so what exactly does make it *official*?'

'It's just a decision you come to after a few dates, or maybe longer than that, and then you tell everyone else when you feel ready.'

Her eyes widened again. 'And does imminent fatherhood make you *feel ready*?' she asked scathingly.

Shrugging again, Aiden said, 'It's not an issue. We both agreed we didn't want it to be serious.'

'But now she's pregnant and apparently thinks it's serious enough to send an email to Dad . . . Did she tell you she was going to do that?'

'Never mentioned a word. I didn't even know myself – about the baby thing – until a couple of weeks ago . . .'

*The baby thing? What kind of son had she raised?* 'And you didn't mention it when you found out, because?'

'I guess, because I wasn't the only one she was getting it on with last August. There was Tim Watts and Dylan Fullbright . . .'

Seizing the lifeline, Cristy said, 'So there's a chance one of them could be the father?'

'Who knows? I haven't asked. Maybe there's not even really a baby. Girls make this stuff up all the time.'

'Well, this one has had a scan because she attached it to the email, so I think we can assume there is a child.' To Matthew she said, 'You need to talk to her parents.'

'Me?' he protested. 'How about *we* talk to her parents?'

'You better check first that she's told them,' Aiden advised. 'If they don't already know it'll be a helluva way to find out, you and Dad turning up on their doorstep all *reach for your guns* . . .'

Cristy almost laughed, out of hysteria more than humour.

'What matters here is that we establish whether or not the child's yours,' she declared, knowing she had to calm down, but seeming unable to. 'Is she the kind of person who'd say it was, even if she wasn't sure?'

'I don't really know her that well.'

She stared at him. This was turning into a farce and if Matthew laughed again she might just swing for him. 'Why aren't you taking this seriously?' she shouted at him. 'You surely can't think it's something we can just brush under the carpet and pretend isn't happening?'

'I am taking it seriously,' he insisted, 'but you're right, there are a few steps to go through before we start getting excited . . .'

'*Excited?*'

'Sorry, wrong choice of word. I should have said . . . something else. Anyway, I'm with you that we need to find out if Aiden's really the father. As that's going to involve a DNA test we need to make sure she's on board for it. If she isn't, well then she won't have any claim on him, will she?'

'Which doesn't exactly put him in the clear, and I for one want a definitive answer. So, this is what we're going to do . . . You, Aiden, will contact her tonight to ask for the test, and you, Matthew, will reply to her email telling her that's what we're doing. Unless, of course, she's ready to admit there is no baby and the scan is just something she downloaded for . . . I don't know, a bit of fun? Would she do that?' *Really grasping at straws now.*

Aiden regarded her thoughtfully. 'I guess, she might,' he said. 'I mean, I'm not saying she did, but . . .'

'Stop! Just stop,' Cristy cried, holding up a hand, and she turned to the fridge to snatch out a bottle of wine.

'I'll have one of those,' Matthew told her as she filled a glass. 'And you, Aiden . . .'

'Yeah, sure,' he said readily.

'I'm not offering you a drink,' Matthew said, 'I'm telling you to get going on the contact Mum's just suggested. With any luck, once this girl knows we're getting into the science, she'll come clean and admit it's some sort of prank.'

*Prank. Oh please God let it be that.*

As Aiden slouched off to his room, already texting someone,

Cristy took her glass to the sofa and slumped down wearily. She could hardly believe that this, and the farewell to Janina, were happening in the same day, but they were and as disorientating as it felt maybe it was also grounding in its way. She'd become far too caught up in Sadie's story, was perhaps too focused on David as well, when what she ought to have been doing was putting a lot more effort into making sure her son didn't go off the rails. He had so much potential for it that the only surprise was that something like this, or worse, hadn't happened before.

*Could it actually get any worse?*

Knowing it could, she took a gulp of her wine.

'Do you think he is the father?' she asked, as Matthew came to sit with her.

'If there really is a child, then apparently it's possible,' he replied, watching her move along the sofa to put more space between them. He moved too, closing the gap, and tapped his glass to hers. 'Grandparents,' he smiled, looking exactly like his son and sounding just as absurd. 'Never imagined that this soon.'

Going to sit on the other sofa, she said, 'Why am I the only one who's upset about this? I'd have thought you, of all people, would realize what a disaster it's going to be if he really is the father.'

'You mean because I've recently had a baby I didn't plan for?' he countered. 'A bit different in my case, but yeah, I guess you're right, it will be disastrous and expensive and consuming . . . It'll be a lot of things we can't even foresee right now, but at least he's not talking about getting married.'

*Was he for real? Had he* actually *just said that?* She eyed him carefully, and finally, as the penny slowly dropped, she realized why he wasn't anywhere near as worked up over this as she was and she almost wanted to weep.

'You're seeing this as a way of keeping us together, aren't you?' she challenged. 'You think, if there is a baby we'll both be responsible for it, because Aiden isn't capable, and we'll share custody visits and baby bathtime and nappy changes and he can meet Bear, his uncle who's practically the same age as him . . .'

'It might be a girl,' Matthew put in quickly. 'And I'm not sure Bear will be the uncle, will he?'

'I don't know, and I don't care. I just want this to stop, now, and you to accept that there is no going back for us.'

Looking crestfallen, he sipped his drink and turned to stare out at the garden.

She watched him, wondering what he was really thinking and trying not to care about how lost he suddenly seemed. In the end she broke the silence, just as he knew she would.

'What's happening with Marley?' she asked, hoping a slight change of subject might help calm things down a little. 'You mentioned at some point that you had plans to go over there.'

He nodded. 'I also invited you and David to come with me,' he reminded her. 'Generous of me, don't you think?'

Incredulous, she said, 'Why would you even want that?'

He shrugged. 'I guess being with you, even if he's there, is better than being without you.'

Not wanting even to try processing that, she closed her eyes and forced all the strange images it conjured out of her mind.

'She's going to Santa Fe,' he said after a while. 'Apparently she's been cast in a movie that's shooting there and she wants me to have Bear while she's away.'

Cristy's eyes narrowed as she saw where this might be going. 'How long's she planning to be gone?' she asked cautiously.

'A few months, I think.'

'So she wants you to bring him here?'

'I guess so. We haven't discussed it yet, but it can't happen any other way.'

Sounding snappier than she'd intended, she said, 'I thought she had a fantastic nanny.'

'She does, but it's not the same as a parent, she says, and she thinks it'll be a great opportunity for some bonding between Papa Bear and Boo Boo.'

Cristy stared at him, caught now on the names, and aware she shouldn't laugh, but it was already happening. *Papa and Boo Boo? Really?*

'It's OK, go right ahead,' he told her. 'We have to try to see the funny side of all this or we might just go mad.'

Knowing she would – go mad – if there was a chance of two babies to contend with in the not too distant future, a grandson and whatever Bear was to her . . . Actually he was nothing, no relation at all, so why was she even considering it? Probably because, knowing Matthew as she did, once the child was here at his home in England, he'd find a way to trap her into parenting with him whether she wanted to or not.

*God spare me*, she thought, taking another gulp of wine, but she was too tired now to argue any further, and was actually missing David too much to want to speak to anyone else. If only Matthew would go home and take Aiden with him.

David rang a few minutes later.

'I'm going to take this in the bedroom,' she told Matthew.

'Is it him?'

'Mind your own business, and if you want to be a really good dad you might go in there and try talking some sense into your son.'

'He's doing everything right, isn't he?'

'Only you would think that,' and leaving him to puzzle it out she swept off to the privacy of her room and lay down on the bed.

'Are you OK?' David asked when she answered. 'You sound tired.'

'Just a bit. There's quite a lot happening here that's . . . Well, let's say I wasn't prepared for it and I'm not sure how well I'm handling it.'

'Do you want to talk about it?'

Realizing she did, she gave him a shortened version – not that there was a longer one yet – and as she waited for him to respond she found herself hoping he wasn't laughing . . . *Please, please, don't you find this funny too.*

If he did, he was clever enough not to let her know. 'How's Matthew dealing with it?' he asked carefully.

Sighing, she said, 'I think he's angry, but he's also treating it as a bit of a joke. Well, not a joke, but it's like he doesn't seem to realize what this could do to *our* lives, never mind Aiden's.'

'Well, maybe the time to start worrying is when you know for certain if Aiden's the father. Meantime, is it possible you're also trying to get over the shock of him actually having sex?'

She laughed. 'I think I've known that for a while, but I assumed he was taking the proper precautions – actually that Matthew was making sure of it. I should have known better and talked to him myself. As for the girl, whoever she is . . . Pearl Something-or-other . . .' She stopped, realizing she really didn't want to talk about it any more, that actually what she wanted was to forget about everything for a while and think only about David. 'Why don't you tell me what's going on in your world?' she suggested, feeling some of her tension unravelling simply by asking the question.

With an ironic sort of tenderness he said, 'You mean apart from how much I'm missing you?'

Smiling she said, 'Well, you could start with that.'

'OK, here goes . . .'

'No!' she cried laughing. 'I didn't mean it . . . Well, I did, but if it's as much as I'm missing you then I kind of already know.'

'Good, I'm glad we're both having a difficult time being apart again – a subject we'll need to revisit, I feel. But for now, why don't I update you on what else is happening here?'

'I'm listening.'

'Well, apparently Gabe, Lukas and Evie are planning to stay for at least another week, and Sadie's going to have another go at trying to talk to Mia tomorrow. She's sent her several messages saying she believes Lottie was behind everything in the hope it'll make Mia more willing to see her, but so far she hasn't heard back.'

'Do we know if anyone's actually been inside the house since Connor and I were there?'

'I'm not sure, but I don't think so. Sadie's seen her though, looking much as you described with her hair like a nest and some sort of ghastly make-up. God knows what she's up to, I suspect she doesn't even know herself.'

Wondering how true that was, Cristy said, 'We're meeting with the lawyers in the morning to discuss what we can put into the next episode. Obviously we have the big reunion and the clifftop farewell, but we're hoping to include at least some excerpts of Janina's contact with the sisters without running into a lawsuit.'

Sighing, David said, 'I guess it says quite a lot about Sadie that she still feels protective enough towards her aunt, even now, not to fight the injunction.'

'She is remarkable, but some people are just made more forgiving than others. As Evie has put it several times, nothing any of them do will bring Janina back and seeking revenge on an old lady is no way for any of them to go forward.'

'I suppose you have to agree with that. It's about the future now, not the past.'

'Which doesn't help those of us making a podcast very much.'

'You really do sound tired. It's making me wish you were here – or I was there – so we could . . . end the day together?'

Sinking into how wonderful that sounded, she said, 'I need to tell you how glad I am to be the sweets in your pocket and wind in your sails.'

With a laugh, he said, 'You've been talking to Rosie.'

'Guilty,' she smiled. 'It's a lovely phrase. She's a lovely girl, and I'm so glad for your sake that at least *she* isn't pregnant. It's just a pity Aiden didn't learn the facts of life from Ludo.'

Laughing, a lot, he said, 'I'm sorry, I probably shouldn't have found that quite so funny, but it was good.'

Still smiling, she rolled over on the bed and closed her eyes. 'If you knew what I was thinking now,' she said, 'you might blush.'

His voice was quieter, softer, as he said, 'Why don't we give it a try?'

Aware of the words gathering and warming her in all the right places, she said, 'If we do I'll make myself blush.'

'Would that be so bad?'

'No, I don't suppose so, but with Matthew and Aiden still here . . . Maybe I can call you back when they've gone?'

'Sure. Meantime I might send you a link to Amanjena to see if it really is somewhere you'd like to go.'

'I know it will be, but I'd love to see it so I can start to imagine us there.' She frowned as someone knocked on the door.

'Mum? We're sending out for pizza. Shall we get one for you?'

'Sorry,' she said to David, 'I have to go, but please send that link. And if I don't manage to call back tonight, let's speak tomorrow.'

Ringing off, she went to open the door and for no reason she could name, seeing Aiden standing there looking sheepish, and tousled and all grown-up, but not, made her want to hold him closer than she had for a very long time.

'Cool,' he murmured as her arms went round him. 'Clearly got to offer you a pizza more often.'

Smiling, she said, 'Why don't you guys pick one up on your way home? It's been a long day and I've still got things to do before I go to bed.'

'Actually, I was thinking of staying here, if that's OK?'

'Really? But you have school in the morning?'

'Yeah, but I can Uber it if Dad lets me use his account.' He met her eyes tentatively, a little playfully. 'I missed you while you were gone and I don't want to leave while we're still kind of . . . like this.'

Loving him for that, she said, 'Staying here for the night isn't going to sort things out, you must know that. But of course, if you want to – this is your home as well as mine.'

'Good to know. And my pizza's yours if you only want your usual slice.'

It wasn't until much later, after they'd eaten and somehow avoided the subject of his disgrace, and teased Matthew about being Papa Bear to Boo Boo, that Cristy was finally back in her room and ready to slip into bed. She lay quietly for a few minutes, already starting to drift into sleep, while wanting to call David back. Maybe she was too tired, but she could at least text, or leave a suggestive voice message with instructions for him to delete as soon as he'd heard it.

Reaching for her phone, she turned onto her side and found an email alert from him, presumably containing the link to a holiday in Marrakech. Wanting to see it, to fall asleep dreaming about it, she started to click through but suddenly came jarringly awake, as she noticed another text had arrived from the anonymous sender.

In spite of knowing she shouldn't open it, especially not at this time of night, she went ahead and felt a burn of unease as she read the few short words, *Aaah, Cristy, back in Bristol, safe and sound.*

How did he know that? Was he *physically* stalking her, watching her every move? Could he even be outside right now?

Knowing it was much more likely that he was tracking her

mobile, she quickly turned off the Find My iPhone app – except if he was using some other sort of spyware that wasn't going to do it.

Deciding to let Jacks take a look in the morning, she was about to move the latest message to the folder when she realized there was an image attached. She opened it and revulsion surged through her. Not quite a dick-pic, but the closest thing to it: a man's hand on his crotch suggesting he was about to lower the zip of his jeans.

# CHAPTER THIRTY

It was after eight on Tuesday evening by the time they uploaded to the various platforms. For the past two days the entire team, along with two lawyers and four back-up technicians, had been editing, re-editing, recording and re-recording in a way that wouldn't – or shouldn't – end them up on the wrong side of the law.

'And you're certain it won't?' Meena asked, as Iz handed out much-needed drinks while Clover wandered around with sandwiches from a nearby deli.

'As certain as we can be,' Cristy replied. 'All we've said is that Janina's car went off the road while she was in Guernsey. No mention of her being on her way to meet Lottie – or Mia. Nothing about where the accident actually happened, or of the police questioning the sisters after the event.'

'But you did include a reminder that Lottie met with Janina and Gabe in a café, just prior to the so-called accident. Do you know who took those photos now?'

'According to Lottie's journal it was Mia, in an effort to thwart a blackmail attempt.'

Meena wrinkled her nose. 'OK. Not seeing it, but from what you tell me about Mia she's . . . different. So, as things stand we're left with Lottie writing about being unable to live with herself if she denies Janina access to her daughter. That's one hell of an early cut-off considering what comes next.'

'It can't be helped,' Cristy responded. 'Everything else is covered by the injunction.'

'So are they just going to get away with it?' Iz asked incredulously.

'For now, yes,' Cristy replied, sounding as frustrated as she felt. 'Although anyone with half a brain can work out that there's more, and that it very probably involves the sisters.'

'Or Albescu,' Jodi pointed out. 'You're kind of suggesting he might have caught up with Janina.'

'It can be seen that way,' Cristy agreed, always grateful to Connor's wife for the way she pointed things out for clarity. 'It was what Sadie wanted. Obviously we weren't going to lay it at his door when we know it wasn't him, but we decided we could include what Lottie had written about him.'

'I take it Mia's lawyers have had previous scrutiny of the pod,' Harry said, side-eyeing Jodi's nappy-changing process on the sofa next to him.

'We sent it over at five,' Connor told him, 'and let them know at the same time that if we didn't hear back by seven-thirty we'd be running it as is. So, I'm guessing they either had no problem with it, or they didn't receive any instructions from their client.'

'Or they've opened up a very big hole to bury you in,' Harry grunted.

'It'll be great for the ratings if we are sued,' Iz pointed out, eagerly. 'Advertisers will be falling over themselves to get a spot in something sensational.'

Deciding to let her reflect on that in her own time, Cristy said to Meena, 'David took Sadie, Gabe and Lukas to see Guernsey's chief police officer earlier today. They thought it would be a good idea to give him a heads-up on what could be coming down the tracks. Apparently they left with the feeling that a prosecution, based on the journals, is unlikely.'

'But if it's written there in black and white,' Jodi protested. 'Lottie couldn't have made it clearer . . .'

'There's no way of corroborating her story,' Connor explained. 'Even if what she's said is true, it can't be proved, especially not with Mia claiming it's all lies.'

'And according to our lawyers,' Cristy continued, 'if they go after Mia the case will be thrown out long before it gets to court, either due to her mental state, or because there are no witnesses to what happened so it can't be proved it was her, and of course there's no body.'

'Didn't Mia try at one point to say that it was Sadie who wrote the journals?' Meena asked curiously.

'It was Lottie,' Cristy told her. 'The handwriting, the syntax, the whole style matches her other works, and as you've already pointed out yourself, Mia doesn't really know *what* she's saying half the time.'

'How's Sadie feeling about everything?' Jodi said, handing a lovely fresh baby Aurora to Harry while she packed up the changing mat. 'It must be really hard for her trying to deal with it all.'

'When we spoke to her earlier,' Cristy replied, 'she said that what really matters to her now is the fact that she's found her real family and her mother is no longer forgotten, or not mentioned, or even denied, as has been the case for most of her life.'

'Please don't shoot me for saying this,' Meena put in, 'but lovely as that is, it's not shaping up to be a particularly sensational end to the series?'

Hating hearing it, Cristy said, 'We've established that Janina and Gabe are Sadie's parents, that the sisters faked her identity and lied to her all these years, and that they knew Janina was on the island at the time she lost her life. We've even made it clear that Mia is not willing to be interviewed, which strongly suggests she knows more than she's telling.'

'It's true, you've achieved a lot,' Meena agreed, 'but I feel we're missing the big finale that gets everyone gasping and talking and, let's face it, gagging for another series of *Hindsight*.'

Jumping in, Iz said, 'I've already got a whole slew of possible sponsors lined up. That's how well things have gone so far with this series. If you can properly wow us with the last episode – no pressure – we can probably double, even triple your buy-in rates next time around.'

Cristy looked at Connor, knowing he felt as irritated and frustrated by that as she did.

'We can't just ignore the law because it's not working for us,' he pointed out tightly. 'It's not a drama. It's true-life, and sometimes life is just . . . shit.'

Cristy watched Jodi turn to him, the baby in her arms now, a surprised and worried look on her face. 'Should I be taking that personally?' she asked carefully.

'No, of course not,' he retorted. 'None of this is about you. It's about the fact that we're sitting here feeling that we've backed the wrong horse because we can't get it over the line the way everyone wants us to.'

'But what were you actually expecting when you decided to take the case on?' Harry asked. 'It was always about finding out who the girl really was and what sort of crime had been committed by her aunts, or her parents, or some vile intermediary. You've done it, for God's sake. Her mother was murdered by at least one, if not both of her aunts so the aunts could keep her. You might not be able to put it out there as plain as that, but people aren't stupid. After tonight's episode they'll all be jumping to the same conclusion. I don't think you're helping here, Meena.'

Shrugging, Meena said, 'Just voicing my opinion, that's all.'

After a brief and awkward silence, Iz said brightly, 'How about we regroup tomorrow, or the next day, when we've had some listener feedback, and *then* we can decide how best to approach the last pod?'

'Let's do that,' Cristy said, appreciating the suggestion, 'and by then we might have clearer heads. We've been pretty full on these past ten days, especially yesterday and today.'

Iz beamed. 'Have I ever told you my teapot theory?' she asked cheerily. 'I always say, if you're feeling blocked it's probably because you're trying to go too fast so everything's getting all clogged up. So what you have to do is pull the teapot back, give the leaves a swirl and next thing you know it's all pouring out perfectly and no more block.'

Cristy looked at Connor, willing him not to say something cruel, but he clearly didn't quite get the message. 'I've already pointed out that this isn't a drama,' he snapped angrily. 'No one's *blocked*, *Iz*, the law is the law, and no matter how many times you swirl the pot we're not going to get around it.'

As Iz coloured, Cristy said, 'But it's still a good idea to meet after we've had time to think things through – and after we've interviewed Sadie for the wrap-up. We don't know what she's going to say yet. OK, no one's expecting her to give us the conflagration Meena's hoping for, but who knows? Maybe she'll have talked Mia into letting the journals be aired in their entirety. Would that be an explosive enough climax for you, Meena? To leave everyone speculating on which sister was guilty rather than whether they were actually involved in Janina's death or not?'

'I think they're going to do that anyway,' Clove pointed out.

'She's right,' Connor said. 'And whatever we can or can't run, it's still a truly dark tale of abduction, insane wealth, entitlement, human trafficking, murder . . . It's got everything, so let's stop doing ourselves down here. One way or another we'll make the last episode a winner, and I'll lay money now that by this time on Wednesday, or maybe Thursday, we'll have worked out how.'

*

Early the next morning Cristy was alone in the office, stressing over Aiden's situation again, or she had been until another text arrived from the stalker, this one so ghastly it was actually making her feel sick.

*Oh, Cristy, you're a dirty, dirty girl. If anyone knew what you got up to when alone in your bed . . . Shall I send the photos?*

Photos! Was there a camera in her bedroom, for God's sake? Had someone actually managed to break in to set up some sort of surveillance . . .

*Stop!* She hadn't actually done anything to warrant this message. Sure, she'd thought about it, and had even mentioned it to David, but it hadn't happened, so this *person* was either playing mind games, or did it mean he had a tap on her phone?

The next step, obviously, was to let Jacks and his shadowy team of geeks see if they could trace the source; and she would, were it not for the fact that she simply couldn't bear for anyone to see this latest message. At the very least they'd wonder if there was some truth to it, or, worse, *much worse*, they'd picture her in a state of writhing and moaning masturbation with God only knew what sort of stimulating devices. Who knew how vivid and graphic their imaginations might be? They might also want to call the stalker's bluff and ask for photos! Obviously he didn't have any because it *hadn't happened*. However, he could easily Photoshop her face onto some hideously pornographic images and even if, in the end, it could be proved it wasn't her, people, Jacks included, would still feel they'd seen her like that.

So she couldn't ask Jacks to get involved. What she had to do was change her phone and the number . . . Except everyone would want to know why she'd taken such a bizarre decision at this stage of a series. It would make no sense to them, any more than it would to Aiden if she asked him to check the flat for some sort of bugging device – or devices, plural.

She looked around the office, wondering if she was being watched even now. It was impossible to tell when she had no idea how covert surveillance was set up, much less carried out. But maybe she was in danger of blowing this out of proportion. Whoever was behind it hadn't threatened her physically, nor was he suggesting he might. In fact, in the grand scheme of things, these messages weren't actually that bad; no rape or murder threats, no mention of her children, nor even a suggestion of going public with fake masturbation photos. Nevertheless, she still didn't want anyone seeing the latest text, so the best thing to do was drop it into the folder with the others, and feel thankful that she had plenty else going on right now to distract her.

*

It was on Thursday afternoon while everyone was at their desks working on ways to create a big finale that Mia rang.

Immediately scrabbling to take the call, Cristy alerted the others and waited for Mia's image to fill her computer screen.

'Mia?' she said, when nothing happened. 'Are you OK?' She could hear breathing and the sound of someone moving, but still no one spoke. 'Mia?' she called again.

'She's coming for me,' Mia cried, still not in vision. 'I know she is, but I'm not going to let her in. Tell her, she *can't come in*.'

With a quick glance at Connor, Cristy said, 'Are you talking about Sadie, Mia?'

'*I'm talking about Lottie*. She's coming for me . . . You've poisoned her against me, told her all your ugly lies . . . Those people she's with are *imposters*. You brought them here, so you have to make them go away.'

Realizing she was talking about Sadie, even if she didn't recognize it herself, Cristy said, 'Mia, listen. Sadie just wants to talk to you, to make sure you're OK after the shock of everything . . .'

'Tell her to go away!' Mia yelled. 'I don't want her here. She wants to kill me.'

'That's not true,' Cristy argued gently. 'She still cares about you . . .'

'She wants to punish me for keeping her away from that doctor. I regret it now, but she won't listen.'

Back to Lottie. 'It was a long time ago,' Cristy said. 'What happened then . . .'

'It wasn't my fault what happened to her mother! I didn't do it. You have to tell her that.'

'Please, just let Sadie come and talk to you,' Cristy said. 'If you like, David Gaudion can come with her . . .'

'No! I don't want her here. I just want you to know that if anything happens to me it'll be down to you and everything you've done to turn my niece against me. Lottie is very angry about it. Very angry indeed.'

As the line went dead Cristy looked at the others, feeling as mystified and disturbed by the call as she could see they were.

'She's clearly completely lost it,' Clove said quietly.

Cristy nodded. 'When I spoke to Sadie last night she told me this was happening and it's upsetting her quite a lot. The ridiculous part of it is that she's as afraid of her aunt as Mia now seems to be of her, which is why I suggested David should be there when they meet.'

'Is Sadie up for that?' Jacks asked.

Cristy nodded. 'So's David, it's just a matter of getting Mia to open the door.' To Connor she said, 'Did you manage to record any of that?'

He nodded. 'Most of it. Do you want to send it to Sadie?'

'It won't be anything she hasn't already heard, but I think we should.'

An hour later, having listened to the playback, Sadie came through on FaceTime looking tense and pale. 'I don't know if you want to get my response on record,' she said, 'but if you do, I've already prepared something that I can read out.'

As Connor hit the right buttons and Clove got ready to make notes, Cristy said, 'Where are you?'

'At home. Dad and Jasper are with me. We went down there a few minutes ago to try again, but everything's bolted from the inside and she didn't even answer when we called out.'

'We saw her watching us from an upstairs window,' Jasper added.

Faintly spooked by that, Cristy said, 'OK, we're recording now.'

SADIE: 'I've made four or five attempts to see my aunt since the last episode about my mother coming to Guernsey was dropped, but without any success. I've no idea if she's heard it, but I think she probably has and that's why she won't see me. She's managed to convince herself that I'm blaming her for what happened, but as I keep telling her, I don't blame her for anything, and all I want now is to move on with my life. Having said that, it's not my intention simply to abandon her; she isn't getting any younger and nor is she in great health, so it would be cruel of me to carry on now as if she never mattered at all. She did matter, a great deal, and she still does. You can't just wipe out all the good someone has done in your life, as if it never happened, especially not when there has been a lot of good. So I want her to understand that we – I'm speaking for my father and uncle now as well – wish her no harm and we never will.'

CRISTY: 'When you went to see her earlier, did she realize that the man with you was your father?'

SADIE: 'I'm not sure, but I thought, if she met him and saw for herself just how gentle he is she'd be more likely to let us in.'

CRISTY: 'Will you try again?'

SADIE: 'Of course. I have no plans to leave Guernsey yet, and I certainly won't without seeing her first. Dad, Lukas and Evie are flying back at the weekend and Jasper's going with them to look at a few job opportunities that Lukas is setting up for him.'

CRISTY: 'So your long-term goal is to relocate?'

SADIE: 'I think so. We'll need a fresh start after all that's happened, I just want to be sure that Mia is properly cared for before I go and that might take a while. It doesn't matter though, there's no rush, and obviously I'll come back to visit on a regular basis.'

CONNOR: 'So when do you intend to try seeing her again?'

SADIE: 'Are you asking because you'd like me to record it?'

CONNOR: 'I confess it did cross my mind.'

SADIE: 'I'll do my best, and if I can't do it myself I'm sure David will help out. He's bringing Cynthia over in the morning. It's possible Mia might be more willing to open up if she's there too.'

CRISTY: 'Just to explain, David and Cynthia are good friends and long-time neighbours in Guernsey.'

CONNOR: 'OK, well, let us know how it goes and if anything happens in the meantime, you know where we are.'

SADIE: 'Thanks – and thanks too for all the support you've given me throughout this. I feel as though you guys are more like friends now than anything else.'

CRISTY: 'We're OK with that, and obviously really glad we were able to play a part in helping you to find out who you really are.'

After the call was over and the recording checked, Cristy sat back in her chair and said thoughtfully, 'That could be a sign-off for the last episode.'

'Just what I was thinking,' Connor agreed. To Jacks he said, 'Bookmark it for a quick find. Any thoughts, Clove?'

Looking up from her notes, she said, 'Not about Sadie's input, but I'm worried that airing anything Mia said just now is going to be considered exploitation of someone with profound mental health issues. Something like that could backfire on us horribly.'

'We'll take advice before using anything,' Cristy assured her. 'If it turns out we can't run her actual words, we'll do as we did after Connor and I paid a visit and found her sitting under a noose. We'll describe it the best we can and try not to sound in any way judgemental or unsympathetic to someone who's . . .'

'Completely fucking nuts?' Clove suggested.

With a wry smile, Cristy said, 'Yes, but obviously not in those words.' She glanced at her phone, tensing as a text arrived, but it was only Aiden letting her know that he'd be staying with her again tonight.

Happy for that, she sent a quick message to Matthew asking if he'd managed to make contact with Pearl or her parents yet.

*You mean the other grandparents?* he replied.

Deciding not to grace that with a response, she reminded Connor that they had some final promos to record for Iz and followed him through to the studio.

*

'Wow!' Connor declared in amazement, when he walked into the office later and Cristy practically leapt out of her skin. 'Nervy or what?'

'Sorry,' she gasped, pressing a hand to her thudding heart, knowing it was an overreaction, but there it was anyway. 'I didn't hear you . . . I thought you'd gone home.'

'Just about to. What's going on?' he asked, clearly noticing the way she'd quickly shut her phone down.

'Nothing,' she insisted, aware of Clove and Jacks regarding her as if she'd just grown another head. 'Or I guess everything,' she admitted in a rush, 'from not knowing if my son is going to become a father at sixteen, to worrying about what my ex is planning to do with Boo Boo Bear while he has custody, to missing David, to feeling distinctly edgy about what is happening over there in Guernsey.'

Sinking into his chair, Connor said, 'I've got to admit, the

Sadie/Mia thing is getting to me a bit too and I can't really put my finger on why.'

'It's got a strange sort of undertow to it,' Clove observed. 'I can't stop thinking about it.'

'Nothing to do with the fact that we're totally focused on shaping a last episode,' Jacks commented dryly.

'Do you think we should be over there?' Connor asked Cristy.

She was distracted by another text arriving and had checked it before she could stop herself. '*For God's sake*,' she muttered under her breath when she saw it was from *him*. A gushing thanks for the 'hot tit-pics' that she hadn't even sent. How could she, when she didn't even have his number?

Connor said, 'Are you still getting those anonymous texts? Is that what's going on here?'

Knowing her cheeks were burning, she said, 'They're vile. At least some of them are. I know I shouldn't read them . . .'

'Give me the phone,' he demanded.

'I actually don't want you to see them.'

'Too bad. Hand it over.'

Realizing how ludicrous she'd seem if she outright refused, she opened up the thread and half threw the phone at Connor, already feeling the shame of things she *hadn't actually done*.

'*Shit*,' he muttered as he read the messages. 'What a fucking psycho. Jacks, you need to get onto this, find out who it is so we can shut him down.'

'But I need the phone,' Cristy protested as Jacks reached for it.

'Who are you expecting to hear from tonight?' Connor asked.

'David. Matthew. Aiden. Possibly Hayley. There's also a chance Sadie will call.'

'Then text them one of the burner numbers,' he told her. 'You only have to say yours is going through some sort of routine check, and will be back on air . . . When?' he asked Jacks.

Jacks shrugged. 'No knowing how deep we might have to dive, but I'll get right on it.'

'I just want you to know,' Cristy said, looking from Connor to Jacks and back again, 'that nothing – I mean, *absolutely nothing* – he's saying is true. OK?'

'Got it,' Jacks assured her.

'So what's he saying?' Clove immediately wanted to know.

'It's your typical scumbag fantasy stuff,' Connor replied dismissively. 'Nothing to worry about, but I've got to admit, I wouldn't want to be on the receiving end of it. Let's run him to ground asap, Jacks, and then do whatever it takes to make him rethink his career choice.'

'Could be a woman?' Clove suggested tentatively.

'Doubtful,' Connor told her, 'but you won't want to see the proof unless dick-pics are your thing.'

With a moue of distaste, Clove said, 'Could still be a woman, hiding behind someone's dick.'

'It's not *that* big,' Connor quipped and even Cristy had to laugh. It turned to a shudder of revulsion as the thought of it made her feel as though she'd been contaminated, violated even, in an actual physical way.

'We need to keep this in mind for a future series,' Clove told her gravely. 'There's so much of it now and some people, kids, are getting seriously damaged by it.'

Agreeing that it was worth looking into, Cristy glanced over at her phone as another text arrived.

'Shall I?' Jacks asked.

She nodded, and as he opened the message she became so tense it actually hurt.

'It's Matthew,' he told her, holding the phone out, 'wanting to know if you're free for a bite to eat later.'

Holding up her hands to block it, she said, 'Text back to say you have the phone, but you'll pass the message on and you're sure I'll be in touch.'

Going to take a spare phone from the store they kept, Connor passed it to Jacks for set-up and said, 'If you're worried this creep is actually following you, why don't you come and stay at ours tonight?'

Cristy gave a laugh, without quite knowing why. 'Thanks, but Aiden's going to be with me, and now it looks as though a family dinner is in store. Does that mean you think there is someone following me?'

Jacks was shaking his head while staring at the phone. 'No way of telling at the moment,' he said, 'but whatever he's got in mind it'll be me he's coming home with tonight. Wonder how much he's gonna like that.'

*

'You're kidding me,' Cristy groaned, looking from Matthew to Aiden and back again. 'Please tell me that's not what she said.'

Matthew regarded her helplessly, while Aiden only shrugged as if to say, 'nothing to do with me,' when it had *everything* to do with him. They were in a tapas bar they used to come to regularly as a family, with an assortment of small plates between them and three portions of *patatas bravas* just for Aiden. Cristy, unable to face food right now, refilled her glass with wine as Matthew said,

'It's not that long to wait . . .'

'We shouldn't have to wait at all,' she snapped. 'We want to know *now* if he's the father, not after the baby's born. And *that*,' she added forcefully, 'is still three months away, but OK, if you don't think that's long—'

'I'm just saying,' Matthew interrupted, 'that we don't get to call any shots here. She's the one carrying the child so if she doesn't want to subject it to a DNA test before the birth, there's not much we can do about it.'

'What do her parents say? Surely they want to know who the father is.'

'If they do, it's a conversation they're having with her, not me.'

'Have you actually spoken to them?'

Sighing, he said, 'I've had an email saying they're aware of the situation and, as regrettable as it is, they don't feel any questions can be answered until Pearl is ready to do so.'

'Jesus Christ. Who are these people?' She glared at Aiden. 'Have you met them?'

He shook his head, picked up another *patata* but clearly thought better of eating it when he caught his mother's expression.

'What about the other boys?' she asked. 'Surely they want to know if they're going to be landed with a child they don't want.'

'Course,' he agreed. 'But like Dad said, we don't get much of a say in it.'

Looking at Matthew again, Cristy snapped, 'This is starting to feel like a game of Russian roulette.'

With no small irony, he said, 'Except in this instance the last one standing gets a cigar and brandy instead of a bullet.'

As Aiden guffawed she cried, 'It's not funny, for God's sake. In fact it's so far from funny that I have to wonder at what point you two are going to see the seriousness of it all.'

'I do,' Matthew told her, 'and so does Aiden, but right now we're as incapable as you are of doing anything about it.'

'Which you don't seem to mind, whereas I'm not ready to give up just like that. We – *he, our son* – must have some rights, for God's sake.'

'Then name them. It's too late for a termination, even if she was willing, and if we start pressuring her for a DNA test it could be seen as intimidation of a pregnant girl and that's not a route we want to go down.'

'What about the other boys' parents? Maybe we should speak to them, see if we can act together in some way?'

'Intimidation,' he reminded her.

'And they haven't all fessed up yet,' Aiden added, 'so you have to back off for now, Mum. I know it's against your nature . . .'

'Oh shut up,' she snapped at him.

Doing just that, he helped himself to a few more *patatas* and brazenly checked his phone for messages.

'We need to meet the girl and her parents,' Cristy said to Matthew. 'No more emails. For all you know she's sending them herself and . . . Aiden, are you listening?'

'Sure,' he answered, 'it's just there's a text here from David saying he can't get hold of you.'

Remembering she was supposed to have let him know her temporary number, while not wanting Matthew and Aiden to ask why she had one, she said, 'Tell him I'm out of battery and I'll call as soon as I get home.'

After sending the message, Aiden looked up as Cristy said, 'Where do her parents live?'

'I'm not sure. Siston, I think. Or out that way somewhere. But do you know what, Mum? I seriously think you should chill for a bit. I know you're in shock and it's kind of not ideal, but it is what it is . . .'

Wanting to throttle him, she looked at Matthew as he said, 'We should still let the girl know we'd like to meet her. With any luck it might frighten her into . . .'

Cristy waited.

'Something,' he said lamely.

'Like a miscarriage?' Aiden suggested, with an anxious glance at his mother.

'Well, I wasn't exactly thinking that,' Matthew responded, 'but . . .' Catching Cristy's eye he quickly recalibrated and said instead, 'It might persuade her to see how lucky she'd be if you are the father, to have us as grandparents, and your genes . . .'

Cristy gaped at him in disbelief, until, realizing he'd got himself all mixed up with trying to put a positive spin on things, she started to laugh. 'I'm not sure you're for real,' she told him, as relief and confusion nudged him into laughter too.

'But you know that came out wrong,' he said, 'and that's what's so wonderful about us. We always end up on the same page . . . Son, this isn't a good time to be answering your phone.'

'It's David,' Aiden told him and looked at Cristy as he clicked on. 'Sure, I'm good thanks. Yeah, she's right here, I'll pass you over.'

Taking the phone and turning away from the others, she said quietly, 'Hey, is everything OK?'

'Say hi from me,' Matthew called out.

'I've just heard from Evie,' David said gravely. 'Something's going on at the villa, so I'm heading over there.'

'What do you mean? What's happened?'

'I don't have any details yet. I just thought I should let you know. I'll call again as soon as I have more news.'

# CHAPTER THIRTY-ONE

CRISTY: 'It's almost midnight on Thursday and I'm with Connor at his home recording this. We're hoping for news from Guernsey after receiving a call a couple of hours ago telling us that something was going on at the Villa des Roches. We still have no idea what it is, or if the incident – I guess that's what we should call it for now – is over yet. We just thought we'd share the wait with you guys so you'll get an idea of the build-up to whatever is coming down the track.'

CONNOR: 'Since getting the tip-off we've been trying all our contacts on the island – including Sadie, Gabe and Lukas – but so far all we've had is a text from our original source telling us that things aren't looking good.'

CRISTY: 'What the hell does that mean, you must be asking, and believe me, we are too. Our imaginations are running out of control. Is everyone safe? Has someone set fire to the villa? Where is Sadie? What's happening to her, or her aunt? Are Gabe and Lukas still there? It was Evie who raised the alarm, apparently, so we're guessing they are, but she's not responding to messages either.'

CONNOR: 'As a quick recap: the last we heard from Sadie was earlier today when she told us she was planning to go to the villa again in the morning in the hope of speaking to her aunt. So, did she go this evening instead?'

CRISTY: 'I know it's doubtful we can use this next bit, but just in case: now could be a good time to share a call we had from Mia, also earlier today, in which she was clearly confused between Sadie and Lottie, and ended up accusing us of turning Sadie against her. She claims to be afraid of what Sadie might do to her, and insists that Gabe and Lukas are imposters. A quick reminder here that the results of a DNA test on both men show that they are indeed who they claim to be. Anyway, have a listen to some of Mia's distress call, because that's what it sounds like – a woman in distress.'

As Connor stopped recording Cristy noted the time code and wrote, *She's coming for me*, next to it, a guide for where to edit in the call later. That done, she sat back on the sofa, tired and worried, and annoyed with David for keeping them in the dark for so long.

'What the hell's going on over there?' she muttered, glancing up as Jodi put her head round the sitting room door. The baby was in her arms, goggle-eyed and dribbly, and smiling in a way that caught Cristy's heart.

'More coffee?' Jodi whispered, as if someone might be sleeping.

'What are you doing up?' Connor asked, going to take his daughter.

'She's hungry,' Jodi replied, 'so I thought I'd come and sit with you guys while she feeds.'

Nuzzling, kissing and cooing over his girl, Connor said, 'Then I'll make the coffee.'

Jodi smiled her thanks and went to sit with Cristy on the sofa, taking Aurora back as Connor said, 'I'm guessing you won't want one?'

She shook her head and yawned while opening her top ready to nurse.

Watching, Cristy couldn't stop her mind leaping from Aiden to Bear and on to the awful possibility that she was going to be drowning in babies in the coming weeks and months. Thank God this sweet little angel wasn't her responsibility, was completely loved and cared for by her parents and had no need of anything from her soon-to-be godmother other than to be doted on and spoiled.

'Connor told me about Aiden,' Jodi said, after settling Aurora against her breast.

Cristy's eyes closed, then quickly opened again as her phone rang.

'David!' she shouted to Connor, and clicking on, cried, 'Thank God. What on earth is happening over there?' She glanced up as Connor rushed in and set to record.

David's voice was hoarse and low as he told them what he could.

DAVID: 'It's been pretty chaotic. The police and emergency services are still all over the place, but mostly they're searching the cliffs under the villa . . .'

CRISTY: 'Christ! What are they searching for?'

DAVID: 'A body. I guess it can only be that, the fall is too great to survive and the rocks . . .'

CRISTY: 'Who are we talking about, David? Please, for God's sake, don't say it's Sadie . . .'

DAVID: 'Sorry. No, it's Mia. Apparently she contacted Sadie earlier and told her to come . . . I'm not sure how long Sadie was there, or what happened between them . . . All I can tell you is what a detective told me, that apparently Mia threw herself from one of the balconies.'

CRISTY: 'Oh my God! In front of Sadie?'

DAVID: 'I'm afraid so. Sadie's been in a pretty dreadful state since. They've given her some kind of sedative now. As far as I can make out she went down there alone, but it's possible Lukas was with her . . . I haven't got that straight yet . . .'

CRISTY: 'Have you managed to talk to Sadie at all?'

DAVID: 'A few minutes ago, but she was pretty out of it by then. Exhaustion, shock, the drugs kicking in . . . She seems more worried about Mia than anything else.'

CONNOR: 'Where are you now?'

DAVID: 'On my way home. The police want to talk to me again tomorrow, and there's a good chance someone will contact you . . . I told them about the podcast, and the noose incident, I hope that's OK. It kind of goes to her being suicidal.'

CRISTY: 'Of course. We can let them have—'

DAVID: 'Sorry, Lukas is trying to get hold of me. If there's anything to report I'll call back, otherwise let's speak in the morning.'

CRISTY: 'Please ask him if he was with Sadie at the villa earlier.'

DAVID: 'Will do.'

As the call ended Cristy and Connor stared at one another, processing all that had been said, all it could mean, all that might or might not have happened earlier that evening. For the moment it was difficult to get their heads around anything, although a standout for Cristy was the fact that Mia had thrown herself to the very same sort of end that had been inflicted on Janina, and she could see from his expression that Connor had very probably zeroed in on that too.

*

It was late on Saturday afternoon before the events of Thursday evening began to come clear. By then Cristy and Connor had shared all relevant material with the Guernsey police and had also spoken to Gabe and Lukas. Both men were clearly badly shaken up, they could see that on the video link as well as hear it in their voices.

LUKAS: 'No, I didn't go down there with Sasha. I wanted to, so did Gabe . . . We just weren't sure how stable the woman was, or why she was so insistent that Sasha should go alone. I had a bad feeling about it from the moment she left our hotel to drive back there. We all did. I only wish we'd ignored her instructions and gone with her anyway. Or at least followed.'

CRISTY: 'How long was she there before you heard what had happened? Actually, *how* did you hear?'

LUKAS: 'Sasha rang me . . . She was so distraught I could hardly make out what she was saying . . . Obviously we jumped in the car and went straight there. Jasper let us in the gates. She'd called him too, so he came to the villa with us, but none of us knew until we got inside what had actually happened.'

CRISTY: 'And what had happened?'

LUKAS: 'We found Sadie curled up in a ball on the floor of Lottie's study. She pointed at the open doors and kept saying, "I tried to stop her, I tried to stop her." I went to look, but it was too dark to see anything. Jasper got straight on the phone to the police, while Gabe and I did our best to comfort Sasha. She could hardly catch her breath she was so upset. She told us she hadn't realized what was happening until it was too late. She asked us to stay with her until the police arrived, so of course we did. Evie drove over as well, as frantic as we were. By the time the police came . . . They must have already called out the lifeboat and helicopters because we could hear them, the noise, blinding lights on the water . . . We were asked to wait in another room while Sadie talked them through what had happened. They wouldn't even let Gabe be with her. It was very hard for her, but I think they treated her well.'

CRISTY: 'Where is she now?'

LUKAS: 'At the lodge with Jasper. Obviously we've cancelled our flights to Florida. We'll be here for as long as she needs us.'

CRISTY: 'Do you think there's any chance she'll speak to us?'

LUKAS: 'Yes, yes. She's told us everything she told the police, and she says she wants to share it with you when she's ready. I'm not sure when that will be. She's been a little calmer since the body was recovered this morning, but I'm sure you understand this is still a very difficult time for her. So much to process . . . The trauma of it all. How could her aunt have done such a terrible thing to her? Thank God we're all here.'

After the call was over Cristy and Connor, at the office now, continued to record, while Jacks and Clove joined in the discussion of what they'd just heard, and how their initial thoughts were playing out.

CRISTY: 'The first question I'm asking myself is, did Mia get Sadie down there with the sole purpose of making her witness her suicide?'

CONNOR: 'It's the kind of mad and cruel thing she'd do.'

CLOVE: 'Do we know if Mia contacted Sadie by text, or did she call her? I'm bringing it up because a text will show whether or not Mia asked her to go down there, whereas a call won't.'

CRISTY: 'Are you thinking Sadie might have gone, uninvited?'

CLOVE: 'I'm just saying, it'll look a lot better for her if there is a text asking her to go there.'

CONNOR: 'Unless it's found that Mia died before she went off the balcony, I can't see how they'll be able to pin anything on Sadie, if anyone's actually thinking that way.'

JACKS: 'Do you believe that neither Lukas nor Gabe were at the villa with her when it happened?'

CRISTY: 'I did, but now you're asking . . . The police will no doubt establish how their movements corresponded with Sadie's, presuming their phones were on.'

CONNOR: 'Hey guys, do any of us actually believe that Sadie would have pushed her over?'

JACKS: 'Yes, but no. I mean, what would be in it for her? Why create all this fuss and put herself in danger of going to prison when a whole new life is just starting to open up for her?'

CRISTY: 'It doesn't make sense for her to do that, but it's true, her being there alone with her aunt before it happened, especially with everything that's come to light lately . . . But no one knows about the most incriminating parts of the journals so why would they suspect her of anything?'

CONNOR: 'Actually, the police do know. Remember, Sadie tipped them off herself about what could be coming down the line.'

JACKS: 'If she'd taken someone to the villa with her, like Lukas or Gabe, she'd have an alibi of sorts . . . Actually, it's unlikely they'd be considered reliable witnesses when their revenge motive is, arguably, as strong as Sadie's.'

CRISTY: 'And I don't think any of us believe that Sadie did want revenge. She just wanted her aunt straightened out – as if that were ever possible – so she could move on with her life.'

CONNOR: 'I'm not arguing with that, but I think from hereon, we're going to have to record two ways – one taking the view that Sadie was the victim of her aunt's madness and guilt, i.e. suicide. The other asking, did she punish Mia for what was done to her mother? OK, I get we're not really believing in that, but the police are almost definitely going to open an investigation, and I'm sure once they delve into the detail the similarity of the two deaths – Janina and Mia – won't pass them by.'

A lengthy silence ensued as they considered the impossible situation Sadie was now in, her presumed innocence very probably hanging in the balance, and how they were actually discussing exploiting that fact as events unfolded. They would also, Cristy realized, with mounting apprehension, need to take a long hard look at their own investigation, and the role they might have played in pushing Sadie to where she was now.

*

'We've made the national news!' Iz declared triumphantly, as she bounced into the office on Monday morning looking only marginally less eccentric than usual. 'It's making every bulletin – *Hindsight* at the heart of another murder mystery; inside scoop from our favourite podcasters: what more can Cristy and Connor tell us about the mysterious events in Guernsey? You must have heard it?'

'Of course we have,' Connor retorted, 'and we're being bombarded with requests for statements, interviews, exclusives. Probably thanks to you?'

Flushing, she held up her hands in innocence. 'I'm sure these guys can find their way to you without my help,' she pointed out. 'But if you do feel like speaking to one of them, I've made a list of those who are likely to give us the best coverage – and I'm negotiating with a couple of broadcasters for a full hour sit-down after the last pod has dropped.' She gave a little squeal and shimmy of excitement. 'We've definitely got our big finale now. Did she jump or was she pushed? Revenge or karma? So many questions, and everyone's going to think they know the answers . . . By the way, I listened to the recording of your team chat that you did on Saturday – it's going to be perfect for the last episode. I've already tipped off a couple of outlets . . .'

'Wait! What?' Connor cut in sharply.

Iz looked startled, immediately worried.

'Please tell me you haven't been discussing what was in that recording,' he growled. 'It hasn't been edited yet, and it definitely can't go anywhere until we've spoken to Sadie, which is supposed to be happening later today.'

Iz drew a quick zip across her lips. 'No details given,' she assured him. Then added brightly, 'Tell me the difference between *Hindsight* and Wuhan?'

Everyone regarded her incredulously.

Joyfully she cried, 'What happens in *Hindsight* stays in *Hindsight.*'

As Connor blinked Cristy found herself laughing, as did Clove and Jacks until Connor finally cracked a smile too.

'OK, as long as we've got that clear,' he grunted. 'And, for the record, we're happy to do as many interviews as you can lay on once we've got the last episode nailed down, but be aware that that might not happen as fast as you'd like. As far as we know the police haven't finished questioning Sadie yet, and we still don't have the pathologist's preliminary report on how Mia actually died.'

'Did she jump or was she pushed?' Iz repeated excitedly, and peeled off her tricornered hat and bobbly coat, to go and tuck herself behind her desk. 'I know it's wrong to be so . . . *thrilled*, by someone's death,' she whispered to Jacks who was closest to her, 'but you have to admit Mia did us the biggest favour by jumping when she did. Unless she was pushed of course, and that would be even better.'

Jacks's eyes widened as he looked at the others, clearly not sure how to deal with this.

Having no suggestions, Cristy said to Connor, 'Let's go over what we already have for the last episode . . . Actually, here's David.' She clicked to answer his call and as his face filled the screen she saw right away how badly he must have slept the last few nights.

'OK, pathologist has reported death by drowning,' he informed them, 'which means she was alive before she went into the water, but probably not conscious, possibly due to hitting rocks on the way down. There are trauma injuries to the head and torso, consistent with a heavy fall. Toxicology showing nothing sinister so far, they're still working on it, and no mention of what might or might not have happened during the lead-up to the event.'

'Where's Sadie now?' Cristy asked. 'Do you know what's happening to her?'

'As far as I'm aware she's still at the lodge with Jasper and the others. Anna's just gone over there and Mum's planning to join them later. At some stage there will be a funeral to organize, but we're probably a way off from that yet.'

'Do you know if anything's happening at the villa?'

'Lukas tells me there's still a police presence, so it's off limits for now, although I can't imagine Sadie, or anyone else will want to go down there.' David glanced at his watch. 'I'm sorry, but I have to get to a meeting. If I hear any more I'll call.'

*

It was much later in the day when Sadie finally appeared on their screens looking perhaps less shellshocked than she had over the past few days, but still dazed as though it hadn't all completely sunk in yet. Her lovely face was ashen and her shoulders seemed weighted by all the emotions she was battling.

'Are you sure you're OK to do this?' Cristy asked carefully.

Sadie nodded and attempted a closed-lip smile. 'Does it make sense to say that I want to try and put it behind me?' she asked. 'Obviously that can't happen yet, but talking it through with the police, and with my . . . family, and now with you . . .' Her voice broke and she lowered her head to take a moment.

'Is anyone there with you?' Cristy asked.

'Yes, Jasper, Evie and Anna. Dad and Lukas have popped over to the hotel, but they should be back soon. Anna's been the very best friend anyone could wish for throughout all of this. I'm really going to miss her when Jasper and I make the move to Florida, but she's promised to come and visit and I expect I'll be back and forth myself for a while.' She stopped, looking slightly bewildered, as though talking about the future was an alien concept when her whole life could be about to implode.

'There's a lot to sort out,' she continued, 'and it'll probably take some time to get everything straight . . .' She touched a hand to her mouth as it trembled. 'I wonder who'll want to buy the villa after what happened there.'

Knowing how scattered and even irrational a person's mind could be following a trauma, Cristy said, 'We're already recording, so whenever you're ready to start talking us through last Thursday night . . . Just take your time.'

Sadie nodded, inhaled another deep breath and glanced off to her right where, presumably, the others were watching and listening and lending their moral support.

SADIE: 'I got a call from Mia about eight o'clock – actually it was five past, according to my phone – the police checked. All she said was, "I think it's time we talked. If you can come now there's something I want to show you, but please come alone." My first thought was of what had happened to you when you went to see her – the noose and everything. I was afraid she might do the same to me, so we decided that Jasper should go with me regardless of what she'd said. Then, at the last minute, I realized that if anyone else was there she might start putting on a crazy act, the way she does. With only me as an audience, I felt she'd be more likely to behave . . . I want to say rationally, but I'm not sure it's the right word. Anyway, it's why I ended up going alone.

'When I got there the front door was open. I called out as I went in, knowing she probably wouldn't hear me if she was in the kitchen, but then she answered and I realized she was in Lottie's rooms. I'm not sure why that spooked me – I guess it was because she so rarely goes in there and after everything . . .'

Sadie pressed a hand to her mouth, as though steadying her lips, then sucked in a breath and pushed on.

SADIE: 'I wondered if maybe she'd found something else, another bombshell to hit me with, and because I was afraid of what it could be I almost turned around and left again. Now I wish I had, but I had no way of knowing what she was planning, so I braced myself and went to find her.

'She was on one of Lottie's sofas, surrounded by what turned out to be the contents of Lottie's desk and cabinets. She'd pulled it all out . . . Photographs, files, letters, old notebooks, postcards . . . I have no idea why she'd done it, it didn't seem to make any sense, even less so when she told me she was looking for Lottie's will.

'I reminded her that Lottie was dead and the will was probably locked up in a lawyer's vault somewhere, but I don't think she was listening. She just kept picking up the papers and dropping them, not really seeming to search, just . . . dropping. I went to try and help her up, but she pulled back so sharply that I almost stumbled over her. Then she started to cry, big howling sobs, that made me cry too. I sat down with her and held her . . . I tried telling her that everything would be all right . . . I promised we wouldn't share what was in the journals, that she was safe. She begged me not to leave, and I felt so awful, so sorry for her, that I wanted to say I wouldn't, but . . . Obviously, I wish I had lied now, told her what she wanted to hear, but I had no idea what was in her mind, how she'd probably already planned what she'd do if I refused her. She didn't give up right away, she started telling me that I'd inherit everything if I stayed, that the entire estate would be mine . . . I told her that it wasn't about that, I didn't care about money, but she shouted over me saying that all I had to do was send Gabe and Lukas away and stop making up stories about her and Lottie.

'I said we should go and make some tea and continue our chat in the kitchen. I thought that was happening, I really did. She was with me, all the way to the door, and then suddenly she wasn't. I turned around and saw her scrabbling at the French doors . . . She tore them open and half-fell out onto the balcony. I raced over, but she was already leaning into the railings, tilting forward, arms wide apart as if she was going to fly. I grabbed her, but she snatched herself free . . . She said if I touched her again she really would jump, so I held back, not knowing what else to do. Her back was turned, I couldn't see her face, but I heard what she was saying. She said, "Why did you do this to me? Why, Lottie? Why?" Then she looked at me and said, "*You* have done this to me. *You.* Let my death be on your conscience. See how you like it," and then she . . .'

As Sadie started to cry Jasper came to put his arms around her. Cristy and the others watched quietly, almost numbly, as the scenario she'd described continued to play in their minds, the horror of those final moments resonating in all their ugly and vindictive power.

SADIE: 'The stupid thing is, I couldn't believe she'd done it. I thought . . . it was some kind of trick and she was . . . I don't know where I thought she was. I just couldn't accept that she really had thrown herself over. I made myself go to the railings and look down . . . It was too dark to see anything, but I could hear the sea, and this . . . this strange sort of whining . . . I thought it was her, then I realized it was me. I ran back inside and called the others . . . They came as fast as they could, but there was nothing anyone could do. She'd gone, and I was . . . I was hardly able to speak I was in such a state . . . I kept seeing her going over. I couldn't get it out of my mind.

'Then the police arrived, and the coast guard . . . I can't remember the exact order of things, but I know I probably wasn't very coherent when I tried to explain what had happened. A doctor turned up and gave me a shot of something and the next thing I knew I was here at the lodge and it was morning. The police came to see me again, they've questioned Dad and Lukas as well . . . There are so many questions . . . I know they probably don't mean to make us feel guilty, but I do anyway. Those awful words, "Let my death be on your conscience. See how you like it." They keep going round and round in my head. I mean, I know I'm not to blame for what she did, but the fact that she wants me to think I am . . . Through most of my life she's been kind and generous, devoted . . . eccentric, yes, and unpredictable, but always there for me, no matter what . . . So I do blame myself now, because she's a truly good person in her heart, and I brought all this on us by making her think she wasn't enough – by trying to find out who I really am when being her niece should have been the best and luckiest thing in the world. And it was, it really was. There was just something in me that needed to know the truth. I wish she could have understood that, but it made her angry and afraid . . . Of course we know why now, but she was so lonely and lost without Lottie and I didn't properly recognize it. I just dismissed her feelings and pressed ahead with what I wanted, telling myself it would be all right in the end, that she'd come to terms with everything and maybe even embrace my family when she finally met them. How naïve and selfish I am.'

Cristy watched her closely, tears of grief and self-recrimination shining in Sadie's eyes and causing her mouth to quiver.

SADIE: 'Please don't think I'm not grateful for everything you've done to help me, for giving me this incredible chance to share my story with your hundreds of thousands of listeners around the world. Is it OK to thank them for all the messages of understanding and encouragement they've sent my way over the last few weeks? I don't know how anyone's going to feel once they know how much my search has cost my aunt. Maybe they'll think it wasn't worth it, or they'll decide that she shouldn't have held back on me. I still can't get to grips with how I see it, but I do know that sometimes terrible things happen and it's only with the benefit of hindsight that we can see how they might have been done differently. You know I'm talking about what they did to my mother now, but please don't use it.'

She stopped again, and as she dabbed her eyes, Cristy glanced at Connor to see if he was still recording. Receiving a nod, she asked Sadie if she was OK to continue.

SADIE: 'I think so. I mean, no, but yes . . . Oh God, it's all still so mixed up and awful and strange . . . I keep thinking I should hate her but I don't. I just feel desperately, desperately sad for her.'

EVIE: (out of shot) 'Maybe that's enough for now? She's been through a terrible ordeal and I'm not sure that reliving it, over and over, is doing her as much good as she seems to think.'

Signalling for Connor to stop recording, Cristy waited for Sadie to look at her through the camera and said, 'We really appreciate you sharing everything with us the way you have, Sadie. I know it's been difficult to do and things probably won't get any easier for quite a while, but I have no doubt you'll find the strength and courage to embrace your new life with all the integrity and honesty you've shown throughout this series.'

Forcing a smile through her tears, Sadie said, 'I'm going to miss you so much. You've been like family these past few weeks . . . I feel as though I've known you for years. I hope we'll always be in touch.' She sobbed on a breath. 'I'm not sure when we'll speak again, but if you need any more for the series you know where to find me.'

Minutes later, after the screen had gone dark, and the random sounds from outside the office began to fade back in, Cristy looked at the others and wondered if they were all thinking the same as her.

# CHAPTER THIRTY-TWO

'I don't believe her,' Cristy stated, throwing a pen onto her desk and sitting back in her chair, angry and frustrated, and alive to the repercussions of her own doubts already gathering force.

Clove and Jacks regarded her, wide-eyed.

Connor seemed still to be processing it all.

'What exactly don't you believe?' Clove asked, clearly needing to understand what she'd missed.

'Any of it,' Cristy replied, with a dismissive wave at the screen. She truly didn't like how she was feeling, wished it would stop, but it was there and she couldn't shake it. 'In fact,' she continued, 'the only verifiable truth in Sadie's story was the time Mia called her, because it was registered on her phone. We'll never know what Mia actually said when she rang, any more than we'll ever know what really happened at the villa, because there's no one to corroborate any of it, and nor will there ever be.'

Carefully, Jacks said, 'So you think she made all that shit up because . . .'

'. . . she could,' Connor finished for him. He looked at Cristy, making it clear that he was with her on this.

'Are you serious?' Clove cried. 'Are you actually saying you think it was a push, not a jump?'

Cristy nodded. Yes, that was what she thought, much as she might not want to.

'But why? What did Sadie say to make you think that?'

'What she just told us,' Cristy replied, 'had been carefully thought out and there's no doubt it was convincing. I could even swallow it myself if it weren't for the fact that I just *know* in my gut that she wasn't telling the truth. For whatever reason, it's serving her best now to have Mia out of the way.'

Since they all had experience of Cristy's hunches bearing out, no one argued. 'I don't see we'll ever have a way of proving anything,' Connor said, 'and I guess there's a chance she didn't intend for things to end the way they did – Mia called her, remember – but either something was said . . .'

'Or Mia showed her something,' Cristy put in.

'And whatever it was Sadie – lost it!'

'Jesus,' Clove muttered, slumping back in her chair as if all the wind had gone out of her. 'I mean, I can see where you guys are coming from, but . . . *Really*? After all the swearing that she doesn't want revenge, that she still owes her aunt for a wonderful childhood . . . It couldn't all have been lies. Could it?'

Cristy was asking herself the same question: could it all have been an act? Had Sadie known about the journals and her aunts' part in her mother's death right from the start? Was it possible the whole thing had been an elaborate, near faultless manipulation designed to punish Mia and provide herself with a cover, a victim role even, so she'd . . . what? End up with everything?

The girl Cristy had come to know wasn't that devious or coldly calculating, she had a heart, an innate and wrenching need of the family that should have been hers . . .

'Cristy?' Connor prompted.

Quickly assimilating, she found, to her dismay, that she was no closer to believing the story Sadie had just told. 'I'll concede,' she said, 'that Mia might have been in Lottie's rooms when Sadie got there, and it's possible there was paperwork everywhere, although that could have been staged after the event to support her story. It's highly likely they talked, or argued, got into a terrible fight about something, most likely the journals, and Mia ended up saying or doing something that pushed Sadie over the edge – poor choice of words, but you get my meaning. It's the timing of it all that I'm having the biggest problem with, and the way she just delivered her version of events.'

'It was too pat,' Connor agreed. 'And I agree about the timing. Why would Mia jump now when Sadie was promising to protect her from the real damage the journals could do? Sure, she didn't want Sadie to leave, but taking her own life to try and stop her? What kind of sense does that make? OK, we know she was nuts, but she wasn't as far gone as she kept trying to make out, so I'm going to say that something happened to blow everything wide open in a way that . . . Actually, I've no idea what it might have done, but we do know that Mia will never be able to tell us.'

Feeling her heart clench around the truth of that, Cristy said, 'Her suicide threats play very neatly into Sadie's narrative now, and *we*, as luck would have it, are key witnesses to the fact that her aunt was mentally unstable and threatening to do away with herself.'

'So you reckon she could have been playing us along ever since she met you?' Clove cried incredulously. 'Is that what you're saying? Like she had some gross manipulation thing going?'

Cristy's distaste for her own fears showed. Then, out of nowhere, she was picturing Sadie's reaction when she'd seen her father and uncle for the first time in over twenty years. It was a reminder of how deeply she'd felt for Sadie, for them all, in those moments.

'I'm prepared to believe,' she said, 'that Sadie didn't know about Gabe and Lukas before the series started. In fact, I'll go as far as to say that right up to when we found them in Florida it was highly likely the search for her roots was as genuine and heartfelt as she portrayed it.'

'But?' Connor prompted.

She shook her head, wishing that she wasn't seeing things the way she was. 'It was very soon after discovering she wasn't alone in the world, that she "found" Lottie's journals. So was the timing of that simply coincidental, or had she been waiting for the right time to use them?'

'Shit,' Connor murmured. Then, 'Who the fuck is that girl?'

Long moments passed with no one attempting to answer the question.

In the end Clove said, 'So where the eff does this leave us?'

Connor shrugged. 'Well, whatever happens next,' he said, 'it still remains one hell of a story – putting the likelihood of us being strung up like turkeys to one side. *Abducted child murders her multi-millionaire captors and walks off with all the dosh*. This is presuming she messed with Lottie's meds, the way Mia claimed.'

'Seen through that lens,' Cristy said, 'you're right, it is a great story – if only we could tell it that way.'

'I wonder if the injunction will be lifted now,' Clove said. 'We could tell it then.'

'Small point,' Jacks said, 'actually, fucking great big one really, *does* Sadie get all the dosh?'

'I presume so,' Cristy replied.

'Whether she does, or doesn't,' Connor said, 'we have to ask ourselves if we're sitting here crediting her with more . . . *malice* and powers of cunning than she's actually capable of?' As Cristy's eyes came to his, he said, 'It's not the way we've seen her until now, so we have to put it out there that we could be wrong.'

No one commented, in fact there seemed no more to say for the moment as the reality of how they might have been duped spread all its ghastly ramifications over their hard-earned reputations, and their futures.

In the end, Connor said, 'Time's running down on prepping the last episode so we need to start making decisions. I say we record as many accounts as we can of what happened last Thursday night – police, coast guard, David if he's up for it – and then follow up with Sadie's version of what went down. It's all we've got, so it's all we can do.'

The silence that followed showed how unenthused they all felt.

'Getting away with murder is one thing,' Clove grumbled. 'Pulling one over on us is another altogether.'

Cristy almost smiled. After a moment she said, 'I know, it's disappointing to end with "did she jump, or was she pushed" when we're all thinking the way we are, but it's not a bad ending for the series. As Iz pointed out everyone's already asking the question . . .' She stopped, frowned and looked at Connor. 'Call up the last episode and go to where Sadie reads the journals to Mia. I'd like to listen to it again.'

*

By five the following afternoon the so-called grand-finale was more or less ready for release – just a few sound edits to smooth over and the closing dialogue between Cristy and Connor to add. Although no one was experiencing the high that generally whooshed them to the end of a series, they were all agreed that listening to Sadie's reading of the journals again had straightened a few things out in their minds and allowed them to pack a bigger punch to their closing than most would be expecting.

With some time to spare while the techies took over, Cristy nipped out to meet Matthew at the Harbourside Kitchen. He'd texted earlier practically begging to see her before he left for Heathrow later – he was flying to LA early in the morning. It was a meeting she could do without, knowing he was probably going to try to persuade her to go with him, but she didn't quite have the heart to let him go with no more than a curt *Bon voyage* on the phone when she knew how much he was dreading the trip.

'Thanks for coming,' he said, as she joined him at a window table. 'I know this is a busy time for you, especially with it being the last episode . . . Everything good with it? Happy with the way it's ending?'

'Sort of,' she replied, unfastening her coat, but keeping it on. 'Is this the coffee I ordered?'

Matthew nodded and pushed it towards her, and then managed to look sad, probably because he was.

As she watched him she could feel the scrutiny of those on neighbouring tables who'd probably recognized him, possibly her as well, but she deliberately avoided eye contact. Instead, she found herself seeing him as the man she'd always loved, the father of her children, the husband she'd always trusted and respected and had fully believed she'd spend the rest of her life with, until he'd become the bastard who'd cheated on her and broken her heart. It might all be in the past now, but she couldn't deny that it still had the power to hurt her. Just as his angst could move her, the way it was now, proving, as if she didn't already know, that there was still a connection between them, and probably always would be.

Clearing his throat, and making an attempt to sound cheerful, he said, 'I've already spoken with a nannying agency, so someone should be in place by the time I get back with Bear.'

Feeling for how worried he was about trying to cope on his own, she said, 'That's good. You're going to need someone to help out while you're at work.' She could say more, so very much more, but she was afraid she might end up offering herself as a back-up. 'How much time are you taking off?' she asked.

'Two weeks is all I could manage, having been in LA over Christmas. Hayley's said she'll try to come down for a few days mid-March, and Aiden's obviously going to be around. Not that I'll be expecting him to babysit with his exams coming up, and I didn't get into it being good practice for him. He keeps telling me we'll cope, which kind of suggests he's not planning to decamp on me and come to you full time.'

Moved by the children's efforts to support their father, and feeling guilty for not doing the same, Cristy found herself saying, 'I'm sure I'll come to visit too.'

He looked at her in surprise and with so much hope that she immediately wished she could take the words back. 'Will you?' he said. 'You're welcome, any time, you know that.'

'I just hope there aren't going to be two babies by May,' she said, 'or whenever Pearl's is due . . .'

'I'm sure that one will live with her and her parents,' Matthew put in quickly.

Suspecting he was right, she said, 'Shame they're standing by their daughter's decision to put off a DNA test until after the birth. You'd think they'd want to know themselves who the father is.'

'I'm starting to get the impression that young Pearl calls most of the shots in that family.'

Thinking of what an awful girl she sounded, and how bloody unfortunate it was going to be if she, thanks to a few quick shags with Aiden, ended up being permanently in their lives, Cristy said, 'Let's talk about it some more when you're back. Maybe by then the other boys will have told their parents so we can join forces to put the pressure on . . .' She broke off and groaned aloud. *Stop with the intimidation.*

Matthew put a hand over hers as he said, 'Whatever happens we'll work it out,' and she was reminded of how much comfort she used to take from this very gesture, and those very words, for he always had seemed to find the answers one way or another. He was a different man now though, thanks to his own schizoid aberrations, so much as she might want to lean on him, or at least trust him, she knew she couldn't.

Instead of taking her hand away, she turned it in his and linked their fingers. 'You know you'll always mean the world to me, don't you?' she said, meaning it. 'Apart from all the times I want to brain you, of course, but I need you to understand that even if I weren't with David now, there really is no going back for us.'

He swallowed as he nodded, and his voice was unsteady as he said, 'He's a lucky bloke, I just hope he knows it.' He removed his hand and picked up his coffee. 'So, I won't ask you to come with me tomorrow,' he said, as if only coming to the decision now, 'but if you and David would like to join me out there before I come back . . . OK, de-lulu, as Aiden calls it.'

Breaking into a laugh, she said, 'Do you honestly think David would even want to?'

He shrugged. 'I thought we got along pretty well when we met.'

'Which is good, I'm glad you did, but it doesn't mean he wants to be your best buddy, or go on holiday with you.'

'His loss.' He thought about that. 'Actually it's mine, but hey, as long as you and I stay friends and you understand that I'm ready to take you back any—'

'You're married,' she interrupted, 'and now would be a good time to remember that. I take it Marley will still be in LA when you get there? She hasn't gone to Santa Fe yet?'

'Not as far as I know. Well, someone has to be taking care of Bear, and last time we spoke it was her.' He sighed heavily. 'And soon it's going to be me. Do you think I might be able to rename him before I give him back?'

'You can always try,' she smiled, checking the time. 'I'm sorry, but I have to go, we'll be uploading soon and then, I guess, it won't be long before we find out what the public at large thinks of the series finale.'

'Any surprises in store?' he asked, dropping a twenty on the table as they stood up.

'One or two.'

As they left together Cristy was aware that they were still being watched, and once outside, probably because she knew it would mean something to him, she kissed him on both cheeks.

'Have a good flight,' she said, 'and message to let me know when to expect you back.'

'I will,' he promised.

As she started towards the office she could feel his loneliness and regrets as if they were stretching out between them, even trying to pull her back. She kept going, only turning at the last to give him a wave, but to her surprise he'd gone – and for one peculiarly disorientating moment it was as though he'd left her all over again.

*

An hour later everyone was gathered in the office, drinks in hands, feet up on desks or chairs as they listened to the closing minutes of the pod. Sadie was thanking the *Hindsight* team for the 'incredible chance' they'd given her to share her journey, 'with your hundreds of thousands of listeners around the world . . . Sometimes terrible things happen and it's only with the benefit of hindsight that we can see how they might have been done differently.'

'Neat how she slipped the series title in there,' Harry commented dryly.

Cristy nodded and continued listening to her own voice as she began winding things up.

CRISTY: 'So there we have Sadie's final words on the search for her roots, the surprises and joy it brought her along the way, the confusion, frustration and sadness – and last of all the way it resulted in the untimely and tragic death of her aunt. I wonder if you're finding yourselves as moved by her retelling of what happened at the villa that fateful night as we were when we first heard it. It must have been terrible for her, having no one there to support or guide her, or to help persuade Mia not to jump. I'm sure the trauma of it will stay with her for a very long time.'

CONNOR: 'I have no doubt of it. We don't know whether or not Sadie and Mia talked about Janina that night, but it's hard to imagine they didn't, considering what Sadie found in Lottie's journals. As the key points remain unavailable to us we still can't share any details, but what we know already is that Lottie met Janina and Gabe while they were in Guernsey. You might have seen the photographs on our website of them in a café.'

CRISTY: 'The fact that Janina lost her life not long after the pictures were taken could be put down to a tragic accident, caused perhaps by careless driving on dangerous roads that she was unfamiliar with. Or did someone force her over the edge? Matis Albescu, her old tormentor? There's no evidence of him being on the island at that time, and why would he want her dead instead of returned to the captivity he'd kept her in for the previous five years?'

CONNOR: 'As we've read the journals we believe we do know what happened to Janina, as does Sadie, of course, and we understand why she's choosing not to share the details publicly. That could change now that her aunt Mia is no longer with us to be hurt by the revelations, and if it does we'll certainly let you know.'

CRISTY: 'Before we go we can reveal that questions have arisen around the way Lottie Winters died back in 2020. They were posed to us by Mia days before she died. I'm afraid we can't be specific about what was said, nor can we say for certain that Mia was thinking straight when she brought the matter up. It's just left that lingering doubt in our minds over what might have happened to cause Lottie's collapse when her heart medication had allowed her to live a full and healthy life until suddenly it didn't.'

CONNOR: 'Naturally we wish Sadie – or Sasha as she'd now like to be known – all the happiness she deserves with her new family, and I'm sure you do too. We hope to be back later in the spring with a brand-new series, a whole new crime to unravel and hopefully solve.'

CRISTY: 'For now we'd like to thank our sponsors for making this production possible, and all of you for listening . . .'

As Connor faded out the sound, Meena let her breath go in a long, loud exhale of amazement and said, 'Well, a redefinition of subtle, if ever I heard one. I can't wait to see how all that plays out when it reaches the parts most other pods wouldn't dare to go. *It must have been terrible for her, having no one there to support or guide her, or to help persuade Mia not to jump*. Wow, if no one guesses from that what you think then they're not paying attention.'

'Did Sadie know you were going to talk about the journals like that?' Jodi asked, clearly surprised and impressed. 'I mean, you didn't say what the missing parts are, but you'd have to be an idiot not to work it out.'

Cristy shook her head, and felt a quick pang of unease as she tried to imagine how Sadie, Gabe and Lukas might respond when they heard the insinuations, never mind what she'd said about Lottie's death. She'd yet to hear what David thought of the episode, having sent him a copy just before the upload.

'How do you think Sadie's going to react?' Iz asked, glancing up from her phone.

'She's lucky we didn't go any further than we did,' Connor retorted.

'Everyone's been asking, "Did she jump, or was she pushed?" since the last ep,' Jacks put in. 'All this will do is create more volume.'

'Because you're convinced she actually did push her aunt over?' Iz grimaced as they all looked at her. 'Sorry. Just needing to be clear.'

Connor eyed her warily. 'We are, but if you're thinking of putting our suspicions into some kind of press release, rein yourself in. We've got no evidence to support them and I guess there's still an outside chance we could be wrong.'

'What, you?' Jodi teased. 'Never let it be said.'

Connor crooked an eyebrow, and downed the rest of his drink. 'Any more going?' he asked, holding out his glass.

'Coming right up.' Iz headed for the fridge. 'I'm so happy to be celebrating with you all,' she declared in a burst of exuberance. 'It's been a brilliant series in so many ways, and with all the interviews we've got lined up over the next few weeks . . . The advertisers are going to carry on fighting for space forever more. That's the great thing about pods, isn't it, there's no actual end to their lives. Unlike poor Mia and Lottie. Which reminds me, how *do* you think Lottie died? Was it really suspicious? Could Sadie actually have been behind it?' Her cheeks were so flushed with excitement and her tongue running on so loosely that Cristy had to wonder if she was actually connecting with what she was saying.

'Just imagine, if it turns out she offed both the aunts!' Iz gushed elatedly. 'There won't be any Florida for her then, that's for sure. And we, on *Hindsight*, will have exposed it . . .'

'Exactly what part of reining in did you not get?' Connor interrupted. To Cristy he said, 'Do you have to be somewhere? You keep checking the time.'

'I'm meeting Robert Brinkley at seven-thirty,' she replied. 'He's leaving at the weekend and asked if we could get together before he goes.'

'The drop-dead gorgeous heart surgeon?' Jodi teased.

'Who was in love with Lottie,' Clove added. 'Do you know what he wants to see you about?'

'I think just to say goodbye. I've put the journals on a memory stick so he can read what she wrote about him. Before you ask, no he doesn't have the crucial entries, and no, we won't be adding his starring role to the website. It's not relevant for one thing, and they're way too . . . personal.'

'Amazing, isn't it, the stories behind the stories,' Iz commented thoughtfully. 'There's so much the public doesn't get to see or hear about that they'd probably find every bit as fascinating as the main theme. I remember thinking that when I listened to your last series, the one about David . . . Actually, that reminds me,' she said, looking suddenly worried as she turned to Cristy. 'I've had a few calls about you guys, wanting to know if it's true that you're seeing one another. Obviously, I'm denying all knowledge, but frankly all that's really surprising here is that no one's cottoned on to it sooner.'

Dismayed, while knowing it had always been inevitable, Cristy said, 'Let's just feel thankful it's not happening in the middle of a series.'

'Wait till they find out he was in Florida with you,' Connor grinned. 'Anyway, the fact that Sadie and her aunts live in Guernsey should have flagged it up at the get-go. Just goes to show that not everyone's paying attention.'

'They will once they know you're getting it on with the man you cleared of a triple murder,' Harry commented dryly. 'What?' he demanded as Meena scowled at him darkly. 'I'm right, aren't I?'

'You are,' Cristy told him.

'It's your phraseology that needs some work,' Meena chided. 'Anyway, aren't we going for an end-of-term dinner at The Ivy? If we are, we ought to be on our way.'

'I'll just be a few minutes late,' Cristy told her. 'And I suggest we turn our phones off for the evening unless we want to deal with Sadie and her family tonight.'

'Talking of phones,' Jacks said, 'I'm picking up your old one tomorrow. I'm not sure what they found yet, but apparently there was something and the advice I'm getting at the moment is that you should abandon the handset and the number altogether.'

'Really?' she said, not sure whether to be alarmed by that or not. 'Did they trace the stalker?'

'I'll know more when I go there, but the good news is, you're already up and running with a new phone, so nothing more to worry about.'

*

'Well, that was a very close sail to the wind,' David commented dryly when Cristy called after saying goodbye to Robert at the White Lion in Clifton. It had been an unexpectedly emotional parting, with him glad to receive the memory stick and her still sympathizing with his loss of a woman he'd so clearly loved. She hadn't told him about Mia's claims regarding Lottie's death, there was no point when it was doubtful anyone would ever be able to prove it.

'I know you warned me it might ruffle a few feathers,' David continued, 'but I confess I wasn't expecting anything like that. Have you heard from Sadie since it aired?'

'Not a word.' She stepped off the kerb to cross into Princess Victoria Street. 'Have you?' she asked.

'No, but Anna's had quite a lot to say about it.'

Cristy winced. 'Do I want to know?'

'Probably not, but I expect she'll tell you herself once she's managed to get hold of Sadie.'

'So she hasn't spoken to her either?'

'She keeps trying. I guess you know what you're doing, so you have to be aware that you could be facing a whole lot of trouble over this. OK, you didn't outright accuse her of anything, but the implications are clear and I'd be amazed if Lukas isn't already talking to a lawyer.'

'You could be right, but think about it. If they start kicking up a fuss they'll only draw more attention to it and I'm not sure they'll want to do that. Dealing with flak from social media is one thing, getting lawyers involved could take it to a whole other level.'

'OK, but tell me, do you seriously think Sadie was behind both her aunts' deaths? Because I have to say, it's a hard one for me.'

'I understand that, but once you've had time to think about it you might find it's not so far-fetched. The trouble is, we'll never be able to prove it.'

'OK, well I guess we have to wait and see what happens over the next few days. As you say, giving it more oxygen probably isn't the way to go so you might not hear anything from them. Where are you now? I can hear traffic.'

'On my way to meet the others at The Ivy. Wish you were here.'

'Well, I can't make it happen tonight, but it turns out I need to be in London on Friday, so I thought, when my meeting's over, I could take a train to Bristol and fly back to Guernsey on Sunday or Monday. Will that work for you?'

Loving the thought of seeing him again so soon, Cristy said, 'Even if it didn't I'd make sure it did. Oh, and by the way, I should probably warn you that there's been some press interest in our relationship. Cristy Ward falls for man she helped clear of murder, that sort of thing.'

'OK, I like the falling-for bit, and I guess we were always going to be outed at some point. Pretty amazing, in fact, that it hasn't happened before now. It's not as if we've put much effort into hiding things.'

'We haven't,' she agreed. 'Maybe we need to talk to Iz about how best to play it, whether we want to brazen it out and give someone an exclusive, or beg for privacy, or something in between.'

'I'll be guided by you, or Iz. Why not set something up for when I'm there, if she's going to be around?'

'I'll talk to her tonight and let you know. I should go now, I'm at the restaurant. We're going to turn our phones off, by the way, so if there is any blowback from Sadie and family tonight, we won't have to deal with it until tomorrow.'

# CHAPTER THIRTY-THREE

SADIE: 'You can choose to use this video in a pod, or on your website, or maybe you won't use it at all, we'll leave it up to you. We just want to express our disappointment and hurt – yes it was very hurtful – that you chose to end the series the way you did.'

Cristy's eyes moved carefully between the three faces on the screen, Gabe and Lukas either side of Sadie who was making no secret of the fact that she was reading from a pre-prepared script. Each of them appeared solemn and, on the parts of Gabe and Lukas, perhaps bemused by the fact that they were having to make this video at all. They'd sent it half an hour ago, with a follow-up text alerting Cristy to the fact that it was attached to an email. She'd waited until she was at the office before opening it and this was now the second time she and Connor had watched it. Clove was there too; Jacks had rung to say he was running late but would be in by eleven.

SADIE: 'I don't understand why you felt the need to do what you did. I thought we'd become friends over the past few weeks, certainly I trusted you and, as you know, I gave you virtually unlimited access to my life, my thoughts, all my emotions, and my story. I totally believed you would treat your findings, and me, with sensitivity and respect. Throughout our time together it seemed my judgement was sound, you were kind, supportive, and always careful about detail, as well as mindful of my feelings. I fully trusted your honesty and integrity, and never thought for a moment that you would end up using my aunt's death, and my bereavement, to sensationalize your podcast the way you have. The question of whether or not Mia was pushed to her death will now always hang over me. I don't deserve that, and I can't believe that you think I do.

'We all know that you have no evidence to back up your insinuations – you can't have as none exists. You have framed them in such a way as to paint me in the very worst of lights and I'm sure that in your hearts you know I am not the person you are making me out to be. It has been a difficult and often painful journey for me to get to where I am now, but working with you, believing you were on my side every step of the way, was what helped me to keep going. Now, thanks to you, I have my father and uncle and I couldn't be happier about that. But they are as shocked and upset by your betrayal – yes, that's how we see it – as I am.'

LUKAS: 'We won't be taking any action against you, although of course we could. We've decided that it would only cause further heartache to go that route. Perhaps it will serve us better for your actions to be recognized, over time, for what they are: shamefully self-serving.

'We have discussed making this video available to other press outlets and that option, of course, remains open to us. However, before we do that, we'd like to give you the opportunity to go on the record with an apology for the way you misled your listeners in the latest podcast and with an admission that, in spite of knowing your implications were without foundation, you went ahead with them anyway in order to create more interest in the series. If you are prepared to make a statement to that effect, we will not publish this video.'

As the screen darkened Cristy turned to the whiteboard where photographs of Sadie, Janina, Mia and Lottie were lined up along the top. Three dead, only one still alive: the child on the beach who'd grown into a beautiful and, as it turned out, very astute young woman. And now, presumably, a very rich one too.

*But what if they were wrong? What if Mia really had jumped?*

'There's no way we can do what they're asking,' Connor stated. 'And no reason why we should.'

'I say we call their bluff,' Clove urged. 'Do nothing, let everything stay as is . . . If they want to put out their little statement they can, I don't see it making any difference to the way people are seeing things. Listeners know they're not getting a full picture of the journals, and now they have a pretty damned good idea why. Half of them are already posting about it, they're even outright saying Sadie killed her aunt for revenge as well as personal gain.'

'All that is true,' Cristy said, turning back to them, 'but I'm afraid she's outmanoeuvred us with this. Its tone, its subtlety and incisive attack on our integrity are powerful enough to do us a lot of damage going forward.'

'But . . .' Clove protested, and stopped when Cristy's hand went up.

'Sadie's right,' Cristy continued, 'we don't have any actual evidence to support why we – to quote her – painted her in the very worst of lights. And by calling our honesty and professional integrity into question – something we should have seen coming – she's opened us up to the kind of scrutiny that'll be hard to withstand.'

'Why?' Clove objected. 'We haven't lied about anything . . .'

'And how could we, in all good conscience,' Connor said, 'have let her last interview run unchallenged when the fact that there is only her version of events absolutely needed to be acknowledged? We wouldn't have been doing our jobs if we hadn't gone for it, no matter how we phrased it. Just about every listener we have would have been calling it out before the episode had chance to finish. Even without the journals they're thinking the sisters did away with Janina, and therein lies Sadie's motive for punishing her aunt in the worst possible way. We had to do it.'

'If that was her motive,' Cristy stated.

Clove and Connor stared at her uncomprehendingly.

'I'm not saying it wasn't,' she explained, 'it would certainly have been a part of it, but without knowing what went on between them prior to Mia's "fall" . . .' She broke off with an impatient sigh, knowing there was no point speculating any further over that now.

'Whatever we might think,' she said, 'if we let them run that video the public will turn, mark my words. We'll be perceived as having treated Sadie Winters badly, or as Lukas put it, in a shamefully self-serving way. And ask yourselves this, where will that leave us with future investigations? Trust is at the very core of what we do. And we all know how spiteful some of the tabloids can be, how hungry they are to bring down success. So as soon as it's known a new series of the "increasingly popular *Hindsight*" is underway, out will come the Sadie Winters video to show how we treat people.'

'Well, I for one am not up for putting out the kind of statement they're asking for,' Clove declared defiantly. 'Apart from anything else, it's too soon. It would be a knee-jerk on our part when we still don't know how the police might have reacted to the pod. For all we know they've already pulled her in for further questioning.'

'You're right,' Cristy agreed and reached for her phone. 'Let me speak to David, see if he can find out what's going on over there. If the investigators are still all over it, it could at least buy us some time.'

*

Almost an hour had passed by the time David rang back.

'I'm putting you on speaker,' Cristy told him, 'Connor and Clove are here.'

'Hey, guys,' David said. 'Here's what I've got. Apparently the detectives have requested sight of the journals. I'm not sure if it was prompted by last night's pod, but I got the impression they were interested to hear your views, and obviously they know you've seen the unpublished entries.

'Not quite as helpful,' he continued, 'was that even if the journals claim that the Winters sisters sent Janina's car off the road, the Procureur – prosecutor – thinks it still might not be seen as a strong enough motive for Sadie to act the way she did. For some it might, but it's felt that a good lawyer would be able to trash the theory in a trial, if it came to that. So, as things stand, the chances of the police acting based on the unreliable nature of the journals alone are not very high.'

Seeing her own disappointment reflected in the others' expressions, Cristy said, 'Well, at least they're not completely throwing it out.' Maybe she wished they were: how hopelessly conflicted she kept feeling over this.

'They're not,' David agreed, 'and actually, there's more. I had a chat with Victor Dubois this morning – you'll remember he's head of the law firm Mia uses – and he told me that it wasn't Mia who sought the injunction on the journals, it was Sadie.'

Cristy stilled as she took this in, trying to work out what it could mean. The most obvious explanation chimed with what Sadie had always said, that she wanted to protect her aunt – after she'd vented her fury by practically demolishing the sitting room and kitchen, of course. But why had she never mentioned she was behind the injunction? She must have known they'd understand, had even been expecting it.

Connor said, 'Remember when we told Mia about the injunction? She seemed not to know what we were talking about.'

It was true, she hadn't, although it was hard to see how that was relevant now when the fact that Sadie hadn't told her didn't change anything . . . Unless . . . Cristy needed to get this straight in her head, could see the reason, almost hear it, but the others were still talking . . .

'Have you heard anything from Sadie or Lukas since last night's drop?' David asked.

'Actually we have,' Connor replied. 'I'll send it over as soon as we're done with this call.'

Cutting across David's response, Cristy said, 'Did Victor Dubois say anything else you can share?'

'Not to do with this, but I'm having lunch with him later if there's anything in particular you'd like me to ask?'

'There is,' Cristy replied. 'I'd like to know if Mia had been in touch with him in the last couple of weeks about her will.'

'Sure. What are you thinking?'

'All kinds of things right now, but getting an answer to that might explain a lot and help us decide how to respond to the video you're about to watch.'

*

‘Hey, team,’ Jacks sang out, going to drop his backpack on his chair and fishing out various objects.

‘You need to see the little gift of a video we’ve received from Sadie and family,’ Clove told him.

‘OK, cool. Here’s your old phone, Cristy. Like I said last night, highly recommended that you abandon it from hereon, but there’s something that came in while it was being worked on that I think you’ll want to hear.’

‘Who’s it from?’ Cristy asked, taking the mobile as if it might burn her. ‘Please tell me it’s not the creep who’s been texting . . .’

‘No more from him,’ Jacks assured her. ‘I mean, I think there were a couple, but Clyde – he’s the one who’s been checking it out – assured me he’s been shut down. Apparently there was some sort of spyware on it that’s gone now, but he doesn’t think it’s worth going with that phone again in case there was something he missed.’

‘OK, fine. We’ll get into how it got there later. Where’s this something you want me to listen to?’

‘Regular voicemail. First one. Is that coffee still hot?’

As he went to fill a mug for himself, Cristy called up the message and put the phone to her ear. Moments later, as she registered what was happening, she felt herself turning faintly dizzy.

‘What is it?’ Connor wanted to know.

Hitting the playback again, and putting it on speaker, she set the phone on her desk so everyone could hear what was happening at the other end of the line. It began with distant, indecipherable voices, and the sound of someone moving around, footsteps, items being shifted. There was some talk, Mia saying she hadn’t been sure Sadie would come, and Sadie asking why she’d think that. Sadie again, ‘Come along, it has to be . . .’ There was more movement followed by Mia saying, ‘We shouldn’t be in here, Lottie won’t like it.’

The gentle rasp of Mia breathing filled the next few minutes and a faint noise that wasn’t possible to decipher. Sadie spoke, but her voice was too far away, too faint for them to make out what she was saying.

Cristy rewound and replayed, but it did no good. She let the message run, and Mia's voice was suddenly and briefly clear as she said, 'What are you doing?'

After that only the occasional words were audible '. . . waiting,' 'mother,' 'afraid'. Mostly it was like a background mumble; they couldn't even tell who was speaking, only that a lot was being said.

Filled with frustration Cristy held the phone out to Jacks.

Taking it, he said, 'I'll do my best, but don't hold your breath.'

*

Almost an hour passed as Cristy, Connor and Clove walked the harbourside, giving Jacks the space to download, enhance, remove, audio-cleanse, test, search for more software, even make a couple of calls for additional expert advice. No one spoke, they were too tense, almost too afraid to share what was going on in their minds, to state what they were expecting, or hoping for. Cristy wasn't even sure she knew, and guessed it was the same for the others. It was best simply to try not to think about it, not to let their imaginations run wild, although of course it was impossible not to.

Finally, Jacks texted to summon them back and as soon as they entered the office he gave them a thumbs up.

The unravelling of relief was almost palpable, as they sank into their chairs and Jacks hit play.

Cristy's eyes widened with amazement and awe as both Mia's and Sadie's voices came through, stripped of the stifling muffle of background sound. It was the audible version of a film being processed, first nothing, then something, then a perfectly intact image. Yes, a few flaws here and there, some words missing . . .

'Stop! Stop!' Cristy cried, as the recording went past the last they'd heard. 'Go back a few seconds.'

Jacks hit the keys and the message picked up where they'd left off.

'We shouldn't be in here, Lottie won't like it,' Mia said.

'Lottie's gone, Mia,' Sadie responded.

A few moments passed. Mia said, 'What are you doing?'

Sadie's voice was further away, but clear enough. 'Waiting for you to tell me why I'm here.'

Mia's next words were lost, until she said, '. . . so please don't go, Sadie . . .'

Long moments of nothing until Sadie spoke, almost inaudibly, '. . . can't ignore what's happened . . . did to my mother. And it was you, wasn't it?'

Tearfully, Mia said, 'Lottie made me. I didn't want to . . .' She either leaned onto the phone, or perhaps her hand covered it for a few moments, before she could be heard saying, '. . . past. Can't we put it behind us?'

'No, Mia, we can't. I'm sorry . . .' Some muffling and echoey distortion until she said, '. . . Why are you afraid? I took out the injunction to make sure you were protected from what you'd done.'

'Yes, that was very good of you, but if you leave . . . I've already told Victor that I want to see him . . .'

Sadie's laugh had no humour. 'Are you about to pull a Lottie on me?'

'What do you mean?'

'If I don't do as you ask – if I don't stay – you'll cut me out of the will? You think it's all about money, don't you, Mia. . . always have. Lottie . . . same. . . had enough.'

There was another long silence before Mia said again, 'What are you doing?'

Sadie's voice was more distant as she replied, 'We need some air in here.'

There was the sound of doors unlocking and what was surely wind whooshing into the room.

Mia cried, 'Sadie! Everything's blowing around . . .'

Closer now, Sadie said, 'I thought you understood that if you changed your will, I would get the injunction lifted, and then everyone would know what you did. I thought you wanted to avoid that, to get away with what you did. And now you're threatening me . . .'

'Let me go. You're hurting my arm.'

'You could go to prison for what you did to my mother. Maybe you should.'

'Please, Sadie, stop. I don't want . . . Don't make me go out there.'

There were the unmistakable sounds of a struggle, Mia sobbing in terror, shouting for Lottie, Sadie grunting with effort, saying, 'It's for the best, Mia. You know it is . . .' Then, 'I don't want you threatening me any more . . . You did it to my mother. Now see how you like it,' and then the terrible, heart-wrenching sound of Mia screaming before the call ended in an abrupt and deadly silence.

'Jesus Christ,' Cristy murmured, clasping her hands to her cheeks. Suspecting was one thing, being proved right another altogether.

'I've never heard anything like that before,' Clove practically wailed. 'It was awful. Shit! I feel like I was there.'

Clearly still shaken, Connor said, 'Maybe there is a God.'

Cristy looked at him.

'I think we have the response to Sadie's video,' he explained.

*See how you like it.* The words kept going round in Cristy's head, along with the horrific image of Mia's final moments. That poor, demented woman, trapped for so many years in the guilt of what she'd done to an innocent girl; she was a murderer herself, but had she really deserved to die like that?

Had Janina?

It was making Cristy feel sick, and strangely exhausted, weighted by all the lies and deceit, the tragedy and the terrible, inexplicable fate that had bound them all together. The note Janina had tucked into her little girl's pocket all those years ago . . . *I know you are good people. Please take care of her until I can come back for her.*

It was too tragic, too awful to think of what had happened when she had come back.

Janina and Sadie, Lottie and Mia. In a sane world they'd never have known one another; in that same sane world Sadie would never have been born. Lottie might have made a life with Robert. Mia might have found someone to love her in the end, and she, Cristy, might not be feeling so wretchedly, painfully mixed up about her own feelings for the girl who had never had the chance to know her mother. Being so close to her own daughter, and in no doubt about how much Janina had loved Sadie, it was tormenting Cristy to think of what Sadie had missed out on – and what was likely to happen to her now.

'Cristy?' Connor said quietly.

She looked up, saw his concern, and for one crazy moment she almost told Jacks to erase the call. In the end, because she had to, she made herself say, 'We don't have a choice, we need to send it to the police.' She nodded to Jacks, an instruction for him to do the honours.

Out of nowhere she thought of Gabe and Lukas and found herself close to tears. This was going to be so devastating for them that she was already regretting bringing Sadie into their lives.

'Why did she do it?' she asked, barely above a whisper. 'She had the journals . . . She was already using them to stop Mia changing her will, and yet she pushed her over anyway. Why? I don't understand it.'

'Because she'd had enough,' Connor replied. 'I'm sure that's what she said. And if there was no more Mia, there would be no more threats, no more anything to stop her from getting – and doing – exactly what she wanted.'

Looking up from his computer, Jacks said, 'It's ready,' and they all fell silent as they waited for Cristy to give the final instruction to press send.

She gave it and closed her eyes. Mia's final moments, and Sadie's fate, were now in the hands of Guernsey's law enforcement officers – there was no going back.

*

Oddly, unnervingly, thirty or more hours passed with no word from anyone. The silence seemed to have a power all of its own, making them feel as though they were holding their breath, hardly daring to move, as they waited for something to happen.

'Someone has to be in touch with us soon,' Cristy remarked to David over a FaceTime call on Thursday evening. A whole week since Mia's death that felt more like a year – and strangely like it had all been a bad dream.

'There's been a lot more police activity in the villa today,' he said, 'and around the cliffs below.'

Picturing it, wondering what they were hoping to find, she said, 'They're surely interviewing Sadie by now. Have you heard anything about that?'

'No, but I do know that Victor Dubois has already told the police he had an appointment set up with Mia for Friday of this week – tomorrow in fact – to discuss a codicil to her will. So it's possible she did mean to cut Sadie off if she refused to stay.'

'I'm pretty sure that was behind it all,' Cristy said.

'Go on,' he prompted.

'We've wondered if Sadie was playing us right from the start – she lied about the pages, remember – but I think she really was just foolish where they were concerned. No, I'm certain everything changed for her when she read the journals to Mia and let rip with her fury. At some point then, or shortly after, she began to realize how useful the journals could be if she took out an injunction that she could hold over Mia. The journals – or the incriminating parts of them – would never be made public as long as Mia never changed her will. And it would probably have worked if Mia hadn't gone ahead and threatened to cut her off again, as she did that night. Whether Sadie decided in that moment to put an end to the threats once and for all, or whether she went to the villa already knowing, even fearing what she was going to do . . . I guess only she knows. But whichever way you look at it, I'm sure, in the end, it was every bit as much about the money as it was about revenge.'

David audibly sucked in air as he considered her thoughts. Finally, he said, 'I can see it, I only wish I couldn't. Are you going to share this with the police?'

'If I'm asked to, but I'm not sure they need anything from me now. The pocket-dial speaks for itself.'

'That's true. I don't suppose Gabe or Lukas have been in touch since they sent the video?'

'No, but I wouldn't expect them to be.'

'And the video's lost all its power now anyway. Or it will once it's known Sadie's under investigation for murder.'

Glancing up as Aiden came into the flat, Cristy said, 'My son has just turned up looking very wet and hungry so I'd better feed him. Are you still coming tomorrow?'

'Of course. I should be in Bristol by six at the latest.'

'Great. Jodi and Connor have invited us for a bite to eat, so maybe take a taxi straight there.'

*

By the time David arrived the following evening, there was still no word out of Guernsey, not from the police, nor Sadie and her family, nor any of David's contacts.

'You'd have thought someone would want to speak to us by now,' Connor remarked, putting a drink in David's hand as Cristy gave a pained look and pointed at the phone while mouthing, *Matthew.*

'We've been discussing doing another pod,' Connor continued, gesturing for David to sit down, 'but we can't use the phone call at this stage. Probably at any stage if it ends up being needed in court – and it obviously will be given everything's going to swing on it. Jody's upstairs with the baby, down any minute.'

'Sounds like Dad's got himself in another fuck-up,' Aiden commented, glancing up from his homework to give David a wave of welcome. 'Good to see you.'

'You too,' David responded.

Connor said, 'Doesn't feel right, leaving everything hanging like this, but unless there's an arrest, better still a charge, we've got nowhere to go, nothing new to say. Series over. I don't suppose Anna's spoken to Sadie, by any chance?'

David shook his head. 'She stopped taking Anna's calls on Wednesday, and since Anna heard Mia's message – I hope you don't mind me sharing, I think we can trust her – she's given up trying. I left another message with my contact at police HQ on the way here, but he either doesn't know what's going on, or he's not in a position to tell me anything yet.'

'You know what we keep wondering,' Aiden piped up, 'is whether or not Gabe and Lukas still believe Sadie's story. You know, that Mia jumped.'

'It's a good question,' David remarked. 'I guess they do if they haven't heard the phone call yet. If they have . . . Well, it'll be very hard for them to take, that's for sure.' He looked at Cristy as she ended her call and closed her eyes in despair. 'What is it?' he asked carefully.

'You're never going to believe this,' she groaned. 'Matthew can't take the baby out of LA. Something to do with when he was arrested after the birth . . . There has to be some sort of hearing before it can happen, and Marley has to be there, but she's already in Santa Fe and is saying she can't leave. So, wait for this, he wants me to fly over there so I can bring the baby out.'

David's eyes widened.

'Don't worry, I told him I have no intention of being arrested for attempted kidnap, or anything like it, and there's no guarantee that won't happen, especially if he, Matthew, is with me. He's suggesting we take different flights, but I've told him that he has to take a reality check and sort this out for himself, because *I* am going to Amanjena next week.'

'Where?' Aiden asked, all ears.

'Morocco,' David answered, still looking at Cristy. 'That soon, huh?'

She shrugged. 'Why not? If the police want to question me I'll be just as contactable over there. Presuming we want to be, and maybe we don't?'

'Hang on,' Aiden interrupted, 'does this leave me going to LA to bail out Dad? I wouldn't mind, I mean LA's great, but I'm kind of busy right now with mocks and everything.'

'Dad's a grown-up,' Cristy reminded him, 'or he sometimes pretends to be, and so, as I said just now, he has to sort this out for himself.'

'Cool. So who's going to take care of me if you're off to Morocco?'

Cristy regarded him askance. 'You're sixteen years old *and* you can cook.'

'You're also very welcome to stay here,' Jodi told him, coming into the room. 'So what have I missed?'

'Dad's up shit creek again,' Aiden told her, 'and Mum and David are planning some sort of romantic . . . Ah, here's Dad now. Just knew he'd call me as soon as Mum knocked him back.' He clicked to answer the phone. 'Hey, my man, how's it hanging with the Bear?'

As the others laughed, Cristy rolled her eyes and said to Connor, 'Are you OK with me going away next week, presuming we can get into the Aman resort?' she added to David.

'We'll try,' he told her.

'That's fine,' Connor replied, 'you just leave all the police enquiries to me, not to mention working the press with Iz . . . She'll probably want to hold my hand through every interview.'

Cristy grimaced. 'You're right, I shouldn't just take off—'

'He's winding you up,' Jodi broke in. 'And anyway, isn't it about time Clove and Jacks got some public recognition for all they do? So why not rope them in for some of the media gigs?'

'We're seeing Iz tomorrow,' Cristy said, 'so we can discuss it with her then. In principle I think it's a great idea, although I think Clove might be more up for it than Jacks.'

'Out of interest,' Jodi said, curling into an armchair with a soda, 'how much is Sadie likely to inherit if things happen to go her way?'

'They can't go her way,' Connor objected. 'It's just not possible now – unless some clever bastard lawyer is managing to pull something out of the hat even as we speak and that's why nothing seems to be happening.'

'We can't rule it out,' David responded. 'In fact, it's highly likely.' To Jodi, he said, 'I don't have any details, but it could be somewhere in the region of forty, even fifty million.'

'Wow,' Aiden gasped, as Jodi choked on her drink.

Cristy said, 'Well, even if there is some clever bastard lawyer on the case who manages to get her out of a murder charge, at least the "Did she jump, or was she pushed?" isn't going away any time soon. She'll always have to live with that. Not that I'm vengeful, you understand, in fact I can't make up my mind from one minute to the next how I feel about it all.'

She was about to go and sit with David when a text arrived on her phone. Presuming it was from Matthew now that he'd apparently finished talking to Aiden she clicked on, wishing she could just ignore him, while not quite having the heart to.

She saw right away that it was from a No Caller ID and as she read the message she started to turn cold. It couldn't be. This was a new phone, almost no one had the number yet, and hadn't they traced and stopped the stalker? It seemed not, because here he was saying, *Hi Cristy, did you miss me? It's lovely to see you again. Are you having a nice evening at Connor's?*

'What is it?' David asked, clearly sensing something was wrong.

She looked up, and seeing his concern quickly smiled. Now wasn't the time to get into this. She'd forward it to Jacks in the morning. 'Nothing,' she said. 'Just more unfinished business. The story of my life these days,' she added with a pointed look at Aiden. He wasn't listening.

Putting her phone aside she arched an eyebrow as she said to David, 'Much more important right now, is there availability at the Amanjena?'

'Looks like the earliest is for a fortnight from next Thursday,' Aiden informed them.

They turned to look at him.

'I've got it here,' he explained, gesturing to his laptop. 'This gaff is the business, Mum. Totally out there. They've only got suites – *pavilions* – with their own private pools – and, listen to this, one of them has *two* bedrooms with—'

'And guess what,' Cristy broke in quickly, knowing exactly where this was going, 'you, my darling, won't be in one of them.'

'I'm not sure we will be either,' David said, reading the message that had just come into his phone. He looked up. 'It's from my contact at police HQ. Apparently Sadie's just been charged, so my guess is you guys will be busy doing other things next week.'

*TWO MONTHS LATER*

BONUS EPISODE

'OK, recording,' Connor announced. 'Over to you.'

CRISTY: 'Hi, it's Cristy.'

CONNOR: 'It's Connor, and welcome to this bonus episode of *Who's That Girl*.'

CRISTY: 'A lot has happened since the series officially ended, but I'm afraid we haven't been in a position to share anything with you until now.'

CONNOR: 'Legal reasons, you understand.'

CRISTY: 'All will soon come clear, but for now, we're going to start with something we don't normally do.'

CONNOR: 'It's very popular on other pods and because we've had so many requests to do the same, we've decided, for this episode only, to share an update on what's been happening to us since Sadie Winters was charged with murder. Should you not be up for hearing our personal chitchat, and no one can blame you for that, please feel free to fast forward now. If you are, here goes: Cristy, you're much more interesting than I am, so why don't you take it away?'

CRISTY: 'Ha! Not true that I'm more interesting, but one of

us has to set the ball rolling. So, what can I tell you that you haven't already read about in the press?'

CONNOR: 'For those who somehow managed to miss the blitz of tabloid fascination with Cristy's love life a couple of months ago, she is now happily involved with the extremely eligible and disgustingly photogenic David Gaudion. You might remember him from our series *Nothing to See Here* in which he was proved not to have committed a triple murder. Great guy, who's helped us quite a bit with *Who's That Girl.*'

CRISTY: 'I have to admit it was much easier, and even more enjoyable, being the focus of a new romance than it was being the pitied victim of a broken marriage, as I was for so long.'

CONNOR: 'Speaking of Matthew Jennings, which we kind of were – FYI he's Cristy's ex, also known as husband of actress Marley Dukes and anchor of TV news – I guess most of you are aware that he became a father again at the beginning of the year.'

CRISTY: 'It was a boy, his name's Bear, and he's currently in the UK bonding with his dad and half-brother, Aiden.'

CONNOR: 'Have you seen much of the baby yourself, Cristy?'

CRISTY: 'Now and again. He's very sweet – aren't all babies. In fact we took him to Guernsey a couple of weeks ago where we all – Matthew, our daughter Hayley and Aiden – spent some time with David and his family.'

CONNOR: 'Amazing. So everyone's good friends and the past is in the past where it belongs?'

CRISTY: 'Something like that. Actually we had some extremely welcome news while we were on the island – Aiden, who is sixteen, is NOT about to become a father. Any parent who's been through similar angst with a teenager will know what a relief it was to find that out.

'You know, Con, I'm really uncomfortable with that, so let's edit it out. No one needs an update on Aiden's careless attitude to sex.'

CONNOR: 'Got it. Noted – and . . . moving on. There was something else going down with you during this time, Cris, do you want to tell us about that?'

CRISTY: 'Yes, I was the victim of a phone stalker and it really wasn't pleasant. In fact it was downright scary at times . . . We're considering giving much more coverage to this truly despicable way of menacing people, even hounding some to their deaths, during a future series. For now I'll just say that in my case, Jacks, one of our researchers, managed to track the stalker down. It turned out to be someone Jacks himself had long trusted to carry out deeper dives into phone and technology issues for the series.'

CONNOR: 'Apparently the guy had some sort of unhealthy fixation on Cristy and Jacks was so upset by it all that he offered to withdraw from the series. Fortunately, we've managed to talk him out of it. He's a fantastic and highly valued member of the team, as is Clover, our other researcher, who will also be on board the next time *Hindsight* sets sail.'

CRISTY: 'So, how about your news, Con?'

CONNOR: 'You know, I reckon we should get into mine at the end, because what everyone out there really wants to hear about now is what happened to Sadie Winters after she was charged with murder.'

CRISTY: 'Sure. Your turn to take it away.'

CONNOR: 'Actually, you have the first link.'

CRISTY: 'Ha! So I have. OK, well, almost as soon as Sadie was remanded in custody for murdering her aunt, we were inundated with requests for as much inside intel as we could share. Most particularly, you wanted to know if we at *Hindsight* had played any part in helping to answer the question of "Did she jump, or was she pushed?"'

CONNOR: 'An electrifying question if ever there was one, and it got so much debate going on our social media channels that for a while there they looked in danger of going into meltdown. Well, the mystery is now solved and we'll be bringing you details later in this episode of *Hindsight*'s role in proving the case against Sadie Winters. It didn't happen in quite the way you might think, and there are others who deserve far more credit than us, namely Mia Winters, and the god-of-mobile-phones. But we'll come on to that.

'For now we're going to address as many of the other questions you've been firing at us as we can. Starting with: "Where was Sadie held in custody?"'

CRISTY: 'The short answer to that is Guernsey Prison – and this is probably a good time to explain, for those keen to know about the island's legal system, that it is basically the same as ours in England. There are a few anomalies, and some different terminology, for example criminal cases are generally presided over by a judge of law – aka bailiff – with between seven to twelve jurats, aka the jury. If you'd like to find out more about the Bailiwick's composition of the court you'll find several helpful links on our website.'

CONNOR: 'I'm sure that most of you will know by now that Sadie entered a plea of guilty to manslaughter due to diminished responsibility. Were we surprised by that? No, not at all. We'd already heard that it was going to happen, and whatever you might think when we play you the evidence we submitted later in the episode, you'll probably agree that there was a plausible case for temporary insanity.'

CRISTY: 'So she avoided a mandatory life sentence and received fifteen years instead with no recommendations, which means she could be out again in less than ten, maybe even sooner than that. We were in court to witness the judgment, and we were also able to record a short interview with her father and uncle after she was taken away. Before we share that with you, let's talk for a minute about Sadie's demeanour during the passing of her sentence: did she show remorse? Shock? Was she emotional? Did she look at anyone? Did she speak at all?'

CONNOR: 'The answers are, yes she appeared quite stricken by what she'd done and shocked, kind of bewildered actually, to find herself where she was. She didn't speak to anyone, and the only person we saw her look at was Cristy.'

CRISTY: 'It was a surreal moment, almost as if time was shifting somehow leaving just the two of us in a space that . . . Well, let's just say it was weird and it still feels weird.'

CONNOR: 'We need more, like what do you think her look was saying?'

CRISTY: 'Actually, nothing at first, it was just . . . empty, and then – I'm still quite blown away by this – she seemed to be feeling kind of sorry for me, as if I was the one to blame for her actions, and she was sad that I was making her pay for them. That's what she made me think, so you see why I say weird.'

CONNOR: 'So she didn't come over as angry, or vengeful, or even a little bit pissed off that you'd caught out her lies?'

CRISTY: 'Not in that minute, no. It was only later, when her lawyer delivered her note, that we got confirmation that she really was – or is – on some other planet. I'll read it out for you.

'"Cristy, I realize now that I should never have trusted you, but we all make mistakes. Being as vulnerable as I was at the time I came to you with an overwhelming need to find my true family, I was perhaps more prone to making them than most. I can see now what easy prey I was for you, and how I continued to be throughout the making of your series.

As I begin to serve a sentence for something you know I didn't do, it will be for you to decide how to live with your conscience. Perhaps you don't have one, so there will be no inner struggle for you. Can I pre-empt any request you might be considering for an interview with me by saying: without trust there can be no further contact. Sasha."'

CONNOR: 'Wow, kind of powerful, definitely delusional – and if she didn't do it, why plead guilty to manslaughter? I guess she'll have some sort of an answer for that, and I'm sure what I'll want to say in response is "*See how you like it*." These are the final words she spoke to her aunt before she pushed her to her death.'

CRISTY: 'We'll play you an actual recording of it in just a few minutes. We'll also be hearing from Sadie's father and uncle about how she is justifying her actions to them.'

CONNOR: 'But before we get too far ahead of ourselves, we thought it would make sense to play you some selected highlights from all six episodes of *Who's That Girl* to bring ourselves back up to speed. We're going to start with the pages, written by Lottie, that kicked the whole thing off when Sadie brought them to Cristy. Incidentally, we only saw a few chapters of that story, Cristy. Do you think there was more, or was the scene when Edwin came to the house as far as Lottie got with her memoir?'

CRISTY: 'If it's true that Mia had all Lottie's computers returned to factory settings after her death, then my guess is this: Lottie could have written more, the entire story even, but then she died and Mia took drastic action to make sure nothing ever saw the light of day.'

CONNOR: 'So Mia knew what Lottie was doing?'

CRISTY: 'It's certainly possible. For all we know Mia wrote some of it herself. She definitely gave the impression of that the first time I spoke to her. What I doubt she knew was that Lottie had printed out the early chapters and hidden them in random places, either to edit, or to make sure a copy still existed if Mia ever went nuts and tried to sabotage things.'

CONNOR: 'Does that lead us to wonder if it was Mia who tampered with Lottie's meds?'

CRISTY: 'It's hard not to wonder that, but we'll never have an answer to it, so we need to edit that last bit out, and get back on script. Pick up with Sadie reading Lottie's account of finding a child on the beach and how it led to all that came after.'

As the pre-prepared insert began to play Connor sat back in his chair to listen, while Cristy and David, finally in Marrakech, did the same poolside. They'd arrived four days ago, and had so far only ventured out of their very private and exotically luxurious pavilion-piscine suite for the occasional meal, or an evening stroll. At the moment, in the lazy heat of the mid-afternoon, they were lying out on their loungers, hands loosely linked over the sound equipment Cristy had set up just before Connor had connected for this bonus recording.

The sun was dazzling, and the heady scents of orange blossom, musk and incense infusing the air seemed to add a sense of unreality to the many voices that had gone into making up the series. Robert and Gita Brinkley; ex-DS Catherine Shilling; Edwin Prosser; Natalie Irwin; Lottie's publisher, Felicity Green; Gabe and Lukas; Mia Winters, even Lottie in her way – and of course Sadie.

Cristy was once again considering, as she had many times over the last few weeks, the words Lottie had written when she'd read the note Mia had found in two-year-old Sadie's pocket. She'd experienced a *confliction of feelings* and this perfectly described Cristy's own response each time she thought of Sadie. There was still anger and despair over what the girl had done, but this was followed all too quickly by a sense of betrayal in itself underpinned by compassion. Sometimes she found herself recalling only the affection she'd felt for the girl, the empathy that had allowed her to connect with her confusion and need, that made her want to turn back the clock and make things right. Without even knowing it she'd developed a maternal sort of feeling towards Sadie, with all the complexity and challenges that entailed.

Now, almost as if it were Hayley at the heart of her confliction, Cristy could feel the confines of Sadie's prison, the shutting down of a young life, the terrible, pointless stifling of so much. And through it all, erupting like sudden tides on a calm day, came surges of guilt, harsh and unforgiving reminders of the part she'd played in putting Sadie where she was. Never mind that she'd had little choice, it wasn't ever going to feel good or satisfactory, or even right, to know that justice had been served when Sadie, her start in life, her upbringing, her motives and her reasoning, were so much more complicated and multi-faceted than the law allowed for.

Cristy guessed all this emotional turmoil was going to be with her for some time, haunting her, testing her conscience and her heart in ways that would serve neither her, nor Sadie. It would simply be a part of who she was going forward, until like all forms of grief it eventually began to lose the power of its hold.

She watched David get up from the lounger, wearing only shorts that he didn't actually need given the privacy of their pool area, and releasing the difficult reflections she took a long, desirous moment to admire his newly acquired tan. It was only when he returned, bringing a pitcher to refresh their cocktails, and regarded her askance, that she realized Connor was cueing her to begin the next stage of recording.

'Yeah, I'm here,' she said, pressing a finger to her earpiece. 'Are you going to lead us back in?'

'Sure thing.'

CONNOR: 'So there you have it, the series in a dozen or more soundbites, but what you still don't have are the so far unshared extracts of Lottie's journals. They are crucial to just about everything and at last we have clearance to use them.'

CRISTY: 'So here they are, read by Sadie herself. Lottie's account of what happened the day Janina, a tragic young mother desperate to reunite with her child, left St Peter

Port to make a rendezvous with Lottie and was never seen again.'

Here Sadie's voice took over, conveying tenderness, passion, angst, confusion, horror, as she lifted Lottie's words from the page, and Cristy could only wonder why they hadn't connected sooner with what a gifted actress she was. In her ear, Connor said, 'How didn't we see this? She could be red-carpeted for this kind of performance.'

Cristy didn't respond, simply listened until the insert came to an end, feeling as far away from knowing Sadie as she ever had.

CONNOR: 'So, now you know what most of you guessed anyway, that Mia, according to Lottie's journal, was responsible for Janina's death.'

CRISTY: 'This is something Mia strenuously denied when Sadie read the journals to her . . . Take a listen to this . . .'

As Connor played in Mia's distraught, terrified voice insisting that Lottie was twisting everything, Cristy's eyes closed and for the next few minutes she found herself transported to the room where Sadie had confronted her aunt. It was as though she was watching, and even believing in something she'd never actually seen: Mia's panic, shock and helplessness; Sadie's steely determination to finish reading, before outrage and fury had made her trash the place.

'Ready?' Connor asked in her ear.

'There,' Cristy confirmed, moving her script into the shade.

CONNOR: 'Pretty dramatic stuff, I'm sure you'll agree, and frankly, after many listens on our part, Mia still sounds pretty convincing to me.'

CRISTY: 'So you think Lottie purposefully lied in her journals to cast Mia as the villain of the piece?'

CONNOR: 'That's the trouble, I'm not sure I do believe that.'

CRISTY: 'On this, I tend to agree with Sadie, that to whatever degree, they were both responsible. I can't say it goes as far as falsifying journals for me, but Lottie hasn't tried to get out of her involvement. She writes about sending Janina to Sark View House, and she clearly knew about Janina's death at the time it happened, so she's every bit as guilty as Mia.'

CONNOR: 'OK, so it was both of them. I think we can all get on board for that.

'Let's move on to what came next, something neither of us will ever forget: that horrifying scene when we went into Mia's house to find the kitchen and sitting room trashed and her sat right under a noose. Jesus, that's an image I don't think will ever leave me.'

CRISTY: 'We couldn't record any of it, Mia refused to allow it, but we did describe it in episode five, and made it pretty clear there that Mia wasn't flying with many feathers in her wings by then, if she ever really was.'

CONNOR: 'And I think we can conclude that Sadie reading out the journals pushed her aunt even closer to the edge. Did she know that would happen? It seems reasonable to conclude that she did, at least on some level, given how well she knew her aunt, and her various eccentricities, as she called them.'

CRISTY: 'So we move closer to Sadie's decision to make her aunt pay for her mother's death with her own life – and in the same way.'

CONNOR: 'She could, of course, simply have handed the journals to the police and let the law take its course – God knows prison, or a secure mental facility, would have been a severe enough punishment for Mia. It would have been the end of everything for her, and Sadie, would well deserve to take control of the Winters' fortune, in the court of public opinion at least.'

CRISTY: 'But – and it's a really big but here – for as long as

Mia remained alive there was always a chance she could be deemed fit enough to change her will and cut Sadie out completely.'

CONNOR: 'Meaning Sadie would lose out on upward of forty million quid. Nice if you can get it. So, to make sure Mia didn't even think about doing anything silly, Sadie acted – it could have been spur of the moment, or maybe it was already planned. We know the court has accepted the former. See what you think as you listen to this next clip. I should point out that it's the recording of a pocket-dial from Mia's phone, so it's not always as clear as we might like. But the salient points are, I think you'll all agree after hearing it, that God, or fate, or the universe can move in just as swift and decisive ways as Sadie Winters managed that night.'

CRISTY: 'A quick warning before we play it, it is distressing. So please, either choose not to listen, or, if you feel in need of support after you can go to our website where you'll find appropriate links.'

Not wanting to hear Mia's pathetic and helpless cries again, or Sadie's gentle coaxing and horrendously vengeful words at the end, Cristy removed her earpiece for the next few minutes. But even as she gazed up at the palm fronds, and listened to their rhythmic rustle, she could still hear the disturbing echoes of that final scene.

David reached for her hand, and as she turned to him she watched him listen until he signalled it was time for her to plug back in.

CONNOR: '"It's for the best, Mia." That's what she said. And then those deadly words, "See how you like it."'

CRISTY: 'As we mentioned just now, if you need help dealing with what you've just heard, please go to our website and click on one of the links we've put there to guide you.'

CONNOR: 'So, you now know why Sadie didn't opt for a trial. She'd never have been able to win if she entered a plea of not guilty. So, diminished responsibility won it for her, if you can call fifteen years a win.'

CRISTY: 'There's a very good chance she'll still be under forty by the time she comes out. Will she then be able to pick up her massive inheritance, and rejoin her family, and get on with her life?'

CONNOR: 'The answer to that is no, she won't. Whatever's left after the other beneficiaries have been paid out will go to the Crown. Although I imagine it'll be the subject of countless lawsuits before that happens, and maybe, in the end, once the lawyers have claimed their share, something will go to her.'

CRISTY: 'So, the bottom line is she will not be able to profit from her crime, or certainly not in the way she presumably hoped to. Or did she? I never got the impression she was driven by money, but there again, with so much at stake I don't think we can rule it out. More likely there was a whole slew of complex and conflicting emotions playing into her motives that probably even she couldn't identify if asked. Anyway, I don't think we need to worry about her financial security. I'm sure she'll find herself a book and TV deal somewhere down the line, and as we know, her father and uncle aren't exactly broke. Quite the reverse in fact.'

CONNOR: 'This is true, but it isn't their wealth that makes them stand out for us, and it certainly has nothing to do with why we've kept their interview to the end. It's how hurt they have been by all this that's probably moved us the most. And how determined they are, in spite of everything, to stand by Sadie. Here's what they had to say the day after she was sentenced.'

This time Cristy listened as the insert was played, staring at the gently rippling pool in front of her, glazed by sunlight, sprinkled with blossom. She wondered what Gabe and Lukas might be doing now. Were they still in Guernsey, or had they flown back to Florida for a while?

CRISTY: 'Thanks for agreeing to talk to us. I realize this is a very difficult time for you, and not at all what you were expecting when we came to you back in February with the news that Sadie – Sasha – was alive and looking for you.'

LUKAS: 'I won't deny that the events of the past few months have delivered us a number of terrible blows. We were so happy to have found our dear Sasha, and to start making plans for a future with her. We are still making those plans, and we shall continue to for as long as she is compelled to stay where she is. She knows, and we would like your listeners to know also, that we have no intention of abandoning her. She is Gabe and Janina's daughter, my niece, and as such she will always have our love and loyalty – and our full understanding of why she was driven, in a moment of utter despair and confusion, to act as she did.

'I know the recording you have paints her in a damning light, but that is because most people won't understand what was happening to her at the time. What had been happening for years under the influence of her aunts. They were a malevolent force in many ways, iron fists in velvet gloves, master manipulators of truth and lies. So much so that after discovering the journals Sasha found herself unable to think straight . . .

'You know yourselves that Mia was suicidal, and the most likely reason for that was guilt. She knew what she'd done was a terrible, wicked thing and no matter how much she gave Janina's daughter she could never make up for what she and her sister had taken from her. It was tormenting her, crushing her from within, and to hear Sasha speak about it it's clear it was doing the same to her. She was stifled by her aunts' deceptions and constant refusal to tell her who she really was, and by the threats they repeatedly made to cut her out of their wills if she didn't stop trying to find out about her past.

'I ask you: how can anyone be relied on to behave rationally when they're under so much pressure and for so long? When all they want is to know the truth and it is always denied? Sasha has a good and kind heart, she is like both her parents in that respect; it was only in Mia's final moments that nurture overcame nature and made our dear Sasha behave like one of her aunts.'

GABE: 'We are intending to relocate to Guernsey to be close to Sasha until such time as she can join us in the States.'

CONNOR: 'Will it be possible for her to get into America as a convicted felon?'

GABE: 'If it isn't, we will all stay here.'

CONNOR: 'So there you have Sadie's father's final words to us on the subject of his daughter, her uncle's, too. Whether or not you believe she deserves such loyalty is up to you. Personally I think it reflects very well on them, and I'm sure, in the long term, it will go some way towards reducing her sentence if it's known that she has a loving family who'll be there to help with her rehabilitation.'

A lengthy silence followed, until Connor said, 'Cristy? Are you still there?'

CRISTY: 'Sorry, yes. So, that brings our bonus episode of *Who's That Girl* to an end. Thank you for listening. Please join us for a new series in the coming months.'

CONNOR: 'Are you serious? That's how you're going to end it?'

CRISTY: 'What's wrong with it?'

CONNOR: 'A bit abrupt, don't you think?'

CRISTY: 'Please feel free to rephrase and say whatever you feel is right.'

CONNOR: (after another pause) 'OK, I get what's happening. You're on the Marrakech Express?'

CRISTY: (laughing) 'Something like that.'

CONNOR: 'Slow on the uptake, or what? So, have a good one guys, and see you in a couple of weeks. Meantime, I'll record a decent end to the series, complete with credits and sponsor beatification. Iz will be proud of me. I'll also fill everyone in on my news, although I don't suppose anyone's interested now. Whatever, don't you worry about us over here in the cold and wind and rain, we're coping.'

He waited for a response, certain it was going to be droll.

CONNOR: 'Are you still there?

'You're not even going to say goodbye?

'Nice.'

# Acknowledgements

One of the most important characters in this book is the location, and it is only thanks to the wonderful Judy Moore – Guernsey resident and much-treasured cousin – that I have been able to bring the island to life. Thank you Judy for being such a dedicated and insightful guide, your remarkable input made all the difference. This thanks also extends to the excellent lawyerly advice I was given by another Guernsey resident – he knows who he is.

A huge and heartfelt thanks to my eldest stepson, Mike Garrett, not only for the many recces around Bristol's harbourside, but also for bringing such remarkable marketing skills to my social media accounts.

Love and thanks to Gene and Marty Tardy for welcoming me so warmly to their beautiful home in Naples, Florida, and for sharing lovely anecdotes and flavours of life there. And also to Jane and Henry Pearsall for their kind hospitality during a very informative chat.

More love and thanks to Chap and Sallie Jo Mitzell for hosting me in Naples, and for being just the best friends in the world.

Of course, no book is complete without the amazing team that works so hard to get it from author to reader, and I count myself truly blessed to be a part of the HarperCollins team. A huge thank you to every one of you – Kate Elton, Roger Cazalet, Lynne Drew, Belinda Toor, Maddy Marshall, Maud Davies, Liz Dawson, Holly Martin, Claire Ward and all those whose involvement even I don't always see. Knowing you are all there sprinkling your own kind of magic over each step up of the process is both humbling and inspiring and a total joy when we come to the end results.

Last, but never least – endless amounts of love and thanks to the world's best agent, friend, confidante and fellow bon vivant, Luigi Bonomi.

Read on for an exclusive extract of the next Cristy Ward thriller from Susan Lewis . . .

COMING SOON

## Never Look Back

**A dead husband. A missing wife.**
**A past that won't let go.**

Romy Kaplan's husband drowned mysteriously six weeks ago. Now Romy is missing.

When posts start to appear on her social media accounts asking everyone to stop looking for her, the police are satisfied she's just a grieving widow in need of some space.

But Romy's friends and family know she would never disappear without telling someone where she is going.

When true crime podcast host Cristy Ward picks up Romy's case, she has the whole world asking . . .
where is Romy?

# PROLOGUE

'I think, my love, that I might have come up with a way out of the unfortunate situation we're in.'

Rudi Kaplan had uttered the words softly, rhythmically, making them sound like part of a song. His wife, Romy Kaplan, looked up from the notebook she was writing in, and her heart skipped a beat as she watched him leave the piano. He'd spent the past half an hour there, playing some of the gently haunting tunes he'd composed in recent times. They were meant to soothe him, as her writings were meant to soothe her, and they did in their way, but the spectre of what was happening to them never truly went away, not even for a minute.

As their eyes met, Romy's were already shining with hope and trust. She had so much faith in him that she sometimes feared it might be more of a burden to him than a blessing. He would insist, of course, that everything about her was a blessing, that the best thing he'd ever done in his life was marry her, over forty years ago, but she couldn't help fearing that the terrible events that had taken them over were weighing more heavily on him because of her.

Casting a quick glance over her shoulder to where his eyes were now directed, she saw that he was staring at their portraits, hanging side-by-side over the dining table. In their elaborate gilt frames, they were too large for this tiny cottage, but there they were, and his, to her mind, was a true work of art. Whenever she assessed them as a pair, she felt that his had been created by a superior hand to the one that had created her own, but it hadn't. The same artist had done both, taking a lot of time to get to know them first, encouraging them to share stories of their lives together, their dreams for the future. In the end, the capturing of

Rudi's charm and irony, the soulfulness in his deep-brown eyes, the enlivening hints of him as a younger man, made Romy love the painting almost as much as its subject.

Hers was – different. Like her, and yet not, as though the artist hadn't quite seen her, or had maybe tried to turn her into someone else. The woman depicted certainly had Romy's naturally high cheekbones, full-lipped smile and silver-blonde hair styled in a wispy sort of bob, but even Rudi, who professed to adore the painting, agreed that the playful light in her luminous violet eyes wasn't quite there. Nor was the infectious energy she exuded, or the natural vivacity that drew people to her; the crafted contours of her slender face made it appear more oval than heart-shaped, even a little harder than she was in reality.

'My love,' he murmured softly, looking at her now as he reached for her hand.

She smiled and put aside her notebook and pen. Even after all these years, the romance in him could cause her heartbeat to quicken, and his voice, at least to her ears, remained as hypnotically melodic as it had ever been. Everyone had always loved it when he sang – folk, jazz, even opera – but he hadn't done much public singing lately.

'The idea came to me a couple of weeks ago,' he told her softly, as though afraid of being overheard. 'I've been thinking it through, and now I feel ready to share.'

Knowing how protective he was of her, how hard he tried never to trouble her with something until he'd worked out a way to handle it, she said, gently, 'Would you like a brandy to sip while you tell me?'

Clearly loving how easily she read him, he said, 'Yes, and perhaps we'll take it outside, over to the lake?'

It was something they often did: enjoy a twilight pick-me-up at the water's edge, no more than a dozen steps from their front gate. With the sun shimmering its last rays over the surrounding valley slopes before disappearing behind the hill, it always felt the perfect place to end the day. Sometimes, they'd put on music and dance, cheek-to-cheek, Rudi crooning softly in her ear. Neighbours from the smattering of nearby cottages would occasionally join them, bringing their own cocktails, music and chitchat. A truly lovely group of new, dear friends who'd made this tucked-away lakeside enclave their home. Some were their age, others younger. No children, which was a shame; Romy had always loved children and was sad never to have had any of her own.

Rudi took himself off to "their bench", almost hidden amongst a cluster of yellow irises and milfoil, carrying jumpers and blankets in case it turned cold. It was still early March, after all. As Romy watched him from the kitchen window, she reflected, as she often did, on how fortunate they were to have found this place at the heart of a meandering and leafy vale with no one to bother them much or to ask too many questions. It was very different to what they'd had before, of course, but it didn't matter; what really counted was that they had one another and were no longer in danger of doing harm to anyone.

'You two are so much fun,' their new neighbours often told them. 'You really know how to enjoy life. We didn't get together much before you came, hardly even knew one another. And you're a fabulous cook, Romy. All your exotic recipes, and Rudi's stories . . . As farfetched as fairy tales, but no less fascinating for that. The places you've visited. The things you've done.'

Feeling a wave of nostalgia approaching, a current of memories bent on carrying her away from the moment, Romy stepped out of the tide and waved cheerily to Nula Higgins, their neighbour from two doors down, as she went chugging past in her old VW Polo. Romy often walked with Nula and her dog, climbing stiles and wooded hillsides up to the common where cattle had priority over traffic and winds blew in from afar.

She knew she should head outside, but she was nervous about what Rudi might have to say. She mustn't let herself hope that there was any real way out of their situation, however hope was hard one to suppress.

Satisfied that Rudi was settled, his wispy hair being gently tossed by a wayward breeze, she turned to survey the room behind her, taking a moment to remember what she was supposed to be doing. This little home of theirs was so quaint and old, with its wooden beams criss-crossing the sloping ceiling, a red-brick fireplace in the sitting area and awkwardly fitting French doors that opened onto a back patio and lawn. There were dozens of photographs and books around the place, along with special mementoes from all over the world and plenty more still in boxes in the spare bedroom. Squashed in under the stairs was Rudi's mother's roll-top desk that served as their office, while the treasured piano sat wedged into a small alcove at the far end of the dining table. Two antiquated chintz sofas flanked the hearth, where Rudi's daily fire was turning to ash. He liked it to remain lit, no matter the weather, so she went to stoke things up with a poker and dropped on a log.

Ah yes, drinks – and she'd take out some nibbles as well.

As she stooped to open a kitchen cabinet, she found herself falling into the trap of paranoia that so often dogged them these days. It was as though they were being sucked back into a dark and distant past, to a time when they'd known beyond doubt that they were being watched and listened to. It was a time when the world had been a very different place to what it was now. And they had been different people.

Today, when the feeling and fear of another presence came over them, they escaped by going to their bench, especially when they had something important to say about "the situation".

After filling a tray with glasses and small bowls of nuts and olives, she spotted Rudi's mobile on the windowsill and decided to leave her own next to it. They wouldn't need them this evening. If anyone called, they could always leave a message. Much better that they had the time to themselves, without interruption.

A few minutes later, with everything set out between them, Rudi tapped his glass to hers and said quietly, 'Here's what I think we should do.'

Romy was hardly daring to breathe. Was there really a way out of the dreadful position they were in?

'I think we should contact Cristy Ward,' he told her.

She blinked in surprise, several times. She knew the name, of course; everyone did – more than that, she'd once known Cristy's mother, someone she'd thought about often over the years, but never as much as these past few months. Had they ever actually met Cristy? They'd come across so many people in their lives, but Romy couldn't immediately recall ever having been introduced to the well-known podcaster.

'Layla could probably put us in touch,' he said, seeming to pick up on her concern.

Her eyes widened slightly as she realized this was true. Her goddaughter, Layla, had worked with Cristy Ward a few years ago when they were both in TV.

'I think Cristy Ward will help us,' Rudi declared decisively.

It didn't take Romy long to see why he thought that, or to agree that he could be right. There was no need for her to consider it more thoroughly; he'd already done that, or he wouldn't have mentioned it.

'But would she want to?' she countered cautiously.

'We won't know unless we ask.'

This was true: they wouldn't, and Romy would be all for it were she not now thinking of the risk involved. They were only enduring this to protect those they loved, and what had already been done to them and others could also be done to Cristy Ward.

'We don't want her to get hurt,' Romy said worriedly. 'And she'd have to . . . How much do you think we can tell her?'

'I'm not sure about that,' he admitted, 'but maybe we should talk to her, without going into *all* the detail, and let her decide if she wants to get involved. If she doesn't, or if we think we've made the wrong decision . . . well, we can just leave the meeting and come home again.'

Romy nodded slowly. Cristy did seem like a good choice of person to go to, for all sorts of reasons, mostly to do with her mother.

'Do you think Layla would set something up?' Rudi asked.

Certain Layla would, if she asked, Romy said, 'She's in Dubai, remember, but that doesn't matter. The question is, how do we stop her mentioning it to her mother when they're next in touch? Beth's already worried enough about us; I don't want to add to it.'

Beth was Romy's best friend of almost sixty years; they were as close as sisters, maybe even closer than that.

Rudi sipped his drink and stared thoughtfully out at the water, where shadows of fish skittered about in the darkness and tiny bubbles of air broke the surface. They seemed to Romy to embody all their memories, their fears, everything they needed to keep hidden that just kept rising up again.

'How was Beth when you spoke to her earlier?' Rudi asked.

'Actually, she sounded quite good. The effects of the last chemo have started to wear off. She's looking forward to our trip.'

He smiled. 'It'll do you some good to get away for a few days too,' he said. 'Is Johnny planning on joining you?'

'I don't think he can, but you know we'd love it if you came.'

'No, no, this is for you and Beth, some time together in your happy place while she recuperates and recharges. I'll stay here and keep thinking.'

'Good idea,' she whispered, leaning over to kiss him. 'I'll miss you while I'm gone.'

'I'll miss you too,' he said and kissed her back.